FROM A WORLD MORE FULL ...

A FANTASY

E.C. Kasalivich

To Veronica
With love, E.C. Kasalivich

ps David says Hi!

:‿:

British Library Cataloguing In Publication Data
A Record of this Publication is available
from the British Library

ISBN 978-1-84685-902-1

First Published 2008 by
Exposure Publishing,
an imprint of
Diggory Press Ltd
Three Rivers, Minions, Liskeard, Cornwall, PL14 5LE, UK
and of Diggory Press, Inc.,
Goodyear, Arizona, 85338, USA
WWW.DIGGORYPRESS.COM

My Mother said I never should
Play with the Fey Knights in the wood.
They'll smile, beguile and lead you away
And won't let you back until Judgment Day.

Local variation to traditional skipping song

Prologue

Karl was tall, slim and blond, and very good looking. And little Rosemary hated him with all her heart. He was here, this German boy, eating and drinking, even doing "things" in the woods with that traitorous land army girl. He was alive and experiencing all the life that Paul should have; feeling, and tasting and living and growing up to be a man. But her big brother was dead, killed in the water before he had even set foot on the Normandy sands while this enemy's mere existence was an affront to her.

What made it worse was that people liked Karl, until she had made up her big lie. Even PC Shadrack had turned a blind eye when he'd caught him and another German in the *Moiled Bull* wearing their prisoner of war jacket with the red stripes up each sleeve. Rubin Tregonhawke had given them each a pint of mild 'on the house.' Every time someone paid a kindness to a German, Rosemary wrote their name in her secret book. Rubin was there, together with PC Shadrack and a lot of other people. They were all dirty traitors and one day they would pay. But today, only Karl would pay.

It was all planned. She told her big lie and the villagers had chased Karl into the wood. Now there he was, hiding under that big oak, panting and very afraid. But not half as afraid as he would be soon, for she was leading him to "them" and they would take him away until Judgement Day – or perhaps they would just kill him. She would leave it to them to decide. She had watched them kill before. It wasn't pleasant, but it was no more than Karl deserved, for being German and for being alive.

CHAPTER ONE

The Long Awaited Day

Times were when a young man could enjoy a tryst in Wymes Park with his girlfriend without interruption. Times were when legends would behave themselves and stay safe within the pages of musty books, or at worst, trip off the tongues of crazy old women. In and around the Shropshire town of Little Rillton it seemed the times they were a-changing.

Christian Wren De'Ath hit the 'off' button before the alarm clock emitted more than a single peep. Excitement had kept him from sound sleep and the night had been a long stretch of half-dozes, fleeting repetitive snatches of dream and exhausting, seemingly eternal tossing. He rose quickly, glad of the dim, pre-dawn light and hoping for another hot June day. A special day carefully planned and long awaited. How would it be?

Chris tensed as the cold jet of water darkened his fair hair and cascaded down his back causing his flesh to contract onto his bones. He caught a shriek and subdued it so that it emerged from his contorted face as a truncated yelp. No sense it annoying the whole family by waking them up so early. After a moment, he had the setting adjusted so that both power and temperature were working in unison to soothe his rudely shocked body. Showering off the last cobwebs of a long, uncomfortable night he made a grab for the soap, but quickly replaced it in its ceramic sea-shell holder. No; today was a shower-gel day. He had to smell right. Everything had to be right; clothes, smell – everything.

Stepping out of the shower, he looked at his dripping reflection in the full-length mirror. 'Great gangling bugger - all arms and legs' is how Dad described him. Maybe later, maybe after, he would ask Gayle for her observations. *An Adonis. A wild stallion. A well-oiled love machine.* Well, maybe. On the other hand it could all end horribly. *Couldn't get it up. All talk. A no hoper.* The corner of Chris's mouth curled up in a lop-sided smile. He knew he'd have no problem getting it up. No, the problem would be keeping it down until the right moment. And even if it didn't all go according to plan, Gayle was not the sort to kick him when he was on the ground.

A hefty bang on the bathroom door shunted his daydream into a siding.

'Oi! Hurry up in there,' his father called.

'Okay. Won't be long.' He had to be polite. Nothing was going to spoil his day. He quickly towelled off, shaved - which wasn't entirely necessary - and then quietly opened the bathroom cabinet. Slowly, so that they would not chink together, Chris took out the half-dozen odd bottles of never-used after-shave to reveal that little nook at the back where Dad's little blue box was always 'hidden'.

He had known about it for years. And Dad knew he knew. In fact, it was Dad who told him where to look - just in case. Chris had been given the father-to-son lecture which every boy dreaded but few received. Pretty much as expected; all that stuff about responsibility, love, worth waiting for the right girl. But then came the unexpected ending: telling him where to find the condoms.

Chris took the slim package and flipped open the lid. The pack was full. Damn! Dad would notice if he took one. He took one anyway then thought of himself and Gayle lying in the long grass that grew inside the old tower. He took another. Oh, what the hell! He took yet two more.

'Have you died in there or what?' came a raised voice at the door.

'No Dad. I'm coming out now,' he said, fumbling to get the after-shave back. He slipped on his carefully selected Tommy Hilfiger boxers, secreted the newly acquired condoms down the waistband and let his father in.

'Morning Dad,' he said with a grin.

'Morning, Chris. How can you be so bloody cheerful this time of the day?'

I'm on a promise, Dad. Today's the day. Chris grinned wider at the thought of his father's reaction to his unspoken thoughts. 'I'm just looking forward to the fishing, that's all.' he said.

'Oh yes? Well I hope your tackle is ready,' Dad said, very obviously aware of the double entendre. 'And I hope the fish are going for latex bait these days!'

Chris looked down. Four little blue wrappers protruded minutely above the elastic of his shorts. *The curse of observant, mind-reading fathers.* Chris grinned widely as Dad pushed past him to get to the bathroom – always his first line of defence; that grin.

It was a well known fact that Lord Wymes's roach loved sweet-corn. Also maggots and doughy bread, and of course worms, mince and even baked beans. Lord Wymes held that his fish had absolutely no sense of self-preservation. 'Put a scrap of paper on your hook with "Bite Me" written on it, cast out and reel in another bugger,' he had been heard to say. The old boy was very particular in giving out fishing rights, so for all the suicidal battalions of roach, tench, chubb and the rest, few could tell of the one that got away to wind it's leviathan body amongst the rushes of Wymes Lake.

One of Wymes's relatively recent ancestors - Lord Harold Wymes of Ypres - had been Chief Constable hereabouts, so angling policemen and their immediate families were in with a chance. It also helped if your father was estate manager, and as far as he knew, Christian De'Ath was the only son of the current holder of that honourable office.

Richard De'Ath, police sergeant (retired), had secured the position two years ago on leaving the force when Chris had been fifteen. Chris supposed that there must be some advantage to being a copper's son but he had never been able to find out what it was. It was partly due to the reactions elicited from less controlled members of school society upon learning of Chris's ancestry that he came to follow two courses of action. The first, a conscious decision, was that he would learn how to fight. He enrolled, entirely of his own volition, into a junior jujitsu class. The second decision, if that was the right term, crept up on him almost subliminally. He would be an extremely bad boy. *Then* make the term 'goody-goody' stick!

He thought he was extremely bad, but deep down badness went against the grain, and was filtered out through several layers so that extreme badness became a general cheekiness. Master of the one-liner, king of the quips - general pain in the arse. He also gathered with a handful of other boys in the toilets at break time to smoke - but he didn't take the smoke down.

Chris's most wicked deed was to organise a game of strip-poker one lunch hour in the sixth form lounge. Several students got down to their underwear, and then Danny Stockdale lost another hand. He stood with manful resolve and blushed as he saw Katie McMerdie's lascivious smile of anticipation. No one knows whether his resolve would have held firm though, for as he gripped the sides of his briefs and stooped to pull them down - Miss Thomas, (Religious Education and English Lit) walked in and had the shock of her life. Both Chris and Danny were excluded for a month and became top of Mr Huddleswick's hit list.

Then that happy day dawned. Dad retired from the force and Chris was no longer a copper's son. The family moved back closer to the Wymes Estate, into the village of Little Rillton, Dad took up his new duties and Chris gave up jujitsu. He'd found new hobbies: sneaking into pubs with Danny Stockdale, fishing - and Gayle Merryl of the upper sixth.

The uncovered Land Rover crackled and popped to a halt on the grit road as the dull, red, beach-ball sun bowled through the distant trees of the estate's woodland filtered by a thick mist.

'I must be bloody mad.' Richard De'Ath muttered almost to himself. 'Five-thirty of a Sunday morning! You must be too. Can't you get into a sport that starts in the afternoon?'

Chris dragged his tackle from the tool locker shutting the truck's passenger door as quietly as possible. He dropped the rods and tackle bag gently by the road and leaned across a five-bar gate which marked the end of the road. Mr De'Ath joined him.

'It's going to be a hot one, Dad.'

'I reckon it will at that. Soon as the mist clears.'

Lady Wymes began to wish she was riding side-saddle. Tomahawk was a seventeen hand, brown and white skewbald gelding with the girth of a battleship's boiler. She took the considerable weight off her rear by standing in the stirrups. Tomahawk threw his head up as high as the martingale would allow, then shook it from side to side to relieve his mouth from the effects of his double bridle. Lady Wymes loosened the reins.

Two figures caught her eye, which surprised her. She had thought to be the only human about the estate at such an early hour. The sun was beginning to fire up, so she shielded her eyes as she peered at the silhouettes. Ah! One was clearly Mr De'Ath; average height, stocky, wearing a cap. But the other? Taller then De'Ath; like a bean-pole and with one of those trendy American baseball caps.

'Come on, Tomahawk.' she said squeezing at his girth. 'Let's see what's afoot.'

Hey, up! Here comes her ladyship,' Mr De'Ath said.

Chris watched as Tomahawk and her ladyship gudda-boomed ever nearer like an overweight centaur. 'Is she always up this early, Dad?'

'She has nightmares. What's your excuse?'

'Morning De'Ath,' Lady Wymes said affably. Tomahawk snorted and sent two steams of steam from his nostrils.

'Good morning, Lady Wymes.'

'Who's this?' she said, pointing her crop at Chris. 'New recruit?' She hoped not. She had an aversion to boys whose knees peeped out of their 'blue jeans', and why they had to wear their vests un-tucked and hanging below their similarly un-tucked shirts she could never fathom. She glanced down skinny legs to inspect his footwear. He wore white, or rather once-white trainers the tongues of which stuck out insolently held lightly in check by orange - yes *orange* laces. God in Heaven he was even wearing an earring! Having looked him down, she looked him up again and this time she noticed his face. She caught her breath as ice gripped her heart. Someone was doing a rumba on her grave but no trace of the shock rippled her countenance.

'No, not a recruit, Ma'am. May I present De'Ath junior.'

'Aha!' said Lady Wymes maintaining perfect composure. 'Number one son.' Poor boy has holes in his trousers, she thought. Maybe De'Ath needs a salary increase. 'How d'you do, young De'Ath?'

'Fine thanks, Mrs Wymes,' Chris said, smiling.

Lady Wymes ignored the faux pas. 'Here for the fishing I dare say.'

Chris nodded.

'Well. It's the last Saturday before we open for the season. Should have the lake all to yourself. Unless that ghastly old tramp comes trespassing again. Oh well. Must fly. Enjoy yourself, young man.' Lady Wymes snapped off a salute with the whip, reined Tomahawk round and cantered off towards the manor. With the boy behind her, his face still floated before her mind's eye and she knew she would face another restless night.

Richard De'Ath swatted Chris with his cap. '*Mrs* Wymes? You ruddy great pillock!'

'Sorry. Forgot,' Chris said imitating her ladyship's clipped speech. A lop-sided grin indicated that he had not forgotten at all. He warded off a second swat.

Mr De'Ath opened the gate and Chris gathered his things. 'What about this ghastly old tramp then?' Chris asked.

Mr De'Ath chuckled. 'Harry's not so ghastly or old really,' he said. 'I was inspecting that crumbly bank we did some work on last year and found him using the lake as a bath. He had all his clothes right in there with him, floating in a big plastic bag. I thought he was a poacher using the bag to put fish in. "Get out of it!" I yelled. He froze - then burst into tears.'

'Big bully.'

'So then I said as how he could earn himself a breakfast by mucking out the stables.'

'Big softy.'

'Aren't I just? Thing is, they don't know about him up at the house, but I've taken him on kind of permanent. I have to keep hiding him whenever they're around.'

Father and son watched as Lady Wymes and Tomahawk dissolved into the mist - a deep black shadow-puppet, then an amorphous impression of movement which strained the eye - then gone altogether.

'Right then! Got all your stuff?'

Chris checked. Yes. It's all here. Okay to pick me up this afternoon?'

'About half-four?' Mr De'Ath asked climbing into the cab of his Land Rover. 'If you're sure you'll be finished fishing ... or whatever else it is you have in mind.'

'Fine. See you then.' Chris said, feeling a blush coming on.

'And mind the Fey Knights don't get you.'

Not that old legend again. It was amazing how often mention of the Fey Knights crept into conversation with the older generations of Little Rillton. Fey Knights this, Fey Knights that; mind they don't take you, dupe you, lead you astray. 'Fey Boys, Dad? I'm more scared of the gay boys. You do know Marc Stockdale and his soldier boyfriend creep in these woods whenever the mood takes them, don't you?'

Mr De'Ath obviously did not. 'Oh my God!' he said, his look something akin to panic. 'Maybe I should ... maybe you should ...'

'Dad!' Chris was rising towards exasperation. 'I *am* only joking. You *really* think I'm bothered about running into Marc and Sean while they're getting down to gay boy stuff?'

'Chris!'

'It's cool Dad. You know Marc. He's a nice guy and so's Sean from what I've seen of him.' *Next time I'll stick to remarks about the bloody Fey Knights*, Chris thought. *Can't go wrong with them.*

Mr De'Ath drove off shouting something about wanting a nice pike for his tea. He would be disappointed; about the only thing unlikely to emerge from Wymes Lake was a pike.

Wymes Lake was a good size - about three times the area of a football pitch. There were two small, tree covered islands in the middle and at one end where the underwater stream came in there was an area of bull rushes. The whole lake was surrounded by woodland.

Chris's trail wound through the woods and he emerged by a tree which had been partially blown down in the great storm of '87. Chris called it 'Drunken Willow'. It leaned over the lake at a seemingly impossible angle - almost parallel to the water surface, but clung on refusing to fall in or die.

Chris stopped and caught his breath. He wasn't one to wax lyrical, but he had never seen the place looking quite so magical. The surface of the lake was covered in a foot-thick veneer of mist. Mist also gathered in the high branches so the sun stabbed through like pale yellow lasers.

By the time Chris had set up his swim, the sun was winning the battle and the mist held out in only a few pockets of resistance. A few bubbles broke the surface from the quarry - or rather, the ostensible quarry. The real quarry was due at half-eleven, and Chris hoped she'd be wearing her tight white T-shirt and jeans.

In went a moderate handful of sweet-corn. After all, eleven-thirty was a long way off, so why not make the effort. He cast out, sat back and waited.

And waited, and waited, and waited. They were there but they wouldn't bite. By eight, Chris had scoffed his first ham and pickle roll. All traces of mist and grey were gone, the sky was an unblemished blue and it was already warm enough for the flies to be a nuisance. He found himself wondering if they would tickle him while he and Gayle were making love. Nearly every thought found a way of leading a few hours into the future to where he and Gayle would finally be entwined, on a floor of soft grass in the old ruined tower, at long, *long* last to go *all the way*. It was about time. He was nearly 18 and unless all the others were lying, the oldest virgin boy left in the town. Not that he admitted anything to his mates – well, except for Danny that is. Danny and Megan had been doing it for six months, but Danny was his best friend and didn't rub it in.

Unlike Chris, the fish wouldn't rise. He persisted, trying various baits and a couple of different swims until ten-thirty by which time he was bored and hungry, having polished off the last of his salt 'n' vinegar crisps. The fish had beaten him, so he decided to walk round the lake to use up some of the time left before Gayle's arrival. He thought of that tight T-shirt again and excitement began to rise, but Chris quickly splashed cool water over his head and face.

Stowing his fishing tackle in the corner of a lakeside folly, which he presumed once doubled as an elaborate boat-house, he set off tying his shirt round his waist. The folly was shaped like a miniature, medieval keep and he wondered if it was modelled on the ruined tower that lay deep in the wood. That the tower was the genuine article and no folly was beyond doubt. Few knew of it. Of all his old school friends only he and Danny Stockdale shared the secret. Being roofless and therefore exposed to the elements, soft springy grass formed the floor and the walls were home for all manner of rock-plants. It was a perfect love-nest, where he and Gayle could become one; surrounded by nature, but safe from chance discovery.

By the time he had completed half a circuit, the sweat ran off him, attracting flies and those horrible little white midge things that land on you for a drink and irritate like mad. He ambled on to the rickety punt-pier and walked to the end carefully avoiding the missing slats. Spreading his shirt as a ground sheet, Chris sat dangling his feet over the edge. He was hot. He was sweaty. He grew ever more excited with thoughts of Gayle. Those miserable flies. Cold water; refreshing - and by all accounts, the enemy of lust. It would be nice to go in for a swim.

Why not? Nobody around so why not? His decision was made. His shirt was already on the planking and was joined so quickly by his T-shirt, trainers and socks you would think they were full of ants. He was going skinny dipping. His jeans came off a little more slowly as he looked round for intruders. His boxers were even more reluctant coming down to his knees before being pulled firmly up again. Chris suddenly felt vulnerable, though logic told him there wasn't a living soul within a mile. He stood for a few moments with his thumbs down the elastic waiting for the nerve to whip them off and walk as nature had made him. It was suddenly very appealing to be dressed only in the sun-light, if only he could summon up the bravado to overcome the inhibition and embarrassment of being observed by unseen eyes.

Bravado came in a swirl of action that ended with his boxers crumpled around his ankles. He stepped out of them and the breeze caressed his skin, tickling those recently exposed parts. For a few moments it felt so good; he stood, naked and free, at the pier's end and made ready to dive in.

Alas, bravado today was as elusive as the fish. Chris's experience as a true naturist lasted about fifteen seconds. He snatched up his boxers and pulled them back on as an image came to his mind. This vision had him swimming nude, mid-lake, while the girls of the 1st Little Rillton Brownie pack made something novel for mother's day - out of *his* best underpants.

With his boxers firmly in place and serving as trunks, he jumped off the pier, went under and then broke the surface letting out a gurgling yelp. The water was cold - but not freezing. Tolerable he thought, as the sweat slicked off. He trod water until the 'tolerable' became 'refreshing', then struck out to one of the islands. As for the lust, although the outward manifestations of his condition lost vigour, far from quenching his drive, the fresh water fired his longing still more.

Gayle, her smiling face; Gayle, her firm body: she filled him and surged through his blood until even the cold water could not keep him down. He struck out hard for the island - a furious crawl that succeeded in channelling and using up his excess energy, but before he reached his objective he stopped and began treading water again.

The water had suddenly become considerably warmer and as he pondered the cause he had the strangest feeling that the world had just contracted around him. Bird song took on a discordant and drawn out tone, the woods surrounding the lake were thicker and even the air seemed denser. Something – a bird or a large insect – flew over him close to his head, but just out of his field of vision, its wings beating a vibrant thrum into the air and on the far bank the reeds parted and a face stared at him. Chris blinked; the face was gone, but the eerie, off-kilter feeling remained. He swam slowly for the little pier making as little noise as he could, feeling as if a million hidden eyes were staring at him. Something in the water brushed his legs and sent his heart racing He broke into a crawl as the thing in the water touched him again and he struck out as fast as he could.

Heaving himself onto the planks he couldn't get his feet out fast enough so sure was he that something was about to snap them off. Once on the hot, dry planking his panic attack melted away with his fear, and Chris laughed at the power of his imagination. Gathering his clothes he scurried to the bank and found a space between some rhododendrons where he whipped off his boxers, wrung them out and slipped them on again before quickly pulling the rest of his clothes over his damp skin. So much for the shower gel: Gayle would have to have him smelling of fresh boy and lake water instead of Thai Spice or whatever stupid name they'd given the stuff this month.

Chris tucked in his orange laces and stepped out of the bushes feeling refreshed and invigorated, but something was still not quite right. There had been that face in the reeds: it looked like a lad of about his own age or a little younger, with long black hair. Suddenly a memory emerged from a long neglected crevice of his mind. One of the three Fey Knights was supposed to have long black hair. 'Bollocks!' he said under his breath. *Next I'll be seeing the other two and the little ones with wings.* He smiled at this latest piece of nonsense dished up to him by an overactive imagination. Still, something was just not right and Chris felt troubled by it.

He looked across the bank to the clump of reeds. Nothing; not a flicker. The fey boy or whoever the Hell he was had been no more than a trick of the light. Gayle would have a good laugh when he told her about his little mid-lake scare. Then another thought squeezed out into the daylight: according to the legends the Fey Knights nearly always ensnared courting couples. Chris slapped the thought back down where it belonged, for if there was one thing guaranteed to cramp his style it was the thought of three dirty little elves watching him from the bushes as he got it on with Gayle. He smiled again. Once he was safe in the secret tower with Gayle, nothing would cramp his style. *The Fey Knights can go fey themselves!*

He heard voices. About to shuffle back into the cover of the rhododendrons, Chris thought better of it. It was too early for Gayle and he wasn't expecting her to bring a friend, so he sat on the edge of the pier and waited to see who would come along. He did not allow himself to spare a single thought more to Fey Knights or other impossible creatures, even when the voices came closer and it was obvious they were both male.

Emerging from the narrow wooded path just behind a burst of their own laughter came Danny's brother Marc and Shaun his soldier-boyfriend. Chris was about to stand and throw them a friendly wave but he noticed they were holding hands and thought maybe they would prefer not to be disturbed. He shrank down so they wouldn't see him, and sure enough they passed by without noticing his presence. Then they scrambled over Drunken Willow and Chris developed a bad feeling. There was only one reason to climb over the horizontal trunk of that hardy old tree, and it was to get to the tunnel in the thick stand of shrubs that led to a path which was no more than a virtually indiscernible trickle through thick undergrowth. Of course, once through the first couple of hundred yards, the path opened out just a little, but it led to only one place, and that was the secret tower. Who had told these guys about the tower? Well, that was obvious. It had to be Danny. *I'll kill the little bastard!*

Marc and Shaun were making their way to the tower. They had to be. There was no other explanation. 'But it's *my* tower', Chris mumbled, and he meant it to be a special place for him to be with Gayle for their first time. He suddenly felt very angry with the two lads. They obviously intended to use it for the same purpose. His lip curled in a cold sneer and he was ashamed to find himself thinking unkind, bigoted thoughts about them. A robin landed on a nearby twig and caught him out. He watched it cocking its little head as it watched him.

'Amazing how a bit of jealousy can screw you up, isn't it?'

The robin let forth a short burst of chirps.

'Yes mate, that's right. You give me a bollocking. I deserve it. Thing is, where can I take Gayle now? Do you know any good places?'

The robin twitched and flew off.

'I guess that's a "no" then.' He checked the digital display on his mobile phone. Still an hour to go before Gayle was due. Maybe Marc and Shaun will be done by then, he thought, and then he found himself wondering just what it was they might be done with. Did they use their hands? Kiss? Did they go the whole way? Chris shuddered, but at the same time his curiosity flared. Was it wham, bam thank you mam – sir? – or did they take their time? Did they love each other or was it just sex?

That last was a question he'd asked himself about Gayle. He wanted her so much it hurt, but was it just sex or did he love her? Yes, he liked her company. He loved their long conversations and their delicious cuddles. Her touch thrilled him and their all too infrequent sessions of heavy petting left him deliciously drained. But none of that helped him answer the question. Maybe later today he would know. When they had made love and been together, joined as one being, then he would know. Again his thoughts turned back to Marc and Shaun. Were they together like that, even now?

'I'm bloody well going to find out,' Chris said to himself. He'd decided to creep through the woods and do a bit of peeping. It would be a bit of a giggle; something to tell the lads in the pub. On second thoughts, it would be something to keep a secret. He wasn't going to get cheap laughs at someone else's expense. He ran round the bank past the folly and sprang over Drunken Willow. He felt very naughty, but sometimes naughty was fun, and anyway, he might learn something.

Half an hour later Gayle sat on the pier planks wondering where Chris could be hiding. She had found his fishing gear stashed in the folly, so he wasn't far off. In fact, she felt sure he was watching her. She giggled as she thought of him stripping off and coming to her through the bushes, naked and sporting an erection like a half-pulled beer tap. Typical Chris. She couldn't help being a little surprised that he wasn't waiting for her though. After all, this was going to be their very special day, and she hadn't left him in a lot of doubt that she was willing to go all the way.

Gayle jumped as something crashed through the bushes. Seeking the source of the commotion she caught sight of Chris on the adjacent bank just as he tumbled headlong through the air and came down in the dusty dirt with a crump audible right across the lake. He scrambled to his feet looking back as if he were being chased by a pack of ravenous Rotweillers and spying her he cried out her name with such fear that it froze her heart.

Gayle ran to him though every fibre in her body was screaming for her to turn and run the other way, away from the invisible horror that snapped at Chris's heels. They met with such force that Chris nearly bowled her over, and he wrapped his arms round her and clung tight as if she were a lifebelt. His eyes were wild, round and terrified and as they locked into hers, tears came like a flood.

'They ... they ...' he said through laboured breath.

'Oh Chris. What *is* it? What on earth's happened?' She took him by the shoulders and felt for him as he fought to regain composure. When he did speak, it came out in little more than a whisper.

'They... Something came ... took them away. Marc and Shaun have gone. I saw them. I saw them.' And with that Chris looked over his shoulder and then high into the trees. When he looked back something about him had changed.

'We have to call the police. They fell in the lake. I think they ... drowned.'

Gayle used her mobile to call the emergency services and then noticed Chris's jaw muscles working hard, and saw fear in his eyes. She pulled him into a hug but he resisted and was unresponsive. All she could do was hold him and try to comfort him, looking all round for signs of what could have terrified him so much.

CHAPTER TWO

No Wisdom in Books, No Truth in Legend

Chris was taken to County Hospital where he was assessed for post-trauma related conditions. He was given a stitch in a nasty deep wound on the heel of his right hand and a tetanus injection. He said he couldn't recall where he'd picked up the injury saying he must have fallen. It was a lie.

PC Chapel, who also happened to be Chris's old jujitsu instructor, came that afternoon, straight from the scene of the 'accident'. Oscar, his Alsatian dog sat quietly in the corner of Chris's bedroom as the policeman took down his statement. Later the same day a captain from the Army came by. Not from Shaun's regiment: he was a redcap and he asked all the same questions PC Chapel had and then a few more. Of course, Chris lied some more.

They dragged Wymes Lake and police divers went down, but Chris knew they'd find nothing. At least, nothing that had anything at all to do with Marc and Shaun's disappearance. The Army went in as well. Dad said there were strange comings and goings in windowless vans and soldiers dressed all in black with balaclavas and machine guns. All very hush-hush. The Army did not like to lose promising young officers, but there would be no return for Lieutenant Shaun Ashton.

No one questioned the details of Chris's story. He kept it simple. He'd seen Shaun fall in the lake and Marc jump in after him. They started to have difficulties and thinking he heard voices Chris went for help. No one was there and he came back in time to see Marc going under. He panicked. They drowned. End of story. Marc and Shaun had drowned in Wymes Lake, like many others in the past, and like the others, drag and dive and search as much as you liked, you would never recover their bodies.

'Underground streams, you see,' PC Chapel said. 'Who knows where they end up?'

Only Gayle had a problem with his account and so like the subject of religion, it became taboo. He couldn't explain why she had not seen or heard anything while she had been waiting by the lake. Chris told her he must have passed out. No other explanation, but Gayle sensed he was holding something back. They began to argue. Gayle resented his reticence believing there should be nothing they could not discuss, and Chris got angry at what he called her prying and nagging. They never did go all the way, and they began to drift apart.

Weeks passed. School broke up and the summer holidays began. A memorial service was held at St Luke's and Chris went even though he had no time for religion. Danny was his best friend, and it would be rude not to go to the memorial of his best friend's brother. Gayle was there of course, and they spoke briefly like newly introduced strangers. It was embarrassing for both of them. Most of the school crowd came along and Chris even spotted Cappy Shirakawa, barman from the *Moiled Bull*, his spiky, died blond hair contrasting absurdly with his sober cut black suit. Cappy in a tie! The world was indeed turning on its head. Chris acknowledged him with a nod. Cappy's almond eyes were serious and sad as he nodded back, a curt little movement that looked like a samurai bow.

The vicar, old Charles Knapper, gave a good sermon and came to the wake afterwards where he made a beeline for Chris who stood next to Danny biting into a dry sausage roll and longing for the whole thing to be over. The Reverend Knapper took him gently by the arm and with apologies to Danny, drew him to one side.

'It came over really well, Vicar, that stuff you said. Thanks, and thanks for the things you said about me too.' He felt a total fraud.

'Not at all, dear boy. It's all too easy to forget how painful it is to witness a tragedy, and the feelings of guilt that often follow.' Charles Knapper was as tall as Chris, and slim with an unruly mop of white hair and penetrating eyes that beamed from under bushy, white eyebrows. Chris wondered how deeply the old man could see into his mind. 'Aby tells me you're not yet back to your old self.'

'Aby? Oh, Aby Knapper!' Chris said an instant before the penny dropped. 'Of course! Your last name's Knapper too, isn't it? So Aby from my class is your grandson.' Chris had always known Aby's family had something to do with the church, but he never went to church, had never met the vicar before and just hadn't made the connection. He felt silly for missing the obvious.

'No, no. He's my youngest son. I was, as they say, a rather late starter. Margaret and I didn't meet until I was in my late forties.' He smiled and there was humour in his eyes which quelled any embarrassment Chris might have felt before it had time to develop.

'I'm surprised we haven't met before now,' the vicar said. 'Aby's always talking about you.'

Chris was rather puzzled. He didn't know Aby that well; not friends, more on friendly nodding terms.

'Anyway Chris, it can take a long time, you know, to get over such a terrible event.'

Chris shrugged. This old vicar didn't know the half of it.

'Especially if for some reason, one doesn't feel able to relate *all* the facts.'

The old man's words went from comforting to a bucket of cold water in one sentence. 'I'm sorry. I'm not sure I follow.' Chris followed very well in deed, but hoped with all his heart he was wrong. He felt the vicar's eyes were shining beams into the dark, secret corners of his mind and feared they might illuminate the truth.

'It is just that witnessing tragedy sometimes brings down blinkers, so that there are details that you don't recall until later. Wymes Park has that effect on people.' Charles Knapper turned the beams on full strength. 'May I ask? Are there any details you may have kept from the police?'

'What kind of details?' Chris said, his voice raising a pitch. 'Marc and Shaun fell in the lake and drown. Anything else doesn't count.' The vicar's probing put Chris on the defensive.

'And yet, the details may count for a great deal. You are, of course, aware that mystery and legend has surrounded our dear old Wymes Lake for centuries. It's a wonder they haven't drained it or filled it up with concrete.'

Chris began to feel afraid. Just what did old Knapper know? 'Bloody Hell, Vicar! I hope you're not going to go on about the Fey Knights.' *Bugger! I've sworn to the vicar.*

Charles Knapper inclined his head and raised an eyebrow, indicating that Chris had hit the nail on the head. He didn't seem to take offence at the mild oath, even though it sprang from "by Our Lady, Hail!"

'Look, you're a flipping vicar,' Chris said in a little above a whisper, just managing to stop himself adding *for Christ's sake*. 'You shouldn't be going on about stuff like that.'

'You mean I shouldn't believe in the legend of the Fey Knights?'

'Of *course* you shouldn't!'

'Too fantastic? Too silly and impossible?'

'Flipping too right it is.' Flipping? Chris never said "flipping" but he was speaking to the vicar. All his usual epithets were entirely unsuitable and he wasn't even going to risk a second go at the mild one.

'Whereas, I suppose you will forgive me if I believe in a man who walked on water? And turned water into wine? And came back from the dead? Nothing too fantastic there I suppose?'

Chris just stared. He couldn't work out where the vicar was coming from. He had the distinct feeling he was the butt of some kind of a joke, but he knew in his heart the vicar wasn't mocking him. He hardly broached his other certainty: the vicar knew he had seen something more than a drowning.

'Here. I've brought something for you.' The vicar held out an A5 sized magazine, old, worn and browned with the passing of years.

Chris took the offering and looked at the cover. 'St Luke's Parish Magazine, June 1912,' he read out loud. 'What's this?'

'Read it when you get a spare moment. There may be an article or two of interest. Then, if you have any questions, pop into the church or if you'd rather, collar Aby and he'll tell me you need to chat. Now if you will excuse me.' Charles Knapper smiled and left Chris in the corner as he joined a group of Stockdale family members.

'What was that all about?'

Chris jumped. He hadn't seen Danny's approach. 'Don't have a clue. He gave me this.'

Danny examined the document. 'Wow! It's a 1912 copy of the parish magazine. Aby once told me this thing has been in print ever since 1872 without a break, not even for the war.'

'Want it?' Chris said, holding it out.

'No thanks, mate. If he gave it to you he must have a reason. Funny old git, isn't he?'

'Could say.' The vicar's words were still sinking in, and Chris still struggled to make sense of them. One thing was for sure, he really did need to tell someone the whole truth, and if anyone deserved to hear it, Danny was the man. 'Look Danny. You busy tomorrow?'

'I was going to do a bit of course work, but any feeble excuse to put that off. What you got in mind?'

'Let's meet up somewhere. I need to talk.'

'Sure thing. The old tower?'

Danny may well have struck Chris across the face for the effect his words had. 'No way!' he said a little too loudly and then continued in a whisper. 'I mean, no. Anywhere else but there.'

'Okay, okay! Keep your knickers on. You suggest a place.'

'The old swim under the giant willow, where we used to watch the Kingfishers.'

'Cool. About eleven then. That'll give us time for a lay-in, and after we can pop into Dolly's for a pie and a pint.'

'See you then, Danny. Thanks. Look, you don't mind if I –? '

'No, it's cool. You shoot off. It was good of you to come in the first place.'

'Tomorrow then.'

'Tomorrow.'

'It's something about Marc and Shaun.'

'I guessed it might be. Take care, bruv.'

Chris got home to an empty house. Mum and Dad had stayed on at the wake, and no doubt they would come home and give him a hard time for leaving early. He could hear them already. *Danny is your best friend. How could you?* and *You've broke Gayle's heart and now your walking all over the Stockdales. Just snap out of it!* He could also hear his furious riposte: *keep your fat noses out of my business. Just piss off!* Chris could feel himself turning into the kind of person he despised, but it was downhill all the way to Hell on an icy road, and he had no handholds. Maybe tomorrow. Maybe Danny would throw him a lifeline.

He turned on the TV and watched a documentary about the Boxing Day tsunami. A volunteer in a dog collar made Chris think of Charles Knapper and then he remembered the parish magazine. Retrieving it from his jacket pocket he thumbed through it, feigning disinterest but hoping beyond hope that something would help.

There were childish poems, and line drawings of bucolic scenes and bunny rabbits; there were articles cautioning against the evils of alcohol and there were obituaries. One such caught Chris's attention. It was about the untimely death of a 17-year-old railway porter called Frank. According to the article, he was a popular lad who decided to go for a swim in Wymes Lake and – surprise, surprise – went and got drowned. His body had apparently been got at by the fishes, but unusually for Wymes lake's many victims of drowning, it turned up. It was the very last paragraph that hooked into Chris's guts and pulled hard.

> The Vicar has asked that the people of both Great and Little Rillton refrain from entering into discussions linking Frank's sad death to the worn out and somewhat childish legend of "The Fey Knights of Wymes Forest" as it is most hurtful to the families concerned.

It had taken summer a long time to arrive but now it was here and the next day came in hot. Chris was up early, once again unable to sleep, and he rehearsed over and over his forthcoming meeting with Danny. How to broach the painful subject of Marc and Shaun's ... drowning? How to phrase it? Trying to guess Danny's likely, unlikely and downright impossible reactions to his revelation. He couldn't remember a time before Danny. They had been born days apart; had cots next to each other in the County Hospital and had gone through all the important phases of their lives as firm friends. He would rather a thousand strangers believe he was an utter tosser than risk losing Danny's friendship, but this thing had to be done; Chris had to tell the truth to someone.

Chris found himself on the towpath sooner than planned and he slowed to an amble. He wanted to get to the giant willow before Danny and establish himself with a modicum of comfort, but he didn't want to be ridiculously early. A large beetle flew by and Chris nearly jumped out of his socks. Something about that noise of heavy, whirring wings smacked a vision of *that* day into his mind. He tried to shake it off and enjoy the blue sky and the hot sun. Maybe he would keep an eye on the river and watch out for a Kingfisher as he used to do when he was little, but nothing came close to lightening his mood.

He arrived at the swim half an hour early, and there was Danny sitting on the pitch-boards dangling bear feet into the water. He looked up and snapped off a salute. Chris sat next to him but kept his trainers on, folding his legs under like they used to do at assembly in the infants. It was a long time before they spoke. Words were not always necessary between them, but today Chris wished Danny would make a start. Eventually he gave up wising.

'Remember when we were kids?'

'I thought we'd agreed never to talk about that.' Danny picked up a few pebbles and skimmed one. It bounced three times before sinking. 'You're not going to tell me you're gay, are you? I could believe anything after the way you dropped Gayle.'

'Of course I'm not, and I never dropped Gayle.'

'She drop you then?'

'Well, no but ...' Chris looked off down the river wishing right now that he was in a boat and catching up with his thoughts.

'Spit it out, Christy. But, if you are, you know, like my brother, I'm not going to drop you like a greasy spanner. Don't forget I've got a good track record. Marc thinks ... used to think ...'

'It's nothing to do with that, Danny. I'm talking about Dolly's Gary's party. He was home on leave and we were invited to his 17th.'

'Oh, yes. The tabs.'

'That's right. Some knob-head dropped acid in our drinks and we both tripped.'

'Great laugh for all the big boys to watch the two little fifteens get out of their heads. Pretty bad trip as I remember it.'

Chris looked round as if worried about being overheard. 'Me too. I was sick. The thing I want to ask is, have you ever had a flashback?'

Danny chewed on his lower lip and stared at his friend, trying to work him out. 'I thought we were here to talk about my brother and Shaun, not prat about talking about old times best forgotten.'

'It is about them. Come on Danny. This is important. Have you ever tripped since?'

'No! Why? Have you?' Danny glared and threw a pebble hard into the opposite bank. He wasn't in the mood for reminiscing, not now he'd started recalling his brother and hearing a voice in his head that would never come again.

Chris withdrew into himself a little and his eyes glazed over. 'Perhaps. Maybe. For God's sake Danny I don't know, but I have to tell someone – you – what I saw. The whole lot. The thing is it's all so stupid you'll think I'm crazy.'

Danny's irritation fled before his friend's obvious pain. 'Give it a try bruv. If it's all too nuts we'll just put it down to that tab, shall we?'

'Sounds fair, but let's go to the tower. We really need to be there.'

'But you said ...'

'I know, I know. Kind of flipped a bit, didn't I. But I don't want to just tell you. I want to show you. Come on, off your arse. Let's get going.' Chris leapt up trying to energise his spirit by the actions of his body. 'And on the way, I want you to tell me a bit about Marc and Shaun. How they met. How you felt when you found out about Marc. All that kind of stuff.'

Danny stuffed his socks in his pockets and slung his trainers, suspended by the laces, round his neck. 'Okay,' he said cautiously. 'But why?'

'Tell you later. Trust me. I'm going to have to trust you, so trust me first.'

Danny shrugged. 'If that's what it takes to get the old Chris back.' He made for the towpath. It was a good day for walking barefoot. 'I suppose you *do* know I was about the last person on the planet to work out my own brother batted for the other side?' Chris's lop-sided grin answered that question in the affirmative.

CHAPTER THREE

The Story of Marc and Shaun
or
See the 'Fisher

Danny recalled a day only a few weeks earlier. So much had happened in so short a time. The grass tickled his feet and he led Chris along the towpath his mind drifted back.

How do you ask the question? No, that wasn't quite the problem. How do you ask the question without big brother kicking the crap out of you? That was it! That was the question about the question that had been bugging Danny for days. The first hurdle was to get Marc on his own, so when Marc had suggested a day out fishing, Danny had, uncharacteristically, jumped at the idea. What with Marc's work and Danny's A' level studies and busy night life, who knew when the next chance would come along?

It was a scorcher, the kind of day best spent by, or better still, in a lake. Danny and Marc had set up swims a few yards apart, Marc's on a bank which projected slightly. Surprisingly, there were few other anglers about.

From his swim, lying as it did behind and to the left of his brother's, Danny could watch Marc without fear of being caught staring, for staring it certainly appeared to be. Studying; that was a more accurate word. Observing; like a naturalist, looking for clues as to the nature of the beast. Danny watched as Marc made a long cast look easy, his broad back moving almost in slow motion.

Danny's float wobbled, then bobbed, then whipped away under water. Danny did not even notice. He did notice how three small moles on Marc's cheek looked like the mathematical symbol for 'therefore'; he did notice how Marc's large nose (a feature which Danny shared and which so clearly marked them as kin) protruded from the shade of his narrow brimmed jungle hat. Danny unconsciously ran his middle finger along the bridge of his own nose, well protected by a Washington Redskins baseball cap. Damn nose! Spoiled an otherwise ruggedly handsome face. Still, it didn't stop him pulling the birds.

A splash brought Danny's attention back to fishing. Marc's broad, open face snapped round, his smile wide and reflected in his eyes. 'You've got something, you jammy little git!' Six foot one, an inch shorter than Marc - still a jammy little git. Danny chuckled as he reeled in a decent sized rudd.

A well appreciated diversion; for the first time that day, Danny thought about something other than 'the question'. Marc was there with a landing net and after a minute of co-ordinated effort, the monster was in the keep.

'Can't let you get away with that!' Marc said. 'Ten quid on the biggest haul of the day!'

'Game on!' said Danny. 'Only if you win I'll have to owe you. Fancy a coffee first?'

Marc grabbed the flask while Danny set his rod on the stand.

Wymes Lake was surrounded by woodland, and the brothers were glad of the shade to be had just a few yards from the bank. Sitting with their backs against an oak, they enjoyed their coffee in silence.

Danny felt his heart beating faster, could actually feel the thump of it pulsing at his ribs. Marc had taken his hat off, his blond hair stained a few shades darker with sweat. As 'the question' formed, almost at Danny's lips, the thumping rose to his throat. It had to be asked, but the asking was torture. Anyway, he knew the answer; all the clues were there, the evidence all pointed in one direction. But still, he had to have the confession. The consequences? Things between Marc and Danny would never be the same.

'Marc ... oh shit.' The question , cut off after the first syllable.

'What's up, mate?' Marc said, curiosity furrowing his brow.

'Oh, nothing really.' Shit, shit, shit.

'Need to borrow some dosh?'

'No, no. It's nothing. I just ...' *Damn, bugger, sod it.* Saint Peter's cockerel crew in a saltier tongue these days, but the question would not be denied for much longer.

Marc licked his teeth. Something was bothering young Danny, but Marc knew from experience some problems were best left to emerge in their own time. Sometimes, if you probed for a winkle with a pin, it would pull deeper into its shell. Leave it, make no attempt to coax, and out it would come, millimetre by nervous millimetre.

'Refill? said Marc holding out the flask.

'Thanks, Marc.'

The silence resumed, broken only by slurps and the buzzing of insects. Marc's float submerged then surfaced with a plop. They both saw, they both ignored. It seemed important that for a while the silence remained unbroken as if to disturb it would scare away an important truth of the verge of revelation.

Just as Danny felt sure he knew the answer, Marc anticipated the question. On the edge of apprehension, he felt a kind of relief. He too needed the confession.

'How's Shaun?' asked Danny at length. The kraken stirred.

'He's fine, as far as I know.' Marc said slowly. 'Why do you ask?'

Danny shrugged. 'No reason. Just wondered why he's not here. He is on leave, isn't he?'

'Yes, but we don't live in each other's pockets.' said Marc becoming defensive against his will. 'Anyway, he's got some business in Oxford and then interviews at the Ministry.'

Danny could tell Marc was feeling uncomfortable. It was getting away from him. He would have to tread carefully, or Marc would clam up good and proper.

Danny drained his coffee, breathed deeply. 'Hope he does well. "Captain Shaun Ashton". Got a nice ring to it.' The brothers shared a smile, tension climbing down a rung. 'He's a nice bloke is old Shaun.' Marc nodded then gazed away from his brother fixing on some object on the opposite bank. 'How long have you known him now?'

'Since the fifth-year at St. Martin's - that's coming up for eight years.'

'Really?'

'Yep.'

'As long as that?'

'As long as that!'

Danny paused, pondering the years, phrasing at long last *the question*. 'You two are, well, sort of close, aren't you?'

'One way of putting it,' Marc said, the hairs on the back of his neck bristling.

'Are you, I mean, is Shaun ... Are you both ...'

'Come on Danny! Spit it out. Get it over with. It will make you feel better.'

The kraken burst up through the surface.

'Are you and Shaun ...?'

'Yes. I am and he is. And yes, we are, if that was your next question.'

'There's more than one gay in our village, then,' Danny said in an exaggerated Welsh accent.

The brothers held each other's gaze for a beat then the tension was burst in a torrent of laughter. And for the next hour, no more was said as they returned to the serious business of fishing for fish, the answer having been successfully landed.

I'm too hot for this.' Danny said tipping his rudd out of the keep net. 'I'm all fished out. Let's go for a drink.'

'You mean you don't mind being seen in public with your raging queen of a brother?' Marc smiled his wide smile but there was something else in his eyes - an uncertainty - a shield for the newly bared soul.

Danny saw the something else. He wanted to do, wanted to say the right thing. As he paused, groping for the right response, the smile began to fade from his brother's lips.

'Don't be a prat!' Danny said, slapping Marc's shoulder. 'Of course I don't mind, so long as you don't put your hand on my knee!' They laughed. 'And if you're buying, I might even let you!'

'Tart!' Marc said.

The *Moiled Bull* at Little Rillton was as unexplainably free from custom as Wymes Lake had been. Mr De'Ath, the estate manager down at Wymes Park was treating old Harry to a pint, and a couple of lads from the village were playing Go, the audible clicks as they placed their stones as regular as a metronome. That was it, and on an afternoon guaranteed to bring flocks to every available watering hole. So much for guarantees; perhaps there was something good on the box.

'There you go lads. One mild, one four-ex and two salt and vinegar crisps. That's four pound on the button, my loves,' Mrs. Tregonhawke said.

'Thanks Dolly,' Danny said, handing over the money.

One of the Go players waved a greeting. 'One of you two care to take on the winner?' Colin called optimistically. His opponent was Cappy Shirakawa, the Japanese-American barman who'd introduced the game to the *Moiled Bull* in the first place, so it was clear Colin didn't stand a chance.

'No thanks, Col. We're going to make the best of the weather,' Danny said.

'He's doing good,' Cappy said, his deep voice and Texan accent always a surprise coming from a 5'8" skinny Japanese guy. 'This time I think he's got me!'

Colin preened, but he couldn't see the fat ironical wink that Cappy chucked over his shoulder.

The brothers settled at a wooden bench at the far side of the garden. It overlooked a river and was overhung with willow branches and there they sat for the space of half a pint, listening to the water gurgle round the feet of a stone bridge. The silence between them had just began to threaten comfort when Danny felt the kraken stir once again.

'How do you feel Marc, now that you've told someone?'

'Now that I've told you? Bit of a relief really. I mean, it's been difficult, in all sorts of ways.'

'Tell me.'

'What's all this? "The psychiatrist is in and awaits your call". Doing your Samaritan bit?' Marc said gently.

'No, I'm doing my brother bit. Come on Marc. I want to know.'

Marc mulled over a mouthful of real ale, took a deep breath, exhaled noisily. 'Well, for example, when you came home all full of it after your date with Megan. Head over heels like. It would have been nice if I could have told you that I knew how you felt, because I was in love as well.'

Danny flushed and looked over his shoulder away from Marc.

'And all those couples things. You end up going on your own, and there're all your mates with girls. It all just goes to make you feel a freak. Which I suppose is right.'

'There you go again! Being a prat. This is 2005, not 1945. Any road, when they were dishing out sex drives did you go up and order a "V-8 Turbo Charged Poof 2-litre" or did you just end up tuning what you were given?'

Marc's smile returned. 'You always were one for the original turn of phrase.'

'Well, it hits the mark, doesn't it?'

'Just about. But I tried like hell to fit a "Straight-Six" - just wouldn't go.'

'You find me the mechanic who can turn a V-8 into a Straight-Six and I'll catch you a fish with feathers. Come on Marc, your round,' Danny said, draining the last of his lager.

While Marc was getting the beer, a kingfisher blue-streaked down the river, the sun glinting on a small silver fish held like a nose-cone in its beak. Marc had never seen a kingfisher, while Danny had seen dozens. Marc was always looking the other way, or getting the beers. Dad had a phrase for it: "like the bus-conductor; never sees the accident because he's upstairs collecting fairs."

'Here you go. Get yourself outside this.' Marc placed a tall, water-beaded glass in front of his brother.

'Saw a kingfisher.'

'You never!'

'Did.'

'You *did* didn't you?'

'Yep.'

'You jammy little git!'

'"Only those who tell no lies can see the 'fisher as he flies",' Danny quoted with mock superiority.

Marc stood at the bank for a minute or so, looking up and down the river without really expecting to see anything, before joining Danny. 'This is the life. Blue sky, hot sun and cold beer.'

'And a river full of kingfishers.'

'Shut up!'

Another half-pint interlude went by during which the noise of a passing airliner swelled the hot air. As its thunder eased to a distant whisper, Danny's curiosity waxed once more. He was brave, if not tactful.

'So, when did you first realise you were turned on by boys?'

Marc tutted and rolled his eyes. 'I woke up one morning after having sexy dreams about James Bourne from Busted romping round my bedroom dressed in just his jockeys and thought "Yum, yum! I think I'll be a poof" and then the Angel Nancy came down and awarded me my pink fluffy slippers and a free subscription to *Gay Boys in Bondage*.'

'You crease me!' Danny spluttered having trouble laughing through a mouthful of beer.

'Well, come on Danny. It's hard for me to talk about all this crap. You sound like a lawyer or a cop with your questions. And I know my rights. I don't have to say anything unless I want to do so.'

'Are you now or have you ever been a communist?' drawled Danny in his best FBI agent impression. Then, snapping back to common or garden Danny: 'Seriously. I'm not just being nosy. We've both grown up in the same house. Generally speaking Mum and Dad treated us the same. I want to find out when we started ... going different ways. I want to go back to the cross-roads and read the signpost.'

'Deep, Daniel Stockdale - very deep. My kid brother, the philosopher.'

'I mean, oh Christ, it *is* difficult, isn't it? Maybe I could have gone the same way as you. When I was younger, I thought I might be ... you know?'

'Gay? You and Chris De'Ath?'

Danny flushed deep crimson and snatched looks over both shoulders as if the thought police were about to strike. 'How did you know? Was it that obvious? Anyway, we didn't ... there was nothing ... I mean ...'

'Danny. Shut up!'

Danny shut up and returned to beer supping while the heat dissipated from his face.

'You and Chris were what, twelve or thirteen, when you were big mates? We all go through that ... if we're lucky.'

'Yes. I've read the books.' Danny said, subdued but on the rise again.

'Right, so if you've read the books, and gone through the routine adolescent phases, you'll realise it's impossible for me to answer your "when did I first know" question. I know, because I've asked it to myself a million times.'

'All right,' Danny said, persisting. 'When did you first decide? I mean, I remember you going out with girls. And what about Jenny when you were at university?'

'Smoke screen.'

'So when did you decide to come out of the smoke?'

'You're not going to let go, are you? Okay, it kind of crept on me. I wasn't like one of these guys who claims to have known since he was an embryo or something. I kept making excuses to myself, until I was watching a guy on TV one day and I started ... having thoughts. Like, thoughts I couldn't put off as something other than what they were. If you know what I mean.'

Danny nodded knowingly. 'Busted?'

'Ah ... well ... I never said ...'

'James Bourne?'

Marc blushed.

'Marc, the kid used to leap round like a frakkin monkey!'

'Marc took a long draft of beer then put on a little boy voice. 'Take me to the zoo, Daddy?'

Danny shook his head and sucked on a molar. 'Well, all I can say is, I'm glad you grew into Shaun and out of Jimmy boy. I can't see me taking to such an annoying ...'

'Careful, little brother! Don't walk on my fantasies.

'... such an energetic and bouncy young dude.' He drained his beer. 'One more pint and then home?'

'Okay. I've definitely got the taste. But I'll be good for nothing this afternoon.'

'Your round.'

'Actually it's yours, but I'm feeling generous. I'll get the beers again so long as you swear never to say anything horrid about Jamie, ever again. And as for "young dude" he's at least a couple of years older than you.'

'I'll try to be nice about him bro, but it might be a bit difficult. Eeek, eeek, eeek!'

Marc picked up the empties. 'And if you see another kingfisher while I'm gone, keep it to yourself.'

The sun had sweltered past its peak, but it was definitely mad dogs and Englishmen time. Shafts of sunlight stabbed through the willow canopy and swifts swooped low over the river screaming like manic devils at the abundance of food.

Danny stretched - yawned. Beer mellowed and sun warmed, he felt glad his friendship with Marc had proved to be based on foundations of rock. He thought of his brother and Shaun together, found himself wondering about them. Did they kiss? Hold hands? What did they do in bed? He pondered the possibilities without being revolted or judgemental but with a kind of voyeuristic curiosity.

The beer had lowered the barriers maybe a little too far because he decided to ask Marc when he came back. Hey Marc, he'd say; how's Shaun in the sack?

He was pre-empted. While he drew on his fresh pint, Marc pipped him to the post.

'Okay, Danny. So far it's been me and Shaun under the microscope. What about you and Megan?'

''What about us?' Danny shrugged.

'Well, is it going to be wedding bells or just broken bed springs?'

Danny giggled - the beer. 'Too early for wedding bells, and as far as broken bed springs - chance would be a fine thing.'

'You've been going with her for a year. I can't believe my little brother has been a perfect gentleman for that long.'

Danny rolled his eyes. 'Of course not, but can you imagine us at home, really going for it and in pops Mum asking if we want a cup of tea? Nah! We do it in the car - it's safer.'

Marc choked on a mouthful of ale. 'What? In your clapped out Mini Cooper? You over six feet tall and you do it in a matchbox toy? I don't believe it!'

'Believe it.' Danny said smiling lop-sidedly at the thought of his last session. 'Let's just say, the missionary position is out.'

'You randy little beast! British racing green, but more steam on the back seat than under the bonnet.'

'And by the lake if it's a warm day.'

'Wymes Lake? Where abouts?'

'There're loads of places. Our favourite is the old ruined tower. We have a picnic - and take hours over desert.'

'I've never seen an old tower,' Marc said, his brow furrowing.

'Proves what an ace place it is then doesn't it? The walls are covered all over with moss and ivy, so you can be almost on top of it and still not know it's there. It's got no roof, but inside the grass is like a lawn. Grazed by rabbits I suppose.'

And you and Megan ...?'

'All the time! Sometimes we'll spend the whole afternoon there. Mum and Dad think I'm fishing - well, Mum does. I think Dad suspects I'm dipping another kind of maggot. You know how he is with his winks and sideways looks.'

No I don't, Marc thought. 'Sure.' he said.

'And she'll wear something silk. It drives me crazy!' The inhibitions were gone, beer-dissolved, and Danny was getting himself hot under the collar.

'Got a silk-fetish then, have we Danny.' Marc ribbed, noticing his brother squirming in his pants as the hormones surged.

'Fetish smetish.' Danny said pulling at the crotch of his jeans. 'The way that stuff feels - the way it slides over, and off the skin.'

'Danny, don't drink the rest of that pint. Pour it over your head.'

Shared laughter. Danny was having a good time and felt closer to Marc than he had ever felt before. He felt there was nothing he couldn't share with him, nothing too embarrassing to talk about. After all, Marc had just opened himself up, right down the middle, guts on display for the hawks to peck at - and Christ he had some guts - and Jesus Danny would swipe the first hawk that showed its nasty beak!

'What about you and Shaun? Where do you go for a bit of fun?'

'The flat mostly, when he's on leave. It used to be our rooms when we were at Uni if the others were away or somewhere safe and out of the way. It all has to be top secret - at least until he comes out the Army. It's not against the law in the Army anymore, but it doesn't exactly make life easy either.' He drained all but a mouthful of his pint. 'I tell you what though.'

'What?'

'I like the sound of your ruined tower. I don't suppose ... ?'

'Your on, bro! I'll show you where it is on the way home. We'll take a detour through the estate. But it's out of bounds on the days I'm fishing - in case I'm not fishing.'

'You got it.'

Dolly rolly-polled over to collect the glasses and stopped for a bit of gossip. 'That little trollop from the Gables was in here again last night, she was, eyeing up anything in trousers. Ended up the night going off with Colin Bain she did, but she was staring at my Gary like he was a Cosmopolitan centre-spread. I told him if he wasn't careful he'd take something back to his regimental surgeon as he didn't bring home.'

'Gary's on leave then, is he Dolly?' Marc asked.

'Yes. Couple more days and it'll back to Germany. Can't stop! Someone's hollering from the bar.'

The brothers waited while Dolly hauled her great bulk back indoors. They had good reason to be circumspect in her presence. She had a bloodhound's nose for scandal.

'So it's love ... you and Megan?' Marc said at length.

'I reckon. But don't tell her I said so.' Danny was suddenly chilled by the thought of early marriage. 'So it's love ... you and Shaun?'

'Yes. And you *can* tell him I said so. Totally, wholly, a hundred per cent.'

'Wow. Lucky guy!' Danny's eyes sparkled as he smiled at Marc - then the lop-sided grin re-emerged to give him an impish look. 'But there must be *something* about him that gets on your nerves.'

'No ... well.' said Marc, a note of uncertainty creeping in.

'There you are! I knew it. Go on, what's he do that's a pain in the arse?' Danny's face set into a portrait of pure horror no sooner had the last phrase left his lips. 'Marc, I didn't mean ...' He blushed deeply and was mightily relieved when Marc began to chuckle.

'It's all right, mate,' Marc managed. 'As it happens, we don't go in for that very much. But yes, there is something that grates. He doesn't wear pyjamas.'

'I didn't think you did.' Danny said, his face subsiding to a delicate pink.

'I don't. But I don't keep my socks and shirt on either!'

'What's that, an old Army habit?'

'An old Shaun habit more like.'

'Bit of a turn-off, is it?'

With their glasses empty and feeling more than a little tipsy, the brothers decided it was time to be getting on. They walked along the river's edge towards Wymes Park. The large private estate was made up mostly of broad-leaved woodland although there was a fair expanse of formal deer park round the mansion. Fishing rights were hard to come by and access was restricted, but some of the local lads had secret ways in.

Danny and Marc were two of the few who didn't need to resort to covert access; they both had permits to fish. Old man Stockdale and Richard De'Ath, the estate manager, had been good friends at school, and people did favours for each other in Little Rillton.

The brothers, despite their open invitation to enter via the grand gate, hopped a ditch and parted some ivy which formed a living, unofficial door through a past-it's-best stone wall, and entered the estate from the south. They soon reached the lake - not a soul in sight. Marc followed Danny along the bank, hopped Drunken Willow via a series of twists and turns to a steep fall in the land overgrown with rhododendrons.

'From here on, you're sworn to secrecy; otherwise everyone and his great aunt will get to know about the place,' Danny whispered.

Danny led a traverse round the outcrop of ancient shrubbery, then almost on his belly, ducked under the low branches. Marc followed to find himself in a dark tunnel of knurled roots and twisted trunks. Twigs snagged his hair and spider-silks tickled his face, so that he found it a relief to get into the open again. The brothers emerged into sunlight, but there was a deal of scrambling yet to be done, more rhododendrons to skirt, a crumbling ivy covered wall to vault and then a bracken-dressed incline to scale.

Then, all of a sudden, it was before them, about ten metres in all from mossy foot-stones to green-flecked battlements. Here and there the tower showed through dark grey, but for the most part it wore the colours of the forest; varied hues of moss and lichen, ivy and even some thick strands of mistletoe gave it a perfectly camouflaged coat.

'This is amazing. I thought you were on about some piddly little out house, but this is the real thing,' Marc said, not quite sure whether or not he was dreaming.

'I told you. Come round here and I'll show you how to get in.'

It was not as easy as one might expect, for the only practical entrance was a portal some three metres off the ground.

'Remember your rock climbing rules: "three points on at all times",' Danny called from the portal, he having scaled from the ground in a little over ten second.

A little over fifteen seconds later, Marc's head reached the step. To his surprise, Danny stood within the tower, but still looked down on his brother. Although it was a three metre climb up to the portal, it was a drop of only half a metre to the grassy floor within. Marc heaved himself up on the stone uprights and jumped from the step.

'What did I tell you? Perfect place to make love or what?'

Sex was the last thing on Marc's mind at the moment. He couldn't imagine how such a structure as this ancient tower had remained unknown to him. The woods and lake of Wymes Park had been his playground throughout his boyhood. All those games, playing out the stories and legends, pretending to be Fey Knights or looking for the lost tribe of Indians, even getting lost in the place for crying out loud! But never once had he seen or even heard about a medieval tower.

'How did you find it?' Marc said running his hand over the cool walls.

'What, do you mean the first time? It was Chris and me. We were in our last year at junior school waiting for the summer holidays to start. Old Rosy had our class. What started off as local history soon turned into local mythology. She ...'

'Not mad Christy and the Fey Knights?' Marc laughed.

'You too! And the creature from the stone age?'

'Yes,' Marc said, chuckling. 'And all about people disappearing never to be seen again.'

'And others turning up out of nowhere.'

'"The Mysteries",' Marc said. 'She called them "The Mysteries".'

'That's right. She'd get dead serious and say "Beware the Mysteries, for they walk abroad. I know, for I have seen them".'

The young men chuckled in shared memory of their ancient and slightly dotty junior school teacher.

'So me and Chris decided we'd go hunting for some of her Mysteries. Chris was pretty pissed off at the time because his old man was a copper then, and he'd had to pull out of a camping trip for some duty or other. To make up for it, he pulled a few strings so we could camp out on the estate.'

'I remember. Mum was worried, her darling little boy out in the big wide world.'

'Shut up! But do you remember what happened when we got back?'

'No, not really,' Marc said, but then a faint memory began to form. 'Ah yes! There was some fuss about something. Got it! The tent hadn't been used.'

'That's right, and we got a grilling about where we had slept if not in the tent, and we kept getting caught out telling lies. Dad and Mr De'Ath got right out their trees.'

'So where did you stay?'

'Right here. It was brilliant. A real castle to ourselves. It was as if rambling Rosy's stories were all true, like living the legend.'

'Weren't you frightened?'

'Not much. We made a fire here.' Danny pointed to a ledge which probably had actually been built as a hearth. 'And I slept with my sheath-knife in my sleeping bag.'

Danny crossed the circular, grass carpeted floor. 'Come here and read the names,' he said pointing to what looked like aeons old graffiti. Marc walked over and joined Danny, who turned away from the writing. 'Check me. I know them all.' Danny began to recite from the list of names that adorned the stone wall in two, long lists. 'Then, in the second list: "Fonlak, John-with-an-E" - I reckon that's from about the seventeen-hundreds - "Stormcloth, Christy" as in mad Christy and the lost Indians, then a few names you can't read properly, and finally "Daniel and Christian". That's me and Chris - we were feeling a bit formal at the time.'

'Not "finally",' Marc said. 'There's another name after yours and Chris's.'

'Never! Where?' said Danny pushing Marc aside in disbelief. Sure enough, another name had been carved deep into the stone. 'Who the bloody hell's "Harry"?' Danny said running his index finger along the newly gouged lettering.

'Another mystery?'

Danny shrugged, snapping out of it. 'Place is full of them. Look here for example.'

Marc followed and read. Familiar stuff; two names separated by a heart. '"Gayle loves Chris". So, what's the mystery? She probably does.'

'The point is Marc. It was scrawled up there when Chris and I first discovered the place, long before Chris and Gayle ever met.'

Marc took a closer look at the writing. Old it was, and very worn - older and more worn even than John-with-an-E. Another Gayle and Chris no doubt, but strangely, there was doubt.

Marc came away from the tower head spinning with questions. 'Shaun would love the place - and the mysteries surrounding it. How did old Rosy know half the names from that carved list?'

'She must've been to the tower, when she was a girl maybe, and just made up the stories to fit the names.'

'She said this mad Christie told her the stories, and there is a Christie on the list.' Marc said.

'I know. Chris and I got quite enthusiastic about it all when we first found the place, so we asked loads of questions, and guess what?'

'Go on.'

'Dad says there was a bloke who lived in these woods during the war. No one knew here he came from and when he disappeared, no one knew where he went.'

'Mad Christy?'

'That's what everyone called him.'

The secret shared and the mysteries yet unsolved, the young men picked their way back through the bracken and round-under the giant rhododendrons to join the path leading home. When they reached the lake they noticed a figure kneeling at the end of the punt pier. It was old Harry and he seemed to be clutching a bundle of rags to his chest. The lads skirted by silently and left the old fellow to it.

'What you doing Saturday, Danny?'

'Nothing planned. Why?'

'Shaun's coming over for the weekend. Why don't you join us for dinner?'

'You're on!'

'And bring Megan.'

'Great!' Danny hid his apprehensive feelings about what Megan's reaction might be.

'It's going to be a big weekend for us, Danny. It's our ... anniversary. We've been going together for exactly two years on Saturday.'

'Congratulations.'

Marc began going over the details when female laughter peeled through the wood. 'Hold up, Danny! Someone's coming.'

It was Lillian, and Aby Knapper. There were rumours about Lillian. Nobody knew where she came from, but here she was shacked up at 'Lofty Gables', a rambling house set in generous acreage on the outskirts of Little Rillton. She was, according to whose opinion you sided with, a little scrubber up from the Smoke, the house-keeper ever aware of her master's pleasure or a runaway from an approved school. But about one fact everyone seemed to be in agreement; she was boy-crazy, and more than one of the village lads boasted first hand knowledge.

Lillian smiled at the brothers as they passed in the narrow lane, and it was very apparent where her eyes went; first they caught Danny's gaze, then they swept down to fix very obviously on his crotch, and this while she moistened her red-stained lips with a suggestive slide of the tongue. Instant crutch-crickets for Danny; mild amusement to Marc. Aby looked like a rabbit caught in a truck's headlights. He replied sheepishly to Marc's greeting and looked over his shoulder as if silently calling out for rescue, as Lillian dragged him off the path.

Danny snatched a look over his shoulder noting the tight black pedal-pushers and fluffy but form-hugging pink woolly.

'How do you reckon you measured up in *her* book then, Danny?'

'I feel like I've just been mentally stripped, tickled up and had! Mind, she could have me gift wrapped and eager without a lot of trying,' Danny said almost watering at the mouth.

'Not my type.' Marc said sporting his brother's lop-sided grin. 'But Aby, on the other hand ...'

'He's the vicar's son so he's out of bounds. And with a girlie in the woods, double out of bounds.'

'And I'd always though Aby was "guys like us".'

'Like you, not us,' Danny said, a little too forcefully.

'I meant me and Shaun. Anyways, where do you think that little vixen is dragging the gorgeous son of a preacher man?'

'Into the woods to get him out of his boxers, I should imagine.'

Marc tried hard not to imagine Aby out of his boxers but failed abysmally. 'You don't think she's taking Aby to our tower, do you?'

'No way! I don't even think Mr De'Ath knows about it. No; me, Chris and his girlfriend Gayle, Megan and now you. And perhaps half a couple other people ... tops. And I kind of get the feeling that Shaun might be let into the secret. Apart from that, the place is like the Lost Ark.'

Marc hopped over a style and leaned on it with both elbows. 'About dinner. We're inviting Mum and Dad too.'

Danny grabbed the style from the other side. 'Do they know, like, you and Shaun?'

'Nope.'

'Going to tell them?'

'Nope.'

Danny frowned. 'Won't they guess?'

'That's what we're hoping. We'll walk the walk to save us having to talk the boring talk. It won't be the family at Marc's. It'll be the family at Marc and Shaun's. Lots of clues, but nothing obvious.'

Danny nodded. 'So, no screwing on the dining room table, but the sound track from "The Wizard of Oz" as background music ... kind of thing?'

Saturday was wet. The rain was light but with that 'in for the day' feel, and the train was half an hour late. Squirrels on the line again. It eventually pulled in to the station and shunted Marc closer to the edge of expectation.

A dozen people got out, one of them a tall dark haired lad wearing a college scarf, a dark grey duffel coat and well pressed olive green cords. Spotting Marc he smiled and homed in, a spring in his stride. Marc felt his heart leap but stayed outwardly cool - so practised, so in control. Shaun transferred a heavy looking sports bag to his left hand and extended his right in formal greeting, the precision in his movement hinting at a military connection. The young men shook hands.

'How do you do, Mr Stockdale?'

'How do you do, Mr Ashton?' Marc replied, then softer - just above a whisper - 'Have you missed me?'

'Just a tad.' Shaun said. 'Give us a kiss.'

Without a look either to the left or right, Marc leant forward and gave Shaun a peck on the cheek.'

'Blimey! You're getting brave in your old age!' Shaun did the looking round for both of them. 'This can mean only one thing. You're out! No more pretending.'

'Not quite. Come on - let's get out the drizzle. I'll tell you all about it in the car.'

Marc's flat was the downstairs of a large, converted Edwardian house on the outskirts of Shrewsbury, fully furnished, rented by the month and a forty minute drive from Little Rillton. Danny was worried. He worried about embarrassing silences round the dinner table, about stony looks from Mum, about the brave but transparent face likely to be worn by Dad. He worried that Megan would hate the whole scene and perhaps even review their relationship: if Danny could accept what she could not, who could tell where it would all end.

Megan nibbled at her thumb nail. She was full of apprehension. She had met Marc many times and never once guessed he was gay. He played rugger for Christ's sake! And now here she was, going to his house for dinner, to meet his boyfriend. She shuddered at the thought of them kissing and hoped to high Heaven that they didn't get that friendly during the visit. Would she giggle, would she wretch? She did not know.

Rob Stockdale eased the nose of his big Peugeot estate round into the almond flanked avenue leading to Marc's close.

'I really do think Marc was lucky to get a flat in such a nice area. It makes me feel quite jealous.' Irene said.

'Give me Little Rillton any day.' Rob replied.

'Oh yes, of course! But I mean, to think how we started out. A horrid little bed-sit above a dry cleaners. All those fumes and - ah! - here it is, darling. Number thirty-three.'

'Here they are Shaun. Good luck,' Marc said with one hand on the door catch.

'God, I'd rather be somewhere else. Are you sure it's a good idea?'

'Yep. Like we said, nothing overt, nothing they can't explain away if they really want to, but plenty of little clues.'

'Like the two of us at the door to greet them? Subtle. How do I look?'

'Great. Get 'em off!'

'Timing's not great Marc, but ask me again later. Cripes, the door bell!'

Marc had done the right thing asking Danny along; there was no chance of the feared silences with him all quips and banter. Shaun too helped to keep the atmosphere light. In fact, Danny and Shaun made a good double act. The clues though were there and they remained unveiled by the alternately convivial and jovial atmosphere; the exchanged glances between the hosts, little gestures which indicated a great care each for the other, even their places at the table.

Danny, the keen observer, eyes closely scrutinising the faces of his parents even as he joked and played his close fought role as life and soul of the party, could say with fair precision when the penny dropped with each of his parents.

With Mum, it was an arrested smile as she read the truth in her eldest son's face while he watched Shaun pouring wine. And Dad, a slow furrowing of the brow together with the smallest nod of his head as realisation dawned. And then, on with the party! Each regained composure almost immediately. Everything was going to be all right, Danny knew it, and he suddenly felt a great pride in his parents.

Danny and Megan stayed until gone midnight. Mr and Mrs Stockdale had left earlier so that 'the youngsters could enjoy themselves' as Irene had put it. They had parted on the best of terms and Rob, to the everlasting surprise and equally lengthy spell of gratitude from Marc, had actually clapped Shaun on the shoulder in a farewell gesture, and that from a man with an aversion to social touching.

'Thanks lads,' Danny said at the open front door. 'It's been a great evening.'

'Thank you Danny. Thanks for coming. And thanks for a hell of a lot more than that,' Marc said.

'Yes, and it's been a pleasure to have met you at last Megan,' Shaun said, kissing her hand. Megan blushed,

'Shaun, you old smoothy,' Marc said.

'Unhand my woman, you cad!' cried Danny, hamming it up. 'Pistols at dawn.'

'Leave Dawn out of this, poor girl,' Shaun responded.

They laughed as they waved their goodbyes, the volume of their mirth in exact proportion to the amount of wine they had consumed and nothing to do with the somewhat tired witticisms. Only Megan had kept to orange juice and lemonade having volunteered to do the driving.

'Whoops! Nearly forgot,' Danny shouted forgetting that his brother had neighbours who were probably long a-bed. Running over to his well polished ten-year-old Mini, he flipped the driver's seat and took out a small gift-wrapped parcel. Megan settled into the driver's seat as Danny skipped back up the garden path. 'Sorry Marc,' he said. 'I was going to get you both something but I blew all my readies on these. Here you are Shaun. Happy anniversary.'

Shaun took the parcel and Danny was off, running back to the car even as Shaun was saying his thanks.

'Coffee?'

'Please, Marc.' Shaun collapsed into an arm chair. He opened Danny's gift.

Marc filled the kettle. 'What's Danny been buying you then?' he shouted through from the kitchen.

'Damned if I know.' Shaun examined the contents of Danny's parcel. 'Well, I know what, but not why. It's a bit strange. Some hidden message maybe.'

Oh no. He's not been up to one of his tricks, thought Marc as he hurried into the lounge. 'What's he been up to?'

Shaun held up the gift. 'White silk shirt and a pair of white silk socks. Weird anniversary present. I suppose I'd better wear them next time young Daniel visits.'

Marc shook his head, smiling. 'I think that maybe you're supposed to wear them in bed.'

'Good suggestion,' Shaun said.

Marc bought in the coffees and flopped down on the sofa. Shaun joined him and slipped an arm round his shoulders. 'It all went pretty swimmingly, I thought. But I'm glad it's over. I'm cream-crackered.'

'Not too creamed!' Marc said, sliding his arm round Shaun's waist, snuggling in close, kicking off his retro sneakers to bring his feet up.

'You've got a family in a million you know? And that brother of yours – he's something else. One of a kind.'

'What about the aged P's? Do you think they guessed?'

The phone went early next morning. Marc extricated himself from Shaun's sleeping embrace and scuttled to the living room to pick up without bothering to put anything on first. On hearing his mother's voice he snatched up a cushion and held it in front of himself. Dad wanted to meet, she said. So soon after seeing him, it didn't bode well. And there was something in his mother's tone that set the warning bells jangling.

Here it comes, he thought. Dad's had time to think about me and Shaun, and now he's going to get heavy about it. *Meet me at the Moiled Bull. Come on your own.* It had to be trouble, he thought. How wrong can a person be?

Rob got the pints in and he and Marc took the same bench under the willow that Marc had so recently shared with Danny. There were many parallels between the two meetings; the stumbled starts, the half-pint silences; but this time, when he realised what it was that Rob was opening up about, it was Marc who asked most of the questions.

And then the talking was done, the reflection begun. Marc felt an unprecedented closeness to his father and a deep sorrow on his behalf.

'So you see, I understand completely and I just wanted to say I wish you both all the happiness in the world.'

'And Mum ...'

'She wishes you well, but it might be a while before she can speak about it. Give her some time to loose all her dreams about grandchildren and all that.'

Marc was just about to say she still had Danny when something caught his eye. At first he thought ... but no, that was absurd. Trick of the light ... or something. Then he saw it again, a blue dart streaking through the air.

'Dad!' Marc hissed through his teeth in a strained, excited whisper. 'Look over there, on the reed by the opposite bank.'

'God's teeth! It's a kingfisher! I've never seen one of those little beggars before in all my life.'

'Me neither! There she goes. And there's another. Danny will *never* believe this.'

'Remember that rhyme your Granny used to torment us with?'

'"Only he that tells no lies can see the 'fisher as he flies".'

'"Only he that's pure of heart can watch the fire-and-azure dart",' Rob continued.

Marc finished his beer and wiped his lips on the back of his sleeve. 'I always did think that rhyme was a load of rhubarb,' he said.

CHAPTER FOUR

The Knights and the Old Tower

Danny sat on Drunken Willow to pull on his socks and trainers. The going had been soft underfoot until now, but the young men were about to scrabble through to the path leading to the old tower and in that direction there were holly trees.

'I thought you wanted to keep away from the old tower.'

'I did, but now I feel different. I want to tell you what happened in the place *where* it happened.'

'But you said ... the lake. They drowned in the lake.'

'No. They didn't. I made that up.'

Danny's face hardened and he looked ready to explode in anger.

'Hold on Danny. You'll know why I lied when I tell you what happened.'

'Tell me now Chris. Stop farting round it. We're talking about my brother and I haven't got time for all this.'

'When we get to the tower.' Chris was as determined as Danny was angered. 'Not before. Let's get going.' Chris swung over the trunk with Danny close behind. They were soon through the rhododendron tunnels and in the thick of the wild wood the trees seemed to close in around them. The air was hot and heavy and sounds were muffled. A blanket of peace and quietness tucked them away from the rest of the world and the usual sounds of the wood were largely absent. Any bird that did venture to sing seemed to regret its bravado at once, and cut its song short. The sharp drone of a large insect came so sudden and so near that Chris jumped and swatted at the air.

'It's only a beetle. Don't wet your pants.'

'I head that noise before. On the day it happened.'

'Marc and Shaun disappearing? So you heard a beetle. We *are* in the woods.'

'Did you see a beetle just now? I mean, actually *see* one?'

No, but ...'

'Button it then! I heard that noise when the guys were ... when they went missing. And I saw something too.'

Danny was on the verge of lashing out, but it was clear Chris needed support. 'Still, it's only the middle of the day and those big bastards usually fly at night. So, it's a bit unusual them coming out in the day, I'll give you that.'

Chris turned away and led off along the ill-defined path, hardly more than an indentation in the leaf-mould. Danny followed, shaking his head.

It was usually a thrill to reach the old tower. A secret shared by very few. An objective achieved. When Chris and Danny had gone there as boys they had never arrived without a sense of excitement and anticipation. It was old stones dressed in the clothes of the forest, but it was also a place of mystery and magic. This time though, Chris felt oppressed and Danny had a nasty feeling of foreboding.

Hundreds of years ago lightning had helped topple a section of the crenellated battlement and now thick with moss a fallen merlon made an excellent seat on a dry day. Chris sat with his legs dangling over the edge and Danny scrambled up and sat cross-legged a half-turn away from Chris. For some moments neither of them spoke and Chris felt the tension mounting. There was no getting out of it now. He had to tell Danny what happened, but now it came to the crunch he found it almost impossible to get the words out. He made several false starts before deciding to ease into it.

'Thanks for telling me about Marc and Shaun.'

'Yeah, well. I've never told anyone about our day fishing. That was something only the two of us shared – me and Marc. Now three of us know. Well, two again I suppose is what I mean, now Marc's gone.'

'Dad told me the Army spent a good while searching the forest and they've put a guard on the old grotto. I wonder if they came here to this old tower.'

'They wouldn't, would they? Not unless someone told them where it was. Gary Tregonhawke went up in a little plane once. He said you can't even see the tower from the air.'

'You told Gary about it?'

'No. When I heard he was going up I asked him to look for anything like an old building in the woods. He said they looked the whole place over and there was nothing.'

Chris tried to find the right words but still they wouldn't come. 'Sometimes I think this place is a dream that only me and you can see.'

'And Marc.'

'Of course. And Shaun. I followed them here that day.'

Danny's head snapped round. 'Followed them! Why?'

'I just wondered ...'

'Wondered if they were going for a shag?' Danny's voice was raised. 'Tell me you weren't going to perv off them, you bastard!'

'No, course not! Danny, give me some credit.'

'What else then? If you weren't going to squeeze one off the wrist while you were watching them, why be sneaky?'

'Okay, okay. I'd planned to go there with Gayle. Marc and Shaun beat me to it. I was annoyed so I wanted to see if they were really going to the tower. If they'd gone somewhere else, me and Gayle could still ...'

Danny took a deep breath and calmed down. 'I get the picture. I'm sorry.'

'No probs. Look, I want you to keep quiet while I tell you what happened. I don't want you to say anything, or ask any questions, or pull any faces or just walk off and leave me. Promise me you'll stay and listen until I've finished, then after that, it's all up to you. Go. Stay. Ask anything you like. Give me a slap. Call me a nutter.'

'You've got it.'

'You promise? Because what I'm going to tell you, you won't believe.'

'I think we've already pretty much established that you're going to talk a load of bollocks and I've got to believe you, so get on with it. We've always got the acid-tab explanation to fall back on.' Danny's face went instantly from dark and concerned to the brightest of his smiles. He clapped Chris on the shoulder. He was doing his best, under the circumstances. 'So get on with it already.'

The subject broached, Chris felt the first hurdle receding and saw the next one up ahead. It was now or never. 'When I got to that little bit of a clearing over there, Marc and Shaun were already climbing into the tower. I thought I'd wait a while, just in case they were just having a look round.' Chris didn't notice Danny's sceptical look. 'I heard that noise a couple of time, that whirring beetle noise, and once I caught something out the corner of my eye. It was no beetle. More the size of a thrush, but I couldn't get a good look before it was off again.

'Then I heard a noise from the tower. Shaun I think. It was like "whoa" as if he'd been surprised by something. Marc came shooting out the tower like his pants were on fire. He'd taken off his shoes and socks and t-shirt. Shaun came down after him. Again, no footwear and his shirt unbuttoned. I thought ... well, you can guess what I thought, but I was curious as to what had disturbed them. It was soon pretty obvious.

'Now here is where you have to keep your trap shut. It was a deal.'

Danny clamped his lips tight shut and nodded.

'Marc and Shaun edged slowly towards the thick shrubs over there. And as they moved towards the undergrowth, three figures came out. There were these three guys, all about our age, a bit shorter than us but not a lot, all with black hair and all looking just the same except one had his black hair loose and long – way down past his shoulders, one had it done up in a kind of Samurai pony tail and the other one had his hair collar length, thick and scruffy. They looked like they were dressed out of a charity shop – loose stuff, old fashioned and worse for wear. All browns and greens.

'First thing I thought was they were a gang of lads who'd caught Marc and Shaun ... who'd caught them and was going to give them a good kicking. The second thing I thought was "Slap me all the way to Shrewsbury and back! They look like the bloody Fey Knights!" I soon discounted the first thought because they looked friendly enough – all big smiles – and they didn't look to be squaring up. As for the second thought, it kind of whooshed through without sticking.

'I couldn't hear what they were saying. I was too far off, but I could hear voices drifting across and it was clear they'd started having a chat with Marc and Shaun. They all sat down on the grass in a little circle, and it was then I thought they must be old mates of Marc's as they were sitting a bit too close for strangers. I also noticed these bird things flitting in and out. Again, too close to see the details. I know what you're thinking Danny, but keep it shut. You promised.

'Then the boys stood up, and Marc and Shaun stood too, only they were moving weird and slow. The guy with the Samurai took Shaun's hand and the one wearing his hair loose took Marc's. Okay, so this is weirdness upon weirdness, and they start leading Marc and Shaun into the woods. Then, Mr Collar-Length sees me. He's there across the glade to the left of the tower and then, without anything happening in between he's in my face! Close enough to reach out and touch.

'He's smiling at me and it makes me feel ... it makes me feel good, somehow, like I've known him all my life. Like he's Jesus or something and I love him like you're supposed to love Jesus. It's like I know him even better than you. He holds out his hand and I take it and he leads me right across here to where we're sitting now and he doesn't have to use force. I'm going with him because I want to.

'I then sort of come out of it for a second and the world's all skewed and wonky. I hear Marc cry out and this guy is a stranger again. I stop, pull him up short and pull my hand away from him. He turns on that smile again and I feel it doing its thing. "Not this time bro!" I think, and I slug him one, right in the face. He looks shocked and there's blood and my hand hurts like Hell. Then I'm on my back. He didn't hit me as far as I can remember but I'm up looking at the blood on his face, then I'm down looking up at the blue sky and the tree tops.

'Then I hear that noise again, and … oh Jesus Danny. Jesus, Jesus, Jesus.' Chris looked close to losing it, but only for an instant. Danny moved in to comfort him.

'No, Danny! Leave me!' He took a deep breath and let out an indignant snort. His emotions were not going to get the better of him. 'I look up and there is, for want of a better word, a faerie. No, let me finish. A flaming flesh and blood faerie, its wings a blur, is hovering a couple of feet above my head. It looks like the guy I just whacked, except he's only about fifteen centimetres from tip to toe. He's wearing nothing but a little Tarzan-thing round his middle made of fur. I remember thinking "mouse-fur" and giggling for a second at the stupidity of it all. This one, little giggle in the middle of a world of fright. He hovers there looking down at me, okay, and I can feel the wind of his wings on my face. Then "flit" he's gone. I sit up and see more of them – three all together disappearing into the wood, same direction they took the lads.

'I start to think the three boys turned into the three faeries and I think I've gone nuts and all sorts of other stuff, but whatever is going on I've got to get to Mark and Shaun. I run after the little flying bastards, crashing through the bushes and I come to another tiny clearing – I'll take you there in a moment – and there is Marc and Shaun with the boys. They haven't turned into faeries after all, but the three tiny flyers join them. They all huddle really close and I run at them. I've got no plan but to barge into them, scatters the fey lot and bowl our lads over, maybe bringing them to their senses.

'But I don't get the chance. The closer I get the fainter becomes this little gaggle of Fey Knights and real lads until they are gone. Right in front of me, they faded into nothing. I look all round the clearing, feel the ground, everything. Not a trace.' Chris took a deep breath. At last, it was out of him, and now he only had to wait for Danny's reaction. 'Well, that's it mate. I hope you can see why I didn't tell the truth, because I know as well as you do, the truth can't be possible.'

Danny said nothing. Fiddling with the moss by his foot he looked totally bemused as if gauging how to react.

'So Danny, are we going with the acid-tab theory, or is your best friend a total nutcase?'

'Who said you were my best friend?'

Chris shrugged.

'Well, after Megan, you are. But tell me, the boy you hit. You sloshed him one in the gob, didn't you?'

'Yes. Palm-strike straight to the mouth. That's what gave me this.' He held out his right hand and Danny could see the half-inch scar. 'Guess I got him in the teeth.'

'Not much doubt about that. Look,' Danny said. He pulled something out of the moss and wiped the dirt away with his thumb, then held up a tooth.

'Human?'

'It's a tooth. And if Fey Knights are human, I guess it's a human tooth. Looks like the acid tab theory has to go.'

Once again, his emotions got the better of him but this time it was relief. Chris let a couple of tears out this time before pulling himself together. Danny squeezed his shoulder briefly expressing the support Chris needed.

'So you believe me. I wish I'd told you a lot sooner.'

'I believe you saw what you saw, but that's not the same as accepting your story at face value. Bruv, I'm sorry but I don't believe in faeries.'

'There! You just killed another one, you bastard.' Both young men chuckled.

'I think it's a combination of things. I've no problem with the black-haired boys. But I reckon one of them smacked you, and the little flyers were due to concussion or something. Who knows, maybe the blow triggered an acid flashback after all. All I'm really sure about is we have to tell the police. You have to say what you saw so they can come here with all their equipment and scientists and look for clues. Something happened to my brother, and I have to know what.'

Chris nodded. He was reluctant to tell his story to anybody else and bringing the world and his granny to this secret place felt like a betrayal, but he saw the sense in it. 'Let's take a look at that tooth.'

Danny handed it over. Chris examined it carefully. There was nothing unusual about it; a perfectly normal, human adult incisor as far as he could tell. 'Can I keep it?'

'I guess. But show it to the police when you tell them what happened.'

Chris pocketed the tooth. He shuffled off his stone seat and nodded towards the undergrowth. 'I need to whiz,' he said.

While he was attending to his business Danny decided to climb up into the tower. Well practiced and intimate with all the handholds he was up to the portal in five seconds, and it was seconds later when he found more evidence in support of Chris's bizarre story. Damp and dirty from exposure to the elements, Danny saw Marc's t-shirt spread over the ground. Lifting it, the grass was yellow below, etiolated from lack of sunlight. Nearby were Marc's trainers and socks, and Shaun's walking brogues with a sock tucked into each one. He heard a scuffle behind and turned to show his friend the discovery.

'Chris ...' It was not Chris. 'Oh. Hi! What are you doing here?' Danny smiled sheepishly.

'I was just about to ask you the same thing,' Lillian said. Danny couldn't place the accent. Was it west-country? At once, her eyes drifted to his crotch.

'I was just ...' Danny was unable to finish his sentence, for Lillian, the girl with the bad reputation who worked up at Lofty Gables, closed the distance between them and pressed a finger against his lips. It soon became clear, she deserved every inch of her reputation.

'Better use for lips than talking with them,' Lillian said. And from her first kiss, Danny was trapped. As Danny dropped his brother's t-shirt Lillian's fingers were working the zip of his jeans. While part of his mind screamed out that this was all ridiculous it was a part of his mind that was no longer under control.

'Come on! I know a better place – and don't be worrying about your pal. We'll be done before he knows your missing.'

'DANNY!' Chris yelled at the top of his voice while he hovered somewhere between annoyance and fear. Fear was beginning to get the upper hand. Chris crept round to the overgrown side of the tower's base, once again, absentmindedly fretting with Marc's damp, limp t-shirt. He moved slowly, and as silently as he could and then sprang out into the clearing with only the most forlorn of hopes that Danny would be there.

He empathised with his friend and could see the scene unfolding, as if through Danny's own eyes. Danny climbs up into the tower. He finds Marc's things. He is overcome by a terrible and profound grief and runs away, not wishing to be seen even by his best friend. It was a good theory, but it didn't fit Danny's character. No, it would be much more like him to play the fool and jump out from the undergrowth for a bit of rough-and-tumble. That would be Danny alright, but that would be Danny on a normal day which hadn't included bared souls and spoken secrets. Chris was worried about Danny. It was nearly an hour since he'd returned from relieving himself in the bushes to find his friend gone. If he'd been gone three minutes it was stretching it, and Chris couldn't understand how Danny had moved so quickly and so quietly.

When he started to imagine the Fey Knights dragging his friend away, he knew it was time to head for home. Danny was probably already back home playing Resident Evil on his Playstation having a good laugh at Chris's expense. Chris made his way back to Wymes Lake hoping that every forest noise was a precursor to a sneak attack from Danny. He swayed between anger and concern all the way home and ducked his head indoors to see if there had been any word. Daniel Stockdale had made no contact with the De'Ath household in Chris's absence, so he walked up past the war memorial until he got a signal on his mobile. No, Danny's parents had no word of him either. Chris checked at the *Moiled Bull*, the cricket club and even the garage where Danny had a part time job, but nobody had seen him.

'You're dinner's on the side,' Mrs De'Ath called as she heard the door go. Chris recognised the stony tones. 'Heat it up in the microwave. Pudding wouldn't keep. It's in the dustbin.'

'Sorry Mum.' He heard the living room door slam. Dinner was on the work surface with a Pyrex plate over the top. It was fish fingers, chips and veg and as Chris slid it into the microwave he noticed it was coming up for half-past six – well past normal dinner time. Sliding back the bin lid he saw what was left of his ruined portion of pudding. Chocolate steam pudding with chocolate sauce. His favourite. Mum was just being bloody minded. That would have kept perfectly well and he could have done that in the microwave too. He considered scooping it out with his fingers, but it was all mixed up with broken egg shells.

Chris didn't bother with a tray or the dining room. He ate at the work surface favouring a lonely meal over another run-in with Mum. That was something he could not handle right now. He ate without enthusiasm and watched out the window across the pasture towards the forest that bordered Wymes Park. The De'Ath residence was a large detached, fairly rustic house set like an outpost to the village of Little Rillton and a hundred metres from the nearest neighbour. From the kitchen window though, the only neighbour hinted at was the estate of Lord Wymes and Chris kept an eager eye fixed on the woods, hoping that at any minute, Danny would come loping out.

He was washing up his dinner plate when Richard De'Ath returned from his post-dinner beating of the Park bounds. 'Hi Chris. Had a good day?' he said as he filled the kettle and switched it on.

Chris shrugged and shook his head,

'Oh, sorry to hear that. You and Danny ... had a row over ... something?'

'No! What made you ask that?'

'I just saw him ... and, well, I just saw him.'

'Where? When?'

'Ten minutes ago. In the High Street.' Mr De'Ath poured boiling water over the coffee granules in two mugs. 'Want a cup? There's enough water for a third.'

Shaking his head Chris suddenly felt a huge surge of relief. 'Are you a hundred per cent it was him, Dad?'

'A thousand! I've known him since he was in nappies. Thing is ...'

'What? He was alright, wasn't he?'

'Yeah, yeah. He was smiling his usual happy smile, but ... and this is why I wondered if things were okay between you two ... he was with Gayle.'

Odd, thought Chris, but at least he was okay. There was no law against his best friend talking to his ... ex? ... girlfriend. 'When you say with ...?'

'He was passenger in her little black Ka. Gayle was driving towards Wymes Park and Danny leaned out and gave me a big wave.'

Mr De'Ath took the coffees through to the living room and Chris was alone once again with his thoughts. He tried to put Danny and Gayle out of his mind and get on with the rest of the evening, and it wasn't until gone ten that his concern was lifted another notch. The phone rang. It hardly registered with Chris; it wouldn't be for him. He heard his father's voice in the next room; recognised the concerned tones. It was Irene Stockdale. She wanted to know if anyone had seen Danny. It appeared he and Gayle had gone off for a drive and nobody had seen them since. Gayle's car had been found, parked in a lay-by by the boundary of Wymes Park, but there wasn't a trace of either of them.

In the early hours of the next day, just after dawn, PC Chapel was at the front door, Oscar waiting patiently in the little police van. The officer wanted Richard De'Ath to help organise a search of Wymes Forest. Dolly Tregonhawke had already been heard, muttering about the Fey Knights.

CHAPTER FIVE

A Question of Stability

To Chris it was like Marc and Shaun's disappearance all over again: police asking questions, large numbers of people searching the woods, telling half-truths about what he saw or knew or did. The truth would mean taking the police to the old tower. The truth would mean disclosing the reason for his and Danny's meeting there. The truth would mean exposing himself to disbelief and ridicule. He couldn't blame them, because the truth of his own senses was a lie in the face of reality, and reality would win every time. How could Chris blame anyone for taking his truth with a pinch of salt when he was his own chief doubter?

Richard De'Ath came home late; exhausted and depressed. The police and local unit of the Territorial Army and many volunteers had poked and prodded and grubbed through the woods all day without a trace of Gayle or Danny.

'If I hear one more whispered reference to the flaming Fey Knights I think I'll blow a gasket,' Dad said at dinner. 'You'd think people would have more sense.'

Mum muttered something Chris didn't hear while he remembered the pain of that "Fey Knight's" tooth embedding into his hand. He rubbed the scar unconsciously. He went to his room as soon as dinner was over and asked himself the old questions yet again. Am I going mad? Was it a flash-back from that old acid-tab prank? There was never a question as to whether his eyes had told him the truth, but in any event there were two things going on here: what had Chris seen and what had taken four young people in the space of six weeks? He knew he had his priorities wrong, but it was the former question that troubled him most. Taking up a pen and a notebook, Chris began to jot down a plan of action. For six weeks he had moped about, never facing the question square on. Not any more.

'I'm going to get to the bottom of this, Danny,' he whispered into the air. 'That's a promise.'

It was long past the time he usually went to bed and his eyes were heavy. Mum and Dad had called in goodnight hours ago. Chris made a half-hearted effort to fold his jeans and dropped them on the floor next to the bed. Hoody and t-shirt joined them and he slid under the duvet wearing socks and boxers. He sat up in bed for a while, knees drawn up to form a lectern for his notebook. Reading the notes and adding a few more he tried to draw out a plan of action. What next? Where was he to look for more information? Who might harbour away little secrets that were the very clues he sought? It was no use: his thoughts kept running round in circles and his eyelids grew heavier still. Taking a deep breath, he let it out slowly and decided to shelve the lot until tomorrow. Slipping off his socks and boxers he let them fall onto the rest of his clothes and slid under the covers revelling in the warmth while at the same time enjoying the chill feel on his legs as he shuffled down. He reached out and switched off his bedside light.

No matter what his worries, Chris never had trouble sleeping. He would block out his concerns by pretending he was in bed with someone he loved and fall asleep cuddling his pillow or wrapped in the warm embrace of his own arms. He was asleep within moments and for an hour or so his slumber was untroubled by dreams. When dreams did come, they were intensely erotic. He was on the top deck of a London bus making love to Gayle. Chris stopped worrying about other passengers spoiling their fun as soon as he realised he was in the middle of a dream that had every sign of becoming a wet one. He sat up at the front row on a single seat of a kind that did not really exist on busses.

With his pants round his ankles and his legs spread wide, Gayle was kneeling between his knees, using her hands. Well, that had happened in real life, if you counted heavy petting through denim, and what was the point of having a sexy dream if you couldn't go just that little bit further? Or a whole lot further for that matter? Chris willed Gayle to go that little bit further – but she would have to be quick. He was close and he didn't want to waste the opportunity on a re-run of reality. He wanted her dream-self to be more accommodating then the real Gayle, who had always wanted to wait until she was ready to commit to a long term relationship. The dream Gayle smiled and licked her lips, and then moved slowly closer, and closer. And the closer Gayle came to making his dream one to remember the more quickly Chris drifted through the borders of the realm of sleep towards wakefulness. He did his best not to wake up, but it was out of his control and Gayle faded away to nothing and Chris was left unfulfilled and in the dark.

But pleasure still pulsed like electricity and his mind fought to make sense of it. Was he still asleep? No, absolutely not; he was awake and the wet, warm feelings that had been produced by dream-Gayle continued, only now he was closer still to a climax. His breathing increased rapidly as the moment came nearer. He forced his consciousness into his hands, believing that he had somehow lost control of them and he was pleasuring himself, but his hands were by his side, so the only remaining explanation was that someone was actually down there, doing it.

Opening his eyes he could see only a vague, human shape in the darkness of his room. He parted his lips to speak but another shock of intense pleasure radiated out from between his legs and stole away his words. His thoughts raced, considering and discounting one explanation after another. Only one was viable: a stranger had entered his room and was subjecting him to an unsolicited if not altogether unwelcome union. Slowly reaching out to his left he found the switch to his bedside light and clicked it on.

It was Lillian. She hesitated only for a moment, one hand holding his flesh while her blood red lips pursed an inch above. She appeared more beautiful than Chris remembered, with long black hair and ivory skin given a warm glow by the yellow light. Chris's duvet was gone and she had pushed his legs wide apart. She crouched between them, naked and lithe with passion. She smiled, her full lips parting to show even, white teeth and then she extended the tip of her wet, pink tongue to begin where she had left off. Chris held his breath as she took him in and once again waves of pleasure overwhelmed him.

Moments passed as she worked her magic while her eyes never lost contact with his. The pleasure was so welcome he kept blocking the vital questions. Who was this Lillian? How had she come to be here in his room, in his bed, filling him with so much raw pleasure? ... Why should he bother with such questions now, when they could wait for a few more, vital, explosive moments?

But something was wrong. Had it been a trick of the light, or had her eyes just flashed amber? And there was a dreamlike quality to the scene that affected only the girl, as if she was solid and real but cloaked in something less so. With this new concern Chris moved back from the precipice of climax, and the woman appeared to sense the fact. She let her lips slip off him gently and took her eyes away from his as she continued touching, her fingers playing with his wetness. She smiled and cocked her head, watching her work intently, and freed from her mesmerising look, Chris saw below her skin to something else that lay at the heart of her. Suddenly he was appalled and repelled. Galvanised to break free of her lascivious ministrations he pulled away and kicked out at her with both feet. He kicked a horror from the midst of beauty and with a sickening, inhuman scream the horror was propelled off the end of his bed, while the beauty froze in place then quickly faded away like breath-mist on a cold morning.

He had no time to react because the beast came back at him almost instantly smashing him hard against the headboard and pinning him there by the shoulders. The now undisguised amber eyes burnt evil intent into the back of Chris's skull and he felt all strength leave him. He slid down under the beast unable to move and as limp as a dead fish. He could blink and move his eyes but he had forgotten how to command the rest of his body, and the only part of it that interested the beast was at the mercy of small, black racoon-like hands. Perching back between his legs, the black fingers tightened round him and worked his fading erection back to hard functionality once again and all Chris could do was watch in abject horror.

The beast was as repulsive as its assumed form had been beautiful, and Chris cursed his body for responding to it. But friction and pressure elicited responses that revulsion could not overcome and the beast appeared to revel in dominance over the boy. The size of a small adult and covered with grey skin, the thing had large, bat-like wings and a head and limbs in the same proportions as those of a human. The raven-like, lustrous hair was now no more than straggly, black, wispy tufts inadequately covering a narrow head. The nose was better described as a snout and the mouth, Chris thought, could have been designed for no other purpose than the one upon which it was now engaged. With no lips, there was just a circular hole, like a letter "oh" with a double line of fleshy, glutinous tentacles round the perimeters. The creature had breasts, arid, sagging and pendulous, but no discernable genitalia. It was swathed in a miasma of damp, fetid corruption.

As involuntary muscled bunched his stomach and threatened to make him vomit, the circular mouth took him in and the tentacles stimulated him until he exploded with liquid fire. Chris bucked with the white hot intensity of it again and again until his stomach ached, and then the loathsome creature, at last satisfied with its work, slipped off, circular mouth pressing tight until disengagement.

It didn't leave though. Instead it sat up and grasped Chris's knees in its long-fingered, black hands and watched. He feared that it had not been sated by its stolen union, and that it would wait for him to recover and put him through it all again, but it just sat there. Once his sex had fallen fully flaccid and lay beached on his lower belly like a wet eel, there was no movement from either Chris, who was still incapable of commanding his muscles or of the creature which crouched without the slightest twitch. Chris watched the watcher, for that was all he was capable of, and waited wondering if the thing would kill him. He watched, and wondered and waited at the beast's will until after an hour he noticed something changing in its appearance. Its grey, membranous skin began to take on a more Caucasian hue. After another hour it was the same colour as Chris, even the little formerly black hands and they were no longer racoon-like but had somehow broadened and elongated to become very human. The breasts were less pendulous, slowly being absorbed into the rest of the body.

Another hour passed and the sexless expanse between its legs sprouted embryonic male genitals and the wings were being absorbed into the beast's body. Hair started to grow and the snout formed into a nose. By first light the creature had transmuted from the hideous beast it had been into a strangely featureless and indistinct human male. As dawn light suffused through the curtains, Chris realised with horror that this beast was turning into a replica of himself. Fear, never far from the surface during all this time, redoubled; he knew that when it had completed its metamorphosis there would be no more use for him and it would kill him. *He* would kill him. He would be murdered by himself and the intruder would take his place in the world, being him and exacting horrors on his parents and anybody else who got in his way. He struggled to move, to make a grab for the evil beast, but his mind was still disconnected from his body, and he made not the slightest movement. But some involuntary muscles still operated, and tears flowed freely.

Another hour went by, and as he heard his father moving about downstairs, he watched his naked double pad silently round his room getting used to a new body shape. It stretched its arms; it – he – rotated his head and pulled faces in the mirror. He came and pushed his face into Chris's peering intently at the hair, then went over to the mirror in the wardrobe door and flicked his own hair into place. He came back again comparing hand to hand, forearm length and belly button shape. Having eventually seen enough he reached over and yanked the ring off Chris's finger along with some skin; he did not care to be gentle. He put it on his own finger then picked up the duvet and threw it over Chris, who waited beneath for an unseen death blow. A vision, of his mother drawing back the covers to reveal a bloody pulp where his head should be, planted itself firmly in his mind.

Chris could only listen as the other Chris walked round the bed and dressed in the clothes he had worn yesterday – blue Echo T-shirt and jeans. Any time now, and the beast-Chris would tire of his presence and kill him. If the impostor feared the noise of inflicting a violent and bloody death it would be such an easy matter just to lean on the duvet and smother him. He heard the noise of the sash window opening, and then nothing else. He listened carefully for a long time and relaxed when he concluded that the beast had gone. In the airless warmth under the duvet, Chris drifted into semi-consciousness and then sleep.

He woke up ... an hour later? Two hours? He couldn't tell still buried under the duvet where the air was stale and his lungs had to work hard to find enough oxygen. He tried to throw the duvet off but still the connection between his brain and muscles was disrupted. He couldn't call out either but his chest heaved for air and he could still blink and move his eyes, so whatever Lillian had done to him, it wasn't progressive. And it certainly did nothing to relieve the pain of a full bladder.

Curare did this to people, Chris recalled from a biology class. It made the synapses impervious to the chemical that transmitted nerve impulses. Maybe she had used curare on him, or something else that had no effect on his ability to think. Mum and Dad were downstairs chatting. He could hear the words, edges smoothed and made indecipherable by the intervening walls. If only he could call out, but it was beyond him. If they didn't find him soon he would wet the bed, and with that thought he realised he still had control of his bladder. He had a dreadful thought: if the bladder required use of voluntary muscles, maybe he would be stuck here long enough for his bladder to burst. He imagined the pain and thought of the long term consequences. It was so unbearable that he had to try; let a little bit out to see if he could, and then stop. Once started, there was no stopping and Chris felt his face blushing hot with shame – hotter than the warmth that flowed down his legs and soaked the bedclothes. Once again, he cried.

It was school holiday time and although Chris's parents had ideas about how long a lay-in was too long, they had lightened up since he witnessed the fate of Marc and Shaun and the morning hours passed like torture. With the constant feeling of being on the verge of suffocation, such air as Chris could draw into his lungs was now rank with the stench on urine. His mind screamed out for someone to come and find him and at last he heard footfalls outside his room and his door being opened.

'Coming up for noon, Chris,' Dad called. 'It's time to shift your lazy arse.'

I can't Dad. Come and help me! For God's sake come and help me! No matter how loudly his mind screamed, Chris knew he might as well have been whispering from a mile away. He heard Dad cross the room and open the curtains.

'At least your window's wide open. It stinks like a bear pit in here.'

Chris felt something inside his head would burst with the effort he made to move or to utter the smallest sound. Nothing came but the tears from his frantically darting eyes. Dad was at the door again. He would soon walk out and shut it and then how many more hours would Chris have to endure?

Richard De'Ath paused at his son's door. 'Chris? You okay?'

No. No. No! I'm not. Dad, don't go!

Chris would never have been able to describe the relief he felt as Dad pulled the duvet clear of his face and he took a full lungful of fresh air. Dad could see the tears, smell the soaked sheets and tell at once that everything was far from alright.

It was all a bit of a blur until the doctor came. Chris felt grateful that Dad had cleaned him up and dressed him in a fresh pair of boxers and a pair of pyjama bottoms before any strangers had arrived. It was bad enough that all he could do was lay there while the doctor prodded, poked, listened with his stethoscope and even stuck a pin in him. The doctor was an irritable man and Chris could see the impatience behind his eyes and hear the scepticism beneath the outwardly caring words. Dad's pyjamas saved his blushes a little more when the ambulance men lifted him into the gurney and strapped him in, but there were legions of indignities waiting for him at hospital: being hooked up to a drip, the fitting of a catheter, nurses speaking about him as if he wasn't there, being given a bed-bath by a male nurse.

After five days Chris's mind started to look ever more inwards and drifted down into the dregs of his own jumbled thoughts. He sank ever deeper sharing the cloudy depths with strings of overheard conversation. *The encephalogram is perfectly normal. There is absolutely no physical reason for him to be in this condition. No CVA. No trauma. Electric shock treatment. She did this to you, did she not? We'll give him another two days and then …*

One of the phrases was out of place, and Chris reached out for it. *She did this to you, did she not?* The voice was softer than the others; a young man's and not like the older professionals who fussed over his results and argued treatment regimes. Chris struggled to surface from the depths of his own consciousness, and opened his eyes. It was night time. Chris was in a room of his own off the main ward and the glow from nightlights trespassed over the threshold by a metre. He became aware of a person in his room and he or she moved to shut the door, slowly and quietly until the light was shut out and only darkness remained.

Chris waited for the intruder to make a move. Apart from any other consideration, he had no choice. As his eyes became accustomed to the dark he could pick out the figure, a shade moving against shadow. And then the lights came on. The first detail Chris noticed about the boy was his hand on the light switch and the fact that he was wearing a patient's identification wristband. The second feature to register was actually by far the most obvious: apart for the wristband the boy wore nothing but a pair of white y-fronts at least one size too large. But the last detail sublimated all the others including his state of undress: Chris recognised the intruder. Feeling the pain in his palm anew, he could only wait and wonder.

The young man approached slowly, warily and then bent over Chris. He sniffed once, twice, like an animal might seeking a friendly scent and then he touched Chris's temple with one outstretched finger.

'I think I can release you, but I shan't allow you to strike me again. You fetched out one of my teeth. Look!' He brought a hand to his mouth and Chris saw the name on his wristband. It said "Forename: Tarn. Family name: ...?" Tarn lifted his top lip and leaned in affording Chris a close look. The boy's breath smelt of toothpaste. There was a gap between the first left incisor and the canine tooth but it was not a complete gap. Chris stared at what appeared to be a new tooth growing to fill the gap.

Tarn stood straight and passed his tongue over the growing tooth. 'It was a most unfriendly gesture, but no matter. I think fear moved your hand, and the desire to champion your friends. Am I right?'

I can't answer you, you little tosser!

Tarn frowned. 'What's "tosser"? Is it "toss-pot"? For if so I tell you, no hard liquor touches my lips – only a little mead or wine at festive times. And beer of course, but only small-beer so that doesn't count.'

If Chris had control of his muscles, his jaw would have dropped. He had to think hard: had he spoken or merely thought his reply? Who was this strange sounding guy? *"What's tosser?" for God's sake!* Without realising it, an image accompanied his last thought.

'Ah! I see now. Yes, I do that sometimes if I have been a long time without company. Don't you? Doesn't every man of our youth and vigour? What a strange kind of an insult, for you used the term thus, I'm sure.'

Chris blushed heavily, and Tarn frowned again.

'I'm sorry. I probed into your private thoughts and saw that which was not intended as communication. I shan't look so deeply again. Those thoughts you wish me to hear, think them *loud* and I shan't listen for the faint or fleeting words or look at the pictures.'

Chris marshalled his thoughts. *Can you hear me?*

'I can.'

A thousand questions competed for attention like a room full of excited school children with hands reaching for the ceiling. Me Sir, pick me! But they would all have to wait. *You said you could release me. Please, do it now and ... I promise not to hit you.*

'Of course, then when you wake, we will speak after the usual fashion of men. But you will sleep for some hours once I have lifted the spell. I might not be here when you first awaken, so is there anything you would know before you sleep.'

Who are you? Where do you come from, and where did you take Marc and Shaun?

'To the first, I am Tarniel. To the second, you must wait until we may converse at length. And your friends from the wood, I think you will meet again. They are quite safe.'

Safe where?

'Again, all will be answered in time.' Tarn flinched as the door handles snicked. The night nurse put her head round the door, but Tarn was already crouching in the shadows. Satisfied that Chris was alright, she continued her rounds.

What about Daniel? And Gayle?'

Tarn's brow creased in thought. 'I know nothing of another couple. Now quickly, is there anything else?'

Not really ... only, why are you walking round in your shreddies?

'These?' Tarn said pulling at the elastic of his underwear. 'They took my other things and would have me dress in clothes that smell of the alchemy. I shan't put them on, lest they burn my skin with their malodorous vapours. Now ...' Tarn moved close until he locked eyes with Chris. 'Look deep, past the sheen of my eyes. Seek the darkness behind them.'

Chris didn't want to look for the darkness. He wanted more answers. He started to think a question but the thought was stillborn, killed by Tarn's grass-green eyes. Could eyes be *that* colour? The green turned to the black of a deep rock pool; Chris fell in ... and drowned.

He woke again to the sound of laughter. Two nurses were sharing a joke outside in the main ward. Early morning sunlight formed orange-red bars on the far wall, shapes determined by the half-opened Venetian blinds. Something tapped at the window and Chris looked to see a wood pigeon parading up and down, strutting along the window sill, chest out, chin in, like a sergeant major of the bird world. Chris smiled at the image before he realised he had actually moved. He had moved his head; a little stiff and painful, but he'd moved it. Raising his hand he watched it as he wiggled his fingers and opposed each one in turn against his thumb. He smiled, felt the corners of his mouth draw apart, and then he laughed. If he had ever known such unqualified joy before, he could not remember when. It was short-lived though and soon soured by worries about his friends and his own mental stability.

The doctor shone lights into his eyes, listened to his heart, took his blood pressure and asked numerous questions, but once that was done and he was given the physical, if not mental, all-clear a nurse – the same one who had given him the bed-bath – began to unhook him from the support systems that had kept his body going whilst paralysed.

'Okay Chris, this will be a little uncomfortable ...' Nurse Kostja Claussen said as he began the decatheterisation process.

Chris closed his eyes and ground his teeth trying to place the nurse's heavy accent – anything to take his mind away from what was happening to him.

'There. All done. You can put yourself away.'

'I thought it was going to hurt more.'

'More embarrassing than painful – for both of us.'

Chris pulled the covers over himself then shuffled into a sitting position, propped up against the pillows. He felt weak and a little light-headed. 'When d'you think they'll let me go home?'

Kostja gathered all the medical detritus, put it in a compressed paper bowl and covered it with some paper towelling. 'You'll need to pee a couple of times and I guess you'll get another brain-scan. But beds are scarce, so you won't be in more than another day or so. Unless you are relapsing.'

Chris shuddered at the thought of enduring another attack from that – thing – and then, once again he began to doubt his sanity. He recalled his second nocturnal visitor. 'How's Tarn?'

'Tarn?'

'One of the other patients. Paid me a visit last night.'

'Did she?'

'It's a guy.'

Kostja shook his head. 'No patient in either ward called "Tarn." What's he look like?'

'Ordinary. He was just a guy, about my age, maybe a little younger. Very green eyes, black hair, skinny and a bit shorter than me.'

'How can you tell how tall he was, you laying down and all?'

Chris wasn't about to say he'd met him before in the woods. 'Oh, well, he seemed like was shorter than me. Maybe not.'

'Well, shorter or taller, there's no "Tarn" round here, nor has there been for as long as I can remember – which is two years. "Tarn" isn't the kind of name you're likely to forget. Do you think you might have …?'

'Dreamt it? Yeah, probably.' Chris knew Tarn had either been here in this room – a real flesh and blood boy – or he was a hallucination far more real than any sane man's dream. 'Do you think they'll do some tests on me to see if I'm nuts.'

'Nuts? We don't call people "nuts" these days, Chris. But yes, I'm sure you'll get a visit from a consultant from the psychiatric wing over the road. This whole paralysis thing has got the doctors flummoxed, but nothing to worry about, okay.'

'Sure,' Chris said quietly. There was a sympathetic tone in Kostja's voice, and Chris wasn't ready to handle sympathy.

'I'll clear this stuff away,' Kostja said taking hold of the drip support, 'and I'll pop back to see if there's anything I can do to make you more comfortable. Okay?'

'That's fine, thanks. If I can have a shower, that'd be good.'

'Easy-peasy. We'll sort that in no time flat.' Kostja began to wheel the drip away.

'There's just one thing,' Chris said remembering something of his encounter with Tarn. 'Can people grow new teeth if they lose one? I mean, I know most people can't, once they've got their grown-up teeth. But can some people?'

'Like, get a third set of teeth? I've never heard of it, but I'll see what I can find out. My big brother still has a baby tooth and he's nearly thirty, so I suppose anything's possible. I'll ask the orthodontist. She's in today.' Kostja passed through the door followed by a squeaky-wheeled trolley and then he was gone, leaving the room empty and silent. Chris appreciated the fact that the nurse didn't ask why he wanted to know about the teeth.

While flexing his wrists, moving his arms and stretching his legs – anything really that reminded Chris he was close to fully functional once again – he tried to remember everything about his encounter with Tarn, not just last night in this room, but also in the wood. He also tried to recall those stories about the Fey Knights. But always uppermost were his thoughts for Danny and Gayle. Surely, by now, they would be safe at home and he would soon meet them.

Kostja was not away for long. 'Let's see you walk round the room. And if you don't wobble too much you can go take a shower. You need help getting out of bed?'

'No, I'll manage thanks.' A shiver passed up Chris's legs as his bare feet came into contact with the cold linoleum. He stood carefully. 'I might wobble a bit, but I won't fall down.'

Kostja chortled. 'You're a Weeble, yes?' He pronounced his w's as v's.

'What's a Veeble?'

'"Weebles wobble but they don't fall down!" ... No? ... Of course, you're too young. When I was a kid ... oh never mind, you seem to be getting about okay. So, you want to shower you go left past the nurse's desk and next door on left. Here's a towel, and take this.' Kostja took a small plastic bottle of shower-gel from his pocket. 'Make you smell nice for when mamma and poppa comes.'

'Hospital issue?'

'Out of my locker. It was a freebie. Now, you will see a fold down seat in the shower. Use it, and if you start to get more wobbly, press the red button.'

'And you'll come running?'

'No, I'll finish my tea, eat some biscuits to keep up my strength, try and get the rest of the day off and if Staff says no, then I'll wander over, see what the Hell all the noise is about.'

'Good to know I'm in safe hands. And thanks for the gel.' Chris took the towel and gel and headed for the door.

'Oh, by the way. I spoke to the orthodontist. She told me there are many documented cases of people having a third set of teeth.'

'You're kidding?'

'I was surprised too. See, every day a new thing you learn.'

'So you can get an adult tooth knocked out and a new one can grow?'

Kostja shrugged. 'Not so. Some people have a third set come in and they have too many teeth and not enough mouth, so they need surgery. Other times the third set just stays up there in the jaw and never comes down.'

'But ... if they were up there in the jaw and a tooth got knocked out, couldn't one come down?'

'I guess it might be possible. Why all these questions about teeth anyway?'

The very question he didn't want to answer. What the Hell? 'Tarn, the guy who I mentioned before. We ... had a fight once. I knocked out his tooth. When he visited me, he was growing a new tooth. So, that's why I was wondering ...'

'Oh yes. Tarn, the boy who visits in the middle of the night. The patient who has no record.' Kostja smiled. 'Are you sure he wasn't one of the ... *Feejugend*? Kostja fluttered his hands at the wrist like butterfly wings. 'The guys who were never there?' As soon as he had spoken Kostja wished he'd kept his mouth shut. Chris looked crestfallen and vulnerable. 'Look, Chris. The mind can play little tricks with us all at times. My Grandfather ... well, it doesn't matter. It doesn't mean you're ... nuts. Okay?'

Chris nodded.

'Go shower. Come back. We talk – it's a quiet day for a change and I've got through all the routine stuff.'

Chris showered; the hot water revived him and pumped strength back into his muscles. When he got back to his room Kostja had changed the bedclothes and remade the bed. He had also laid out a set of Chris's own clothes.

'Your mother brought them in while you were still out of it. How about you dress and I'll get some tea. Then we'll talk.'

'This is all on the National Health I suppose? All this and my own personal nurse?'

'Most days you wouldn't get more than two minutes of my time. Change the sheets, give you your medication. Goodbye. But today, very few patients, so you get my undivided attention, until Staff finds me more work. No extra charge.' Kostja smiled.

Chris was dressed by the time Kostja returned with two steaming mugs of tea. It felt good to be back in his own things.

'What a transformation Chris! You look good, you smell good ...'

Chris took the tea, a little wary at Kostja intentions. 'Look, I ... I hope I haven't given you the wrong impression. I'm not ... like ...You know?'

'Of course not. Nor me, but it goes with the territory. You're a nurse so everyone draws the wrong conclusion. I have a wife. A little boy. Here,' Kostja said taking out his wallet. He opened it to reveal little boy of about three years old, fair haired and cheerful looking like his father. 'My little son, Philip Andrew, and here's my wife. So, you don't have to worry.'

'Cool.' Chris returned the wallet. 'Must be nice to have a kid. But for the record, I didn't draw any conclusions ... until you said I smelt good.'

'Ah, fair point. I hope I neither embarrassed you nor got your hopes up.'

Chris smiled. 'I've got ... used to have a girlfriend. We kind of split up after all this weird stuff started to happen.' The smile soon faded. 'That's what I want to talk about. So long as it's between us, that is. I don't want you telling the doctors. They'd never let me out of here.'

'Well, no promises, hey? But this is my tea break, so unless you tell me you have little voices telling you to kill Tony Blair or something like, it stays between us. Cool?'

'As a snowman's arse.'

Chris intended to be guarded with his revelations, but by the end the whole story had come out. He spoke of the encounter with the boys in the wood, though skimmed over the part about how he came to be at the tower when Marc Stockdale and Shaun Ashton had been taken. He told Kostja about the tiny, flying beings and about the disappearance of Danny and Gayle. He didn't even stop when it came to his night time encounter with the abusive creature which had paralysed him and then preyed upon him. Again, he kept details minimal but left no room for misunderstanding. Kostja looked worried, or perhaps it was guarded. Chris got the feeling that Kostja had heard this kind of a story before.

'So that's it. The lot. Now tell me you don't think my mind's gone.' *Please say you believe me.*

Kostja took a long sup of tea. 'Quite clearly, your mind is not gone. I remember the story of the missing army officer and his friend. It was also in the papers about Danny and Gayle. I have followed the story.' Here Kostja took another mouthful from his mug and looked very uncomfortable. 'As for the rest, I truly believe you are telling me the truth, as you saw it. You're not making it up, but ...'

'I know. That's exactly what Danny said. Then he disappeared.' Chris looked up quickly and locked his eyes on Kostja as if the strength of his gaze would root him to the ground.

'I'm not planning on disappearing, Chris.'

'I don't suppose Danny was either. You don't happen to know if Danny or Gayle has showed up yet, do you?'

Kostja stared at the floor. 'I, er ... It shouldn't be me.'

'Shouldn't be you, what?'

'Who tells you. There's been a development, and the news, it should come from someone else. I had no idea you were connected with them in the way that you were. I would never have ...'

'Something's happened to them, hasn't it?'

Chris needed no more confirmation of the worst than the forlorn look on Kostja's face. 'They're dead, aren't they?'

'Chris, please don't ask. Wait until you parents get here.'

'You've got to tell me. Now! Look, if I flip I'm in the right place. Tell me what happened to them, or I'll *definitely* flip.'

Kostja nodded slowly. 'It's not my place to say, but I'll tell you. They'll probably have my job, but I'll tell you anyway. Chris, it's the worst kind of news.'

Chris swallowed hard. Tears were already pricking at his eyes.

'They haven't found the girl – Gayle. She's still missing, but they fear the worst. Danny, they found ... in the woods. He was dead. No signs of attack or any thing at all. The post mortem suggested he died of exposure. He was found without his clothes, and for all they can tell he just lay down and died in the night when the temperature dropped. Not tied up. Nothing to say why he didn't just walk out of it and get help. Just as if he were ...'

'Paralysed!'

'Chris ... Don't!'

'She ... that thing ... that evil *bitch* got Danny too.' Chris's mind moved into overdrive; so that he could think through the dreadful possibilities; so that it could outrun the horror that threatened to overwhelm. 'How long had he been dead? How long? When did he die?'

'The papers said just hours after he went missing. But I know something else. See, the post-mortem was done by a surgeon from this hospital. There's talk, and the talk is that Danny's results show he died several hours before he was last seen. Right now they're all busy trying to work out solutions to that riddle.'

Just before Chris broke down, he knew with dreadful certainty that the Danny who had been seen with Gayle was not the real Danny at all. That creature used Danny in the same way as it was later to use him. Why couldn't it all be real, or all in his head? This juxtaposition of the actual with the impossible was almost more than Chris could bear.

'I knew I shouldn't tell you. There, sit quiet. Cry as much as you wish. Better out than in. And don't worry. Whatever is going on inside your head, we can help.' *And there's something else I should tell you,* Kostja thought, but it was a story too hard for him to tell, so he said no more.

CHAPTER SIX

The Wheat from the Chaff

Richard De'Ath sat at the workbench in his well appointed garden shed, thinking about his son while he sharpened a billhook. If only he could grind away Chris's worries as easily as the whetstone smoothed an edge onto this tool. He hardly paid attention to the job in hand, moving the blade in little circles against the oiled stone, almost oblivious to the motion but very much aware that Chris lay up in his room, troubled and alone. Julie surprised him when she came in with a brace of hot drinks.

'Cup of tea, darling?'

'Oh, just the thing Julie.' Richard laid aside the half-sharpened billhook and cleared the spare chair for Julie. She sat and they drank in silence for some moments, each thinking of their son, and each knowing just what was on the other's mind.

Julie cradled the hot mug to her bosom. 'You just can't tell, can you? How a beautiful, happy little boy can suddenly ...' She didn't want to say the word.

'It won't be permanent, Julie. I'm sure it won't. He's been through enough to make anyone ...' Richard was equally as shy of using the label, as if to say it would make it stick.

'And poor, poor Danny. What with Marc just gone, and now Danny. The Stockdales must be distraught.'

Richard set down his drink and picked up the billhook, absentmindedly trying its edge with his thumb. 'Do you remember when Danny first used to come round? How shy he was? That time at dinner with some of Chris's other mates?'

Julie chuckled, in spite of her heavy heart. 'Yes. When he was about twelve or thirteen. "Please may I please have an orange juice please?" The other boys had a laugh at that and he went bright red. Then to grow up so confident and friendly. Such a fine young man, only to ...Oh, I can't bear it Richard. What's happening to us?' Julie started to sob.

Richard put down the billhook, gently set Julie's drink aside and took her in his arms and held tight. 'He'll get over it. We'll get over it.'

'But his school work. He goes back in a week. He hasn't done anything toward his local history course work and he's done no revision and ...' Julie shook off her sobs and burnt her hurt away with a burst of anger. 'It's that stinking wood! Why didn't they burn it down years ago?'

Richard loosened his hold, fearing what Julie had in her mind and repelled by it in spite of his desire to comfort her. 'It's just a wood. It's just trees and ...'

'Don't you tell me it's just trees! Everyone round here knows ... People always go missing. Never turn up, or turn up dead. None of this is new.'

'It's more than twenty years since the last person went missing.'

'What's twenty years? Nothing! I remember Jamie. He was in my Beaver Lodge when he was little. Another one who didn't grow up to be a man. And then in the war – my dad used to tell me a few tales from those times. My own grandfather ... The place is evil.'

'Darling, I work there every day. It has its dangers. There's deep water, a fair acreage of dense, wild woodland – but apart from that, nothing.'

'Legends don't come from nothing. The Fey Knights –'

'Don't even mention the Fey Knights,' Richard snapped. 'That's just a load of cobblers. Faerie tales and nonsense, and you know it!'

'I'm not saying they exist, or that they ever did, but the legend has to come from somewhere. It's always youngsters go missing. Often young couples – and what with Marc and his soldier friend, and Danny and Gayle – well, it seems the legend isn't dead. Whatever caused all this in the past, and gave rise to the stories, is still going on.'

Richard returned to his chair and Julie muttered something about slopping coffee on her t-shirt. 'It happens to youngsters because they're the ones who go off into the woods, to lark about and skinny dip and fool around in the bushes. If generations of kids go swimming in a lake it stands to reason there'll be a drowning every now and again. It's not supernatural, it's cause and effect.'

'Maybe, but the causes can go and effect whatever they like. Right now Chris is the one in trouble, and I don't know what to do about it.'

Richard nodded. 'I don't think he's mad, just sadder than any teenager should have to be. He's strong. He'll get over it.'

'In the meantime we'll have to rally round ... and hide all the felt-tip pens.' Julie read Richards's blank expression. 'Have you seen the scribble he's done on the stonework over his bedstead?'

'The three little birds?'

'That's the one. Three tatty little birds and some Arab-looking writing. What did they *do* to him in that hospital?'

'Those scribbles were there before he went to hospital.'

Now it was Julie's turn to show a lack of comprehension. 'They most definitely were not! He's done them since he came home.'

'Well, I suppose I can't swear they were there before he had his bad turn, but they were there two days before he left hospital, for sure.'

'Can't have been.'

'Julie, I saw them.' Richard shook his head. 'Wait a minute! Two nights before we collected him. We thought we heard a noise in Chris's bedroom and –'

'No way Richard. You're not trying to tell me you think that crazy kid running round in his knickers has been in our house, I hope.' Julie didn't want to begin to think that her house had been invaded by a sexual deviant. 'He was a pervert, or a peeper. Not a burglar.'

'I suppose we'll never know. The police didn't catch him.'

'Surprise surprise. They get here more than an hour after we dialled 999 and wonder why there's no trace.'

'Yes, well. I was only saying. But you're right. Not much chance that he got into Chris's bedroom. Just a co-incidence.'

'But ... when we went up Chris's window was open, and I'm sure I'd shut it before. Then I look out and see this half-naked kid dashing across our lawn. Oh Jesus Richard. I think you must be right. He climbed onto the extension roof and got into Chris's room.'

'And stole nothing? The iPod and all Chris's CDs were untouched. And his wallet with a good few quid in it still in place. He gets in, draws on the wall and does a runner? It's hardly a likely scenario Julie, and certainly nothing to worry about.' Richard began to wish he'd kept his idea to himself. Next thing he knew,

Julie would be pestering him to install an expensive alarm system. Two heads turned as the muffled tones of the telephone tone drifted over from the house. Richard returned to the billhook. 'Are you going to get that?'

'I'd never make it before the answer-phone cut in. Anyway, Chris will hear it.'

'He'll hear it, but do you think he'll pick up?'

The telephone rang on and on while Chris ran his fingertip along the bold lines of the image above his bed drawn directly on to the stone. He hardly noticed the ringing and certainly formulated no intention to answer it. The tone stopped abruptly as the answer-phone did its thing, leaving Chris the silence he required to study the crude scrawl.

Three birds. It looked like three birds, with ibis-like curved beaks each bird in total an inch tall. There was no detail, just an outline, simple and child-like, except there was a consistency to the design that would have been beyond a child's skills. At first glance two of the birds looked identical, apart from the fact they looked in different directions. But the third, though it had the same kind of head and similar wings, had a box-shaped body.

'Bird by Picasso,' Chris muttered, and then turned his attention to the writing. Three lines of script, one set to form a base, the others to make up the sides of a triangle, so that the three birds were enclosed within. 'One ring to rule them all …' Chris said as he followed the longest line with his finger; the style reminded him of the Elvish writing that decorated the borders of a film poster. 'Elvish? Or Hindi? Or Arabic?' He had no more idea of the kind of writing it was than he had of how it came to be on his bedroom wall, so he dismissed it for the time being and returned to his desk. He had been back home from hospital for a some days now, and it was high time to rally his thoughts, sane ones right next to the crazy, and see if he could come up with a way of coping with all white noise that assailed his mind.

Shaking off the lassitude as best he could while still putting off the effort of getting washed and dressed, he dragged the duvet off his bed, wrapped himself in it and booted up the computer. Opening a new file he made up a table of two columns and while they had no headings, the column on the left was for known facts, and the column on the right for the other kind of facts; those known only to him and therefore unreliable. After half an hour, the table looked like this.

Marc and Shaun are missing. Divers, the police and the Army searched for them and found nothing.	*I saw Marc and Shaun taken by three boys who looked like the Fey Knights. I knocked out a tooth from one of them.*
Danny and Gayle went missing.	*I saw a bloody fairy for God's sake.*
Danny and Gayle were seen together days after him and me were by the old tower.	*Danny found a tooth by the old tower.*
I was paralysed. Hospital tests showed I wasn't fooling around.	*I got raped in my own bed by a monster who paralysed me. At first it looked like Lillian from Lofty Gables.*
Something un-paralysed me – the doctors don't know what.	*One of the boys – the one I hit – came to my room in hospital. He was called Tarn or Tarniel. He un-paralysed me.*
	Or do I only think Kostja told me that?
The post mortem showed that Danny died before he was last seen alive!!!	

There are local stories about the Fey Knights going back hundreds of years.	*The vicar said some weird stuff to me, like maybe he knew something about what was going on.*
Someone scribbled on my bedroom wall. Mum blames me.	*I did not scribble on my bedroom wall*
I am an out patient at the County psychiatric.	*I do not feel crazy.*

Chris studied the list for a long time, favouring to linger on the left-hand column for everything in the right troubled him two-fold; by content and impossibility. Off balance and out of kilter, he couldn't place the feeling at first, but in wandering the small confines of his room he came to pause by a small toy on the bookshelf, the last of his once vast Star Wars Action Fleet collection. He remembered Christmas all those years ago when he'd received it and was warmed by the echoes of his excitement on that day. Then he remembered his bitter disappointment when he'd taken his tiny representation of an A-wing fighter from its packaging only to find the paintwork damaged. It had been the tiniest of flaws, but it was enough to spoil the surprise. He wanted a perfect A-wing, not a damaged one. That was how he felt now, whenever he scanned the right-hand column: damaged and incomplete. If only he could package up his feelings and take them back to the shop for a new set. Opening his desk drawer Chris found a space for his once-loved toy. He slowly closed the drawer. It was time to clear away the last remnants of days gone by.

He knew he had to make a decision. He needed to take action. Dad had brought him up to take responsibility for his own life and actions and that was what he intended to do, but the equation was incomplete: the two columns were irreconcilable, and yet at the same time, they complimented each other perfectly. The events in the left-hand column were inexplicable, unless the facts laid out in the second column were indeed just that: facts. And yet, the content of the second column was impossible.

'Help me,' Chris said: to providence? To the God he didn't believe in? To a spiritual something that lay outside the understanding of man? 'Give me a clue. Give me a sign.' The eternal utterance of mankind, left to reverberate in the never ending nothingness of space.

Chris drew the duvet closer as his mother knocked on the door. 'Are you decent?'

'Kind of. Come in,' he said minimising the computer file.

'Phew! It's a bit muggy in here. I'll draw the curtains and open a window.'

'Mum! Leave it!' Chris snapped.

'Okay, okay. No need to get stroppy. Here, I've ironed your top and jeans. I know you only wore them a day in hospital, but I don't like the thought of all those hospital germs.'

'Thanks Mum. Drop them on the bed. I'll wear them today.'

Julie placed the clothing at the foot of the bed and hovered.

'What is it now? And please don't mention homework!'

'No it's not that. It's just ... There was a phone call.'

'And?'

'It was the police. They want to come and talk to you again.'

'Why? I've told them everything. And the Army guy. What more do they want from me?'

'She sounded very nice. A chief detective something-or-other. I think she said her name was Boeing – like the aeroplanes.'

'Well, I won't be able to tell her anything new.' Chris hoped the German nurse had kept his mouth shut, and immediately regretted baring his soul to the man.

'Chris, it stands to reason they want to speak to you. You're the only link to all four of the youngsters who've gone missing. It's what police do to tie up all the loose threads.'

'When's she coming?'

'I suppose I should have checked with you first, but I thought, sooner all this is behind us –'

'When's she coming?'

'Four o'clock this afternoon. Okay?'

Chris shrugged. 'I suppose.'

'Right. About time you were washed and –'

'Yes Mum! Thanks. I'll get washed and dressed when I get washed and dressed.'

'No need to be so ...' Julie thought better of it, smiled weakly and turned for the door. She was just pulling it to when she put her head round the door. 'Oh yes. Nearly forgot to ask. Who's Tarn?'

The question struck Chris like a punch in the guts. He checked the computer screen, but no, the file was minimised and she couldn't have read Tarn's name. 'Tarn?'

'Yes. I'm guessing she's someone you met in hospital.' Julie was wearing a thin woollen top over a summer blouse. Delving into the side pocket she pulled out a little strip of plastic. 'I found this in the pocket of your jeans when I did the wash.'

Chris took the strip: it was Tarn's identity wristband. Chris stared at it oblivious to the fact that he'd stopped breathing.

'Hospital romance, was it?' Julie said her tone artificially light.

Chris snapped out of his trance. 'No. Nothing like that. Tarn's not a girl. It's just a guy I met. He ... he helped me get better.'

'How did his i.d. get in your pocket?'

'Don't have a clue.'

Julie smiled and left, closing the door gently. Boys' emotions would always be a mystery to her; never given the light of day, always buried so deep.

Chris eyed the band with suspicion. He tugged it and pulled it as if testing that it was really there; this was definitely something for the left-hand column. Tarn really existed. Unless he had just imagined the whole encounter with his mother, which he knew he had not.

'The tooth!' Chris dropped the duvet and leapt the few steps to his bed. Scattering the neatly pressed underwear and socks and snatching up the freshly laundered jeans he slid a finger into the little pocket-within-a pocket which was the signature feature of every pair of jeans he'd ever seen. There was something hard at the bottom of the pocket and Chris could hardly allow himself to hope. Prodding and poking and hooking he managed to winkle it out, and yes, it was the tooth. He'd put there just after Danny had found it and handed it over. The right hand column was rapidly becoming frighteningly closer to being fact.

Turning the tooth over and over between finger and thumb, he was wracked with emotion. This tooth was the last thing Danny had given him before he disappeared. He wanted to cry, but at the same time felt inexplicably strong.

'I saw what I saw Danny,' he whispered to the tooth. 'It all happened. And I know that thing got you, just like it got me. And I'm going to find out why and what for. And then I'll ...'

Violent images flashed before him as Chris vented his feeling for the evil monster that had assaulted him and killed his best friend.

'I don't know how, but I'm going to get it and make it pay. I promise you Danny.' He thought of Gayle too, but couldn't verbalise the thoughts and fears that swept through him as he imagined the suffering she must have endured. His fear grew: Gayle might still be suffering. 'I'll find you,' Chris vowed in a whisper. 'I'll find you.'

Chris had a mission. He would find the truth and he would deal with it. What he did not have was a plan. 'Draw the curtains. Open the window. Shower. Shave. Dress. Eat ... Make a plan.'

Somewhere, in a place that was not really a place, in a time that wasn't exactly a time, the reverberations of Chris's decision caused oceans to swell.

CHAPTER SEVEN

Sheldrake's Legacy

Richard De'Ath didn't want to say too much lest he put a jinx on it, but for the first time in weeks his son appeared bright, if not cheerful. He returned Chris's smile with optimism. Chris grabbed a bowl, filled it with cornflakes and then sat down at the kitchen table opposite his father.

'Have you had your radio on upstairs, Chris?'

'No. You probably just heard me singing.'

'It's not that. I just wondered if you'd heard the news about New Orleans. It's been virtually washed off the face of the earth by a hurricane induced flood.'

'What? The whole city?' Chris let the milk carton hover over his cereal as he tried to take in the enormity of the disaster. The De'Ath family had visited New Orleans two summers ago.

'Pontchartrain burst in from one side, the sea from the other. They reckon thousands have drowned.' Richard pondered the sagacity of talking disasters on the first morning Chris had shown any sign of returning to normality. But then normality included coping with whatever the world had to chuck. He watched Chris and could almost see the pictures playing though his mind. Then, abruptly, he shook his head and tucked into his breakfast. 'You're looking your old self this morning. Okay?'

Chris spluttered his answer through a mouthful of cereal. 'Not great, but I've said goodbye to Danny, if that's what you mean.'

Danny's funeral had been held yesterday. 'And Gayle?'

'I try not to think about her too much. She might still turn up, you know?'

That's what Richard was worried about. Gayle would turn up, in much the same state as Danny, and Chris would have to face it all over again. Time, once more, to change the subject. 'What's on the agenda for today then?'

'Well, I thought I'd make a start at my history coursework. Before Mum can get another nag in.'

'You've chosen you subject?'

'Yes, but I'm keeping it to myself until I find out if it's acceptable to the board. It's a bit ... off the wall, but I think I've got a chance.'

'Give us a clue? History of medicine? French Revolution?'

'It's a bit more local than that. But don't ask. I'll tell you as soon as I hear from school.'

'But you don't go back to school for a couple of weeks. That's two weeks wasted, and you're way behind as it is.'

'I'm going to make a start on it, and if they say "No" I'll just adapt what I've already done into something they'll allow.'

'If you're starting today, don't forget Detective Superintendent Bowman is coming tonight. You can't put her off yet again.'

'Seven-thirty?'

'That's right. Slap bang in the middle of dinner time.'

'D'you know her?'

'From years back. We were sergeants together in the Met. We got on well and so long as rank hasn't gone to her head, I dare say she's still the same old Dawn. So don't be late.'

'Don't worry Dad. I'll be home by then. Wouldn't want to miss meeting one of your old girlfriends.'

'I never said –'

'Joking Dad! Joking. See you later. First stop, the Rilltons Museum.'

'Except now it's called –'

'Oh yeah. The Sheldrake Memorial Museum.'

Richard was just about to tell Chris to wash up his breakfast things, but decided he'd let it ride. 'Take it easy Chris. Got your mobile?'

'Yup! Bye. I won't be in for lunch. I've got some stuff to do.' And with that, Chris was out the back door. Richard felt a glimmer of optimism. Chris must be well on the road to recovery if he could joke.

Little Rillton's library was located within a large pair of rooms in the same building as the Community Clinic. Pregnant women, outpatients and visitors for the nurse, turn left; scholars and avid readers turn right. Ever needy of more space, the clinic administrators had made several bids to oust the library, but so far it had managed to cling on.

The librarian eyed Chris suspiciously. 'Curious subject matter.'

Librarians should keep their opinions to themselves. Chris had a good mind to ask for a book on sexually transmitted diseases. That would shut her up! 'It's for my history course work.'

'Faeries? History?'

Chris hoped the Year 10 boy, over there in the video section, hadn't overheard. 'Not exactly. I'm researching how folklore and belief in ... certain stories have impacted on society through the ages.'

'Interesting.' The librarian really did appear interested. She was a tiny fragile-looking young woman with elfin features almost curtained by long, dark brown hair. She wore olive green slacks with a lighter green, figure-hugging top. A local authority name badge was pinned above the pocket. Chris imagined her with a set of gossamer wings. She caught his glance and smiled and his next train of though made him blush. She really was quite attractive. It was the first time Chris had thought about sex without being assailed by visions of the winged beast which had attacked him.

'There's a book by Diane Purkiss you'll have to see. Just the thing for you really and we have a copy in.' She then reeled off a list of a dozen other books on the subject complete with authors and publishers. 'Then of course, you couldn't do much better than to visit the National Archive down in London and get amongst the witch trials. Plenty of mentions of faeries in those dusty old records. Might be a tad ambitious for A' level coursework though.'

'Maybe, but I'll take the books please. All those titles you just said.'

'Impressive, aren't I?'

Chris nodded his head, a little in awe of this woman – Miss K. Paterson according to her name badge – who couldn't have been more than 25.

'Well, I'm cheating. I only know about those books because I recently ordered them in for a researcher. You're not the only one interested in the subject.'

'Who? Who else?'

'I can't tell you that! Professional confidentially. How would you like it if, say, you'd asked for a book on sexually transmitted diseases and I went blabbing to the rest of the town.'

Oops! Reality was getting shaky, once again. Chris began to wonder if his thoughts were being transmitted through a hundred Watt amp.

'But ...' Chris said, too loudly. Several other library users looked in his direction, and one elderly gentleman tutted. 'But,' Chris whispered. 'Two people doing the same research. Maybe we could help each other. Can't you just ... give me a clue?'

'Well ... You could leave me your name and address. Or e-mail address. I could pass it on to her when she next comes in.'

'Ah, so it's a "she"?'

Miss Paterson closed her eyelids to slits and looked at Chris sideways. 'You've got me there. I've just narrowed it down to half the population.' She winked. Chris's insides squirmed. Did she ... could she find him attractive? 'Then again, I could suggest that you visit the local museum and speak to Mr Ryan the curator. I think he might be able to help. The museum definitely has something on the Fey Knights.'

'Really?' Chris was actually beginning to enjoy his foray into folklore-detective work. Once again, the Fey Knights.

'Yes, and you're in luck because it's open today.'

'Fantastic, and thanks a lot. I'll take all those books then, if I can, and head off to the museum.'

'You can book out the Purkiss title, but the others are all awaiting return.'

Hoping to secure a whole host of titles, Chris left with one meagre paperback, but so long as he kept his thoughts from straying towards Danny and Gayle, he managed to maintain a feeling of optimism, even excitement. Something *had* happened to him. A little bit "woo" and little bit "wah" but certainly real and not in his imagination. Chris would no longer allow himself to entertain the possibility of mental illness. If he couldn't rely on his own mind he had no starting point. If the things he'd experienced were all an illusion, than his whole life might just as well be faerie dust and imagination. His new battle cry, spoken quietly and only for himself was 'I saw what I saw!'

The Sheldrake Memorial Museum was to be found on Blencathra Rise, a little cobble-stoned close in the last remaining nest of short cobble-stoned streets in the old village. It had been a school until some time between world wars and had then lain fallow until the mid 70's when old Mr Sheldrake – then only middle aged – took out a lease and began converting it into a museum of local curiosities and antiquities. When Ernest Sheldrake had died five years ago the museum was mothballed while the parish council pondered what to do with the collection. There wasn't long to go on the lease and it looked likely the old building would be bought by developers and made into flats. But a saviour came to the rescue, bought the freehold and kept the collection in tact, opening it to the public on Wednesdays, Thursdays, Fridays and Sunday afternoons.

The old building was tucked out of the way and occupied the blind end of the close at the top of a steep hill. Chris paused to admire the splendour of Victorian, municipal architecture. *I was only a village school*, it seemed to announce, *but I'm still here and I'm still proud even if a little worn by time*. Chris lifted his eyes to a concrete escutcheon high on the front gable above a circular window. In black numerals against a magnolia background the escutcheon boldly proclaimed the building's nativity: 1871. There were three doors facing the close, the central one at the top of a flight of a dozen steps and those to either side at street level. The lintel above the door on the left was marked "Boys", and that on the left "Girls". He supposed that the grander central portal, which now served as the main entrance, had been for masters.

Crossing the carpark which had once been a playground resounding to the laughter and the sounds of children skipping, playing hopscotch, and kicking heavy leather footballs, Chris noticed he was not the only visitor. There was a sporty red MG-T parked in the shade of an oak tree, but it was the other car, parked in the "reserved for staff" bay that grabbed his attention. Catching the eye and standing its ground well in spite of its years was a two-tone green Riley Elf, all chrome grill and shiny bumpers. It had to be forty years old if it was a day, and what's more, it brought Chris a strong feeling of déjà vu. He felt sure he'd seen the old crock before. Somewhere from the High Street below the roar of a motorcycle, rounded off to a purr by distance, drifted up to him; the feeling of vague recognition intensified and made him recall Arnie, the golden retriever he'd had as a boy. They'd had some fun, had old Arnie, Danny and Chris.

Nostalgia was the last thing Chris needed. He shook it off and climbed the stairs pausing at the top to look over his shoulder. Above the Alms House rooftop opposite he could just make out The Beacon, its pointed roof poking out above the pine trees. What a commanding position the museum occupied. Beacon Ridge was at least a mile away. It was once a favourite haunt of Danny, Chris and his dog, and ... *Bugger!* Nostalgia was bringing in its heavy guns today. Chris turned his back on nostalgia and The Beacon and hurried inside.

The smell was different. Chris hadn't been here since Mr Sheldrake had passed away and he began to notice the changes. The chrome plated turnstile entrance was new, and the security cameras, some deliberately obvious, some not so. No longer the feel of entering a secret Aladdin's cave of treasures, everything was more professional and business-like, from the mobile rack of leaflets advertising other local attractions to the layout of the displays. Chris was happy to see an item he recognised: there in a display occupying a central and prominent position of the hall was Donald McIntire's brass fire chief's helmet, circa 1877. But no longer in splendid isolation; the new curator had managed to secure the rest of the uniform, or at least a reproduction of one. And next to it was another fine uniform that was entirely new to the collection: short navy blue jacket with a double row of large brass buttons, sky blue trousers with a fine red stripe and a splendidly curved sabre with a polished steel scabbard. Chris guessed it to be French.

He tried to walk through the turnstile, but it was unyielding and wouldn't turn. It was then he noticed the "ring for attention" button on a bar-like desk to the right of the main door. He pressed it and it produced a two-tone chime like the doorbell at his own home. A voice called out from the depths, soon followed by hurrying footsteps.

'Sorry to keep you. I've been helping out another visitor.'

Chris grinned. He hated grinning but try as he might not to, it was his usual response on meeting anyone he perceived as being older and cleverer than himself. He grinned a lot, until he got to know people. The curator had a vaguely absent-minded professor look about him, apart from the designer glasses, and was probably close to forty. Shorter than Chris his well trimmed hair was greying at the sides.

'Just a general visit or can I direct you to a specific part of the collection?'

'I'd like to look around first, but there are a couple of things I'd like to ask.'

'That works out fine. I'll be through with the other visitor in a little while. Then I'll turn on my sensors and come seek you out.'

Chris grinned again, not quite knowing what to make of Mike Ryan. Everyone seemed to be wearing name tags today. Mike disappeared left along a narrow passage and Chris made a beeline for the new display. It wasn't French, this impressive looking uniform. As soon as he saw the gold-bordered red shoulder straps each with an impressively embroidered gold eagle he knew he was looking at an American uniform from about the time of the American Civil War. A black-braided low chasseur forage cap bore a little oval badge of crossed cannons above the peak. Where the cannons crossed was a small circle of red felt that at one time had held a badge or numeral of some kind, but if nowhere else, here time had stolen away this one tiny feature.

"Kindly donated by Lord Victor Wymes" read the little brass plaque.

'It seems young Wilbur Wymes was the black sheep of the family.'

Chris jumped inwardly at the proximity of the unexpected voice. 'I thought ...'

'The other visitor had fewer remaining questions than I anticipated. Going back to Wilbur here, our genuine 100 percent Redlegs Rilltonian ...'

Chris pointed at the mounted card inside the display case. 'It says Wilbur fought in the Crimea as a subaltern in the 1st Rillton Mounted Rifles, then went out to live in the States, got involved in the Civil War then came back again.'

'That's about the size of it. So we had a genuine hero of the United States Army, living here in Little Rillton. Well, up at the Manor at any rate.'

'Wow! Impressive display. That sword doesn't look like it comes from the 1860's, it's so new looking.'

'It could be even older. It's the 1840 pattern artillery sabre, so unless old Wilbur got himself a new one when he joined up, that little piece of steel might be the best part of a hundred and sixty five years old.'

'What about the gun?'

'You can only see the butt tucked in there under the holster flap, but believe me when I tell you it's one of the finest cap and ball Remington pistols I've ever seen. It's stamped 1858 and like the sabre it's weathered very, very well. Still in its original blued condition. Walnut grips, like they were polished yesterday. And it still works ... Or should I say, I imagine it still works. No reason why not.'

Chris got the impression Mike was backtracking on the issue of the weapon's functionality. He imagined Mike taking furtive pot-shots at passing wildlife. 'That's fantastic. Maybe Wilbur came here in a time machine.' Chris grinned widely. Mike did too, but only after a thoughtful pause. 'So, what made him the black sheep of the family?'

'The stories go that he had mid-Victorian Youngest Son Syndrome – couldn't settle to anything. Or anyone. He left his wife for a scullery maid and did a disappearing act.'

Chris was almost afraid to ask. 'The stories don't say if he went missing in the woods, do they?'

Mike made a couple of false starts before answering and when he did manage to squeeze out a full sentence it was obviously designed to change the subject. 'Sorry, what was it you wanted to ask me earlier on?'

Curious, thought Chris. 'I'm researching the influence folklore has ... or had ... on society through the ages. I'm trying to keep it local and as place-specific as I can, so I'd like any information you have about the –'

'Fey Knights?'

And even more curious. 'Well, yes as it happens. I mean yes please, if you've got anything.'

'No ... I mean yes, but you have to have a reader's ticket to access it.'

'Stuff about the Fey Knights is restricted? You're not serious are you?'

Mike Ryan gave Chris a long stare before replying. 'Of course it's not restricted. But it's primary source material and not on display. So, if you don't have a ticket ...'

'But I do. At least, not with me but I can probably go back home and dig it out.'

Mike's questioning look was easy to read.

'I haven't been here since Mr Sheldrake died. I signed up for a ticket when I was in Year 8 and did Fire Chief McIntire for my Famous Victorian project.'

'Hardly famous, but I'm getting the feel that you like "local".'

Chris shrugged. 'I suppose my ticket's expired.'

'Follow me,' Mike said heading towards a computer; something else new since the amelioration of the old museum. 'If it was good enough for Ernest it's good enough for me. I didn't spend weeks feeding his paper records into the computer just to say "Computer says "No". What's your name?'

'Chris De'Ath. That's "Death" with an apostrophe before the "A".'

Mike keyed in the details and hit the return. 'I've got a Christian W. De'Ath.'

'That's me. Here, it's on my buss pass.'

Mike checked the details. 'Christian Death? I don't suppose you have stigmata, do you?'

'I don't suppose you imagine that's the first time I've heard that one, do you?'

Mike chuckled. 'And here's me thinking I'm being terribly original. Okay, there's an interesting tome by our old friend and benefactor Ernest Sheldrake himself. Could say it was his life's work, if he hadn't achieved so much in other fields. Pop along the corridor to the left of the Redlegs Rilltonian display and wait in the reading room if you would. I'll bring it along, and a couple of other goodies.'

Mike scurried off and Chris found a comfortable seat by the window of the reading room. The room was all wooden lecterns and leather bound hardback chairs and this was one place where the slightly musty smell of the original museum lingered. The walls were decorated with old photographs and Chris was attracted to a large sepia photo of the building when it had still been a school. Four rows of raggedy boys sat or stood, some booted, some barefoot, between their master on the left, who wore a wing collar and a bowler hat, and a pair of distinguished looking gentlemen on the right. One of the boys sat in a wicker wheelchair and Chris was surprised that a school of over a hundred years ago could be so inclusive. With half a mind on the photo and the rest gently musing over Mike Ryan's apparently nervous responses to some of his questions, he sidled to the next shot. It was of a cheerful young man in a railway porter's uniform, but Mike returned before Chris to pay it more than perfunctory attention.

'Here we go!' Mike said. '"Wymes Park: Ancient Forest and the Fey Knights" by Ernest A. Sheldrake. And here's a box of interesting press cuttings, snipped by the fair hand or Ernie's daughter and bound by my good self.'

'You bind books?'

'Nothing too flash. More in the line of the Victorian version of a ring binder. Have binder-winder will travel, as it were.' Mike held up a little white metal implement shaped like a miniature starter handle from a vintage car.

Chris examined the thick volume of newspaper pages and soon understood the mechanism. Use the binder-winder to loosen the front and rear covers, insert new page, use binder-winder to tighten said covers thereby holding the pages securely. The volume was four inches thick, had the two-dimensional measurements of a page of broadsheet, and weighed a proverbial ton.

'Do you remember the rules from your younger days as a registered reader?'

'I think so. No food, drink or cameras in the reading room. No ink. Do not mark the documents in any way and take notes only in pencil.'

'Full marks! But nowadays I have to add, please no pointy-clicky with the all singing all dancing mobile phone cum Hollywood studio. I'll leave you to it then. If you need any help, wander back to the bell push and ... push it.'

'Before you go. Can I ask? Someone said there might be another person looking into the same stuff.'

Mike Ryan moved his head in a strange fashion that was neither a nod nor a shake, but a combination of the two, as if he could not decide which answer to opt for. 'One or two perhaps. But that's nothing unusual. It's a well know local topic and you're not the first to take a bead on it.'

'And here's me thinking I'm being terribly original.' Before Chris could press for details Mike grinned and hurried out of the room. He paused to look into the display case containing the Union Artillery colonel's uniform, made it to the computer terminal and paused again. His movements were, at that moment, exactly in keeping with his absentminded professor appearance. But after a few moments of dithering he snapped out of it and strode for the exit as if craving fresh air. Delving deep into the pocket of his green corduroy trousers he fished out a little silver clamshell-style mobile phone and lifting it to his lip activated the voice-dial.

'Home,' he said and then waited for technology to work another of its minor miracles. 'Hi Polly, it's me ... You'll never guess what ... That kid's at the museum, and he's asking all the questions we didn't want him to ... Well, he knows someone else is researching the You-Know-Who-Boys ... No, don't worry about it ... I've already spoken to her. I'll take care of it ... Bye.'

Back in the reading room Chris carefully opened Ernest Sheldrake's book to the foreword. He hadn't been sure what to expect but his expectation of a handwritten tome, all copperplate and pencil-sketches, was dashed. This was a professionally produced book, properly bound and with neat printing throughout and several illustrations, some labelled "In the Style of Mr A. Rackham."

Chris flicked to the bibliography and sources section. There was much mention of the Public Records Office and numerous works of folklore, but one entry in particular caught his eye. Credit was given, several times, to "Lady Rosemary's Grimoire." What the hell was a "grimoire"? Chris dismissed the question and read the foreword, originally penned by one Lady Mildred Spender in 1979.

It is with the greatest of pleasures that I embrace the opportunity to present this fine work by my old friend, the historian Ernest Arthur Sheldrake.

Yes, I intentionally used the term "historian" for the book that you hold in your hand is far more than a whimsical confection concerning our Good Neighbours – the Little Folk – but a serious and meticulously researched treatise of a very specific and geographically confined example of folklore.

We have all heard of Rapunzel and Rumpelstiltskin. Ask anyone along the length or breadth of Britain about Snow White and they will all be able to tell you she spent many happy hours attempting to domesticate seven bachelor dwarfs. They will gladly confess to having at least heard of goblins, gnomes, trolls and other faerie folk, but ask them of the Fey Knights or the Fey Boys as some call them, and all but the Rilltonian will stare blankly while surmising that the subject of your question might well be akin to those young men who are "anxious for to shine in the high aesthetic line" and "who walk down Piccadilly with a poppy or a lily in their medieval hands." On the other hand, they may suppose the Fey Boys represent that other breed of young man oft found frequenting Piccadilly whose intentions are to shine in anything but the aesthetic line. Only the Rilltonian will provide you with an answer approaching the definitive.

How strange it is that the story of the Fey Knights, and their apparently continued activities, should remain so closely confined to the area and communities encompassed by the Fifteenth Century boundaries of Wymes Forest. Great and Little Rillton, Axenwhit and the isolated farms and hamlets in and about Wymes Park: outside of these the Fey Knights set no foot and their shadows do not fall, even upon the minds of the people. Unlike the wine (which hard-nosed sceptics are given to cite as the cause of many a faerie encounter), the Fey Knights do not travel well.

As close as Shrewsbury you will be lucky indeed to find a single purveyor of folklore who has heard of the Fey Knights. Stop at Oswestry and strike up a conversation with a bard of The Mabinogion who is steeped in the lore of Merlin; in all probability he will cast you a sideways look if you mention the Fey Knights. But the Rilltonians, they are all under the spell of the three young men and their sprite-like companions who remain unchanged throughout the centuries. Ever the same, whether described by Elfric Magnussen of the Axe Hewn Thwaite (circa 850), Godwin de Wymes (1329), poor Molly Blackbridge who was burnt for a witch (1636) or Frank Kirkby (1911), the Fey Knights and the tales they engender remain a mystery.

The mystery has nothing to do with their singular and unchanging appearance. It is not related to the fact that they are held with respect and not a little affection by the local populous despite the apparent fact that they diminish that same populous by spiriting away a selection of its youth. No, the mystery is this: how has such a rich seam of folklore remained untapped for so many generations by the Nation at large?

How can these stories remain relatively – nay entirely – unknown outside such a small area? Do Rilltonians lose memory of the Fey Knights the further away from home they travel? In fact, even as I write I find the images in my mind fading and blowing away like smoke on the wind. Fey Knights? Who are the Fey Knights?

Who indeed! Without further ado, and with apologies to William Butler Yates, allow my friend Ernest to take you by the hand. In the space of but a few hours, give yourself over to immersion in the work of a lifetime, and …

Come away, O human child!
To the waters and the wild
With a faerie, hand in hand,
For the world's more full of weeping than
You can understand.

'Old Ernie's done all my work for me,' Chris whispered and he browsed the pages that followed Lady Spender's foreword. He suspected it was all here, but he was reluctant to look in any depth. Instead he took up the bound volume of newspaper extracts. Mostly from local papers the earliest was dated 1825.

Turning the pages just to keep his hands occupied while he pondered the next move, his attention was snatched by a headline from an August 1986 edition of the Rillton Gazette. It concerned the disappearance of 16-year-old James W. McDowell. It was one of several headlines concerning similar young people – one disappearance every twenty to fifty years – and he would as soon have moved on to the next sheet, but his mind being tuned to notice anything of a personal nature, he was immediately drawn to the missing boy's middle name. It was "Wren" – just like his own.

'Now that is way beyond coincidence.' He jotted down a few details of the story excited that, in some way he did not yet understand, he had stumbled across a major clue in his search for the truth. Turning the broadsheet he came to the front page of the following week's special edition and found himself staring at a photo that elicited a visceral tightening throughout his chest, intestines and lions. There were two colour photos. One was as a picture of Jamie McDowell in school uniform. "His most recent photograph" proclaimed the title, and it was obviously the last of his annual, school shots. Unsurprisingly for a boy from one of the Rilltons, he had attended the same school as Chris; the black tie with its brown and gold stripe and the impressive coat-of-arms badge on the blazer told Chris that without him having to think about it. With fair hair in a curtain cut and soft grey eyes went a self-conscious smile on a face that showed the potential to settle into good looks in his mid-thirties. For Jamie, the potential was never realised, but it was not Jamie's photo that made the room spin and had such a drastic affect on his innards.

Next to Jamie was a distant, somewhat grainy shot of a dark haired young woman. As indistinct as the photo was, Chris did not need to read the caption; this was a shot of Lillian. It was his over active imagination, he knew it, but her eyes bored into him across the twenty years since this shot was taken, apparently without her approval from the mild look of surprise on her face. She was carrying a rucksack and in the distance were two boys in blue-grey uniforms. She had to be the mother of the Lillian Chris knew. But he wasn't so sure: he had assumed the beast which had molested him had taken on Lillian's appearance, but perhaps … No, couldn't be.

Chris read the caption out loud. '"Lillian Hunter, snapped just two days before Jamie's disappearance while she helped Jamie with his luggage following a trip with Little Rillton Squadron Air Training Corps. Police do not suspect her of any wrong doing" – what? You're a bunch of dopes then. Whatever happened to Jamie, she was most definitely involved. " – but they would like to trace her as she may hold information vital to the investigation." I'll bet she does!' Chris unconsciously tugged at the crotch of his jeans. Skimming through the rest of the article he found no further reference to Lillian other than the fact that she was working at Lofty Gables – Jamie's home – as an au pare.

He read the article in depth looking for any reference to the Fey Knights and finding none. Without any logical order he began to thumb back and forward through the newspapers scanning for just those two words: Fey Knights. Nothing; no trace, not until he came to a copy of the Rillton Gazette dated Saturday, 25th May 1912. The front page story concerned the tragic drowning in Wymes Lake of Frank Kirkby.

'The guy from the Parish Magazine that the vicar gave me,' Chris said. The article spoke of Frank as a popular and well liked young lad who worked at Great Rillton Railway Station as a porter. It covered his involvement with the local brass band and his association with one Lord Blencathra, who it seemed, had taken the lad under his wing. Travelling up from East London a year before to take up his position with the railway, he had quickly immersed himself into the activities of the community. It was all there. His loss was keenly felt, but all the details of his life and death faded into the background as Chris read of his meeting with the Fey Knights.

Just short of a year before his death when he was still a little homesick, he had been exploring Wymes Park when he encountered three young men in the woods. Being unaware of the local legends he had not been at all abashed to report the encounter – strange though it was – and had been amazed at the reaction his report caused.

Frank had come across an old tower – the hack who'd written the article assumed it to be the lakeside folly, but Chris knew better – where he had found himself surrounded by three, black haired youths whose features appeared identical. Although Frank reported them to be friendly and that he had engaged them in conversation for some time and shared a meal of bread and cheese, he could not recall of what they had spoken or how he came to fall asleep. When he woke up all sign of the boys – he assumed them to be triplets – had gone. On returning to the village and asking about the triplets, he found himself to be the very centre of attention for several days, during which time he heard all about the legend of the Fey Knights.

Chris soaked Frank's story in through his pores. It brought renewed life to his parched spirit and validated the faith he was trying to rebuild into the reliability of his senses. If there had been any self doubts over his sanity, they shrivelled and died. But as confidence grew, so did a vague sense of anger. Reality was not as he had been taught it to be; somewhere, something smacked of conspiracy.

'Sorry Mr De'Ath,' Mike Ryan said. 'It's five to four. Closing time in five minutes.'

'Already? I haven't even started on Mr Sheldrake's book.'

'It'll be there for you tomorrow.'

'I can't make it tomorrow,' Chris said. Was that a look of relief that passed over the curator's face? 'But can I book it for next week?'

'No booking required. Nobody ever looks at it. This museum has a very local appeal, and all the locals know the stories.'

'I thought I did, but I've just found stuff about the Fey Knights in the old newspapers.'

Mike chuckled. 'The good old Rilltons. Only two serious obsessions: Three Steeples White and the Fey Knights.'

Chris smiled at the reference to the locally produced wine. It did occupy an awful lot of conversation time between older members of the community.

'Well, nice meeting you Mr De'Ath. See you again soon. Leave those, I'll sort them.' Mike took the newspapers Chris held out.

'Call me "Chris". "Mr De'Ath" sounds like your talking to my Dad. Oh, and just one more thing.' Chris thrust a hand deep into the back pocket of his jeans and pulled out a folded and well creased piece of A4. Unfolding the scruffy scrap he made a mental note to use a different pocket in the future. 'Any idea what this is?'

Mike set down the large binder and took the paper. Frowning deeply he studied the drawing. 'Looks like, three hieroglyphic birds and some ... Hebrew I think ... yes, Hebrew writing. Where did you get this?'

'I saw it somewhere and copied it.'

'Do you mind if I copy it, on the photocopier? I can show it to a friend who might be able to help identify it.'

Chris told him to go ahead and off he went to whichever hidden cranny of the old building hid the photocopier. Chris gravitated once more to the uniform of that adventuring Rilltonian, Wilbur Wymes. It really was a splendidly preserved piece of history. The jacket with its domed, brass buttons, the sabre, the ... pistol? It must have been a trick of the light, but Chris could not see the butt of the Remington inside the holster. In fact the holster looked empty now.

'Here we go!' Mr Ryan's unexpected voice made Chris jump. He certainly had the knack of creeping up on people. Chris took back his crumpled drawing and left Mike with the photocopied version. 'If you've got an e-mail I can beam you the results of my friend's research.'

Chris gave Mike his e-mail address and stepped out into the hot sunshine. The sky was deep blue, with not a cloud in sight, and the only sound came from the muffled hum of the motorway a mile off to the east, and the excited chirping of a flock of chaffinches gathered below the bones of the dead tree. Chris had a head full of discoveries to assimilate and digest, and many, many more questions than when he had entered the museum. A motorcycle revved explosively and chaffinches rose from the pavement like a cloud of dust from a smacked rug. Despite the summer warmth the outside world felt cold, unreal and hostile and Chris wanted to dive back into the fusty protectiveness of the old museum. Spooked like the birds, he turned to see Mike Ryan standing with his back to the now closed and securely locked doors. He was frowning and stern-faced for a moment before breaking into a friendly smile. The welcome of the

Sheldrake Memorial Museum was in the balance. The very building itself assumed a personality and Chris was unsure if it was friend or foe.

Nonsense! he thought as he returned Mike's apparently friendly wave. Far from feeling he had achieved much over the last few hours, Chris descended the flight of steps into a world submerged in a sea of confusion. As he crossed the car park towards the wrought iron gates a motorcyclist came to a lazy halt and filled the exit with his presence. Clad entirely in black he looked like a silhouette or a black hole in the bright fabric of reality. His black-helmeted head turned like a lighthouse beacon until a dark beam hit Chris between the eyes causing him to stop in his tracks and catch his breath.

He's after me. Why? What does he want? Chris turned for support. He didn't quite know what to make of Mike Ryan, but any port in a storm. Mike was nowhere to be seen and ice trickled down Chris's spine. Spinning to face the unexplained new threat he was faced ... by nothing. No mysterious motorcyclist; no hole in space: nothing but the chaffinches happily settling once again in the shadow of the dead tree.

'Forgotten something?'

He'd done it again. Crept up on Chris and made him jump half out of his skin. 'No, no. I was just ... looking at the dead tree.'

Mike Ryan cast a glance towards the woody skeleton. It looked like a gigantic piece of black coral. 'Yes, I keep meaning to have someone sort it out. I might even bring an axe in and do it myself.'

Chris nodded, but did not resume his journey.

'Is there something else?'

'No, not really. But, what do you think the biker wanted.'

'Biker?'

Chris shrugged. 'Never mind. Bye.'

'No wait! Biker? What do you mean "biker"?'

'It's nothing. It really doesn't matter.'

'On the other hand it might matter a great deal. Are you telling me you just saw someone on a motorbike?' Mike had become fairly well fired up and took Chris's shoulders as he asked his question.

'Yes. Right there at the gate. You must have seen him! And ... well I can't be sure because his visor was down, but he seemed to be staring at me. What's with that?'

Mike settled down, dropped his hands to his side and contemplated the deceased tree once again.

'So, what about the biker?'

'Oh it's ... nothing. Nothing to worry about.'

Oh for f ...!' Chris kicked the air before realising how childish the gesture must look. 'Two seconds ago it was all important "Are you telling me you saw somebody on a bike" and now it's nothing!'

'Sorry Mr De'Ath. Chris. I've just had this guy snooping round lately. Casing the joint I should imagine. I'll have to tell the home beat officer before I get burgled.'

'You didn't see him just now?'

Mike shook his head. 'My mind was on other things.'

Chris was far from convinced and Mike's reaction to the biker question did nothing but add a gale force wind to the sea he was drowning in.

Depression nipped at Chris's heels all the way home, but he kept up a brisk pace and did not let it catch up. Instead he held it at bay by going through the day's discoveries, formulating and ordering the jumble of new questions they engendered, and maintaining a determination to get to some answers. Inside his own head for the half-hour walk he only came out into the world for a quick peek when he heard a motorcycle purring along in the distance. It wasn't the same one as before so Chris relaxed back into his skull and shut out the real unreal town that was Little Rillton. But try as he might, he couldn't shut out the images of Jamie McDowell or the mysterious Lillian.

CHAPTER EIGHT

The Story of Jamie and Lillian
or
St Michael's Brief War

RAF Grayes Forton was a busy camp, bustling with activity of a mostly routine nature for three-quarters of the year. For those nine months one day was very like another: Victor tankers took off and landed at regular intervals, visiting paratroopers jumped from training towers and a myriad of general duties were performed with RAF efficiency and precision.

Station Warrant Officer Bullock was a man to be feared by all those who wore the grey-blue serge, up to and including (but not necessarily excluding those above) Flight Lieutenant. Every man though, has his Achilles heel and this fierce icon with his signature handle-bar moustache himself lived in fear of those other three months of the year when every Monday morning throughout the summer another busload of gyrating hormones spilled out next to the parade square. The hormones were barely contained within the youthful bodies of air cadets, the majority of whom were boys between the ages of thirteen and nineteen. This being the mid-1980's the Air Training Corps squadron was no longer a preserve for the male gender, and most squadrons numbered a handful of girls amongst the ranks, much to the delight of the older boys. The long awaited enlightened age was burgeoning and equality of the sexes was slowly becoming manifest from the airy words of decades.

The three young ladies who watched the latest arrivals pull in through the main gate had no interest in equality, absolutely no time for female cadets and an agenda that bulldozed rules right out of the camp. Whereas it was the aim of the adult staff in each squadron to direct the energies of their charges into useful and productive channels, it was the sworn duty of these three heroines to cause gyrating hormones to scream, to engage at least some of the boys in a degree of sexual activity and then ... to steal their underpants. Call them trophies. Call them a measure of success. And if there was no success this week? Why worry, for each Monday morning brought a brand new batch of, hopefully, girl-hungry boys.

A council of war met every Monday morning over thick milkshakes in the McDonald's just outside camp. Two old hands were just about to initiate a new member into the fine art of knicker-napping. Lillian was new on the team and therefore, one would think, at a disadvantage as far as the collecting of trophies went. She replaced Wendy who had been kicked off the team in disgrace. Her crime? Found cheating: she had managed to collect a nice variety of boys' underwear including a pair of tanga-briefs – worth a whole twenty points – but then she had been caught in the menswear department of the local Marks and Spencer at the checkout with money in one hand, evidence in the other.

'No wonder she was in the lead, cheeky cow!' Rona said, still bristling with indignation a whole week after the event.

'Yeah,' Carol agreed. 'And all her stories were probably lies too. I bet she's still a virgin.'

Lillian's mouth curled with lop-sided amusement as she watched her co-conspirators dissolve into raucous laughter.

'Never even managed to get a feel!' Rona said between gasps for breath.

'Or a look! Wouldn't know a stiffy from a frozen sausage,' Carol added ever wanting to crown the conversation. Not this time, Carol.

'Leave it out girls,' Lillian said detecting a whiff of the absurd. 'She might be a rotten cheating cow, but it's going a bit far to say that any sixteen year old girl hasn't seen a boy with a hard-on.'

Rona and Carol were, just for the moment, nonplussed. Then Rona re-established command. 'No, I suppose you're right. Anyway, for the benefit of newcomers, Lillian, Carol will tell you the rules.'

'Sure,' Carol said trying to hide a feeling of insecurity with an enthusiastic delivery. 'There aren't that many rules. For today we just look over the latest talent. Tomorrow morning we meet here again and name our targets. If we haven't found out their names by then, we just have to describe them.'

'Then we've got 'til Saturday night to get their pants off,' Rona interrupted.

'Oh you! I wanted to tell her that! Never mind, I'll tell you the points system. It's twenty points if you get the boy you name –'

'Boy? Only one then?' Lillian asked. Her question brought no reply, only a pair of appraising stares: stared that said 'Perhaps we've taken on some real competition here.' Which of course, they had.

Carol continued. 'Fifteen points if you get a different boy. An extra ten points if he's wearing the right pants and –'

'Right pants?'

'Oh yes, I forgot that bit. At the same time you name your target, you have to say what kind of pants he wears. Boxers, French slip, what colour and so on.'

'Baggy string y-fronts, Rona said, and they were off again, rocking on their stools with laughter. Rona swore mildly when a dollop of chocolate milkshake dropped onto her jeans, then returned to the important matter in hand. 'You get extra points if he's in tanga-briefs and you win the game for a poser-pouch,' she said, gasping, whether from excitement or choking on her drink Lillian could not tell.

'Oh and Rona, don't forget the new rule. The trophies.'

'Nearly forgot. Sunday morning we meet up and produce our trophies – the pants of course. And they have to be newly worn.'

'To stop the chance of cheating?' Lillian asked, the lop-sided grin returning.

'That's it Lillian,' Rona said. 'You got it. So, you in?'

'I'm in. Sounds fun.'

'Any questions?'

'Yes. What do you score for sex. When you lay the boys I mean?'

Rona began to wobble on her throne. Lillian had said "when". Not "if" but "when". 'Well, we each go through our stories on Sunday then we produce our trophies as evidence. You don't actually get points for sex. It's trophies that count. I mean, if you've got as far as getting them out of their knickers the rest goes without saying.'

Did it really? Lillian thought.

'The stories about what we got up to just add a little bit of spice.'

Lillian scanned the competition. *No sweat!* 'Right,' she said rising. 'I'm off to meet the talent. Early bird catches the worm.'

'Let's hope they're a little bigger than worms,' Rona quipped.

'I doubt some of them are bigger than maggots,' Carol said, not wishing to be outdone.

The two old hands watched as Lillian sauntered off. The moment she was at a safe distance Rona's amiable mask slipped to reveal pure venom.

'She's a bit of a flash cow, don't you think Rona? Thought you said she was okay.'

'Don't worry about her. She's all mouth, like Wendy. Come on, let's meet this week's batch of totty.'

'Got your condoms,' Carol said making a play of checking her bum-bag and accidentally on purpose exposing her twelve-pack.

'Blue box? They're "Elites" aren't they? I prefer "Ribbed" myself.'

The two friends left the McDonalds discussing the merits and fallbacks of a variety of contraceptives, while each keeping from the other that their condoms were rapidly approaching their use-by dates.

It was becoming clear that Lillian liked to work alone, liked to go her own way, so for a while it looked as if Rona's little surprise might fall flat. Carol glanced at her watch for the fifteenth time. 'She isn't going to show,' she said.

'We've waited long enough,' ventured Josh hoping he wasn't pushing too hard. 'Maybe we should just get on with it.'

Micky, who was Rona's challenge for the week, agreed through a mouthful of chips.

'A couple more minutes,' Rona ordered. 'And then if we go she's got absolutely no cause for complaint. Tuesday night, I said, outside the chippie at half past seven.'

'Now it's quarter-past eight and still no sign … Hang on! There she is,' Carol said waving her screwed up chip bag.

'And all alone I see,' Rona said, her voice steeped in superiority with a topping of sarcasm.

Lillian approached the little group without hurry. What was going on? Rona was with a lad. So was Carol. Lillian recognised Carol's friend as the loud mouthed cadet-sergeant; tall, slim, sixteen or seventeen, light brown hair dyed blond on top and a cheeky knowing face. Getting his knickers off would be as difficult as buying weed in Camden Market. Rona's boy looked a little younger and he was a good deal shorter, but in other respects, apart from the garish hair colouring, he resembled Carol's friend. Another push-over, thought Lillian. Have these girls no sense of challenge?

'Hi Lillian,' Rona called in a voice that resembled an American diner girl telling her customer to have a nice day. 'This is Micky. He's with the squadron that came in yesterday.'

'Wotcha, Micky,' Lillian said. She locked on, eye to eye, licked her upper lip and watched as Micky's smile faltered and exposed a momentary loss of confidence. Then, as his eyes dropped to her bosom, hers went straight for the crotch. *Tightish jeans, nice little bum – definitely a boxer shorts boy.*

'And this is Josh. He's a sergeant,' Carol crowed.

Lillian smiled and nodded a hello, summing him up instantly as a little shit.

'Alright, babe?' Josh said, his leering face almost clown-like. He really fancies himself, thought Lillian. Has to be a bit flash in the underpants department.

'Where's your fellah then, Lillian?' Rona enquired.

'Which one you talking about?' Lillian said, copying the condescending tone.

Rona laughed. 'Well, you say you've got lots, but we don't see any evidence. You coming with us, or will you ... feel too much of a gooseberry?'

'Come on Lilly,' Josh said. 'We don't mind gooseberries, do we Micky?'

Micky was about to answer, but he got a jab in the side from Rona's elbow.

'Thanks boys, but I've got things to do.'

Josh looked genuinely disappointed.

Rona stepped forward. 'Before we go lads, Carol and me must have a quick word with Lillian.' She waved the boys off to the corner of the street before organising herself and the other girls into a tight huddle. 'Right! I'll have Micky's pants off by Thursday, and he's a mini-briefs lad. Josh is for Carol and he'll be y-fronts. What about you? Name your lad and identify his pants.' Rona looked over her shoulder and smiled sweetly at her intended victim. He waved back.

'I can see you've set yourselves an impossible task,' Lillian said, heavy with sarcasm. 'But you're wrong about the underwear.'

'Says who?' Rona snapped.

'Says I. Stands out like as a bulldogs's bollocks. Or an air cadet's come to that.'

Rona and Carol exchanged looks – identical looks which said 'Help! We're outclassed,' which of course, they were. As usual Rona was first to snap out of it. 'Well, maybe we're wrong, maybe we're right. But that still doesn't tell us about you.' She could have been a gambler in the wild west; she could have been saying 'Your hundred and I raise you fifty.' That was the tone of it, but the words? 'Name your lad and name his pants!'

Lillian moved in close, so that her breath triggered a shiver that made Rona's face twitch. 'His name is Jamie McDowell, he's a sixteen-year-old virgin, and he wears ...' Lillian rolled her eyes skywards as if fishing amongst the clouds for the right answer. It was of course an act, for she knew a great deal about young Jamie; all part of the plan to keep the competition wrong footed?

'Come on then,' snapped Rona. 'We've not got all night.'

'Blue silk boxers,' Lillian stated to the astonishment of the other girls.

Carol began to show her admiration for the newest member of the team. 'Blue silk boxers? How can you –'

'Jamie McDowell,' Rona came in forcefully choking off Carol's hero worship before it had properly developed. 'Silk boxers. Blue ones. You know the points system, and you don't get extra for bonking.'

'What, no extra points for bedding a virgin? Bit more of a challenge than having your two alley cats drop their drawers.'

Rona picked up the gauntlet. This was serious stuff and she would have to demolish this brash newcomer to save her face. She flushed with silent fury. 'Okay, we'll see who's all talk come Friday. Blue silk boxers, or you're a lying, bullshitting, fart-faced cow!'

'Don't worry dear. I'll have young Jamie's boxers, AND whatever those two are hiding under their jeans.'

Rona burst out from the huddle dragging a bemused Carol behind her.

'Bye girls,' Lillian called sweetly. 'Bye boys,' she added thick with an undertone of seduction. Then she locked eye to eye, first with Josh, and then Micky. They were as good as hers. 'This is going to be fun,' she whispered to herself.

She headed for the camp and her pre-arranged tryst with Corporal Jamie McDowell. A couple of nights and his boxers would be as irretrievable as his virginity, no doubt about it. But what about Micky and Josh? Maybe, just maybe she had bitten off more than she could chew. After all, there was no competition where Jamie was concerned. But the other two: she would have to find a way to get them away from her rivals who were already softening them up – or more appropriately, hardening them up.

By the time Lillian reached the perimeter fence a plan was taking shape.

'See your pass, love?' the senior aircraftsman at the gate said. As she fumbled for her visitor's pass she smiled and thought about the pass she was about to make.

Half-an-hour later Lillian treated Jamie McDowell to his first French kiss, deep in the darkness of a long forgotten and disused pill-box. It had escaped the fate of so many of its kin because of its location. Being on an RAF base it had never been used as a latrine and apart from the odd cigarette packet, it had similarly dodged use as a giant dustbin.

In the soil-floored depths, Jamie's heart raced while Lillian used her tongue automatically, kissing him deeply but completely without attachment as she refined the details of her plan to de-keg Josh and Micky.

The shower block was deserted but for one tall, thin lad intent on achieving a state of perfection in the art of personal grooming. Leaning forward over the hand-basin he checked his teeth in the mirror then ran a finger over the tiny bump to the side of his nose. A zit in the making. So what? It wouldn't erupt until tomorrow; it was tonight that counted.

Corporal Jamie Wren McDowell was on a promise. He had gone through a long, sticky, sleepless night filled with thoughts of the pleasures he'd shared with Lillian and a day when all he could think about were the pleasures to come: the pleasure; the ultimate act that would see an end to his boyhood and present him with the credentials of a man.

Jamie had mooned through breakfast in the other ranks mess where most of his fellows had sugar on their porridge and one or two had salt. Jamie had a liberal sprinkling of puffed wheat. He'd ballsed-up morning parade: he could have sworn he'd ordered 'right wheel' even though two thirds of his section left wheeled through a flower bed and the rest stood round gaping. Finally he had day-dreamed himself into a state of embarrassingly visible arousal during the afternoon session in the swimming pool. Sergeant Josh Williams was first to notice whereupon he immediately issued the nickname 'Stiffy' to poor Jamie.

Never mind. It was half-past six. He planned on skipping tea and meeting the lovely Lillian at their special, special place. They had been there last night. He had French-kissed her, felt her soft, warm breasts. She had squeezed his bum, and for one delicious moment slid her hand between his legs.

'We can't get serious,' she whispered. 'Not in this dirty old pill-box.' Then she kissed him a little harder, petted a little more firmly. Inch by dangerous inch they moved closer towards the territory from which there is no return. Finally Lillian pulled away. 'No! Not tonight. We mustn't.'

'When?' Jamie said, his voice softly wavering.

'Come back her tomorrow. And bring a blanket.'

Bring a blanket! It could only mean one thing. Jamie could imagine only one thing: Lillian naked, himself naked, together on a blanket in the dark, enfolding secrecy of a long forgotten pill-box.

Jamie returned from reliving the last few hours and peered once again into the mirror. He considered squeezing the zit.

'Watch out Micky,' Josh's insinuating voice came from the direction of the entrance. 'Keep your arse to the wall. It's Stiffy McDowell.

Jamie's heart sank as the double doors clashed together enclosing him in the shower-block with his tormentors. 'Can't you give it a rest, Josh?' he said, resigned to the fact that the sergeant revelled in the power to make others squirm.

'Oh! Can't one give one a west, Joshua? Josh mimicked in mockery of Jamie's diction.

'The sight of all those bare arses in the changing room was just too much for you, wasn't it Jamikins?' Micky added.

Jamie collected his things together and stuffed them into his wash-bag aware that the two squadron bullies hovered just over his left shoulder. He forced himself to stay calm; they were not going to spoil his evening.

'Go on McDowell. Piss off!' Micky said, playing the hard man. 'I want to take a slash and I don't want you staring at my knob.'

Jamie walked towards the doors, slowly in case the dogs gave chase. 'Don't worry Micky. I haven't got telescopic vision.'

Josh laughed, an act that confused Micky sufficiently to stop him lashing out at Jamie for a comment his slow mind had yet to fully assimilate. 'Go on, Stiffy. Get out of it, before you get a slap.'

'On my way, Sergeant. I can see you two want to be alone.' Jamie hurried out before Josh had time to react. He would probably suffer later, but he wouldn't go down without a fight.

Flying Officer Reader was duty officer. He had just finished dinner and was making his way to the duty tent when young McDowell scooted round the officer's mess cutting a corner between paths by running over the grass.

'McDowell, you dipstick! Come here!' Reader yelled, most unofficer-like.

'Sorry Sir,' Jamie said breathlessly. 'In a bit of a hurry.'

'A bit too much of a hurry if you ask me. If the SWO sees you dancing on the green stuff he'll use you for a bog-brush.' He put on a stern face but inside he was laughing. In everyday life Phillip Reader was a fireman, but for three evenings a week (when shifts allowed) and several camps a year he was Flying Officer (Volunteer Reserve Training), 2 ic Rillton Squadron ATC. He was convinced that many officers took their ATC ranks far too seriously. His charges were not there for his amusement, so he could act out his fantasies ordering them about because he couldn't hack it in the real world. Sure, he would point them in the right direction, rein them in if they got a little wild, but that didn't stop him treating them with respect. He did not feel he had to spoil all their fun for the sake of conformity and regulations.

Reader noticed the over-strong smell of shower-gel. Then it dawned upon him that young McDowell was looking exceedingly well turned out for a cadet out of uniform. The jeans were as smart as jeans could be, the shirt was newly

ironed, the trainers were new and un-scuffed, the large bath towel neatly folded
… Bath towel? The penny dropped: McDowell was involved with a young lady.

'Meeting someone, are we Corporal?'

Jamie's ears flushed a little. 'Might be, Sir.'

'Could it be that you have forgotten the way to the swimming pool? Or
perhaps you've got another use for that towel?'

Jamie didn't answer, but the blush spread from ears to cheeks.

'I think perhaps, you are meeting a young lady. Am I right?'

Jamie was taller than the officer but suddenly he felt like a silly little boy. He
nodded, knowing that his evening was in tatters.

After a silence that seemed to last hours, Reader spoke. 'Off you go then.
But don't do anything you'll be ashamed of later. And be careful. Did you hear
me Jamie? Be … careful! I don't want to take you back to your Dad with half
your dangly bits turning green.'

'No Sir, I … Don't get the wrong idea Sir. It's just –'

'Jamie!'

'Yes, Sir?'

'Shut up!'

'Yes, Sir.' Jamie remained before the officer, almost at attention, as if
awaiting a formal dismissal.

'Do you want the full lecture then? About respecting yourself and your young
lady? About acting in haste and repenting at leisure? Of course not! You're a big
boy now, fully aware that all actions have consequences. Yes?'

'Yes, Sir. But it's not what you're thinking. We're just …' He was going to say
"friends", but you didn't kid Mr Reader. Somehow he always saw through it.

At that moment a fat warrant officer plodded into view.

'And don't let me catch you on the grass again,' Reader said in a raised,
withering voice. The warrant officer approved of officers who knew how to give a
bollocking.

Jamie pumped out a 'No Sir!' for the benefit of the ear-wigging WO then
quietly added 'And thanks,' before he spun on his heel and disappeared down
the path heading for the perimeter fence.

Lillian waited by the entrance of the pill-box peering through thick gorse. Jamie
was late and she began to wonder if he had chickened out. Without saying as
much, she made it clear to him that his longings would be satisfied.

The thought angered her. Maybe he was too green even to take the hint.
She had worked hard on Jamie, at home and here at camp, and if the week
ended without him screwing her, all her plans would be up the creek. She began
to resent the silly boy as the minutes ticked by. Not only would she have to
rethink the whole plan but she was feeling in need of a good session. Thinking of
sex made her mouth water.

Lillian hated men, and boys probably even more, but she loved their bodies.
She loved them like an addict loves a fix. She loved the feel of them, the smell
and the taste and the exquisite sensations they could produce when she took
them deep inside. And if she could have her fun and leave them hurt, humiliated
and crushed, so much the better. Use them. Screw them up. Throw them away.
She was after all, her mother's daughter, and although Rosemary had a
reputation as a somewhat prudish old primary school teacher, Lillian knew things
about her that would make the headmaster's hair stand on end.

Josh and Micky would get the full works. Her plan for them was close to completion. Jamie though? She would leave him feeling like a king; the plan demanded it. She would make sure his first sex made him glow with self-fulfilment and pride. That's if the little shit turned up.

When he did arrive he startled Lillian by bursting though the narrow gap between the pill-box and the dense gorse. He was almost on her before she knew what was going on. 'Hi Lillian,' he said with a broad smile and slightly flushed cheeks.

Her immediate impulse was to go for him. He was twenty minutes late and deserved a hard time but she could not risk spoiling things now. 'Jamie! Oh, I was getting so worried. You're late.'

'Yes, sorry. I nearly got captured by one of the officers. He kept prattling on for hours and then –'

Lillian wrapped her arms round his neck and pulling him down sucked him into a long passionate kiss. 'Oh Jamie,' she gasped. 'It doesn't matter. You're here now. I missed you so much.'

Jamie's reply was driven out of him by waves of instant arousal and Lillian kissed him again, satisfied as she felt him harden against her body.

Jamie had lied when he used the encounter with Flying Officer Reader as an excuse for his lateness, although in a way it had been his fault. Had Jamie ran straight here following his conversation, he would have been a few minutes early, but Reader's lecture kept circling his mind, round and round like an old jet fighter at an air show, now quiet and distant, now blasting him with the air-ripping sound of after-burn. In the end – damn and bugger the man all the way to Hell – Reader's words of advice took root. Jamie resolved to slow things down with Lillian. Kissing and cuddling, a little heavy petting but he wouldn't go the whole way. Now, with his tongue entwined with hers and her hand grasping him through denim, he wasn't so sure his resolution would survive the hour.

'Now Jamie. I need you, now. Let's go down. I want you to be my first,' Lillian whispered, while thinking *my first this week*. She kissed him harder and with more passion and then disengaged while Jamie lifted his head to peer over the gorse in the direction of his chat with Mr Reader. Waiting for no more than a moment, Lillian dragged Jamie through the small hatchway and down into the depths of the derelict pill-box.

An hour and twenty minutes later Jamie emerged, hair no longer well combed, trainers scuffed and shirt hanging out. Anyone seeing him would have imagined he had taken part in some terrible subterranean punch-up, but for the enigmatic smile on his face. He crept into the shadow of the gorse bush, pulled at the crotch of his jeans, peered over the top and then with a brief glance back to the hatchway, he ran towards camp his towel billowing in the wind behind him.

Lillian surfaced squinting in the evening sunlight. She carefully parted thorny branches to watch Jamie's retreat. She took a deep breath and ran a hand through her hair then bent to adjust the leg of her black pedal-pushers. She then put one hand into the opposite sleeve of her fluffy pullover and withdrew a pair of blue silk boxer shorts. She held them to her face and breathed in deeply. They smelt of shower-gel, boy and sex – perfect evidence for the validation of her trophy.

Lillian put her head back and laughed silently. She loved it when a plan worked out. She might be a little behind schedule, but she was well on track. Certainly as far as the knicker-napping went, she was home and dry – well, home and a little damp until she got these things ready for presentation. But as for the money making scheme? That needed a little more work. Lillian licked her lips; she could still taste Jamie. She smiled again thinking that the next session would be pleasurable and well within her skills. And then, from nowhere, something stirred in her heart; something unfamiliar and just a little frightening. It did not last long, but while it remained she saw Jamie in a different light and her whole being softened. Surely she wasn't ... No, he was far too young for her, and Lillian did *not* do "love".

The feeling passed, and Lillian's mind was, once again, on the plan. Had it not been for Jamie's remarkable will power, the game would be hers already, but no, he had held out. He was a surprisingly well equipped lad for his age and Lillian recalled of the feel of him through his jeans. She had been a little two vigorously for he had peaked too soon. Still, that had been the perfect excuse to get him out of his boxers and jeans. The rest – the rest was biology, of sorts. They had enjoyed each other in a variety of ways, all initiated by Lillian. But he wouldn't go the Full Monty with her! Just about every other avenue was explored, but whenever Lillian moved towards the full act, Jamie shied off.

How could she pretend she was pregnant and extort all that dosh if he wouldn't do it? No sweat. It was early days yet. She would just wait until they were both back at Lofty Gables. There was no way she would be able to get him alone in the house, but Wymes Forest was on the doorstep and she quite fancied sex outdoors. She would get him into the woods, provide a condom and if it were to bust, well what a shame.

Lillian tucked the damp boxers back into her sleeve and chuckled. When she had used Jamie all up, they got dressed, but search as much as they might his blue silk boxers were not to be found. Still, it was getting dark and the bunker was nine-parts hidden in black shadow. With no torch it was useless to continue the search and so Jamie went commando and pulled on his jeans – expensive 501's Lillian noticed – with no suspicion that she had secreted them away.

'Look boys,' Lillian began, sitting with Josh and Micky in the middle of Greyes Village Green. 'If you know anything about girls, you'll have spotted that Carol and Rona are a couple of teasers. They'll keep you hanging on all week, and if you're lucky you'll get a bit of slap and tickle – that's more slap and precious little tickle. But me, I can't get enough, *and* I like my men in pairs. So, if you aren't busy Saturday afternoon ...'

First the boys had simply looked confused, and then a little embarrassed. But it hadn't lasted long; Lillian knew how to work them. Like two young sheep dogs she knew exactly how to make them come-by. She went through, in sketchy detail, her favourite fantasy. It involved sex in the open air. It involved doing a bit of skinny dipping and nude sunbathing. And it involved two naked hunks stealing into her secret place amongst the thicket and ... more biology, of course.

'And remember, the lads have to be naked when I first see them. I know it's daft, but it's got to be just so. See?'

They saw. They nearly came. Lillian conquered.

'Do you think you two could –'

They were certain they could.

'Saturday then. During the treasure hunt.'

'It's *not* a treasure hunt,' Micky said. Short-lived, his protest was truncated by a dig in the ribs from Josh.

It was a treasure hunt. No matter what military-sounding name Flying Officer Reader gave it, it was still a treasure hunt. Fair enough you had to be fairly nifty at the old map work to stand any chance of winning – sorry; achieving the objective – but you still had to find little clues written on squares of paper: one nailed to the underside of a stile, another folded into a tube and rammed into a knot-hole on a telegraph pole. That sort of thing.

It hardly mattered, treasure hunt or map-reading exercise, it was good fun and if Corporal Jamie McDowell wasn't the best scrum-half the squadron ever boasted, he was pretty hot with map and compass. His section was bound to be in with a chance.

Sergeant Josh Williams was the only real competition and Jamie had seen him sloping off with his side-kick Micky, leaving Pizza-Face Jones to lead their section. Nice kid despite the beacon-like zits. But leading a section? No way! They say there is nothing more dangerous than an officer with a map and compass. You would have trouble convincing Jones's section.

It was a good feeling to have the confidence of your team. Jamie felt like a real leader as he took his men – and two girls – across mole-hill strewn pasture. The place was alive with grasshoppers and the sun so hot that the team was glad, for once, to be wearing their peaked crap-hats. Berets in this weather would have been unbearable. A couple of younger boys unsuccessfully petitioned Jamie to allow removal of shirts. They were lucky; later that day three of Pizza-Face's section were seen by the MO suffering severe and extensive sunburn.

One or two kilometres away an ill-kept wood yielded to scrubby thicket that fell gently to a small river. It was a place well known to poachers – and lovers. Secluded, peaceful, rarely visited, its ill-defined paths were nine-parts overgrown. Many a Greyes Forton babe had been conceived here.

Josh stood with his fists resting on his hip bones. 'This is the place.'

'Yeah, this is definitely it,' Micky said. 'There's the willow.' Now they were actually here, butterflies rose from stomach to chest.

'No doubt about it. This is definitely the right place. What time is it?'

Micky looked at his watch. 'It's the right time.'

'Good,' Josh said while shuffling his feet in the dry grass of this little clearing in the bushes.

'Well, go on then. Make the signal.'

Josh thought about it for a moment then raised his hands to his mouth and gave three long owl hoots. Almost by way of reply came three high-pitched buzzard calls.

'She's here,' Josh said feeling surprised and a little scared all at once. Both boys stood, slack-jawed and furtive, each waiting for the other to make the first move.

'Come on then, Josh.'

'What?'

'You know. Get your clothes off.'

Josh swallowed hard then with trembling fingers started to undo his shirt buttons. Micky followed suit. Their shirts hit the ground at the same instant as Pizza-Face gave the go-ahead for his section to remove theirs.

Josh and Micky needed a little encouragement to complete their strip, just as Lillian guessed they would. So she sang a couple of verses from a Fairground Attraction number. 'It's got to be-e-e-e-e-e … perfect,' wafted across to the boys' shrubby shelter like the call of a siren. They whipped off their jeans and pants and headed for the sound scooting from one bush to the next.

Lillian wasn't at the place they'd expected her to be, but before confusion sent them scurrying back to the security of their clothes, a seductive chuckle from a clump of bushes a little further away drew them on. This happened twice more and twice more the boys made a streaking dash for the next haven of woody seclusion.

'She's taking the piss,' Micky hissed.

'No she ain't,' Josh said with enthusiasm. He was beginning to enjoy this newfound sense of freedom and he frolicked like Pan. 'She'll be waiting for us at the next bush, legs wide and wet as a fish.'

But there was no Lillian at the next bush and no further peels of girlish laughter. Five minutes went by. Ten, fifteen; then the boys heard a sound that made their hearts sink to form a hard knot deep in their stomachs. It was the sound of approaching strangers coming like a heard of elephants; shouting, laughing and fooling around. No: worse than strangers, much worse. It was a troop of cadets.

Without the need for words Josh and Micky were of one mind. No time for stealth; too late for careful observation before exposing themselves to open land. They would have to run for it. They bolted out of their tiny clearing like rabbits scattering from a fox, ignoring scratching twigs and jagged thorns. They covered the distance to their place of disrobing in a fifth of the time it took on the outward journey – but horror of horrors!

'This is the place,' Josh said through gasps for air.

'Yeah,' Micky said, equally out of breath. 'This is the place.'

'No doubt – gulp – about it. This is – gulp – definitely the right place … So where's our frigging clothes?'

'Don't ask us,' Corporal Jamie McDowell said. 'We just followed the clues straight to this clearing. Never saw any clothes.'

The naked lads tried to cover up before the Corporal's section which began emerging from all round, some giggling, some nonplussed, but all lacking the necessary tact to look away.

'Are these two our objective?' piped an undersized leading-cadet.

'What? Two naturist cadets caught having a nice time? I wouldn't have thought so,' Jamie said, revelling in it. 'Come on troops. Let's get out of here. Josh and Micky obviously want to be alone.'

The troop disappeared as quickly as they had earlier emerged leaving Lillian's victims decimated and totally speechless. It was a full minute before Josh pulled himself together. 'I AM NOT … WE ARE NOT … WE <u>DO NOT</u> WAN'T TO BE LEFT ALONE!!!!'

'Piss off Josh! We don't want them coming back again.'

Josh went purple in the face and Micky wondered if it was possible for a boy's head to explode. "I'LL <u>KILL YOU</u> MCDOWELL,' Josh bellowed just before recovering his sense of self-preservation. He dropped into the dry grass. 'Come back, pleeease. You can't leave us like this.'

But they could, and during their return journey to camp the dispossessed died a thousand deaths. Back at camp they made up a story. They said they'd decided to go for a swim in the river and when they returned to the bank their clothes had been nicked. It was only a slight manipulation of the truth and an excuse that minimised future embarrassment.

Later they had to make an official report about their stolen clothes, and they would soon come to regret going into quite so much detail with regard to their underwear, because there was one more misery left in store. Micky's white shorts had been resplendent with a picture of Dennis the Menace and Josh boasted a pair of electric blue tanga-briefs. Their choice of underwear was the subject of considerable ridicule, but there was far worse to come.

Sunday morning came and the council of elders met at their usual HQ. Carol slurped a root beer and looked her usual genial if somewhat thick self.

Rona was a little more subdued than usual and soothed her sorrows with a thick chocolate milkshake. 'Time to tote up the score,' she said, yawning.

'A successful week?' Lillian enquired sweetly.

Rona shrugged.

Carol shook her head. 'Flipping disastrous. It was all going really good, then Josh went all odd and stood me up the next night.'

Exactly the same had happened to Rona with Micky but she was admitting nothing. 'Oh well. Can't win them all. Micky turned out to be a tosser, so I dropped him.'

'Is that so?'

'Yes, Lillian. That is exactly so. I suppose you're going to say you did better. And don't think we've forgotten. You've got to come up with blue silk boxer shorts or you're –' Rona's eyes widened with horror. The look on Lillian's face said it all. She was the cat that got the cream, and a flaming Cheshire cat at that.

Lillian slowly drew open the zip of her bum-bag, then with a magician's flare whipped out her prize and slammed it on the table.

Carol gagged on her beer and coughed a mouthful up.

Rona did a double-take at the dark blue, light blue and red piece of cloth spread triumphantly before her. 'What the sodding hell is that?'

Lillian spread it out. 'I think ... I think they call it a wing commander's pennant.'

'That don't count ... Oh my God! You're not saying you've done it with the Wing Commander, are you?'

Lillian laughed out loud finding it next to impossible to regain her composure. 'No,' she managed through tears. 'Not exactly.'

Station Warrant Officer Bullock took off his cap and wiped his sweaty brow with a radiantly white and crisply pressed hanky. 'Thank Gawd for that. That's the last of the little bastards for this year.' He followed the coach with his eyes as it exited through the main gate and turned right. He was sure one of the little gits was waving him goodbye through the side window – with a V-sign. 'Ignore it! Don't give them the satisfaction of a rise.' He heaved a heavy sigh of relief and not a little satisfaction of his own – but a shock induced coughing fit took him mid-breath. 'For crying out loud! Look what those bleeding little hooligans have done!'

The only person in the vicinity was a young Pilot Officer of the General Duties persuasion. If he knew anything with his newly scrapered sleeves, it was that you never, but never, crossed the SWO. He directed his gaze as he was bid, his eyes climbing a flagpole every bit as radiant as the SWO's hanky, until they came to rest upon the Wing Commander's pennant. What a curious new design. Looked remarkably like three pairs of underpants: one pair skimpy and electric blue, the white boxers bearing the image of the inimitable Dennis the Menace and the others, blue boxers shimmering in the early morning sunlight.

Now the Pilot Officer had a problem. Nowhere in the manual or in standing orders did it tell you how to stop a slavering SWO from climbing up a flagpole.

Jamie chewed his top lip feeling mildly gutted. His shorts fluttering away up there meant only one thing: he'd been well and truly had in all sense of the word. Well, nearly all. Sure she had got him out of his knickers but he never had gone all the way. Maybe old Mr Reader knew a thing or two after all. He smiled a bitter smile. No, she hadn't got all she wanted from him. And as for her job as his Dad's personal assistant and *au pare* – well, the right word to Mum and she'd be out on her ear. He never wanted to see her again. Not here and not back at Lofty Gables.

That's where she had started to work her number on him. That's where the flirting began. 'All these pairs of blue shorts. Don't you like any other colour?' she'd asked recently when she was taking his clean laundry up to his room. She'd flirted, he felt flattered and special that an older girl took so much interest in him – but all this time she'd been having a laugh at his expense.

Still, he thought. He'd had some fun and the ribbing of his mates would soon die down; might even make him a bit of a hero. He hadn't lost that much really. Just a pair of rather expensive shorts, but as his Dad had made a mint importing them and he had a whole drawer full back home, it was a loss he could bear.

His thoughts trailed off and back to that night in the pill-box. As he sank into the seat the passing countryside soothed his mind. 'Do I still count as a virgin?' he asked himself in a whisper.

'What was that?' Pizza-Face asked.

'Oh, it was nothing. Nothing that isn't all over and done with.'

Lillian caught the train home. Staring out at the shifting landscape she wondered if Jamie thought it was all over. If he did she would soon disabuse him of the notion. She wanted more of him and more she would get. Having set the wick burning, there would be no putting it out ... until it was dipped.

CHAPTER NINE

Bus Shelter Reunion

'So I'm related to him then. That explains the middle name. Jamie is ... was ... would have been my ... my what?' Chris leaned on the kitchen table and started to draft out a family tree on the back of an envelope.

Richard dried the last dish, scratched his head and then leaned over the expanding diagram. Mum was in the living room doing the ironing while watching TV. 'Stick your granddad De'Ath in there – that's it. His name was Robin. And Katie's dad was Eric, Robin's little brother. Sooo ... my cousin Katie was Jamie's mum – which means you and him would have been ... second cousins I guess.'

'How many times removed?'

'Don't ask me. I don't even know what that means. Removed from what?'

Chris shrugged. 'How far back do we have to go before we find the family's direct link with Sir Christopher Wren?'

'Further back than I ever managed to get, and I got back to the early eighteen hundreds. It was all visits to St Catherine's House then. No computers. I dare say you could do better these days with all these "trace-your-family" websites.'

Chris nodded thoughtfully. 'You're a first son. How comes your middle name isn't Wren?'

'Well, David Wren De'Ath, your great grandfather, was in the last generation to keep that tradition. I guess when girl sailors started being called WRENs the name kind of lost its appeal. So the tradition died out.'

'Until you revived it?'

'Me and your Auntie ... no third, no second cousin Katie. Wait a minute. If she's your second cousin, Jamie must be ... Oh, I give up!'

'It looks like Jamie's mum and you decided to revive the tradition independently of each other.'

'Looks that way.'

Chris looked out of the open window into the night. 'It's just so, so strange ...' he said dreamily, trailing off into nothing.

'Strange?'

'Yeah – that Jamie got taken by the Fey Knights and I nearly did.' Chris froze as soon as he'd spoken, but like a flying bullet the words were out in the world and beyond recall. Dad looked something between angry and dreadfully sad and Chris was on the verge of writing it off as a joke – until the stubborn streak in him surfaced. He was fed up lying, so he would wait until Dad said something. It was Dad's move. The silence stretched into uncomfortable.

'So, when's your outpatient's appointment?'

'Oh thanks a bloody bundle!' Chris bristled like a whipped Rottweiler and Dad flinched for an instant before attempting to re-establish his position as alpha-male.

'Out of order, Chris. You know that kind of language is not –'

'Stuff the bloody language. You've as good as called me insane! Well, I'm fed up having to lie about it all. And I don't care anymore, if what I saw doesn't fit in to what people are going to believe. But you're my dad. You should ... you should ... *believe* me or at least not treat me like a head case.'

'When you've quite finished –'

'I'm not even f ... I haven't even started yet.' The steam and venom began petering out and where the anger had been, vulnerability crept in once again and Chris felt like crying.

'Okay Chris. Let's start again. I'm sorry, okay? It wasn't very sensitive of me, and I do believe you're –'

'Telling the truth about what I *think* I saw? That's not good enough Dad. I know it's hard to believe, and God knows it's hard for me to say. Why couldn't it be a werewolf, or a ghost or some zombie crawling out of its grave? I could talk to my mates about that kind of stuff. They still wouldn't believe me but I could handle it. Instead I have to stand here, like a little six-year-old girl with a lisp and a pink frock and say "I thaw a faerie." How do you think that makes me feel?'

It was alright to cry. Dad had always said that. Not if you hurt yourself, because then you had to be brave and tough it out, but if you were sad or lonely or moved emotionally, then it was okay. Dad cried buckets at the drop of a celluloid hat when watching films. Anything to do with fathers and sons was bound to set him off, and as Chris looked he saw that Dad was crying now, silently.

Chris shrugged and moments later found himself being hugged tightly. Dad held him and cried, like the last time, when Chris had been thirteen and Arnie the golden retriever had died and just like that time, Dad cried and Chris didn't. It wasn't as if Chris couldn't understand how his dad felt. '*I've seen a faerie*' was no more believable than '*The 1812 Overture was written by a short-sighted chimpanzee, whose head kept falling off.*' Still, Chris was determined not to recant this time.

Dad straightened up, gave a sharp cough as a signal that normal demeanour was being restored and then splashed some water from the cold tap over his face. 'Okay Chris. I'll put the kettle on and over a cuppa you can tell me exactly what you saw.'

Chris told him everything, from the taking of Marc and Shaun by three young lads who fitted all the legendary descriptions of the Fey Knights and the tiny flying man who he still had trouble calling a faerie, to his encounter with Tarn in his hospital room. He even covered the nocturnal visit of the creature that had left him paralysed though did not go into detail as far as the sexual contact was concerned. Now Chris had bared his soul three times: to Danny, Kostja Claussen and now to Dad. He aimed to improve on his hat trick when the detective visited. Richard De'Ath was not impressed.

'Not a good idea Chris. Detective Superintendent Bowman is not going to want to hear about faeries and Fey Knights.'

'She'll have to lump it then. I'm not lying anymore.'

'It's not lying, exactly.'

'What is it then? I tell her something I made up instead of what I saw – what else do you call it?'

Dad cradled his empty tea cup in both hands peering into it as if looking for the right thing to say among the soggy digestive crumbs at the bottom. 'I'll be straight with you Chris. I'm on your side and I'll be here for you –'

'But?'

'But I can't let you go round telling that story to anyone else.'

'Because I'll get committed if I tell the cops?'

'People don't get committed for much these days – at least nothing far short of murder. But "care in the community" might be an option.'

'More like "don't care in the community" if you ask me.'

'Whatever, it's just not an option.'

'It's the only option, Dad. I can barely handle this as it is – juggling two stories is too much to expect, and I'm not doing it. I'm telling that cop lady what I just told you and I am happy to live with the outcome.' Chris lightened up, like a switch being thrown. 'And you should see my research Dad! I'm only a couple of days into it and I've already found tons of stuff. I'm far from the only person round here to have seen the –'

'Don't say it!'

'... Fey Knights.'

Richard clicked his tongue.'

'I've shown you the newspaper cutting about my cousin Jamie, and there's other stuff too. Did you ever meet Ernie Sheldrake?

'Of course; everyone knew Ernest – and he'd have kicked your arse if he'd heard you calling him "Ernie." I suppose you've seen his book?'

'You know about his book?'

'It attracted a bit of attention when Jamie and Lillian went missing. We had the Pebble Mill crew up here and Old Mr Sheldrake got himself interviewed. A publisher wanted to take it on and distribute it all round the globe but it all fell through. Only a dozen or so trial copies ever got printed before the printers went up in smoke.'

'Who did it?'

'Set the fire? Nobody. It was an accident, and anyway, you're changing the subject. I want you to promise you will not tell anyone else, except the doctor, what you told me tonight.'

'No deal.'

Dad looked crestfallen. 'Good job I already cancelled Dawn then.'

'Dawn Bowman? You cancelled the cop-lady? Get back on to her. I want to speak to her.'

'My turn to say "No deal". I told her you were too tired, and that if it wasn't official –'

'You've got no right. I'm nearly eighteen.'

'I have every right to protect my son, even if it's from himself. Chris, we'll get through this. Chris!

It was too late. Chris slammed the front door behind him.

The reverberations hadn't settled when Chris patted his pocket: no keys. *Damn!* He'd have to knock when he came home, so that meant being back before Dad went to bed. He certainly wasn't going to knock now and ask sheepishly for his keys after his dramatic exit. Chris was already beginning to feel rather silly and childish, at least until a somewhat off kilter burst of spookiness was heralded by that sound – that giant beetle-wing thrum that moved in towards him and out again before he could get a fix on it. There was no space for feeling silly when fear was on the up.

'Oh no. Not again,' he whispered to himself. 'Not here.' He got as far as turning back and reaching out for the door knocker before he gritted his teeth and spun to face the world. It was a good day to die, or perhaps it was just a good day to slap a faerie out of the air. As Chris stepped forward the evening closed in round him. If he was in a film, this would be the cue for discordant violins. This would be time for the camera to race forward on a dolly rail while cranking down the focal length: the horizon shrank and the frame of Chris's reality moved in on him – and in the distance a motorcycle engine idled, a little twist of throttle making it roar every few moments.

Chris covered the long driveway to the narrow lane. Turn right and walk for five minutes, he'd be in Little Rillton. Turn left and the woods of Wymes Park were a brisk ten minute jaunt. The woods beckoned while Little Rillton gave him the cold shoulder. The motorcycle continued its guttural stutter from somewhere up on the left, calling to him like a gravel gargling siren. The sound, or some underlying magic, was quite compelling and it joined forces with the confining evening to herd him towards the woods. It was as if the only escape was to turn left at the lane and stride out for Wymes Park.

It was darker than it should be for an early evening in late August and it started raining lightly – the kind of rain you hardly noticed until it soaked you by stealth. Not only had Chris come out without his keys but he hadn't stopped long enough to grab a jacket or even drag on his hoody. *A little rain won't kill me* he thought as he quickened his pace towards the sound of the bike and the shadow of the woods.

And then he slowed to a crawl. There was something about the moment, something about the place he wanted to savour. Home was minutes behind him and as the lane rose he could look over the roof and see the upstairs lights on in the *Moiled Bull* half a mile further on. Family was near, friends were close and yet he felt as if he were the lone survivor in a world where everybody else had simply ceased to exist. There was nobody else; just him and the evening caressing him with an intimate dampness ... and the sound of a motorbike.

Destiny was a short walk up the road but Chris was not yet ready to focus upon it, for if he was about to be absorbed by whatever lay ahead, right now he was the cranesbill scattered in the roadside hedgerow, he was the hawthorn and the crow he heard cawing above. He crouched and laid his hand flat on the damp tarmac and felt one with the ground. The gentle rain was no more than his own breath extending outward from the moisture of his lungs. He had never felt so integrated with his surroundings as he did at this moment. Only the sound of the motorcycle, as compelling as it was, came from some other, from something outside his newfound ubiquiosity.

Chris began to run towards the sound. *It's just you an me then. Me for the Gayle and Danny and the world and you for ... for the Fey Knights or whatever else it is you represent.* He pumped his legs harder until he was at full sprint, and then as if taking up the challenge the motorcycle screamed and without seeing it Chris felt it lurching forward, off the leash and racing to him at full tilt.

All that metal charging towards him; all that steel and rubber, not to mention anything at all about the rider. Suddenly Chris didn't feel so sure of himself and yet still he ran. From the lane through the woods up ahead he saw a movement. Fleet as the wind and speeding towards him like a dark lightning bolt, the bike hurtled. The rider had decided to go without the luxury of headlights, or even sidelights, and descended towards Chris like a buzzard upon a rabbit. Chris slackened his speed as the world began to flee, leaving him to face the rider alone. The hedgerow was just a muddy conglomeration of a dozen species of plant life; the tarmac was just hard; the rain was only wet: none of it part of him anymore.

Chris came to a dead stop and his heart smashed into his ribs like a prisoner demanding release. Resolve and courage all melted away as the bike's engine became thunderous, and then he saw the bus shelter. Made of brick and set here in another age to serve villagers at the west end of Little Rillton and the below-stairs workers of Wymes Estate, it was the only place to hide. Chris made a run for it and dived into its dark interior just as the bike rounded the last bent. He fancied he could feel the wind of its passing through the damp material of his t-shirt.

As the throb of the engine died down, Chris began to relax until shocked right back up to full fight-or-flight alert condition red.

'That was close,' came a voice from the dark shadows. Chris couldn't help but agree; it was indeed very close to him having an embarrassing accident in his pants. He froze, a dishevelled pile of youthful humanity on the dusty floor of an ancient bus shelter. And then a face emerged from the darkness.

'You!' Chris said. 'It's you.'

'Yes, it is me. I usually am me. At least, most of the time.'

Now the motorcycle was but a distant purr that barely stroked the eardrums; for Chris it might as well have been a million miles away. He brushed himself off and sat at the other end of the wooden bench Tarn had chosen as a perch. He sat, birdlike, with his knees drawn up and his muddy footwear soiling the seat.

'Nice to see you got yourself some more clothes,' Chris said, doing his best to sound cool and collected. The guy was smiling but Chris wouldn't be "beguiled" and he was determined not to be "led away until judgement day."

Tarn was wearing khaki combat trousers which were a little too tight, a pair of well worn, black boots "infantry for the use of", circa 1950, and a loose-fitting, heavy duty nylon Belstaff motorcycle jacket, black with a red quilted lining. 'I've found it doesn't go down well with people when I venture abroad in nothing but my ... what was it you called them ... shreddies?'

Chris nodded and sucked on a molar. The boy kept smiling his beguiley smile. 'You *are* a Fey Knight ... aren't you?'

Tarn stopped smiling. 'I *hate* that! Hate it to the depths of my being. Only Sav hates it more than me and he once hefted a welt off a fellow's backside for addressing him thus.'

'Sav?'

'One of my brothers. There's me, Sav and Ret – and you may choose to call us ... "Fey - Knights" ... but we call ourselves Ieladhrim.'

'Yella-thrim?'

'Close enough. To be closer still, say "Ee – ell – a – thrim".'

Chris tried again.

'Almost perfect.'

'And Ieladhrim are what ... a kind of faerie?'

Tarn gacked from the back of his throat as if trying to dislodge a fly stuck to his uvula. 'If there is one thing I hate more than being called a Fey Knight, it being called a faerie. How would you like it? I understand the term has implications to your kind.'

'Well, I suppose –'

'No. And I don't like it either, even though the implication is irrelevant to me. Why oh why do the people from this side so love to label each and every living thing? I am a man. You are a man. We have our qualities and our little bundle of likes and dislikes, but none of them make for an accurate label.'

Chris watched Tarn as the smile slowly spread, past the confines of the boy's face, to warm every corner of the little shelter. 'I'll try very hard not to call you any of the things you don't like then. And a belated thank you for bringing me out of that trance or whatever it was.'

'Perfectly welcome dear chap. And I told you before. It was a spell.'

'A ... spell?'

'Mm,' Tarn inflected by way of an affirmative. 'And you might like to know, she who cast it is dead.'

'You killed her?'

'Certainly not. I'm not the killing type. But I am afraid it's too much to hope that her line is terminated. There are others of her kind, but she was the original and the most powerful.'

Chris shivered at the thought of the ghastly attack he had suffered at its hands; he could not think of the beast as "her" although was not at all sorry "she" was gone and hoped she had died painfully for what she had done to Danny. 'How did it ... how did *she* die?' He shivered again, this time from the damp t-shirt that wicked away his body heat.

'Killed – decapitated in fact – by a little girl. But let's not tarry so on such an unsavoury story. I've but a little time, and much to say. But first, take this.' Tarn shed the jacket, a rainbow hued button-up shirt emerging from the black like a butterfly casting a tough, dull chrysalis. 'I see you are shivering, and as for me – well I don't really feel the chill.'

Chris found Tarn helping him into the Belstaff jacket like a mother eager to tuck her child away from the nasty weather. 'Thanks, but I can do it myself.' Chris was glad of the extra warmth and tugged the zip all the way up to his neck. Tarn had shuffled close and although Chris was now protected from such of the elements that ventured into the shelter, he did not move back to his own end of the bench. Chris felt uncomfortable, his personal space invaded. And then there it was again! That smile: an intoxicant, a soporific, a hypnotic weapon as effective as a stun-gun.

Chris shook off the effect. 'Quit aiming your smile at me. It won't work. I'm immune.'

'Oh. And I was so close.'

'So close to what? Taking me away like you did all the others? You and others like you all back through history, taking kids.' Chris could hardly believe he was having this conversation.

'You were right the first time. At least, almost. You think of me as one of the ... I hate to say it ... one of the three "Fey Knights". Let us, for one moment, own that I am. Then dwell upon this: there have never been any other Fey Knights but us three. Tarniel – that is I, bearing my "Sunday" name – and my identical triplet brothers, Retsutsiel and Savaliel. Though there are others like us, we are the Ieladhrim for Wymes Forest, as ever we have been and ever we shall be. But more importantly, it is not only the Ieladhrim who take "kids" from the woods. I am sure you can hazard a guess upon another culprit.'

Chris nodded, grim-faced. 'Her!'

'Her indeed. She and her kind, who are as different from the Ieladhrim as darkness is from light. Christian, you are in the midst of a war and I, like the man on the posters with the big walrus moustache, need you, just like I've needed all the others from Elfric Magnusson to Marc Stockdale and –'

'And his brother Danny,' Chris shouted. 'My best friend, dead because of some stupid war between the pixies that he didn't choose to fight and –'

Something flared in Tarn. 'Nobody chooses. They are called. And the leladhrim call – or the others do.'

'You're nothing but the captain of a press gang then. Well count me out!' Chris rose to leave before even beginning to ask the first of his growing store of questions.

Tarn rose to as if to restrain him, but before he got the chance the shelter was shot through with the vibrations of a heavy motorcycle engine. No – there were two of them. Tarn appeared afraid. 'Come to me – when you're ready come to me in the wood, by the old tower.'

The shelter entrance was filled by a dark figure. He screamed something incoherent and when Chris looked for support, Tarn was no longer beside him. A fleeting shadow snagged the rider's attention and he made a dash for his machine and gunned it up aiming the bike off the lane. It threw up clods of earth as he took it "rural" and sped across a field towards the wood.

Before Chris could spur his body into any kind of action, the second rider swung a leg off his bike and hefted it onto the centre-stand. He stood for a moment, like a basalt statue or a man-shaped black hole, and then slowly approached Chris, like a wild-west cowboy walking towards his opponent in a gunfight. Chris waited for the draw anticipating the pain that was about to come.

The black-clad rider stopped a metre short of Chris and flipped up his tinted visor giving Chris a hint of the whites of his eyes, but nothing more.

'You're meddling with events you don't understand,' came the voice, deep, smooth and flowing from the slit under the visor like crude oil. 'Stop now or there will be consequences.'

Chris opened his mouth but the words stuck somewhere close to his Adam's apple.

'It will be very dangerous, for you and your family, if you have anything more to do with that one.' The biker flicked his head in the direction his colleague had ridden off, but Chris knew it wasn't the other rider this man was talking about. 'He may look like a weak boy, but he is powerful and ... evil. Let it all go now, and you will be safe. Persist and the result is guaranteed to be painful ... probably terminal.'

The biker remounted, kicked his bike into life although it looked modern enough for a starter button, and sped off across the field in pursuit of his colleague – and without doubt, Chris thought, Tarn. When the bike was almost out of sight, a little of Chris's courage returned.

'You tosser!' he shouted. 'Think you're a big gangster or something? I can work out whose evil for myself, thank you very much!' The last of the sun sent a shaft bouncing off the distant bike and straight into Chris's eyes. He took it as a warning and ran all the way home.

He pounded on the door until Dad came and let him in. 'Alright, alright. No need to bash the door down ... You okay?'

Chris managed to nod, but felt very far from okay.

'Looks like the riders from Hell are on your tail.'

For a moment Chris thought Richard was being serious, but shook it off with a forced smile. 'Forgot ... my ... keys.' He managed between breaths. 'I didn't want to be late. Make you have to get out of bed.'

Richard wasn't listening anymore. 'Whoa! Where did you get that jacket? It's just like the Belstaff had when I was a kid.'

Chris tried to work out a story to cover the acquisition of the jacket. He had given up on truth for the time being. The biker's warning was fresh in his mind and the last thing he wanted was to put his family in danger.

'Bugger me! It's the dead spit of the one I used to have. Even down to this little scuff mark on the sleeve. Got mine cheap because of a little mark *just* like that. Come on Chris. Spill!'

'Oh, it was ... Aby. Aby Knapper gave it me.' Chris knew that of all his school friends and acquaintances, Aby the vicar's son was the last one his dad was likely to come across. 'What happened to your old jacket, Dad?'

'Got nicked, didn't it. And I'd only had it a few days. I went into the off-license for a Party Seven. It was a hot day so I'd left the jacket over my bike seat. When I came back some bugger had swifted it. In Little Rillton, if you can believe it. I tried to report it at the police office, but they had more important stuff ...' Richard came to an abrupt stop and his eyes went glassy as, in his mind, an event from long ago tied up with a more recent one.

'Dad?'

'It was the day Dolly Tregonhawke got flashed at by some bloke who ran through the village in his y-fronts. They weren't very interested in my nicked jacket after Little Rillton's crime of the century.'

'Flashed? Are we talking flasher or streaker?'

'Probably neither. We all know how prone our Dolly is to gilding the lily. He was probably just peeing up a wall. That or he'd been caught over the side with some bloke's wife and was making a hasty retreat.'

Chris nodded. Richard nodded. 'Look Chris. Sorry about earlier. I didn't mean to imply you were two push rods short of a v-eight.'

'Okay Dad. Me too – sorry about the swearing.'

Richard gave Chris's shoulder a squeeze then went into the living room.

Mum popped her head round the door. 'I've been meaning to ask,' she said, the iron still in one hand with the flex stretched to its maximum. 'What happened to those ridiculously pricey undies you shelled out for? Those "Tommy Figaroes"? They're not in your draw and I haven't seen them in the wash since before ... well, you know. You didn't leave them at the hospital, did you?'

'Hilfigers, Mum. Not Figaroes,' Chris said. *No I didn't leave them at hospital Mum, see there was this creature who climbed into my room, got in bed with me, blew me cross-eyed then turned into a perfect copy of me and stole my clothes, including my good-luck knickers.* 'I suppose I must have left them there.'

'That's them gone then. I don't suppose the hospital runs a lost-underwear department. Serves you right for wasting your money.'

Another time and Chris would have bitten. Mum always knew exactly what not to say, and never failed to say it. This time he let her have the last word – almost. 'It wouldn't be called a department anyway. It would be a de-pant-ment.'

'Oh very good,' Julie said sarcastically before closing the living room door and returning to the ironing board.'

Since "the incident" in his bedroom followed by all the palaver at the hospital, Chris had taken to listening at doors. He knew it was sneaky and that he was unlikely to hear anything good, but he had to know what his parents thought about him, and the whole "Fey Knight" thing. He listened now.

He heard Dad talking about the night they saw "that guy running down the garden in his drawers" and mentioned the fact that he may have been into Chris's room and drawn "that bunch of scribbly birds." Dad had gone on to say that there had been another incident of a kid streaking through town, and told Mum about the Dolly Tregonhawke incident back in the mid-70s. Mum said she told him so, and then Dad got a bit stressed when she mentioned the Fey Knights.

Chris had heard enough. He went up to his room.

Chris's heart rate did not return to normal until he'd been sitting on his bed for a good five minutes. He sat with the jacket over his knees and mulled over the bizarre incidents of the last hour. Once again he had missed the opportunity to ask Tarn any of his important questions. Once again he had set out to clear his head and found it stuffed full of more muddle. Now he had those bully-boy bikers to worry about in addition to the Fey Knights in another addition to that beast's sisters or daughters or – what did Tarn call them? – her line.

Absentmindedly stroking the jacket he became aware of something hard in the pocket. Popping the heavy brass press-stud he slipped in his hand and pulled out a pack of sweets. "Spangles" it said on the pack; Old English flavoured Spangles. He wondered what an "Old English" tasted like then fished about in the other pocket. He found himself examining the clean and shiny stub of a cinema ticket. "Row 6H – ABC Cinemas" it said, and it was for the 7.30 showing of "The Godfather, Part II".

Chris lifted the jacket to his nose and sniffed at the arm pit area, perfectly aware of how pervy his mates would think him. *Stuff 'em!* He wanted to know if Tarn was a human boy whose human body exuded human smells. All he detected above the new clothes smell was a hint of his own deodorant, but he did see something that made him screw his eyes tight shut before taking a second look. Below the sturdy, double-stitched loop for hanging the jacket on a coat hook was a label bearing washing instructions, and written bold across the white label in ballpoint pen was a name. "R. De'Ath" it said, and it looked like it could have been written yesterday.

Chris hung the jacket in his wardrobe and tuned off the light so he could think without distractions. 'Okay,' he said softly, for the benefit of his own ears. 'Tarn sees me at the hospital. He lifts the … "spell" … and skidaddles. He somehow gets himself here all the way from County Hospital without being arrested – draws those birds and Arabian words on my wall. Then he does a runner – Mum and Dad see him running off down the garden "with half his arse hanging out" as Dad so delicately put it. Then … then … then he goes back thirty-odd years in time – as anyone would in the circumstances – to nick himself some clothes, the jacket of which is my Dad's, from when he was a teenage biker boy.'

The birds. Why would he draw the birds? What do they mean? 'And why the bloody Hell are they glowing?' Chris reached out a finger and touched the ghostly blue outline of the bird-drawing. It was as if it had been drawn with some kind of glow-in-the-dark ink. It didn't take long for Chris to realise that the ink was not giving off its own light, but reflecting moonlight that poured in through the window from a full moon slung low in the sky over towards Wymes Park. The clouds and the rain had all gone. When he stood between the source of light and the drawing, it became invisible. When he turned the lights on it was just a drawing in what looked like fibre-tip pen. But with the lights off and the moonlight unobstructed, it billowed with diffuse, blue light.

'Like that scary biker-guy said. I'm into something I don't understand. Something very, very dangerous.' *Maybe I should forget about the whole thing.* 'He said there would be consequences.' *Bullying bastard!* 'Who does he think he is? *Well, yeah! Who ... or what ... is he, and why are him and his mates following me all round town with their great big bikes?* 'Maybe I should tell Dad about them.'

There was a soft tap at the door. 'You want to tell me about something?' Dad said. Chris was obviously not the only one to listen at doors.

Now was not the time. Maybe the time would be never. 'No thanks Dad. It's cool. I'm ... I'm just sorting stuff out in my head.'

There was a pause and Chris could imagine the worried look on Dad's face. 'Alright, son. Don't sit up too late. A good early night and plenty of sleep may help you a whole lot better that thinking. Always works for me.'

'I'll give it a try.' Chris waited while he heard Dad move away and go into the marital bedroom.

Nights had been a trial for Chris ever since coming home from hospital after the attack. He slept in a pair of Dad's pyjama bottoms over some Speedos *and* a pair of boxers all finished off with a leather belt done up tight round his middle. If there was such a thing as a male chastity belt he would have been first in the queue at the blacksmiths. His nocturnal attire made for very uncomfortable nights, but he aimed to make it difficult for that "thing" if it ever came to have another pop at him. But tonight, inexplicably, the glowing birds made him feel safe and for the first time since coming home from hospital he stripped off and slipped under the duvet it his preferred attire – his skin.

Chris lay awake for a while. If there was a secret war going on and he had to take sides, he'd be standing with Tarn against those bikers and all the hoards of beasts. He didn't know what Tarn was, but he knew if there was any evil about, it was wearing biker gear. Then came that feeling he'd experienced a lot recently; was he really here? Was any of this happening? Here he was contemplating a war between two factions of impossible beings, just like he might be ruminating on the latest news from Iraq. He shook his head then reminded himself that he must hold all his own experiences to be true and act on them to the best of his ability.

There was one person, just one, with whom he could talk about Tarn. Not Mum or Dad; he couldn't burden them with it. But he had an outpatient's appointment tomorrow at the psychiatric wing of County Hospital and therefore the perfect opportunity. If Dad was too busy to give him a lift, he would catch the bus and report to the hospital wing, just to keep up a show; there was no way he was going to open up to some trick cyclist. No, he'd save talk about Tarn, and the other strange goings on, for the German nurse. Kostja Claussen was a man he could trust to act as a sounding board and not to dob him in to the psychs.

CHAPTER TEN

The Black Princess and the Faerie King

Chris came down to the breakfast table looking and feeling "cool". He wanted to make a good impression at the hospital. Not with the shrinks – they could go fly for all he cared – but with Kostja. He winced with embarrassment when he thought of the impression he must have made last time round and he made no allowances for himself that the whole thing had been completely beyond his control. This time would be different. He wanted Kostja Claussen to see him as he really was, and that meant dressing as he would for a Friday night out with his friends.

'Your best things?' Mum said. 'For a visit to the hospital? Met a nice nurse did you?'

Chris smiled at his mother's guesswork: spot on and yet a million miles off target. Mum was smiling too. So was Dad. And Chris seemed to be the centre of their attention. Mum and Dad exchanged secret little looks and smiled some more.

'What's up?'

'Nothing son. Why should something be up?'

'It's the way you two are acting. You're both ... I don't know, but there's something going on.'

'Go on Richard. Tell him,' Mum said, the cat straining to be let out the bag.

'Breakfast first, dear.'

'Dad! Tell me now. What is it?'

There it was; that look Dad always got when he was deciding whether to stick to his guns or yield to family pressure. 'Oh very well then.' He took a deep breath. 'I'm afraid I can't give you a lift to County today.'

Chris shrugged. 'Okay, I'll catch the bus.'

'We don't want you to catch the bus, do we Richard?'

Chris was beginning to think this was getting silly until Dad slid a set of keys across the table. 'We were going to wait until your birthday, but ...'

Chris snatched up the keys. There were two identical ones on a fob with the Fiat logo. Chris wanted to believe he knew what was going on. Surely, they hadn't? But what else could it be? He leapt up from the table and ran to the front door flinging it open to a bright new morning ... and a beautifully polished black Fiat Punto standing next to Dad's Landrover. He stood in stunned disbelief, his jaw hanging open, his eyes bright.

'Not exactly a Ferrari, but –'

'Dad! It's fantastic. I can't believe ... Mum, thanks. Thank you so much.'

For the first time in weeks, albeit for the space of only an hour, Chris was happy and his mind completely free of the pain that had never left him so fully since that day in the woods.

'She's my little Black Princess,' Chris said as he sat at the wheel for the first time, stroking the leather-bound steering wheel.

'You can't call her that,' Richard said leaning in through the open driver's door. 'I used to have a black Princess. It was an Austin that smelt of Met commanders and pipe-smoke, which in those days was much the same thing.'

'Dad?'

'What I mean is I got it second hand. It was an old police car that senior officers used to be punted around in. It had the shape of a door wedge and was about as much use for pulling birds as a zombie mask.'

'That was your black Princess, Dad. Ancient history. This one's mine and the name's just perfect. I love it.'

Forty-five minutes after taking up the keys, Chris was sliding into the High Street garage to top up with fuel. It only needed a few litres but he wanted to start his first trip with a full tank. He was surprised to find Cappy Shirakawa behind the counter. The first time they'd met Chris tried out his GCSE Japanese only to find that Cappy didn't speak a word of it: Texan, born and bred; went to school in Fort Worth.

'Hi, Cappy. Given up bar tending?'

'Nope. Still do that evenings and Saturdays. Pump gas weekdays and stock shelves at the supermarket during the graveyard shift.' He took Chris's credit card and slotted it into the card reader.

'Lazy git! Can't you fit any other jobs in?'

Cappy gave Chris a wry look over the top of his shades. 'Work at the garden centre Sundays. Hey, you know Rachel Finn the manager? She's a witch and she wants me to go along to her coven one night, but I'm guessing she just wants to see me out of my pants.' Cappy winked heavily.

Chris wasn't so certain anyone would be able to see Cappy naked: he was so skinny he'd surely go unnoticed, like a thread of cotton caught on the breeze. 'So what do you do at her garden centre? Stir cauldrons?'

'Water the plants. Heft compost into little old ladies' cars. Run the checkout sometimes, when I'm not mixing toe of frog and eye of ladybug – or whatever.'

'Sounds like you have a mission to put half Little Rillton out of work.'

'No, I just have expensive tastes, so as I'm no brain surgeon or lawyer and I can't earn the big J-Rock bucks like Camui-san, I have to do what I can. Put your PIN number in.'

'Expensive tastes?' Chris said eyeing Cappy's signature worn out white baseball cap and faded clothes, so baggy on his thin frame that he looked totally swamped. Even his piercings, right eyebrow and left ear, looked a little of the cheap side.

'Not clothes. Other stuff,' Cappy said, reading Chris's look spot on. He suddenly became animated. 'Got me some brand new Go stones. The black ones are best quality slate and the white are snow-white clam shell. No crap stuff. Full honest to goodness raven black and snow white, and as dear as they come. I'm telling you, three whole day's wages.'

Get Cappy onto the subject of Go and he could talk for hours. And he could be very convincing. None of the young guys who frequented the *Moiled Bull* ever bothered with pool or darts or cards these days. It was Go every time, and all because of Cappy's enthusiasm.

'You should play more, Chris. Show a lot of promise, just like Aby.'

'Aby drinks at the *Moiled Bull*?'

'Uh uh!' Cappy said shaking his head. 'I know him from my job at the supermarket. Nice guy, and he took to Go like a duck.' Cappy was suddenly distracted and peered out the window. 'Hey, did you leave your window open?'

'Yes. It's a hot day.'

'Well, a bird just flew in. You better clear it out of there before it craps all over your interior.'

Chris pulled his card from the reader, said thanks and goodbye then hurried to the rescue of the Black Princess. She was quite safe. There was no sign of a bird, so unless Cappy had imagined the whole thing it had flown away by its own volition.

Apart from the fact that the country roads were full of motorcyclists, each one out to get Chris – at least that is how he felt – the trip to County Hospital was uneventful. And yet it was not boring, which is more than he could say for his appointment at psychiatric out-patients. He answered their questions politely and tried to show them a perfectly sane and well adjusted young man, but he refrained from any mention of Fey Knights or bad bikers, or faeries or succubae. There was a limit to his resolution to tell the truth which had nothing to do with looks and appearance and all to do with self preservation. If telling the truth to a psychiatrist meant lock-up and electric shock treatment, he was going to dish truth out in carefully filtered measures.

As soon as his half-hour slot was up, Chris crossed over to the general wards but he was out of luck: it was Kostja Claussen's day off. Chris scribbled a quick note for him and left it with the staff nurse who appeared to feel the need to point out that Kostja was at home decorating while his wife and family were on a three-day jaunt to the in-laws. The note read: *I've met Tarn again. And he was a patient here. I've got his hospital wrist band.* He appended his phone number and e-mail address.

Chris began the return journey wondering if Kostja would ever get in touch. If not, it wasn't the end of the world. Chris was curious as to why Kostja had either lied or been mistaken about Tarn's status as a patient and County Hospital. He was also in desperate need of someone – anyone – to believe his story fully and unequivocally and so far nobody had. Apart from his dad, Kostja was the only one in whom Chris had confided and he wanted not just support, but his belief. If it took so much courage to tell the truth, was it too much to ask, that somebody believe him?

'Bloody faeries!' Chris said under his breath. 'Who *would* believe in them?'

'Call us something else and people might.'

Chris's head snapped round in the direction of the voice, and sitting on the back of the passenger seat was a tiny man with wings. Chris slammed on the brakes and would have skidded out of control if it wasn't for the ABS. Luckily, the road was empty. The little man just sat there smiling.

'O-kay,' Chris said slowly, forcing himself to look at the road ahead. He noticed a sign announcing a parking lay-by quarter of a mile ahead and willed himself to drive that short distance without looking anywhere but straight ahead. He came to the lay-by, pulled off the road, stopped and applied the handbrake. He threw the stick to neutral, killed the engine and then looked straight ahead for a little while longer. When at last he forced himself to look to his left, the faerie was still there.

'Nice wheels!' the faerie said. Chris stared. This was not the same being he had encountered by the old tower. That one had dark hair, like all three of the

Fey Knights. This one had long white hair. He wore a tiny pair of tight, mouse-skin trousers and a loose-fitting shirt that seemed to be made from cobwebs. His wings were birdlike, with long, elegant gold-brown feathers, and they appeared to emanate from an area near his shoulder blades. He wore boots and was no more than fifteen centimetres from head to foot.

'You ... like my car?'

'I do. What's its naught-to-sixty?'

'What's its ...?' Chris glanced away; glanced back; glanced away once more. 'Look. Before I'm even going to talk to you, I'm going to list a whole bunch of reasons why you are totally impossible and cannot exist. Okay?'

'Fine by me.'

'And if after that you're still here, then we can talk.'

'I'm not planned on leaving. Not just yet anyway.'

'Here goes then. With a body as small as yours you would burn up in a mildly sunny day or freeze to death in a cool breeze. To be able to fly you would have to have huge muscles round your chest, so huge you wouldn't look like a man at all, more like a pigeon. With a head the size of a marble you'd have a brain the size of a pea – a small one at that – and you would be no cleverer than a mouse. With vocal chords as minute as yours, your voice would be too high pitched for me to hear. And being so puny –'

'Puny?!'

'... just about anything from a crow to a fox could have you for dinner.'

'You want to take me on then,' the faerie said putting up his dukes like a boxer.

'No, I *do not* want to take you on.' Chris rolled his eyes.

'Come on you lanky streak. I dare you. Bring it on!' Now he was on the wing, hovering at arm's length from Chris – that's Chris's arm's lengths. Actually, just under arm's length, because Chris's anger got the better of him and he shot a hand out and flicked the annoying faerie with the tips of his fingers sending him flying into the side window with a splat. He stuck momentarily, like a character in a cartoon with arms, legs and wings akimbo, then slid down the glass and got tangled up in the door pull. It was so unexpected and absurd Chris would have laughed were he not so concerned that he might have damaged the little chap.

'Oh my God! Are you okay?' Chris reached out a hand to help but pulled up short. How did you help a six-inch faerie in a tangle? 'I didn't mean to hurt you.'

'If I was as frail as your theory suggests, that blow should have broken all my ribs, snapped my neck and caved my skull in.' He hopped down onto the passenger's seat and dusted himself down. 'As you can see, you've barely rumpled my shirt.'

Chris shrugged. 'Shall we start again? I'm Chris De'Ath, but then you already know that. Pleased to meet you anyway.'

The faerie held up his tiny hand, as if for a high-five. 'And I go by the name of Sem. Have done for a few years now.'

'And what are you, Sem? You said earlier "Call us something else" so what should I call you?'

'Sem would be good. And as to what I am, faerie will do, I suppose. Thousands of storytellers over hundred of years have to be acknowledged. It's just unfortunate that the word conjures up images of fluffy pink flitting beings dressed in flower petals.'

'Excuse me for mentioning it Sem, but a see-through shirt doesn't do much for your street cred. You're not exactly Conan the Barbarian.'

Sem flitted into the air and alighted on the top of the steering wheel. He sat there cross-legged. 'I could be if I wanted to.'

'You're a shape changer?'

'No. I'm a personality encapsulated in a physicality of my own choosing. I could have chosen to look like Arnold Schwarzenegger, a frog, a fly or ... or even a house brick.'

'And you chose to look like a faerie?'

'It's a very popular form,' Sem said defensively. 'And anyway, my choice was restricted on account of my lover. She chose a similar form before me, and somehow I couldn't see a frog getting it on with a faerie. Then of course, if you choose the wrong form you might get eaten, or swatted or –'

'Sorry about that,' Chris said, still feeling guilty at swatting Sem out of the air. The thought of a pair of faeries "getting it on" sort of slipped into his mind, and he wondered if they had all the usual bits and pieces. His eyes inadvertently slipped to Sem's crotch and he estimated a full-on size of just under a centimetre – if he was all to scale, that is.

'Think nothing of it. I'm virtually indestructible. Add *that* to your list of impossible facts. But please don't feel the need to test me on that one. I can survive most things, but not with any degree of comfort.'

'Did it hurt when I swatted you?'

'Well, it didn't tickle. But then, I was kind of begging for it, wasn't I?' He chuckled and his actions were somehow out of sync with the sound.

Chris wondered if the explanation for Sem's soft but deep tones was that his words were being implanted straight into his mind.

'When I was new to all this, I was creeping through a vegetable patch looking for Wenna – that's my other half; very keen on hide-and-seek – when the gardener crept up on me and thwacked me with a spade. I took me ages to extract myself from the mud and then ages more to fill in the faerie-shaped impression I left. It took Wenna even longer to get over her laughing fit.'

Chris feared it was going to happen again, just like with Tarn before. They would waste time talking drivel and nonsense and then Sem would disappear before any of the serious questions were answered. He politely told Sem that it was all very nice to chat, but could they first get down to business? What was going on? Why were Marc and Shaun taken and Danny killed? Where was Gayle? What did Tarn, and Sem himself for that matter, want with him? Before all this started happening he'd just been an ordinary guy, he explained, with ordinary concerns and ordinary hopes for the future. He had a sexy girlfriend who he was almost sure he loved, a best mate he'd take a bullet for and things were okay at school and good at home. He wanted to get good A' level grades, get into Writtle or Newton Rigg for a decent, practical degree and then find himself an interesting outdoor job and earn enough dosh to have fun. Now life was spoilt, mucked up, twisted all around: different. Now his expectations were fears and his hopes were for answers. He wanted answers from impossible people – Tarn, the other Fey Knights, this Sem – and he wanted one, just one real human person to believe in him.

'I don't have all the answers,' Sem said. 'But I'll tell you what I know. First; what am I? I am of the Selost Host. Selost: good old English word that, but strangely enough, coined by a Viking. It was a Norse settler called Elfric

Magnusson who lived in settlement that eventually became Axenwhit who first applied the term to us, and it just about sums us up, so we are happy to keep it. Selost means good, and wholesome; clever and skilful. We are, in short, the Good Folk, though some of us are better than others and one or two are downright unpleasant. But by and large, any personality from the Selost Host will do you no harm, and quite possibly a lot of good.

'On the flip side of the coin is the Unselost Mass. Personalities from the Unselost are very nasty bunch indeed, and Tarn tells me you met one of them.'

'Her!' Chris said, the memory alone bringing in a wave of nausea.

'A huge variety of forms draw their power from the mass, but nearly all of them need your blood – or ... erm ... other fluids – to complete their purpose. Demons, Vampires, Werewolves: the list goes on and on. But their purpose is universally identical. They mean to lure their victims along the Hidden Paths and to use them to achieve the ultimate goal of the Unselost Mass. Of that I'll speak later. Some they lure successfully, some they use as bait to lure others and then discard them, usually dead or insane. It won't be easy for you to accept, but it's highly probably that Danny died in that way. They needed his essence to form a copy of him, so they could lure the one they really wanted.'

'Gayle! They wanted Gayle. First they tried making a copy of me. Well, they succeeded, but they must have abandoned the idea because everyone knew I was in hospital. So they copied Danny instead, lured Gayle away and left Danny to die.'

'It seems probable. But he wouldn't have suffered.'

Emotions rose and spilled from Chris's eyes. 'That's bollocks! Believe me, he suffered. When I was her ... her victim, I knew *everything* that went on but couldn't move. I was in my own bed and that was bad enough. But can you imagine all that happening out in the woods? In the cold with crows and rats and things pecking and nibbling ...' Chris couldn't bare the images that coursed through his mind. He buried his face in the crook of his arm and forced the thoughts away. He clamped his jaws tight and pumped himself up with several deep breaths. Now was not the time to break down, and he would not give in to it.

'The succubae touch the mind with different degrees of darkness. There is every possibility that Danny was completely oblivious to his situation, once she had what she wanted.'

Chris convinced himself that was the case, and bid Sem to continue with a brief nod. He hoped for Danny's sake that the Unselost bitch had kept the form of a beautiful girl until she had what she wanted, and then left him unconscious and without pain.

'Tarn told me you lot wants us too. If the bad guys don't get us, you do.'

'We need help to overcome the Unselost Mass, but not just for our own sake. The fabric of the world is at stake.'

'And it's all going to leak out through a rip in the space-time continuum? I've seen all the Brannon Braga stories on Star Trek.'

'Me too!' Sem said. 'I *loved* those stories.'

Every time Chris thought he was getting a handle on this fantastic situation, it slipped from his grip. 'You, a faerie, watch Star Trek?'

'Next Gen, DS9 – Voyager used to be my favourite. Old Janeway could certainly kick arse. "Send them my compliments Mr Tuvok. If that doesn't work send them a photon torpedo." Ha!'

'Kick ... arse? Listen Sem. You're a bloody faerie. Aren't you supposed to speak ... different somehow? More archaic, like Tarn?'

Sem shrugged, his feathered wings stoking the air with a sigh. 'I wasn't always like this. I used to be pretty much the same as you; same kind of guy, but an orphan. Things happened, like they're happening to you. My story would take volumes, well at least three, and we haven't got time.

'Just think of the Selost Host as alpha and omega. We were there at the beginning, and there at the end – and all through the middle. Things happened; I got absorbed. The Selost Host is forever.

'The Unselost Mass on the other hand sort of invaded, and spread, like a creeping vine through an oak tree. It wasn't meant to be there, but it came and before anyone could do anything about it, it had a curling tendril round every branch, every twig and shot though all the roots.

'You see, the Mass represents the remnant of a once mighty evil that spread throughout time and space.' Sem frowned. 'Oo-er; that does sound a bit Star Trek, doesn't it? Anyway, the evil was defeated. Proud to say I played my own small part in that, prior to taking on this form. But in removing the great evil ... well, it was like pulling a tick out of a dog. The main body was destroyed – the intellect, personality and driving force – but little bits of it were pulled off here and there, and remained to fester.

'Over time, the remnants gravitated towards each other to coalesce and form the Unselost Mass. It's a power more than a being, a source more than a body, and it's a source from which the Unselost forms derive their strength. The Mass itself appears to possess only a basic sense of purpose, and that purpose is to feed. So, like a giant slug, it feeds rooted throughout time. It came to exist in parallel with the being from which it originated, and even that being feared it, not knowing it for what it was.

'Those who draw their power from the Mass are driven by the same basic need. They crave, they hunger; they lust. But they can never satisfy the painful need within them and perceive it can only be quenched when the Unselost Mass is able to feed on the Selost Host.'

'The old battle between good and evil,' Chris mused.

'Pretty much. I'm simplifying it a bit but then, what were you expecting? Shakespeare?'

'I'll settle for Brannon Braga any day.' *Here I am*, Chris thought, *bantering with a pixie who's also a Trekkie.* 'Where do I fit in? How is it that you can't deal with this ... this Mass thing, and I can?'

'There's a place where we can't go, and you can. We can lead you, but only you can get there.'

'Why me?'

'Not you, singular. You plural, as in people like you.'

'Humans?'

'Humans plus. There is no sense in me explaining the "plus" just yet. For now settle for this. You have the "plus" and we need you to help us vanquish the mass.'

'Now "vanquish" is the kind of word I'd expect from you. That's not you as in Sem, but you as in all the faeries.'

'Are you game for an adventure?'

'Here I am. Let's go!'

'Not as easy as that. We can only go from near the Tower, where you saw Marc and Shaun crossing. And you can't go until you're ready.'

Cue the disappearing act, Chris thought. 'When will I be ready?'

'You'll know when. When you know, come to the Tower and be prepared for a long, dangerous trip.'

'You mean, bring my sun-block?'

'Now you're just being silly.'

'Whereas, talking to a faerie is perfectly normal? Okay, when I know I'm ready I will bring everything I need to fight a giant slug. I'll just pop along to the library and check out *Demon Fighting for Dummies*.'

'It's a start. Before I go I have to tell you this. I have to come a long way to find you, and there are only two ways it's possible. First and best, you're near the Tower with the Unsullied Jewel. Last and worst – like today – I home in on hatred.'

'I don't hate anyone. Except that demon-bitch, and she's dead.'

'No. But there are people who hate you. And whether there be a valid reason or it's just for show, they like to ride round on great big motorbikes.'

'I've met a couple. Are they from the Mass?'

'No, but they seek to serve the Mass. And I found you today because you were being followed by one of them. Steer clear of them. My brothers and I will do what we can, but we are limited.'

Out to get him? He knew those bikers were bastards.

'The bikers call themselves "Wiergan" and they seek the power of the Mass without knowing much about what it is. But there is always a flip side. There are those who seek to serve the Selost Host – people who are equally ignorant of the truth but who may be of great help to you. I'd be surprised if you hadn't met one or two of them already.'

Chris began running lists of acquaintances through his mind, discarding every one as a possible servant of the Selost Host. His thoughts returned to the obvious question. 'I'm going to ask you a straight question, Sem. It's all very well telling me I'll know when I'm ready, but what is it I have to do now? Where do I go from here?'

Sem thought for a while. 'I can't answer you. Can't tell you a thing. See, when a journey crosses back and forth through time, you have to be very careful what you tell people because knowledge has to originate.'

'I don't follow.'

'An example then. Say Frank Whittle invented the jet engine.'

'He did!'

'And say someone from the future goes back in time and tells Frank Whittle all about jet engines and how they work, before Frank Whittle actually did the inventing. Where did that knowledge originate?'

'Okay, I see what you mean. If Whittle didn't know the theory before this guy from the future told him, how was the knowledge there for the guy in the future to know about, if Frank Whittle didn't … It's kind of complicated, isn't it?

'Bottom line is,' Sem said. 'You are best finding out certain things for yourself. The knowledge gained then has a firm origin and you are likely to have more confidence in it.'

Chris nodded as if he grasped the fundamentals with clarity. Sometimes he was such a good actor. 'And what can you tell me about the Unsullied Jewel? Can't you even give me a clue?'

'Absolutely not. In a manner of speaking, the jewel is the key. But if I even hinted what it was, your chances of finding it would be zilcho. And as for where you'll find it, I haven't got the tiniest little clue. You're on your own there, mate.'

Thanks for nothing, you twerpy pixie! 'Carry on as I have been then? I just keep on grubbing round for clues?'

'It's got you this far. Don't forget to keep dodging the bikers as well. They're real as steel and they'll hurt you if you get in their way, and you're bound to get in their way, if you haven't already.'

Just what Chris needed: a comforting thought.

And then it was all over. Sem said it was time for him to go and flitted though the open window reminding Chris that it was important for him to continue his quest, to find the secret of the Unsullied Jewel, and to come, fully prepared, to the old Tower. Chris sat at the wheel, more stunned now Sem had flown off then when he had actually been in conversation with him. Then, there was no doubt as to the reality of the encounter. Now, even moments after Sem had gone, it all seemed so distant, so long ago and so impossible.

Sitting astride a heavy black and silver motorcycle concealed from Chris by a dip in the road, Edmund Warwick flipped open his clamshell and tapped out a number with his gloved thumb. As soon as Chris had pulled into the lay-by Edmund had come to a stealthy halt and removed his helmet for a better view. He'd seen everything, his tiny pair of binoculars quite sufficient to show Sem up as anything but a bird.

The phone connected, gave the dialling tone and was answered almost immediately. Edmund didn't wait for a reply. 'The boy is in contact with "them", so now he's in play. We have to deal with him, and we have to do it soon.'

CHAPTER ELEVEN

The Son of a Preacher Man

Chris didn't know where it came from, but he knew he was acting on an impulse that materialised as he passed the village sign. "Little Rillton", it proclaimed in big bold enamelled letters. "Twinned with Sternhügel and Ville-de-le-Golas." The idea might just have well have swanned in from Germany or France for all Chris could fathom. All he knew was that Sem had told him to be prepared for a long and dangerous trip, and if there was anyone in Little Rillton who knew how to survive in the big outdoors – which Chris imagined amounted to much the same thing – it was Aby Knapper. He had the gear and he had the knowledge; shame he was about the one boy in the whole school, if not the whole town, he'd never had anything to do with.

Chris drove through town and into the section known as the Old Village. Flint House stood at the edge of the Old Village where the houses thinned out and a finger of parkland slid in from the forest. The vicar lived at Flint House; everyone knew that, and chances were the vicar's son would be in residence. Either that or he'd be blatting through the woods on his 250cc dirt bike. Chris felt he would be lucky.

The vicar's son was in his bedroom. Abe Knapper gave every outward appearance of sitting at his desk painting a 1 to 48 scale model of an RAF Jaguar fighter pilot, but in point of fact he was standing at a crossroads. It was a place many young men had stood and tarried for a little while before resuming the path nature had set, but Aby was close to taking root. This morning nature's path was all too clear but it didn't go in the direction he had intended and so he did all he could not to take that first step, despite the hefty push he'd been given last evening at work.

Aby set down the fine sable brush on the rim of the enamelled tin plate he used to mix the colours. He took a long sip of the tea Daisy had brought him and sat back from the desk top which he'd cleared for painting and model making by stacking the mouse and computer keyboard on top of the scanner, pushing the monitor back and covering the resulting space with several layers of newspaper. The rest of the SEPECAT Jaguar kit was in a box on top of the keyboard, and Aby now took this up and lifted the lid. He'd already painted the ejector seat while still on the sprue. It was dry now, so he twisted it off and set it next to the drying pilot. The inside of the cockpit was also done, and the spaces where the undercarriage folded away in flight, but while he looked at the various pieces of the model kit, his mind was back in the stockroom, with Cappy Shirakawa, last night.

The paint was drying on the tin plate and he had one more detail to add to the pilot to make him perfect. Replacing the box he took up the brush again, swirling it lightly in a chipped egg cup full of white spirit. Setting both elbows on the newspaper and bracing one hand against the other for maximum stability, he held the brush in one hand and the model pilot in the other. Holding his breath

Aby ran the sable hairs over the visor leaving a mixture of green, white and silver paint which made for a fair representation of tinted glass. Add a little gloss varnish later and the effect would be perfect.

Aby paused to admire his work as a glint of light slipped off the flying helmet, the size of a very small pea. It looked good, a mix of gloss and matt white to give just the right sheen. It reminded Aby of the tiles on the stockroom wall. And come to think of it, wasn't that flight-suit the exact same green as those carefully stacked and positioned beer crates? Aby held the model close and compared the flesh coloured mix to the back of his own hand. A little too highly toned perhaps, but the lips were just right. Just like Cappy's. Aby ran the tip of his tongue over his own; if he closed his eyes he could still feel Cappy's there. The contact had only lasted a moment before Aby pushed him away with force and explosive use of the eff-word, but Cappy knew just as surely as Aby: the pause between the approach and the rebuff, short as it was, came only after a millisecond of doubt. Cappy had smiled warmly ... and winked knowingly, as Aby's shell cracked.

Now, in his bedroom with the little pilot drying in his hand, Aby kept his eyes closed. Lights were going on, lining both sides of the path Aby feared to tread, and there at the crossroads, waving him on like a traffic cop was the image of someone who was never very far from his mind.

Aby opened his eyes again, took one last look at the model pilot, and then dropped it into the waste paper basket. He paused for a beat before consigning the rest of the kit, the paints, the brushes and the old tin plate to the same place. As he put one tentative foot on the path, it was as if a ton weight had been lifted from his shoulders. Picking up the mug of tea he crossed to his wardrobe and stood in front of the full length mirror. He moved close and studied his own face, a finger absentmindedly rising to an unsightly zit on his chin. He looked at his hair, dark and short around the back and sides, longer and lighter on top. 'What shows below your beret is ours,' the warrant officer used to say on parade. 'And what's hidden is yours and you can do what you like with it.' Aby ran a hand through the longer, blonder hair that never showed below his beret and wondered if the RAF were as lenient as the ATC in that respect. Somehow he doubted it.

Moving closer still to the mirror, thoughts of commitment to the Air Training Corps quasi-military rules and hair length faded as he looked deeply into his own brown eyes. He had a narrow face with well proportioned features and black eyebrows that contrasted with the much lighter hair. By and large, Aby was quite happy with what he saw, apart from the zit that looked like Krakatoa just before it erupted.

'Abraham Knapper,' he whispered to himself. 'You're gay!' He smiled. He began to chuckle and then as he started to laugh out loud with sheer relief and – yes – even delight at finally accepting himself fully for what he was, the front doorbell rang. The last shards of his old shell lay freshly shattered about his feet, but far from feeling vulnerable and newly exposed, he felt confident and strong, perhaps more so than ever before.

'I'll get it Daisy!' Aby shouted along the hall. As he descended the stairs three at a time he wondered who would be first to meet the new, reborn Abe Knapper.

Chris reached out to tug the ancient bell-pull once again but jumped back of the front door was flung open like a sprung trap. The young man who leapt into the doorway looked both surprised and delighted to see him.

'Chris! Hey!'

'Hi Aby. Okay?' Chris couldn't help catching Aby's grin which proved highly contagious.

'It's "Abe", but no biggie.' Abe shrugged but his smile stayed as wide. '"Aby" is okay for a twelve-year-old, but I decided it was time for me to graduate into "Abe". Come to see my Dad? He said you might ask me to set up a meet, but I figured you'd grab me at school.'

'I guess I should have a chat with your dad in the not too distant future. But it's you I've come to see. I need a favour.'

If anything, Abe's grin just got wider. 'You want to see me? Cool! I mean ... come in.'

Chris crossed the threshold of Flint House wondering if Abe was "on" anything. *What? The vicar's kid?* He quickly dismissed the idea. Showing the world a hard, bleak exterior the house lost all its austerity but nothing of its oldy-worldiness on the inside, with low beams and open fireplaces, antique furniture and bookshelves packed with ancient volumes. Upstairs was a different matter, for here neither austerity nor antiquity had any claim.

Abe bounded up the stairs and Chris followed at a more leisurely pace wondering what had got into the boy he remembered as quiet, in a self-possessed kind of way, dependable and – and well, a bit boring: never one of the in-crowd; not exactly a geek, or a swat, or an anything in particular; just dependable, part-of-the-school-furniture Aby. Now though, he was zipping round as if he had a rocket up his arse.

'My room,' Abe said holding the door and allowing Chris to go in first.

It smelled of white spirit and paint, but was neat and modern with a flat-screen computer, a portable CD player and a small TV. Chris was relieved to see that the neatness was marred by various items of clothing strewn about the floor and over the back of the computer chair: it made him feel quite at home. There were bookshelves, some fulfilling their intended role, one short shelf bearing a row of Blackadder DVDs – all four seasons - and others acting as display surfaces for models of jet fighters, all intricately painted, right down to the control panels visible within the cockpits.

Chris went over to one. 'Wow! This ones a ... Phantom?'

'Buccaneer.'

'You do these?'

'When I was a kid, yeah.'

'Bloody hell Aby ... I mean Abe. They're amazing. You still do them? Like, for a hobby?'

'Not any more,' Abe said balling up the newspaper from his desk and stuffing it into the bin. 'I guess my room's due for a rethink soon. It's time I threw out all the clutter.'

'These are all modern planes. Do you do any old stuff?'

'They may be jets, but they're not modern. These buggers were around when my ... your dad was a kid.'

Chris noted the catch and last second change in Abe's last sentence but Abe seemed to anticipate the next question.

'Sometimes I think Oliver and Wilbur were still at school making paper darts when my dad was a kid. The way he goes on about history, you'd think he experienced it half the time.'

The boys settled to a momentary silence that lurked on the borders of awkward before Abe asked if Chris wanted a drink. Chris declined.

Abe dropped heavily on the end of his bed as Chris took the computer chair offered. 'It's pretty amazing Chris, because I was thinking about you right before you rung the bell.'

Chris frowned quizzically. Was this going to start getting weird?

'You ever thought of joining the police? Because you sort of just popped into my head, dressed as a traffic cop.'

'Weird!' Chris said, and for the first time Abe's grin lost its shine causing Chris to backtrack. 'Not exactly "weird" but ...'

'Weird enough, I have to agree. This random thought shoots into my head, and then "ding-dong" you're standing at my door and it's not even as if we were ever mates or anything, but ... Well, weird.'

'At least I'm not dressed as a cop. How weird would that have been?' Chris picked up on Abe's earlier question, just to get off the subject of weirdness. 'I thought of joining the police once but Dad went ape, which is pretty rich seeing as though he did thirty years on the force. He says the job's f ...' Chris caught the obscenity in mid-air, figuring a vicar's son wouldn't appreciate it. 'He says the job's not what it used to be.'

'The job's fucked?' Abe said, his face all butter-wouldn't-melt.

Chris shook his head and appraised Abe with a lop-sided grin. This was a guy he could be friends with, and during all that time, going though nursery and infants and junior school, and right up to the present they had hardly ever exchanged words. 'Did you ever think of being a vicar?'

Abe just laughed and shook his head. 'So, what's this favour I can do you?'

Chris became serious, seemed to look into himself, appeared to be casting round for the right approach. The moments stretched into minutes and just as Chris appeared to be ready Daisy knocked and asked if they would like tea. This time Chris accepted the offer and Abe did too.

Until Abe's sister returned with the drinks, Chris asked about the various aircraft displayed around the room. He hadn't realised SAAB made jet fighters as well as saloon cars, he was amazed that the plug-ugly, antique looking jet was in fact a modern tank-buster and he thought the sleek, black SR-71 was something out of a sci-fi movie until Abe told him is was an out of date and long obsolete spy-plane.

But as soon as they resumed their seats, each cradling a hot mug of tea, Chris was back on track. 'Abe, have you still got that camp out in Wymes Forest?'

'You know about that?' Abe appeared quite shocked, as if a guilty secret had just been exposed to the daylight.

'There's not an inch of Wymes Forest me and Danny don't know about.' Empathic pain streaked across Abe's face as soon as the words were out, and Chris felt it like a hot knife through his guts. It looked like Abe wanted to say something, to ease the hurt Chris surmised, but he just sat there looking vulnerable.

'Well, you know what I mean,' Chris managed at last.

'Yeah. Sure. I ... I know what your saying.' Abe forced a smile 'My secret hideout, not such a secret after all. I suppose it was you two kept mussing my stuff up and hiding things?' Abe kept it light, kept it running like banter, without accusation or recrimination.

Chris chuckled and nodded. 'Your mess tins. We –'

'Filled them with mud. And you stuck my rucksack up a tree ... how did you climb that high? And made a smiley face with the stones from my fireplace.'

'It seemed funny at the time. We never meant any harm, mate.'

'Forget about it. At first I thought it was a pain in the arse, but after the smiley face I used to wonder what I'd be faced with next. I was even kind of disappointed when things stopped happening.'

'We grew up, me and Danny. We thought, you know, live and let live. We also got a kind of respect for you, Abe. We stayed in the woods once, together for a couple of nights, but to stay out there on your own. Neither of us would have had the guts. Too bloody spooky.'

'It's okay once you get used to all the different animal noises and when you learn not to camp under old trees. Pretty safe, so long as the Fey Knights aren't a-prowling.' Abe didn't notice Chris freeze at mention of the Fey Knights. 'But back to business. Just what is it you want me to do?'

'You're still in the ATC, aren't you?'

Abe seemed to think about it for a moment. 'Actually, no. Well yes, but I decided to leave.'

'When?'

'About five seconds before you called. Things have changed. Time to move on.'

'I thought you loved it? You're a sergeant, aren't you?'

'Cadet Flight Sergeant. But like I said, time to move on. See, just before you came round, something happened to me. Something amazing and ... well, life changing.'

'Whoa! And then I come along and spoil it all. Can you talk about it? Do you want to?' Mr Boring of Little Rillton had suddenly become an interesting guy with a story to tell. Chris grew more at ease and began to feel a little of that special something he'd always had with Danny.

Abe took a deep breath. 'I kind of do, but it's kind of scary too. Tell you what! You stop faffing around and tell me *exactly* why you came to see me and after, I'll tell you about my "road to Damascus" experience. Deal?'

'Deal!'

The boys shook on it.

'Go on then,' Abe said after a couple more silent moment.

'Okay. I need you to help me get some gear together. Emergency survival gear. And perhaps give me some tips on roughing it outdoors. In the woods or the wilderness, like.'

'That's easy enough. But why?'

'That's the hard bit. I'll tell you, but first you have to promise. You'll help me with the gear and advice, even if you think I'm a raving loony, yes?'

Abe held up his right hand and placed the left once over his heart. 'I Abraham Knapper of Flint House, Park End, Little Rillton, do solemnly swear to help my friend become a second Ray Mears, even if I think he is Mr Wibble McLoony from Loonyhampton-on-the-Wold, Nuttinghamshire.'

Chris chuckled again, feeling flattered at the unexpected description of himself as "friend" from this guy who he'd always seen as a little dull. Before today he'd been nothing more than "acquaintance" and it was clear there was a lot more to him than the sensible and somewhat diffident person he had previously seemed to be. 'You're off the wall Abe. Before I start though, I've got one final question. When you've camped out in the woods, have you ever seen anything odd?'

'What kind of odd?' Abe asked suspiciously.

Chris chewed his bottom lip as he tried to guess Abe's reaction to his story. 'Well, Fey Knights kind of odd.'

Abe came close to giggling, but he could see that Chris was deadly serious. 'Nothing even close to that kind of odd, Chris.'

'Shame. Nevermind. Here goes ...'

One again Chris's expectations crumbled and instead of spinning a yarn just sufficient to persuade Abe to lend out his gear and his experience, Chris told him everything: more than he'd told Kostja Claussen; more than he told Dad. He left nothing out, and went into the details of his most recent visitation, and by the time the story was all laid out, two empty, cold mugs sat on the floor by Abe's desk.

'That's the lot,' Chris said. 'Now you know more than I've told anyone else.'

Abe seemed pleased by that. 'Now you know Chris De'Ath is a head case, do I still get your help.'

Abe nodded. 'You get my help. And –'

'And?'

'And if it matters at all, I believe you.'

Chris waited for the next line. It didn't come, so he filled in the blank. 'You believe I'm telling you what I *think* I saw?'

Abe shook his head slowly, his face the emblem of sincerity personified. 'No. I just plain believe you. End of.'

It only took a moment for it to sink in, and once under his skin the importance of it exploded to every corner of his being. There was every chance that Chris was going to get emotional. But he figured 'exuberant' was easier to handle so he threw his arms round Abe and squeezed him in a bear hug. 'I love you man! I frakkin love you.' It felt right – for just a little while – and then it didn't. As Chris released his grip he felt Abe trembling. He fully disengaged and sat back. 'Well. You know what I mean, Abe.'

Abe loosened up. 'Unfortunately, I think I do.'

'It's just that –' Chris broke off to contemplate Abe's words, but he couldn't quite fathom the meaning, so he carried on. 'It's just that you're the first person to believe me, a whole hundred percent. The hug thing, I didn't mean to –'

'Forget it Chris. It's okay.' Abe's smile said *you'll never know just how okay*, but Chris was oblivious to the undertone. 'I'll get the gear,' Abe said as he slid open the wardrobe door.

Inside there was a section of metal baskets arranged on runners from floor level to ceiling. Chris noticed a basket for socks, two for shirts, another for underwear. The lowest two baskets were the deepest and they were loaded with clothing given a military look by the disruptive patterns of various shades of green and brown.

'You're about my size so these will fit,' Abe said pulling a pair of green combat trousers from the bottom draw. 'The jacket's a bit on the large size for me, so it will swamp you, but no probs, 'cause that just means you'll be able to get plenty of warm stuff underneath.' Abe paused and looked up. 'I suppose you *are* going to a cold place?'

Chris shrugged. 'I haven't thought about the climate. But I guess it can't hurt to be prepared.'

The jacket was a heavy duty, many pocketed affair in camouflage material that Abe called "DPM" with "KNAPPER" in black lettering on a dull green tape sewn above the left breast pocket. Over the right pocket was another tape embroidered "MCXIX ATC" over which Chris ran a finger.

'Is this your unit in the Air Training Corps?'

'Actually, no. I inherited the jacket from a guy who joined us from a squadron in Shrewsbury and I've never got round to taking the tape off. So it's second hand. Now it's third hand,' Abe said as he thrust the jacket into Chris's arms.

'I only want to borrow it Abe. It's not for keeps.'

'Whatever. I don't think I'll need it anymore.' Abe reached for a tab at the front and unbuttoned it removing a slide that bore three chevrons surmounted by a spread eagle. 'You won't need this though. Maybe I'll hang onto it for a memento.'

'Your sergeant's stripes? Yes, hang on to them. And what's this other badge up here on the shoulder. Crossed rifles?'

'My marksman's badge. It's sewn on so it might as well stay.'

'Cool! I'm a marksman. Where's my gun?'

'"This is a rifle, this is a gun. One is for killing, one is for fun".' Abe quoted. 'That's what old Reader says if anyone calls a rifle a gun. I'd better teach you one end of a rifle from the other if you're going to walk round with a marksman's badge.'

'Who's Reader?'

'He's our Flight Louie. He's been with Little Rillton Squadron since Pontius was a cabin boy. Could have been a Wing Co by now or even up at Group, but he's turned down promotion a couple of times. Used to be a fireman in the day job, but he's retired from that.'

A lightbulb went off in Chris's head. 'Has he been there since the 80's?'

'Probably longer.'

'So he might have known my cousin. Jamie McDowell.'

'Oh yeah! The kid who went missing. I've seen pictures of him in the squadron albums. There're a couple of pages dedicated to him, with press cuttings and stuff. So he was your cousin?' Abe rifled through the open basket-drawer looking for something before looking up again. 'Do you suppose the Fey Knights got him too?'

'Has to be a possibility,' Chris said without the slightest whiff of self-consciousness. 'It's one of the questions on my list, for the next time I run into Tarn.'

'You reckon that will happen?'

'I don't see why not. It's been three times now, and he seems to need me for something, so there's a good chance.'

Abe nodded slowly. 'You will take care, won't you?'

'Sure. I'm not about to put all my trust in a faerie!'

Abe looked a little affronted for a moment, but then shook it off and chuckled as if to some private joke. 'You know, this Tarn fellow and his brothers. They're not faeries at all.'

'No? What are they then,' Chris said as he pulled the combat jacket on and tried it for fit.

'They're something else entirely, Chris.' Abe paused for impact, held on until Chris was virtually screaming for an answer. 'They're angels, mate. Genuine state registered angels, complete with paid up membership to the Angels and Heavenly Creatures Union.'

Chris felt the muscles in his jaw tighten up and anger build up. *Now your just taking the piss* was a sentence constructed and on the launch pad, but he didn't let the words out. He studied Abe for a moment, and decided that he was being serious. 'And you would know this as a fact, for why?'

'It's their names. Not the short versions but the "Tarniel" and ... what's the other two?'

'Savaliel and Retsutsiel.'

'See, it's the last three letters. The "i-e-l" bit. Nearly all angels' names end in either "i-e-l" or "a-e-l".'

'Why?'

'God knows, but –' Abe cut himself off with a wry smile before continuing. 'But my Dad has dozens of books about angels. Most people know the main half-dozen or so; Gabriel, Michael, Raphael, Uriel and the rest, but his books have lists of zillions of them. We can look yours up if you like.'

Chris nodded then tried to fit this new information into the puzzle. It wouldn't go.

'First though, let's sort out the rest of your kit.'

Abe brought together a full panoply of clothing and equipment that he thought Chris might find useful, including a hefty knife he called a "Wilkie" and a little tobacco tin full of life-saving goodies. He prised off the lid and began to explain the contents, taking each item out despite Chris feared he would never be able to get them all back in such a tiny space. There were fish-hooks, some line, a combination tool the size of a credit card, needles, a flint and steel, and – what the??? – two condoms!

Chris picked one out and held it up like a piece of incriminating evidence. 'Super-strong condoms? For an emergency shag?'

Abe shook his head then rolled his eyes. 'Do you know you can fit over a gallon of water in a condom?'

'Can't say that I do? So long as it takes about ten cc's I'm happy.'

Abe tried not to hold on to the intimate image that flashed into his head. 'See, you make a little basket-weave container out of supple twigs – nothing too flash – and line it with something soft. Then you stick the first condom in and hang it somewhere in your camp. Then with the second condom you go to the river or lake or whatever and fill it up. Finally you bring it back and decant it into the water container you made earlier.'

'Have you tried this in practice?'

'Nope. But old Reader said it works.'

'Do you think it *would* work?'

Abe's face took on the look one of Alexander's Macedonians might have worn on hearing that, as they were in the area anyway, they might as well add India to the empire ... and *then* they could go home. 'It does sound a bit implausible.' He took the condom Chris was holding and picked the other one out of the tin. 'Anyway, I think I might have another use for them now.'

Chris grinned – more of a leer really. 'Who's the lucky girl? Hang on ... don't tell. Let me guess. It's Lillian from Lofty Gables, isn't it?' The real, non-demonic Lillian, Chris thought but didn't voice.

Abe looked like he'd been slapped. 'What made you say ...? Oh I know. I was in the woods with her when I bumped into the Stockdale brothers.' He immediately wished he hadn't mentioned Marc and Danny, one now kidnapped by the Fey Knights, one dead.

'You named that tune in one, Abe. Danny told me he'd run into the pair of you. He said you were a proper dark horse to get a girl like her.'

Abe could have bathed in the glory; probably would have done a day ago, but the Aby who would have soaked up the admiration for something that didn't happen was gone. 'Except that I didn't "get her" at all.'

Chris didn't pursue it, returning his attention to the survival tin, but Abe wanted to carry on. 'Oh she wanted us to, and I have to be honest, that's why we went into the woods. She got all kissy-cuddly. Even had a go at getting her hand down my jockeys. But it didn't happen. I ... er ... I –'

'Don't sweat it, mate. It happens to us all one time or another: nerves; maybe the wrong mood or wrong surroundings.' Chris tried to come over as the expert while hiding his own novice status. The thought passed his mind: maybe that's what all experts did.

'Wrong sex,' Abe said. When Chris's penny seemed to be teetering on the edge without dropping, Abe gave it a nudge. 'As in she was a girl, and I've come to realise I'm programmed for boys.'

The temperature seemed to drop a few degrees and Chris held his breath, which made coming up with just the right words next to impossible. *For frak sake, I told him I loved him.*

Chris continued to piddle about with the contents of the tin, trying to get them all back in. Abe turned his attention to a set of webbing belts and packs. As the boys busied themselves with jobs that didn't need doing, Chris tried to understand what he was feeling. Far from being repelled by Abe's announcement, he felt closer to him and privileged to be trusted with such intimate information.

'*That* was my road to Damascus moment. I've been dodging the issue for a long time. Then – well, something happened. It all kind of sorted itself out in my head, just before you called.'

Abe had only just accepted the fact that he was gay? Chris had never really thought about it, but close to eighteen seemed way late to come to terms with your sexuality. Of course, he was seeing things from a straight boy's perspective where acceptance wasn't an issue, and trying to empathise with Abe's situation he figured the best he could really do was be supportive.

'If it matters Abe, I don't have a problem with what you just told me. I mean, it's got to be girls every time for me, but ... but ...' Chris felt uncomfortable now – too heavy – so he cast round for the words to lighten the situation. 'Well anyway, you dark horse you. Who's the lucky boy?'

It worked. Both boys grinned and for Abe at least, the foundation stone of a firm friendship was laid.

'I'm not telling you his name – Abe isn't going to be the kind of boy to kiss and tell – but he works at the supermarket.'

'And you ... love the guy?'

Abe looked very serious for a moment, and then grinned. 'Let's just say he started something I'm going to finish. It's something I need to do. And then after that I'll think about the "L" word.'

Chris could relate to Abe's need. He had so wanted to be with Gayle in that way. He had to get past that milestone in his journey towards maturity, and then, he supposed, questions of love would be crystal clear to him. Why should it be any different for any other guy, however they were wired up?

'If it's okay to ask, what do you think your parents will say, when you come out to them?'

'I not going to. Come out to them, that is.' Abe said brightly. Chris felt all the more, well privileged came closer than anything else. But then he began to worry, why him?

'Don't you think you should? I mean, you just came out to me and –'

'No, I didn't.' Abe fixed Chris with confident eyes. 'I did not say "Hey Chris, I have something to tell you, yadder yadder blah blah I'm gay. You asked me a question loaded with assumptions, and all I did was put you right. That is exactly how I'm going to handle it with everyone else. It's nobody's business and why on Earth should they be interested in my sexuality anyway – unless they want to go out with me? So, they make a wrong assumption or ask a direct question, I'll put them right and answer truthfully. But I'm not going to start wearing make-up or do any public out-coming. Why should I?'

Chris found himself liking Abe more and more. 'You've got a point there. I never had to say "Mum, Dad. I've got something to tell you. I'm straight and there's this really cool girl" so why should you have to do the gay version?' *Walk the walk and bollocks to the talk!* he thought, but kept it to himself, never entirely able to forget that Abe was the vicar's son. Walk the walk and bollocks to the talk: a little axiom that Chris decided he would bear in mind himself. It couldn't do anything but help while he followed his quest to get to the truth about the Fey Knights. If he had any doubt at all about following his own perception of reality, Abe's quiet self confidence in blasted it away.

Abe helped Chris stow all the gear on the back seat of the Black Princess and refused to take the money Chris offered. They were just on their way back to the house when the Reverend Charles Knapper swept in off the main road, his black cloak blowing in the breeze like the garment of a Marvel Comic super-villain.

'Hi, Dad.'

'Hello Spike,' the vicar said leading Chris to guess that Abe had a family nickname. 'And nice to see you to Chris.' If the opening address put Chris at ease, the second line, edged with ice, hit him when he was least expecting it. 'I'd hoped to see you sooner. Much sooner.'

'A lot's been happening.' If the old man was after an apology he could go wanting. 'Abe was just about to show me something in one of your books. Something about angels.'

Charles Knapper raised his bushy white eyebrows. 'How extraordinary!' The ice was gone. 'I have something of exactly the same nature to discuss with you.'

Chris followed Abe and his father into the study. There was a neat little writing desk, too small to take a computer, which was not a problem as the Reverend Knapper seemed to make do with a laptop, and three walls solid floor to ceiling with bookshelves. Charles pulled open one of the desk drawers while

Abe made a beeline for a shelf over which there was a painting of an Egyptian ibis-headed god. Abe caught Chris gazing.

'It's Thoth, the god of libraries ... and a bunch of other stuff.'

Chris wondered what the other stuff was.

'And this is a book of angels,' he said flicking through the pages. 'And bingo! Here's Tarniel.'

Chris read the entry, gobbling down the sparse information like a starved dog. *A Wednesday angel resident in the 3rd Heaven. One of the spirits of the planet Mercury. Guardian of the East Wind gate.*

'I wouldn't take too much notice of the text. Utter gibberish for the most part,' the older Knapper said. 'Why the interest in angels, Chris?'

Chris was reluctant to go through the whole story again. 'They kind of cropped up in my research. I mentioned it to Abe and he was just telling me about the endings of angels' names being all the same.'

'Not quite accurate,' Charles Knapper said sitting at his desk and motioning for Chris to join him on a second chair. Abe retreated into the shade of the bookshelf. 'Remember this?' Charles said holding out a scrap of paper.

Chris took it and immediately recognised it as the photocopy Mike Ryan, the curator of The Sheldrake Memorial Museum, had taken of his drawing of the three cartoon birds.

'So *you're* the expert Mr Ryan mentioned.'

'Very nice of him to say so but not quite the label I'd give myself. I have my interests though and in those areas I'm well versed.'

'And these little birds are ... what exactly?'

'Angels.'

Chris looked at the comical birds and pulled such a quizzical face that the Reverend Knapper came close to laughing.

'Or should I say, not a representation of the angels as they might appear, but a symbol which stands for them. You see, what we have here is a copy of an ancient amulet which was used in ancient times to protect people from a very specific type of demon. The birds, and the writing – which is Aramaic by the way – stand for the three angels Senoi, Sansenoi and Semangeloph who were guardians against a fallen angel who became a succubus.'

'A succubus?' Chris said his face just a screwed up and no less comical that a moment ago. 'That sounds dead disgusting.'

'And so she is – or was – or may have been. You see, it was the wont of succubae to attack men while they slept and to ... well I supposed we'd call it sexual abuse these days. The stories say they would sometimes assume the appearance of a man's wife or lover and fool him into union or other times simply incapacitate their victims and subject them to their unnatural lusts.'

Chris's guts turned to water and he felt suddenly and powerfully nauseous. He was glad that demon, that succubus was dead and he found himself hoping that her death had been particularly painful and at least half as humiliating as her attack on him had been.

'Tell him Chris,' Abe said from the shadows. 'I'm sure Dad can help. You have to tell him.'

And so, for the second time in the space of a few hours, Chris told the story of his many ordeals since the day – long, long ago it seemed – when he had gone into the woods with Gayle Merryl and the world turned on its head. He was glad he made the effort, for there were now two people who believed him.

Acceptance felt good, but at the same time opened up a whole new store of questions. 'You've known about the Fey Knights for a long time, haven't you?' Chris asked.

Charles Knapper slid a leather-bound book from a high shelf in bookcase and let it fall open in his hands. 'I've known *of* them, as an actual phenomenon rather than a little piece of local folklore, for about five years, but I have to say in all honesty, you know more *about* them than I do. Perhaps you know more than anybody else, excepting those who've been taken, of course.'

Abe kept quietly in the background, transfixed by his father's revelations. He *knew* of the Fey Knights – as a *phenomenon*, not a myth? When he was little Dad would often look out the window and cry 'Look! A baby dragon!' Aby would race to the window and Dad would tell him, too late, it was above the clouds. 'Shame. It was a ridged blue, quite rare nowadays.' It had all been accepted as one of Dad's ongoing funny ways to amuse the kids. But now Abe wasn't so sure. For God's sake, had he actually seen dragons? Fey Knights and faeries were, after all, in the same league.

Chris De'Ath continued. 'Did you see them five years ago? Is that why you believe me?'

Charles Knapper snapped the book shut and replaced it. 'Never seen hide nor hair of them. But five years ago ... something happened which I am not entirely qualified to comment upon. Let's just say it lead me to focus on old legends and look at them in a new light.'

Charles revealed that since that vague and unspecified event of five years ago, he too had researched the Fey Knights and had come to a few nebulous conclusions. 'All the single victims of the Fey Knights had lived in Wymes Vale their entire lives. Where two were taken together at least one of the pair was a lifetime local.'

'Like me!' Chris said. 'They after me just because I'm local?'

'You'll probably find both your parents were too, and your grandparents. The deeper the roots the more likely you are to attract attention from the Fey Knights, and the other less wholesome creatures. Only a theory, though; nothing in tablets of stone, but it fits every victim I've been able to research.'

Chris mulled it all over. 'So what do I do about it?'

Darkness shadowed Charles Knapper's usually bright countenance. 'I don't know. But there are people who may have a better idea.'

'People?' Chris wanted to know what people, suspecting they may be the same ones Sem mentioned.

'Allow me to set up a meeting.'

Chris agreed. Charles would contact him in a day or so with the venue. Meanwhile he suggested Chris curtail his research and wait.

Chris had other ideas. The tide had turned and with Abe's example, he too was coming out: out of hiding and ready to be the hunter, no longer the quarry. He felt a glow inside that at last he had met people who believed in him, and there was a scent in the air that excited the hunter in him still further. He was on the trail of something fantastic, frightening and outside the borders of the accepted world.

Chris thanked Charles for his help and especially for his support in believing the unbelievable. The elderly vicar escorted him as far as the front door and Abe went with him to the car. He said goodnight to Abe and climbed aboard, and if he needed a little more proof that he was not insane, he got it. Evening light hit the side window at an angle and showed up a perfect dust impression of Sem, where he'd hit the glass – a perfect, faerie-shaped pattern, smudged down the route the little being had slid.

'Abe. Come take a look at this. Proof!'

Abe leaned and peered in through from the driver's side. 'Interesting,' Abe said straightening up. 'But like I said, I already believed you.'

Chris wondered, for the briefest of moments, if the spirit of his best friend had somehow entered Abe. Once in a lifetime you could be blessed with such a friend. Surely twice was too much to ask.

Abe swung his legs out of bed. He could not get to sleep, no matter how many sheep he counted. The euphoria of self acceptance had worn off, and while he was still feeling pretty good about himself, he was beginning to notice problems gathering, peeping over the walls of his newfound confidence. Maybe he needed to tell his parents after all. He would hate them to find out from a third party, and even though he trusted Chris, who represented the sole holder of the title "third party" at the present time, he reasoned that the ranks would soon swell.

Then there was Chris's fantastic story of myths come alive and danger. Abe knew he would have to find a way of helping his new friend but did not know how. Perhaps he could help with the research; help find out what the Unsullied Jewel was. He had to do something. If nothing else it would be a way to be near Chris.

Stepping into his carpet slippers, he shuffled across the bedroom wiggling his feet to get them on properly. He cracked the door and put his head out. The lights were still on downstairs, and he could hear his father's voice. He decided to start with Father, and braced himself: now or never. He'd start by talking about Chris and his quest, and then slide into his first coming out speech: *Dad, I've got something to tell you.*

It wasn't until he got to the foot of the stairs that he realised Father was on the telephone, and he really had no intention of eavesdropping, but Charles Knapper had a voice that carried. Abe didn't like what he heard; he was frightened by it.

'He's had an encounter with the Fey Knights …' Charles said into the receiver. 'No, no, no!' he continued, countering a suggestion Abe could only guess at. 'We cannot prevaricate. We have a situation…'

Abe felt the chill of fear creep over him. He was seeing his father in a completely new light. First he knew about the Fey Knights, and now he seemed to be setting Chris up.

'Agreed. The sooner we deal with him the better.'

CHAPTER TWELVE

The Story of Karl and Beverly
or
Sweet Rosemary, German's Bane

Chris stayed up late at the computer writing up the many events of the day. He recorded his meeting with Sem in great detail, using the exact words of their conversation as much as his memory would allow, and recording the minutiae of the tiny man's appearance, dress, accent and turns of phrase. He was just wrapping up a paragraph about his newfound ally, Abe Knapper, when his computer peeped and a little envelope in the bottom right of the monitor screen indicated he had mail.

If Chris's excitement mounted when he noticed the e-mail was from Kostja Claussen, it went into overdrive as he read the contents. The message itself was short: *There are some things I didn't tell you. I'm sorry. Read the attachments. Call me when you can. We must talk.* The attachments were a revelation.

The first was a scanned-in copy of a family tree showing Kostja's relationship to a German prisoner of war called Karl Hochwald: he was Kostja's great uncle and he had apparently died in the war in very unusual and horrific circumstances. The details were the subject of the second attachment. Accused of a crime Kostja's grandfather – Karl's younger brother – knew he could not have committed, he escaped a mob bent on lynching him into Wymes Forest where at least some of the enraged locals hunted him down, tied him to a tree and beheaded him. Being war time, the murder attracted only a cursory investigation. There were no suspects but the older Rilltonians were full of half-whimsical talk about how the Fey Knights must have done the killing. A young land army girl vanished at the same time; theories and rumours were numerous, but nearly all involved at least cursory mention of the Fey Knights.

Karl's disappearance was followed by a series of bizarre "accidents", invariably fatal, which befell some of Little Rillton's better known citizens. Old PC Sheldrake, Ruben Tregonhawke, George Fennymore and his wife were all dead within six months of the incident and some wondered if the Germans were responsible, coming out from Donnington to commit despicable horrors in revenge for Karl's death and then scooting home again, or maybe hiding out in the woods. None of the prisoners were listed absent but the local constabulary assisted by a detachment of the Home Guard searched the forest anyway. Needless to say, no AWOL Germans were found, and in the end the deaths were listed as accidental.

The last attachment was a scanned page from a wartime edition of the Rillton Gazette. Chris read it and looked at the little girl in the picture. Her eyes: her eyes burned into his mind and kept him from sleep until the early hours, and her name seemed so familiar. Her name was given most often as "Miss Fennymore" in the article but her story was under the headline "Orphan Rosie to Lady Rosemary." It was the "Lady Rosemary" phrase that circulated in and out of his thoughts all night, like an annoying draft.

Rosemary Fennimore dressed quickly and as quietly as she possibly could: It was just before six in the morning and because of the blackout it had been a fairly difficult feat, but now she was ready. She crept down the stairs being careful not to tread on the squeaky step second from bottom and to avoid the snagging frond of the aspidistra planted in an ancient goes-under bearing a print of Prince Eddy and Princess Maud. As she crossed the hall she caught a whiff of her father's pipe tobacco

She tip-toed ever so slowly and peeped into the kitchen. Father stood at the open back door, smoke from his pipe curling languidly in the still air.

'Hello Rosie, my lovely,' he said without turning. Was his hearing really that acute, or – as Rosemary suspected – did her father possess a special secret sense rubbed off from the Fey Knights after living so long with them practically on the doorstep? Before she could reply the early morning silence was broken by a deep throaty rumbling which rose to a roar before dying down through a distant purr and then to the kind of prickly silence that knows it had been rudely disturbed.

George Fennimore leaned out and looked up at the sky. 'Thought so,' he said. 'Couple of Beaufighters. They'll be Sixty-Eight Squadron on their way back to High Ercall.'

'Loose lips cost ships,' Rosemary said quoting a poster she saw stuck in PC Shadrack's front window.

George turned smiling. 'You a German spy then? You going to get us all bombed in our beds?'

'There's been bombs,' Rosemary snapped. Still annoyed at having been caught before she could make a clean getaway, she was in no mood for levity.

'Quite right! I do hear tell that they went and bombed Farmer Bowen's prize bull last week. All of Shrewsbury they could have bombed, but no – they knew about King Billy and they came out to Little Rillton and blew him up instead. So thank the German's for last Saturday's roast beef dinner.'

'I won't thank Germans for anything. And anyway, it was tough and stringy.' She fumed silently for a moment. I hope them Beaufighters drop bombs on Donnington Camp!' Knowing full well that her father hated this kind of talk, she stood defiantly, brow furrowed and face flushed red with anger.

'Well, they will do no such thing, because it would be nothing but murder, the same as if Germans bombed a place where our boys were being held. Can't you see that yet, after all our talks?' He took another puff at his pipe. 'And Mum says stop stealing her dolly-pegs. She's another two short. If you're going to dress them up as Germans and roast them over the fire, she'll not be at all impressed. If you'd done that kind of thing three hundred years ago you'd of been burnt at the stake just like Molly Blackbridge.'

Was her father like all the rest? Was he stupid; blind; a rotten traitor; worried more about witches and dolly-pegs than of Germans? 'We should kill all the Germans we can. We haven't got enough food for ourselves. We shouldn't waste any on them.'

George was losing his patience. He tried, he always tried but she was so stubborn, so hard-nosed and implacable when it came to the Germans. 'You could kill every last German in the world and it still wouldn't bring Paul back.'

She was on him with all the speed and venom of a cobra strike. 'Don't you talk about Paul. You don't care! I've seen you speak to them Germans. Why does everyone treat them so nice?'

'Rosemary,' her father began, but it was too late. She pushed past him and ran off towards the fields. He made ready to call after her but another pair of Beaufighters passed over and by the time the noise of their engines had subsided Rosemary was out of sight. George looked out over the fields, the woodland of Wymes Park dark and brooding beyond, and drew deeply on his pipe. 'Of course I care about Paul, you silly girl.'

'What was that, Mr Fennimore?' George nearly bit through the stem of his pipe. It was Mad Christy sitting to the side of the back steps; his unexpected presence and sudden question made George choke on his pipe smoke.

'Jeez, Christy! What the blazes are you doing, half frightening a man to death?'

The vagrant smiled apologetically. 'Sorry. Just came by see if you've got any jobs I can do. For a meal, I mean, not money. Catch rabbits? Lift your potato sacks?' Bearded and scruffy and dressed in tattered clothes, Christy was not an old man, nor even middle aged. In fact his manner was often quite childlike but he had been a feature of village life for some years now. Some said he was up here avoiding conscription and his simple-mindedness merely an act. Some said he was the bastard son of his lordship – there had always been bastard sons, all the way back through the generations. Some of those old families, such as the Tregonhawkes, had even been overheard describing Christy as a Fey Knights reject – the one they threw back instead of took, but most just allowed him to fill the niche of village idiot, and with such an absence of fit strong young men about these days, he could come in handy when there was heavy lifting to be done. Draft dodger, itinerant Fitz-Wymes or village idiot, nobody knew where he came from or what became of the half-naked Indians he was with when he first arrived.

George looked round the yard chewing on his pipe. 'No work as I can see Christy. Not today. You'd best be off back to his lordship's. If there's no work for you on the estate there's little chance of finding any round the village.

Christy got to his feet, brushing dry mud off the seat of his trousers. 'All right then. But it's not nice there now, with all them dead people walking about.'

A typical Christy comment, and hence the prefix "Mad."

'They're not dead people Christy. They're wounded. Hurt in the war. Now, get away with you.'

George watched as Mad Christy ambled down the path. How old was he? George tried to see beneath the raggedy surface. Not a lot more than twenty-five, he guessed, if that. Tall and slim, hair fair under his scarecrow hat: tall, like Paul; fair, like Paul. The back of George's eyes began to prick as he remembered his lost son. 'Of course I care about him, you silly girl.'

Christy stopped, not suddenly but rather as if he had run out of steam. 'She stole my snare wire, your Rosie did.' Having unburdened himself Christy carried on down the path. What was the boy talking about? George couldn't be bothered with either Christy or snare wire. He had other things on his mind.

Paul had been five years older than Rosemary. He thought himself lucky to snag a job as a Saturday stable boy looking after his lordship's cavalry mounts and dreamed of life as a trooper in the days of heavily braided patrol jackets and sabres. There had always been a Fennimore or two in the Rillton Dragoons, but the old regiment was absorbed, like yeomanries up and down the country, into foot regiments to keep up the supply of men to the trenches. When the time came and the drums of war called, Paul joined the Shropshire Light Infantry. If he was to fight, he once said, it felt kind of cosy to be with the same lot Dad had been with in the Great War, and his grandfather before that when it had been called simply "The Fifty-Third."

Paul trained at Donnington before it became a POW camp and all too soon he was off on active service. Naturally the Fennimores worried about him, but not for long. He had only been gone a few short weeks when the dreaded telegram arrived. All their worries were gathered together and traded for an infinitely more painful emotion. He was only nineteen.

George and Merfanwy Fennimore travelled through dark valleys of grief in the fresh footsteps of thousands of others and in that there were so many others their pain was tempered, if only a little. They grieved hard, but they were not alone. Rosemary on the other hand was isolated in her sorrow and she found no comfort in others. She grieved silently, broodingly and alone and saw every ray of light as a transgressor into the world, which for the loss of her brother should remain forever dark. Rosemary was a changed girl. Sullen, moody, angry and nestling an egg of hatred that would prove to be a dragon's egg for the measure of its destructiveness.

The Germans became more than an enemy to her. They were a filthy, monstrous breed worthy only of death. Imagine then, her reaction when she found out that the new arrivals in the villages and farms – the ones who wore a red stripe down the legs of their grey trousers and the sleeves of their jackets – were German prisoners of war. The yellow-stripers, Italians, hadn't bothered her. If fact one of them she thought quite handsome. But now they were gone: on our side now or repatriated or something else she couldn't quite remember or even particularly care about. But the Germans! She would watch them, follow their comings and goings, memorise their routines. In short, they became an obsession to her, even more so than her friends the Fey Knights.

As time went on the number of guards was reduced and then done away with all together, so that the Germans made their own way from Donnington Camp to the fields where they worked and back again. As initial suspicion subsided, some villagers would even *talk* to them. Rosemary was outraged. On one occasion she saw two Germans go into the *Moiled Bull*. She knew it was against the rules for them to go into a pub so she waited outside. Any minute now, she believed, Rubin would throw them both out. She waited and waited. Fifteen minutes at least. Eventually she stood on a flowerpot to look in the big bay window, just in time to see a smiling Rubin Tregonhawke hand the younger German – Karl was his name – a pint of beer.

She ran all through the village until she found PC Shadrack talking to Ernest Sheldrake outside the apothecary. She barely noticed how smart Mr Sheldrake looked in his khaki guard's uniform with three huge stars on each shoulder and she pushed in front of him to make her report to the policeman. It all came tumbling out, the whole outrageous story almost without the time to draw a breath.

'Thank you Miss Fennimore. I'll see to it this instant.'

Rosemary did not like the way the policeman turned his round face toward Captain Sheldrake and gave him a fat wink, nor the way Sheldrake tapped the side of his nose. PC Sheldrake swung one tree trunk of a leg over the crossbar and cycled off in the direction of the *Moiled Bull*. But Rosemary, fleet-footed Rosemary with her intimate knowledge of all the back alleys and short cuts beat him to it. She would have paid all her pocket money to see PC Sheldrake arrest the Germans. She wondered if they would be shot. She hoped so, and how much more would she have paid to witness the execution.

Hiding behind the oak in the middle of the village green the Germans came out of the *Moiled Bull*, right in front of PC Shadrack. Peeping round she saw their nervous faces.

'Afternoon boys,' the policeman said. They replied in their accented English.

'Now then, I hope you haven't been drinking in that pub. Because if you were, I'd have to get all official. You know I won't have you in there with those red stripes all showing.'

'Sorry, Mr Shadrack,' Karl said.

'Just a warning this time. Mind you cover up before you go in again. Overalls, or an old jacket; old Jessie Mable's smock for all I care. If you go in the pub again you can't be looking like pee-oh double-yous. Got it?'

The Germans nodded and smiled sheepishly.

'Back to work with you then.'

The Germans skittered off towards Dick Bowen's farm.

Rosemary was white with rage. They were all in this together, the whole lot of them. Mum, Dad, the Tregonhawkes, even the police. Well then, it was settled. She had been mulling it over for some time but now her mind was made up. If nobody else would do it, Rosemary Fennimore would have to. She would kill Germans, and traitors. She owed it to Paul. And if she could not kill them all, she would at least start with one of those two. She watched as the hated figures receded into the afternoon sunlight.

Karl Hochwalt woke up chilly. All night long, off and on, he had fought a battle with Farmer Bowen; Dick Bowen in his tractor and Karl commanding a Tiger panzer. Should have been no contest, but the panzer would only fire clods of horse dollop while Bowen's tractor rained down hundreds of marble-sized mortar bombs and squirted a corrosive fluid that ate through iron plate like hot water melting ice.

As he surfaced into full wakefulness the noise of battle continued. Two British fighters on their way back to base. Karl listened for, and heard, the disturbed breathing and low curses of his companions. Almost every morning the RAF pilots would fly low over Donnington Camp to herald the start of another day: another day of tilling British soil or digging British potatoes. Karl never felt inclined to grumble. He'd take a year of digging spuds rather than face another day of battle.

Some of the other prisoners spoke of escape and of getting back to the Fatherland to rejoin the fight, but Karl secretly hoped that for him the war was over. He'd been at Donnington for several months and except for certain rules, life was almost normal.

A loud snore issued from the cot next to Karl's. One ham-fist dangled below the blanket and knuckled the concrete floor. Martin Kaulitz had appointed himself as a kind of adoptive father to Karl, a kindness that had instantly put an end to the unwanted pestering Karl had been receiving from a venomous clique of fellow prisoners. Damned SS bully-boys, Martin called them. His contempt for them would probably have got him shot back home or at the front. When Karl thanked him he said it was the least he could do for a fellow Bavarian.

The door flew open. Who would it be? Grumpy Murphy or cheerful, avuncular Bullstrode. It was Bullstode with his usual "hands off cocks, on socks" wake-up call. The Germans groaned out of their slumbers and threw things at him: bundled up blankets, rolled socks, a Wellington boot. Corporal Bullstrode laughed and went round the dorm tipping unlucky victims onto the cold floor. Except for those unceremoniously introduced to the concrete, the Germans laughed as well. It was usually a good day when Bullstode was early watch-master.

Rosemary checked the village clock. It was half-past six. Good, she thought, I'm not too late. She wasn't the first to rush to Little Rillton and check the clock with a similar feeling of relief and pleasure. Rosemary noticed with annoyance a land army girl sitting on the steps of the memorial to the Great War. Those steps were Rosemary's. That is where she liked to sit.

Rosemary became curious. She'd seen the girl before and knew that she'd been assigned to work at Dick Bowen's farm, as were those two Germans. Rosemary had come here to wait for her victim. She would either kill him herself – though at present she didn't know how - or to lead him to "them" and let "them" do the job for her. Surely the land army girl wasn't waiting for the Germans too, but then, who else came by this time of the morning?

The land-army girl noticed Rosemary and smiled. Rosemary pretended not to see but walked on by. After a few moments of determined striding she looked over her shoulder and seeing that the land army girl was no longer watching, she ducked into the alley between the greengrocers and the hardware store. Peeping out from behind a dustbin she looked first one way then the other. At last! Here they came; the expected pair; the enemy.

'Did you see her, Karl? The little girl?' Martin Kaulitz said in his native tongue.

'I see her of course. Sitting below Herr Harold Wymes.'

'No fool! Not the girl under the statue. Not Beverly, but the one who just ducked behind the dustbin.'

Karl laughed. 'Ah! Little Miss Mystery, always watching and following but never speaking or smiling.'

'Strange child. Perhaps she has heard that we are all child-eaters. Or SS.' Martin spat.

'This is probably so. She comes to watch us like we are dangerous animals, and for the same reason she keeps her distance.'

Beverly saw their approach and nodded discretely, her face freshened by the smile that she almost feared to show. Even this early in the morning there could be busy-bodies about.

'The girl keeps her distance alright. Not like your Beverly, eh?' Martin nudged Karl's arm.

Karl went red and shushed his friend. 'Someone will hear.'

'Which "someone" around here can understand our words? But seeing is a different matter.'

'Whatever do you mean, Martin?'

'You two. You and Beverly are all cow-eyes when you're speaking, and the rest of the world might just as well be invisible. When she is near you have no mind for your job. When you disappear for half an hour, so does she.'

Karl looked so sheepish Martin almost laughed. 'Is it that obvious?'

'Yes boy, it is.'

'Her supervisor ...?

'Is a dried up old toad who doesn't realise she's still alive. Why if you made love to the girl –'

'Martin!'

' ... right under her nose she would believe you were practicing field medicine.'

Karl wanted to rush up to Beverly and kiss her. After Martin's word though, it was all her could do to give up a half-hearted smile. 'You think we should stop ... we should no longer be friends?'

'I think you should go no further than cordiality. Just take care, boy. You must know the trouble such a friendship could bring us.

'Hello boys,' Beverly called. 'I've got good news.'

Karl and Martin returned her greeting in their broken English. 'What news?' Karl said. 'The war is over?'

'Not quite that good. It's just that Mr Bowen doesn't need you at the farm util ten this morning.'

'Ah! We could have slept in. Could he not have told us yesterday?'

'Yes, well ... sorry about that. I was supposed to tell you yesterday. I forgot.'

'So boy, what do we do now? Do we go on to the farm early or trek back to Donnington?

'Well, Beverly said. 'We could all go for a nice walk. It's bright and sunny and it's already getting warm.'

Karl's reluctant smile could wait no longer and it burst forth as bright as the sun. 'Martin, what do you think? Let's all go for a walk.'

Martin looked at Karl sideways and then through narrowed eyes in music hall style portrayal of suspicion. 'I am thinking what you really mean is good old Martin will walk in one place, while young Karl and little Beverly walk in another. Not so?' Martin's mock hauteur dissolved into conspiratorial mirth and in that instant Beverly thought him very like a beardless Father Christmas. 'Then why are you waiting children? I am going this way. Oh see how sweetly the birdies play. I suggest you look at the bluebells in the wood.' Martin waved and ambled off towards Donnington and started to sing, enthusiasm making up for a serious lack of technical ability. 'Der Vogelfänger bin ich ja ... stets lustig heisa hopsasa!'

Beverly grabbed Karl's arm and tugged him in the opposite direction. 'Quick! We mustn't be seen alone together. I'll go ahead, so give me a few minutes. Just outside the village, on the left, you'll see a style ... a little gate for climbing over. Hop over and follow the path.' Beverly hurried off. 'I'll meet you on the path. Just keep walking.'

Karl watched Beverly until she was out of sight, then for want of anything else to while away the minutes he walked round the war memorial. So similar to memorials at home he leaned forward to read the names and his eyes fell to one. Could this soldier, Private Percy Hawkins aged 22, have been killed by his father at Hohenzollern Redoubt? Maybe Percy had shot Uncle Gunter's brains out before he had caught himself a German bullet. It all seemed so pointless and so silly. Before Karl could read another name he caught a movement at the corner of his eye. The little girl.

On impulse he ran lightly to the building line, then tip-toed to the mouth of the alley. He sprang into the gap. 'Ha! Got you!'

Rosemary jumped back and clear of the dustbin overflowing with cabbage stalks and pieces of broken crate. 'Don't you come near me, or I'll scream.' Despite her words she was not frightened by any more than the initial shock of the young German's prank. In fact her racing mind quickly told her that this might be just the opportunity she was waiting for.

Karl on the other hand was quite frightened as he realised the consequences his foolishness might bring. A big mean German deliberately scaring an innocent little schoolgirl. What had he been thinking of? 'Do not be scared, Little Miss.' He smiled nervously. 'I don't mean you any harm.'

'Then why did you shout at me?'

'Just a little joking. For fun. To make you laugh.'

'Oh,' Rosemary said, her calculating mind racing ahead. 'That's alright then.' And then she did something that would have struck her parents dumb with incomprehension. She smiled at a German. 'What's your name?' she asked sweetly, a delightfully friendly expression fully masking the hatred that seethed inside.

They spoke for a while under the long shadow of Major-General Lord Harold Wymes as he stood in paternal protection over the names of his fallen boys. One of only a handful of senior officers who really cared for the men under their command, the statue had been raised after the old man's death in 1932 and was funded entirely by public donation. He was one of Rosemary's heroes and she felt his disapproving, stone eyes glaring down at her while she fraternised. *Don't worry Your Royal Viscount-ship* she wanted to say, totally ignorant of how to address a peer of the realm. *I'm going to kill him as soon as I get the chance.* If she could but know, Harold Wymes would have been first in line to deplore such an act. Despite her serious misgivings Rosemary managed to maintain a façade of friendly inquisitiveness asking about Karl's work and where he was at any given time of the day. Karl on the other hand was restless to be away.

Eventually, and with infinite tact, Karl managed to part from Rosemary and hurried along the lane. Rosemary was not about to let the opportunity slip. She called out a merry goodbye and skipped off in the other direction, but spun in mid-skip the instant she deemed him far enough away to follow.

Karl never once suspected, so keen was he to meet Beverly for their tryst in the woods. Along the lane, over the style, following the ill defined footpath and into the woods he went. Rosemary only came close to capture once when her quarry, just visible through the trees and undergrowth, became prey to another huntress. Beverly the land army girl sprang at him from behind an ancient oak.

'Beverly! You'll kill me with fright,' he said laughing.

Beverly: another name for Rosemary to write down in her secret book.

'Kiss me, Karl,' Beverly said.

Then to Rosemary's utter horror the German pig kissed the land army girl. Made careless through surprise she trod on a fallen branch and it cracked. She ducked down immediately but the couple immediately broke off their embrace and looked in her direction. She held her breath until she heard Karl say 'It's nothing but a bird or some small animal.'

Beverly smiled, reassured. 'Come on. This path goes to our beech.'

They set off again with Rosemary following at a safe distance. Deeper into the wood they hurried, then off the path skirting a clearing strewn with the moss-softened remains of a long abandoned cottage, and then into the wood again. They came at last to a huge beech tree and sat on its exposed roots with their backs against the massive trunk.

With much careful manoeuvring Rosemary got herself into a position from where she could spy on the couple while keeping out of sight. Her stomach was gripped by icy hands as she watched the couple canoodling. They held hands. They spoke soft words to each other. They laughed softly. At one stage they broke off to have a childish fight, throwing handfuls of dry leaves at each other and laughing like two-year-olds. They took much care a few minutes later taking the detritus of the forest floor from one another's hair and then they were back to their cuddling phase – only now the cuddling was more urgent and the hands went to ... certain places. Rosemary did not want to look, and yet she was transfixed. Karl's hand was at Beverly's breast, rolling and kneading. Beverly moved her hand hard between Karl's legs.

A strange and alien feeling passed over Rosemary and she began to wonder how Beverly felt right now and what she felt. Rosemary put her hand to her own breasts and squeezed, closing her eyes and imagining herself into Beverly's situation. The frightening but pleasing imaginings, combined with the hot sunshine acted together as a soporific, and proved to Rosemary that she was not the efficient spy she believed herself to be. She fell asleep on the job. Only briefly, but that was enough for when she woke her quarry had fled the field.

She was not particularly bothered. An important decision had been made: Rosemary was now certain she had chosen the right German to kill. Not the old one with the droopy grey moustache, although he had probably killed more English boys, but this Younger, this Karl who hypnotised English girls and made them do ... things. Yes, she thought, it would be more just to kill a German who was about the same age as ... She immediately extinguished the first glimmering thought of Paul. Paul was kind. Paul was good. Paul wouldn't approve. But for Paul, she would execute this Karl. Just for starters.

Now she had absolutely decided on whom, all that remained was to organise how. Rosemary already had a few ideas and they all involved either poison or the Fey Knights. She set off for Lord Wymes estate where she was most likely to encounter the herbs of her choice or the Fey Knights. She had never seen the latter in any other place, and she knew where the herbs grew aplenty.

Ducking in at home to pick up her basket containing the tools she required, including an acutely curved knife given to her a year before by a nice man on a motorbike, she cut across Bowen's Farm to the estate boundary and squeezed through a loose slat in a barbed-wire topped fence. Wymes Park was a huge tract of land covering a wide range of terrain types. There was one of the largest tracts of virgin forest left in the land, meadows, pasture, marsh and closer to the ancient house acres of mown lawn and formal gardens. Rosemary and one or two select school friends knew all the overgrown, out of the way sections almost intimately, but few ever found the ruined tower, and it was close to the tower where the Fey Knights frolicked and the herbs grew.

In one of the meadows, tummy to the ground to avoid detection, she rooted up twenty-odd dandelion tubers. Shaking off the soil she placed them in her basket then went in search of an oak. An easy quest, she had soon collected a dozen acorns. Saving the most important ingredient for last, she hurried to the lake and followed one of its distributaries to a boggy area, dank and overgrown, where she sought out a spot where the sun could reach.

She soon came across her objective and took the curved knife from her basket. Reaching up she sliced off three of the plant's branches complete with bobbing heads of fruit. Securing them furtively under the tea towel cover of the basket she cast round with wary eyes unreasonably worried that someone might be in this remote, rarely visited spot.

Someone was! Rosemary's gasp was almost a scream.

'What you doing with those old bits of plant?' Mad Christy said. 'I hope you know hemlock's deadly poison.'

For a moment Rosemary's reserve of cunning seemed depleted. She had no idea of what to say or do.

'And there's enough dead people walking round without you being another.'

That was it, thought Rosemary, instantly relieved. Christy was mad and renowned for speaking nonsense. It mattered not a fig what she said to him. Even if he repeated it nobody would believe him.

'I know perfectly well it's poisonous, stupid! That's why I want it. See, I'm going to kill someone.'

'Who? Not me I hope.'

'You're not important enough to kill Christy, You're nothing. But if you like you can drink some of my special coffee and I can see how long it takes to work.'

Christy slowly shook his head. 'I'm mad by profession, Rosie. Not by accident of birth. You keep your laced coffee for yourself.'

Rosemary gave the young vagrant a double take. For an instant she imagined that he shone, as if a fiery globe had been momentarily revealed by the lifting of old sacks. She peered at him, uncertain that she'd heard him correctly, but the dirty sacks were firmly back in place and he was just the same old silly Christy.

'Who you going to kill, Rosie?'

'A German.'

'I used to go to school with a German boy,' Christy said looking up into the sky as if searching him out. 'And I knew a Japanese too.'

You just could not have a sensible conversation with Mad Christy: all over the shop like a terrier that had just sat on some mustard. 'You never did go to school with a German. Unless you went to school in Germany.'

'No. round here. St Andrew's JMI in Little Rillton.'

'There're no Germans here except prisoners. You tell me you went to school with a German. When, and what's his name?'

'In about fifty years, and ... never mind his name. You'd probably kill his granny.'

'Fifty years ago? You're nuttier than a squirrel nest.'

Christy grinned and Rosemary brushed off his comments as more nonsense. 'So why are you going to kill a German?'

'Let me think now ... Oh yes: one, we're at war with them; two, they're filthy evil beasts; three, one of them killed my brother Paul and four you're such a useless lump I might do everybody a favour and practice on you first.' For an instant she really considered the possibility.

'Which one killed Paul?'

'How do I know? It doesn't matter. One of them killed Paul and I'm killing one of them.'

Christy thought for a while. 'I suppose that's fair. But you'll not kill nobody with hemlock. You could kill a cow, or a horse but not a human person.'

'But why? I've read all about how Socrates or some other Greek ate it and died and he was a human person.'

'Ah but he knew he was eating it. He knew if he didn't eat it the soldiers were going to pull his guts all out through his bottom. If you've got that kind of a choice you're going to eat the hemlock. But go on, take a sniff on it. Go on ... sniff.'

Rosemary withdrew a small piece of the plant, squashed it between finger and thumb and held it to her nose. 'Poowee! That's horrible! Like mouse droppings.'

'See what I mean,' Christy said with a grin. 'Anyone who's got a working nose isn't going to chew on that, now are they?'

Rosemary shook her head. 'But I was going to put it in dandelion and acorn coffee.'

'It'd still smell bad. Make anyone sick to put it near their mouth.'

Rosemary began to see her plan crumbling away, but Mad Christy shored it up almost as soon as it started to wobble. 'I know something that's stronger poison, and it don't hardly smell. You could put that it your German's coffee and if he don't take the antidote in just ten minutes, he's dead as a snagged rabbit.'

Mad Christy took his newfound apprentice to a meadow where the secret, deadly herb grew. It was similar in shape to hemlock but just as Christy had said, without the mousy odour; in fact, the smell was quite fresh and pleasant.

'What do you call it?' Rosemary asked as she bagged a couple of handfuls.

'Common name, or scientific?'

There he went again, thought Rosemary, letting a shaft of light out from under the sacking. 'Common name, Mister Smarty-Pants.'

'It's called "Sweet Rosemary" or "German's Bane".'

Rosemary raised an eyebrow before taking her leave without saying goodbye. 'You're mad, Christy De'Ath. Mad as a brush,' she shouted from the fringe of the meadow just before she disappeared into the wood.

Christy watched her go, smiling as the insult drifted to him across the distance. His stomach growled reminding him it was lunch time. Off to the Big House and with any luck he would avoid all the dead people and get a nice bit to eat and drink.

A week passed, and Rosemary was growing quite proficient at finding out anything she needed to know. It hadn't been difficult to learn that Farmer Bowen wouldn't require the POWs until mid-morning, and it wasn't hard to extrapolate the likely outcome. Her quarry had been released into the field, and she knew just how to track them down. She knew Karl and Beverly would make straight for the giant beech tree. And now was the time to tell her lie.

She put on the act of her life. There were tears; uncontrollable sobs; and the telling of her story with just the right amount of fear, reluctance and shame.

'Daddy, the German they call Karl, made me do something horrible.' Within half an hour of seeding the lie, an angry mob of villagers were heading for Bowen's Farm intent on dealing with a depraved child molester.

Going by another route she ran all the way; over some fields, down through the wood and over a brook. She quickly skirted the ruins and crossed to the copse. Finding the hollow clear, as she hoped, she secreted herself amongst thick undergrowth and waited.

She did not have to wait long. Now there he was, frightened and afraid. The villagers would tear him apart. Rosemary smiled, but she had another fate in store for him. Karl ran deeper into the wood, and Rosemary followed. Then she cut across the woods to reach the beech tree before Karl.

Rosemary waited while her racing heart steadied its pace and her breathing returned to normal. Any time now, she thought, but the waiting went on and on. She came close to leaving her hiding place when she heard the approach of soft footfalls and whispered conversation. Rosemary shrunk smaller into the bushes.

Karl and Beverly walked quietly into the hollow holding hands. When they came to their usual spot they faced each other, Beverly placing her hands round Karl's neck. She gently pulled him into a kiss which started soft and gentle and soon burst into flames of passion. They didn't talk this time, or have a leaf fight or sit down with their backs to the beech. They just held each other tightly and kissed. How could they do that when the villagers were after him and meant to do him in?

Their kissing became even more passionate. Beverly whispered something between kisses then pulled back a little. Then she undid Karl's collar button. Letting her fingers drop she undid the next button and the next until his shirt was open at the front. He let it fall to the ground then removed Beverly's blouse with something less than her dexterity. They stood for a moment, arms round each other until Beverly knelt and arranged the discarded garments into a make-shift groundsheet upon which she sat. Karl knelt before her and reaching round undid her bra while Beverly unhitched the fastenings of her uniform breeches.

Rosemary wanted to run away and at the same time she wanted to stay. As she watched Beverly undressing herself and the German, that curiously disturbing feeling came over her again. The couple embraced, Beverly naked and Karl in loosened trousers and underwear. Then without interrupting the fluidity of their lovemaking Beverly further loosened Karl's trousers and in a flowing movement, the mechanics of which Rosemary could only guess at, Beverly laid back holding Karl close by the magnetism of her breasts, and with her thumbs down the waist-band slipped trousers and shorts down to his knees.

Rosemary had caught Paul once, playing with himself in the bath, but she had never seen a grown man in this state of arousal before and for a moment, while Karl hovered over Beverly, Rosemary's universe centred on the solid emblem of his masculinity. Then he sank slowly and deeply into Beverly and Rosemary was shut out.

She stopped watching. She wanted to spoil everything for them, to stride up and denounce them both. Treason! Wicked! Disgusting animals! But she wasn't brave enough. All she could do was bury her face under her arms. An ant in the leafy mould tickled her chin, and she couldn't block out Beverly's soft gasps or the rhythmic rustling sounds. A sharply drawn breath from Karl and a more audible gasp from Beverly seemed to mark the pinnacle of the couple's union, and after some moments of silence, Rosemary ventured to lift her head.

The couple lay still, naked, Karl's head pillowed in the softness of Beverly's bosom. He seemed to be asleep with Beverly caressing his blond hair and fair shoulders. Rosemary watched with utmost care and as soon as it appeared that Beverly too had been soothed into satisfied sleep, she extracted herself from the shrubbery intending to creep over and do what she had come to do. She had her basket. She had her weapons. In the end she had rejected the idea of poisoned coffee, especially when her mother had told her Mad Christy's herb was nothing but parsley. She would drop a heavy rock on Beverly's head then do what she had to do to the German.

But then "they" came. Stopping half-way between her hiding place and her quarry, she froze while the three boys dressed in varying kinds of rags and their three faerie escorts materialised as if from a heat haze. All three smiled at her, and one waved. The faeries treated her to an impressively close fly-past and then dive-bombed the sleeping couple. Karl and Beverly woke, dreamily and befuddled. The Fey Knights did there work, smiling and beguiling and then ... they were all gone, Fey Knights, faeries, her quarry – the lot of them: all gone.

Rosemary was not entirely happy with the Fey Knights. They had taken Karl and the silly Land Army girl but that wasn't enough. She thought she would see death; bloody death and destruction. But when the boys took her enemy and the traitor they were smiling kindly, like guides rather than captors. Rosemary had wanted blood, and now there was only uncertainty. She hoped the Fey Knights would lead the couple on like a kindly shepherd leads the lamb for slaughter, and then deal them swift and sure death. That was her hope, but what if they were treated well in the secret land of the Fey?

As Rosemary retraced her steps and the old tower fell into the gloomy distance, she became more sullen with every step, until she noticed something tied to a tree a little way off the indistinct path. At first it looked like a man but then as she peered through the foliage it was more like an old sack. 'Probably a bag of kittens someone was too soft to drown.' She saw a chance to slake her bloodlust. 'I'll do more then drown them.' She lifted the tea towel and rummaged deep into the basket but then as she got closer she realised her first impression had been right.

'It's a man after all. Not much of a man, but a man nonetheless. Isn't that right Christy?'

He was slumped up against a medium sized beech lashed to the trunk under his armpits. His hands were tied behind the tree and it didn't take long to work out the rope-work had been done by someone with a certain flare for the work. It hadn't been a hurried job. The turns of rope were all neatly parallel with no twisting or overlapping and the knot was neat and unyielding. This man, this youth was a present from the Fey Knights and she felt at once elated, frightened and excited that she would not have to forego the required payment of blood.

'Why, Mad Mr Christy. You've had a shave for me, and got dressed up all neat. You're my pretty little Gift Boy from the land of the Fey.'

Christy was not unconscious, but nor was he entirely with it. His eyes were open, but they moved round slowly and without fixing upon either Rosemary anything else as far as she could tell.

'Have you been at the gin? You look all dopey. And what're these funny clothes you've got on? A nice blue vest with a rhinoceros on it; American blue trousers and plimsolls with funny patterns on; white socks like Americans wear on their days off: I reckon you've been burgling the American airbase. Is that what you been doing Christy?'

Christy didn't answer.

'Well it's not good enough. You can't just get a haircut and put on nice stuff and think you can get away with burglary. You must be punished, and that is just what's going to happen.'

Rosemary put her basket down and lifting the tablecloth she took out a camera. 'First off, I'm going to take your picture. See, a Kodak Six-20. Flat and neat like Mummy's make-up compact but ...' Rosemary flicked a catch and the lens extended on a small bellows. 'Abracadabra! Now it's a camera. But you'll have to hold still for a few moments because it's not so bright in here. I don't suppose there is the slightest chance you'll smile for me, is there?'

Christy did not smile. He merely looked confused as if Rosemary were speaking words from another language.

'I didn't think so. But then, if you've got the slightest idea what I'm going to do to you, no wonder you're not smiling.' She aimed the camera, moved forward until the image looked just right and clicked.

'Steady for a moment … Got you!' She began folding the camera but had second thoughts. 'I think I'll take another one of you when you're dead. That'll make a nice before-and-after set, now won't it?' Setting the camera down in the ankle of a gnarly root that sprang from the ground like a serpent, she reached into her basket once again. She took out two dolly-pegs joined together by a coil of fine wire. She knew exactly what to do. Standing behind the tree she held onto one peg and threw the other round the trunk catching it with her free hand. She let it slip down over Christy's head and pulled in gently until the wire was embedding lightly into the skin of his neck.

'Have you got it yet, Mad Christy? I'm going to cut your head off.' Rosemary laughed, like a schoolgirl who has just been told a naughty joke. The high, keening laughter was cut off instantly as she had a dose of second thoughts. It would be murder. 'But he's just a mad tramp who's a D-Day dodger. Nobody will miss him.' If she got caught she would go to gaol for ever and ever. She laughed. 'Nobody would ever suspect me. I won't go to gaol.' It would be too quick, cutting off his head. 'That's true. Perhaps I should do some things to him first. Cut off his fingers … or …' Rosemary let the improvised garrotte fall to ground and went round the tree to have another look at her victim. Maybe the Fey Knights had given him to her for another reason.

He wasn't bad looking as boys go, she thought, and she swallowed hard as the first thoughts of lust fluttered up into her conscious mind. She licked her lips and swallowed again as her eyes fixed on the almost indiscernible mound under the loose-fitting trousers just at the point where Christy's legs met. She thought of the things she had witnessed between Karl and Beverly and, as the images flooded her mind, waves of desire washed over the previously dry landscape of Rosemary's experience. Without knowing she was doing it she lifted the material of her skirt and felt herself through her knickers.

'But it's wrong! Wrong, wrong, filthy and wrong. Animals do it. And people like Karl and his slutty traitor-girl do it.' As her desire redoubled so too did her verbal tirade against the act. But desire will out, and it provided her with the justification she was so desperately seeking.

'Ah! But I told Daddy and PC Shadrack that Karl did it to me. And Daddy said the doctor would have to see me. The doctor will know if I haven't … if I didn't. He'll know I lied.' Rosemary's desire suddenly solidified into resolve. 'So Christy. You are going to do it to me, like Karl did to Beverly.'

It took her a few more moments to realise that whatever Christy had taken to make him dopey, it wasn't about to lose it's effect any time soon. Looking all around once again, Rosemary felt as secure as she was ever likely to out here in the open in the woods. She had never seen anyone but the Fey Knights and their victims in this part of the woods, and if the Fey Knights wanted to look, so what? She had seen *them* naked before, so she was not about to let the thought of them finding her on top of Christy spoil anything.

'It was my birthday last week, so I'm old enough. My great granny was married by the time she was my age.' Pushing Christy's knees apart, she crouched down in the space between. She thought it was possible; no she was sure it was. Earlier when she'd been peeping, Karl had laid back and Beverly did everything, so yes, it was possible. Reaching out with her hand she let it hover an inch above Christy's crotch – she was sure she felt the heat rising – then lowered it gently until he fingers closed around the soft bulge.

'Yuk!' she said. 'I thought it would feel like a snake, but it's like you've got a warm, fat toad in your trousers. All squishy like ... like ... like marshmallows and warm water in a balloon skin.'

Christy acted as if he was vaguely aware of the touch but there was no real response: only more confusion. He frowned deeper and looked down at Rosemary's hand and it squeezed and rubbed.

Rosemary kept kneading the yielding flesh. 'If it won't get hard, it won't go in me. Then I'll just have to kill ... Ah! It's moving!' The kneading turned into circular rubbing as Christy's bulge assumed a shape more to Rosemary's expectation. 'I can feel you growing and getting harder. That's it Christy. Be nice to me and afterwards I'll make things quick. Otherwise I'll tear you apart strip by strip, starting with Mr Willie.'

Satisfied with his quickening, Rosemary simulated the moves she had seen Beverly use on Karl – as she had once caught Paul doing to himself in the bathroom. She kept up the rhythm watching Christy's face as it twitched every few moments. She gripped more firmly and increased the pace until she was ready to move to the next stage.

'I don't think it'll get bigger than that Christy. So it's time,' Rosemary said moving to his fly. She pulled the belt out of its loops and popped the top button then move down for the next one.

'My, oh my! A zip fly! Who's the fashionable one then? You've *definitely* been on the air base stealing those American boys' clothes.' She played with the zip, up and down, up and down, fascinated by the mechanism. Then, pulling open the trousers Rosemary had one more surprise.

'You *are* a German, you filthy pig! What kind of an Englishmen would have his name writ on his underpants, and what kind of a name is "Hilfiger" other than a German one?' She chose to ignore the fact that "Tommy" was the stereotypical name for an English soldier and to feed her belief that he hadn't been lying about having German school-friends after all. She wondered if she should go through with it, with a German, but then she saw the irony of it. It couldn't be better. Thrusting her fingers into Christy's underwear she grasped him and pulled him out into the fresh air wondering if she would be able to take it all inside her.

'You're bigger than Karl, and I'm smaller than Beverly. I wonder if we'll fit each other.' She wasted no time finding out.

Ten minutes later it was almost all over for Christy. Rosemary's arms ached from bracing them against the tree trunk either side of Christy's head, her thigh muscles were tired from squatting and bouncing, and there was a burning pain deep inside her. Christy on the other hand looked no different apart from his dishevelled clothing, and appeared clueless as if his body had functioned without bothering to report the encounter to his brain.

'It was supposed to be nice, Christy – or Tommy, or whatever you're real name is.' Rosemary stepped into her blue serge knickers. 'But it hurt. *And* it made me bleed.' *I don't think I'll go with a boy ever, ever, ever again*, she thought.

Christy looked about as vague and as confused as he had before with no sign that he was even aware of his public exposure.

'And so now, it's time to die.'

Rosemary was behind the tree and gripping both dolly-pegs in a flowing series of movements that looked fluid and practiced. The wire passed round the trunk and over Christy's neck just below the Adam's apple. Bracing one foot on the truck Rosemary paused as a fleeting doubt tickled at the back of her mind. Killed dead by the burning sensation between her legs and the blood on her lifted knee, her lips curled as doubt faded and she heaved with all her strength. There was a noise like cutting through a marrow, a little bubbling sound as she met resistance – Christy's vertebrae – and then she leaned back, taking all her weight on the dolly-pegs. Something gave with a jolt and she heard a dull thud. Could it really be that easy?

She let one dolly-peg drop then tugged the other. The wire and free peg swung round the tree trunk and she caught it deftly. No blood on the wire? Perhaps … no, she could not have imagined it all. Sidling round the tree she found Christy staring wide eyed at his sex from a position between his knees. His head grew from the ground now, leaving his neck a bloody stump. He still wore the same confused look. Rosemary could hardly make herself believe this was real.

'Did you just move your lips Mad Christy? Are you trying to talk to me? Well, it's too late now.' She crouched and picked up the head, surprised at how heavy it was. She looked into the eyes trying to see past the glaze and then balancing it on a tree stump she spread the lips and looked at the teeth.

'Still warm. If I look at you over the top of my hand, so that I can only see above the neck, it's hard to believe your body isn't attached.'

Standing back in front of Christy's body she held her hand close to her face and squinted under it. There was blood down the front of his blue vest, but not as much as she had expected, and the flaccid penis was still exposed. Rosemary screwed up her face in disgust then put him away and did up the zip fly. Confident that nobody would ever suspect her she didn't want to give PC Shadrack or the detectives who would come any ideas. Let them think he was murdered by Karl!

Turning away from the body she was startled by the radiance of Christy's head. A shaft of sunlight beamed down upon it and the stump upon which it rested. Not wishing to waste the opportunity she snatched up her camera and aimed it. 'Smile Christy … or at least do the best you can.' She released the shutter. 'There. Before-and-after, just like I wanted.'

Stowing the camera she took a small Hessian sack from the depths of her basket. Christy's head rustled the greaseproof paper as it fell into the sack. 'Say goodbye to your body, Mad Christy. You'll never be together again.'

Skipping through the wood she quickly came to the place where the German and the land army girl had been making love. Their clothes were all spread out just as they'd left them, and then she had an idea. Forty minutes later Beverly and Mad Christy's clothes were buried deep in the ground, scatted over with mould and newly fallen leaves. They would never, ever be found. That had been the easy part. Stripping the headless corpse of Christy and pulling the German's POW clothes onto it – now that was difficult. But she had managed and just as a bonus she spotted a nice ring on Christy's right hand middle finger. It was a bit loose for her so she slid it onto her thumb.

And now everything was done and in place. Whoever found Christy would assume he was the German, and then after a day or so they'd notice Christy was missing. They would put two and two together to make Christy the murderer. Neat and tidy.

Without a backwards glance, Rosemary ducked through the bushes in the direction of home, feeling very pleased with her day's work. She had killed. It felt good. And although she had no inkling, she and Mad Christy had made a new life, which even as she skipped was sparking into existence inside her.

Lady Rosemary, Lady Rosemary. The name went round and round, but like a slippery eel Chris could not grasp it and tie it down to the memory that would not be recalled. Not until he stopped trying, that is. In the chill just before dawn, when the chorus has stirred but not yet released its song, Chris sat up with a start.

'Lady Rosemary's Grimoire!' he said out loud. That's why he knew the name. He'd read about it in the sources section of Ernest Sheldrake's book about the Fey Knights. Throwing off the duvet chill air assailed Chris's body. He paid no heed to such a minor discomfort, and scooted across to his computer firing it up as quickly as he could. He called up a search engine with the intention of finding a definition for the word that suddenly perplexed him. He found an on-line dictionary, and typed into the search box. G-R-I-M-O-I-R-E.

The definition was returned in a split second: *A grimoire is a book of magical knowledge. Such books contain astrological correspondences, lists of angels and <u>demons</u>, directions on casting charms and <u>spells</u>, on mixing medicines, summoning unearthly entities, and making talismans.*

Slipping back under the duvet Chris relaxed into the warmth left by his own body. He knew that he would sleep well for what was left of the night, and in the morning he would draw up plans to locate Lady Rosemary's Grimoire. He felt sure the secret of the Unsullied Jewel lay within its pages.

So, Chris thought as he drifted off. *The little girl in the newspaper cutting grew up to be a witch.* He fell asleep certain that he was another step closer to solving the mystery of the Fey Knights.

In a bedroom not very far away another young man had slept badly. But now, at last, decisions had been made and sleep began to claim him. As the last threads of consciousness frayed and snapped, a grey hand turned the bedroom doorknob, and as a deeply indrawn breath resonated as a gentle snore, the door was opened and a demon spied its prey. He crossed the floor in a miasma of fetid dankness and looked closely at the young face. He was only a sprat, but the incubus needed his likeness to lure the mackerel away from the protection of strong magic and an ancient talisman.

His sisters may have preferred the subtleties of deception, but this one ever favoured the direct approach. Deception took longer; he hadn't the time and anyway, he thrilled to the terror in his victims' eyes. This one would give him pleasure, provide the material he needed to assimilate his genes and assume his form, and then he would die. Bending close he sniffed the young man's scent, already stealing information that would be incorporated into his living facsimile. Lust and hunger stirred within the incubus and he moved closer to begin his work, pitying the young man no more that a great white pities a seal. He was an object to fulfil a need, nothing more.

CHAPTER THIRTEEN

A Sprat to Catch a Mackerel

Richard sat on the edge of his son's bed with an old, but remarkably new looking Belstaff jacket on his lap and a cinema ticket stub in his hand. The night before his jacket had been stolen, all those years ago, he'd been with his mates to see the Godfather movie. There was no doubt in his mind. This jacket had once been his, but after thirty odd years it looked brand new. Standing up he carefully put the jacket back on its hanger and hung it in the wardrobe. He decided to pay a visit on the vicarage and ask Aby Knapper just where he'd got hold of it.

He was just leaving the bedroom when he noticed a family tree printed out and laying in the print tray. It was good that Chris was taking an interest in genealogy, but a shame that it all had to do with this Fey Knight nonsense. It wasn't a tree he recognised – certainly nothing to do with the De'Ath family with all those German-looking names. But then he spotted one name several generations back that he recognised. He snatched up the printout as if looking more closely would add a certain degree of validation.

'Blimey!' he said, and then running into the upstairs hall he called out for Chris – just as the front door slammed.

Chris slammed the front door and, it seemed, put something to fright: something large; something in the bushes. He thought he heard a growl just as the shrubbery by the fence began to shake violently. The commotion stopped almost as soon as it started, and then Chris went to investigate.

'Hi Chris!'

'Oh Jeez ...' Chris spun round – another fright right on the heels of the first. 'Abe! What are you doing here? Half frightened me out of my life.'

'Sorry Chris. I just thought ...'

Abe looked different somehow. Chris couldn't put a finger on it. 'Thought what?'

'Well, all the stuff you told me yesterday. There're a lot of leads to follow, so I thought I might be able to help.'

Chris liked the idea; there was an awful lot to do and school was only days away. He'd never get it all done in time. And it would be good to have a partner in this venture; someone who believed in him and Abe certainly fit the bill there. 'Cool! Yes, I could do with a bit of help.'

Abe's face brightened. 'What do you want me to do? Anything at all, I'm up for it.'

'Let's see now. I'm just off to speak to a guy about a family tree and something that happened in the war. But I've also got to find a way to bluff my way into Wymes House to ask about Lady Rosemary's Grimoire –'

'Her what?'

'It's a kind of witch's book. And I've also got to find out what the key is and how to get it.'

'The Unsullied Jewel?'

'That's the one.'

'Well, how about I spend some time in the museum looking for clues? I'll see if I can find a lead to the Unsullied Jewel.'

'It's a deal. I'll drop you off at the museum and pick you up after I've spoken to Kostja. He's a guy I met in the hospital. I think he knows a thing or two about the Fey Knights and he called first thing this morning to set up a meet.'

'Where?'

'*Three Fishes* pub. Middle of Shrewsbury. It's near his house ... I think.'

Driving in town was much more tiring and exacting than following country roads, while finding somewhere to park was expensive and frustrating. Next time he had an appointment in town he'd park and ride. But it was another nice day and apart from one incident of mild road rage, which Chris had inadvertently fuelled by executing a piece of driving of which he was thoroughly ashamed, everything went according to plan. He was on time and Kostja Claussen was waiting at *The Three Fishes*. It was a nice old pub, white with black beams and a snug, comfortable interior. It was early so the lunchtime rush hadn't started and there were few other customers.

Kostja got the drinks in – a lager for himself and a bitter-top for Chris – and they found a comfortable place to sit.

'This has to be a first. Having a beer with someone I've de-catheterised.'

'Thanks for reminding me,' Chris said, his ears and neck blooming hotter with a glowing blush.

Kostja laughed and Chris wished he'd thought of a different way of breaking the ice. Chris and Kostja sipped their drinks and chatted about the weather and how they had each made their way to the pub. Kostja made polite enquiry of Chris's health and asked if he'd had any more encounters with the Fey Knights. It was then that Chris reached into his pocket and pulled out Tarn's wrist band. He stretched it out on the table between their respective beer mats, and asked his question by fixing Kostja's eyes with a penetrating glare and simply raising his eyebrows.

'I didn't lie to you, Chris.'

Chris maintained his accusing stare.

'See, I knew he wasn't a patient in either of the general wards, and it didn't occur to me that he could have been in a psychiatric ward. I've checked the records though, and yes, he was a patient. The police found him when they searched Wymes Forest, after your friends had disappeared. He was committed under Section 136 of the Mental Health Act and taken to County. How he managed to get out of a secure ward and visit you is a mystery. How he escaped all together is another mystery, but then there were a few sighting of a kid walking around in underwear, so I figure –''

'It's not much of a mystery really, Kostja. He's a Fey Knight and I don't suppose there's much that can keep them shut in.'

'And yet, he allowed himself to be found and taken in. Curious, don't you think?'

Chris shrugged. 'I haven't thought about it much. Maybe he was unconscious when they found him.'

Kostja took another sip of beer. 'Somehow I don't think so. See Chris, the Fey Knights are very crafty. Sneaky, you could say.'

'Sneaky? I don't think –'

'Sneaky and ... and above all else, evil.'

'Evil? Now hang on a minute, you can't –'

'Evil, I'm telling you! They killed my great uncle, in a ... despicable manner ... and my grandfather spent the rest of his life searching for evidence about their motives. What he discovered was too horrible to contemplate. Nobody would listen to him, and his stories were so fantastic it wasn't long before he found himself institutionalised.'

Kostja told Chris everything that his grandfather had discovered about the Fey Knights. All through history they had been harvesting the young, and not just from the villages and towns surrounding Wymes Forest. He believed that many other areas had their own brand of the Fey Knights. The Orkneys – way up off the north-west coast of Britain – had selkies, who morphed between seal forms and human ones, luring people to the sea. There were mermaids who gathered souls from all round Britain's coasts and virtually every region, not just of Britain, but the world, had its quota of mysterious folk, and all with an endless appetite for young flesh.

Chris shook his head. 'If you'd told me any of this a month ago I'd have been relieved to find someone even nuttier than myself. Selkies and mermaids? Kidnapping kids. It's all too crazy, but the craziest is that the Fey Knights are evil. I've met one. Tarn's not evil, and nor is Sem.'

'Sem?'

Chris told Kostja all about his encounter with Sem and went on to talk about Sem's description of the Selost Host and the Unselost Mass.

'It doesn't make sense,' Kostja said. 'It all seems a little too convenient to me. Selost and Unselost – they're all the same, and they're all evil.'

'You haven't met them. If you had, you'd know that Tarn's lot aren't evil, but the other lot are. I've met *both* sides now.'

Kostja shook his head, unconvinced. 'Look, why do you think this Sem person won't tell you everything out straight? He had the time. He had your full attention.'

'Like he said, I have to find out for myself or –'

'Utter rubbish! He's hiding the truth from you, and the truth is he wants you for the same reasons all the others were wanted.'

'To fight the Unselost Mass.'

'Don't be naïve.'

Just when he was beginning to feel he was getting somewhere, along came a complete reversal. He sighed deeply and huffed with frustration.

'What then? If I'm so naïve, even though I've met a Fey Knight and a ... and another couple of beings, and you haven't, *you* tell *me* what they want.'

Kostja drained his beer and slammed the empty glass down hard. 'Details? I don't know. End result. You wind up dead. Like all the others. My great uncle. Your friend Danny. Everybody else. Nobody comes back once the Fey Knights have taken them. They either die or they vanish forever.'

Kostja stood and made for the bar leaving Chris to ponder. Kostja had a point. Nobody ever came back. He was half surprised when Kostja came back with two more pints.

'Sorry if I got a bit bad tempered just now Chris. But I know the whole lot of them are tricksters, beguiling people into believing they're good and then taking them away forever. I remember how my father used to get upset when he spoke of his father and uncle. Lives are ruined, and the hurt filters down through the generations.'

Chris nodded half heartedly. He'd set out this morning with such optimism, and now the doubts were closing in like storm clouds, choking out the light. Kostja was right. Life would be better without Fey Knights and succubae and faeries.

'There's nothing we can do to stop them, is there?'

Kostja set his beer down and stroked his chin, like he was deciding if he should confide in Chris.

'There might be. My grandfather certainly thought so, but it involves a stone circle somewhere in Wymes Forest, and he wasted the best part of his adult life looking for it without succeeding.'

'A tower you mean? Not a stone circle, but a stone tower?' Would he really tell this virtual stranger about the tower? Would Danny have approved?

'Not a tower, defiantly a stone circle.'

A wave of relief washed over Chris. The tower could remain a secret. 'I know the forest pretty well. I've never seen anything like a stone circle. You are talking, Stonehenge kind of a thing?'

'Yes, I think so. But a lot smaller. More like –'

'Wait a minute!' Chris interrupted. He raced on excitedly: 'There's a book in the museum. It talks about the mention of stone circle in another book, and that other book is already something I'm tracking down.'

Kostja sat up and his eyes brightened. 'Does it talk of the ceremony? Does it mention the ceremony for closing the door that the Fey Knights use between this world and their own?'

Chris shook his head. 'That doesn't ring any bells, but this book, it could easily have stuff about ceremonies and what-have-you.'

'Do you think you might find the book?'

'I've got a few leads. Just leave it with me for a couple of days. If I hit lucky I'll call you.'

Kostja seemed pleased and they began making plans for their next meet when Chris's bubble burst once again. 'If we close the door between worlds, I'll never get Gayle back. Marc and Shaun will be trapped forever. I don't know if that's such a good idea.'

Kostja sympathised, but in the end, he said, nobody ever comes back. To convince yourself otherwise was to be encouraged by the forlorn hope. Better grab the nettle and accept the truth. Gayle was gone forever. Marc and Shaun would never return, and the place where they all were was unknowable, unless you said goodbye to everything familiar and travelled there yourself knowing full well that you would die there.

The drinks were drained and the conversation waned in that awkward little space of time that often precedes parting. Chris was beginning to feel very dissatisfied with the way things had developed when he was once again hit with the absurdity of it all.

'How many people like us do you think there are in the world, Kostja?'

Kostja did not appear to understand the question.

'I mean, here we are, two guys in a pub, talking about all sorts of impossible crap that we know is absolutely real. Here we both are on the borders of ... of bloody faeire-land and life goes on all round like normal. How many other people are like us?'

Kostja shrugged. 'How's to tell? You read about people who believe in faeries and you think, "Poor soul" or "Book them a room in the looney bin", but who knows? Maybe they're all like us, but haven't learnt there are times to keep your mouth shut.'

'Well, at least we found each other. It's easier to handle when you know you're not alone. Thank God for you and thank God for Abe Knapper.'

Chris drove home feeling lonely and depressed. He had expected the exact opposite. Now he had another piece of the jigsaw, but it didn't fit in with any of the other pieces. Maybe it was from a different puzzle all together. Now there were two people who believed in him. He'd felt better when it was just the one. Good old Abe!

Chris pulled over into a lay-by and realised it was the same one where only yesterday he'd met Sem. He wished, hard, that Sem would come again. There were a few more questions he'd like to ask, but Sem was not to be conjured by the strength of wishes.

After a while he took out his mobile and called Abe. He was all done at the museum and ready to be picked up. After a few moments of conversation it was clear his day had not been fruitful: no nearer to discovering the Unsullied Jewel – nothing new at all. Still, Chris felt better for making the call and better yet when he picked Abe up at the museum. Nobody could ever replace what he'd had with Danny, but with time he knew Abe could come close. Making friends with a gay boy! What would Danny have thought of *that*? Again, he knew. Danny would have been one hundred percent cool, and just a little miffed that Chris had even had to stop and think about it. He dropped Abe off at Flint House and drove home, a bag of mixed emotions. Sad, yes – from today's new discoveries – but also glad and proud that he had once had a friend like Danny. As he reached home silent hot tears blurred his vision. He wiped his wet eyes on his sleeve as home came into view; nobody had seen him crying since he was fourteen, and he wasn't about to let that change.

While turning into his drive, he saw a patrol car parked close to the garage. Once – it seemed like years ago – he would have been afraid that the police were here because he'd been reported for doing a bit of under-age drinking, or maybe the web police had caught him looking at porny mpegs on his computer. These days he always thought of the police as harbingers of an altogether more frightening kind of news. Who was dead this time? Had they found Gayle, Marc or Shaun?

No. What they had found – what Dad had found – was a corpse in the bushes. A corpse with its throat torn out.

CHAPTER FOURTEEN

Hoorah for the Redlegs Colonel!

'He had his throat ripped out, and police *don't* suspect foul play? What's going on Mum?' Chris stood at the front of the house looking towards the bushes where a man in motorcycle gear had met a very bloody death. Julie De'Ath tried not to look in that direction. In fact she stood with her back to the area and made patterns in the shingle with her toe.

'I think I'll get Dad to chop the whole lot down. I don't think I'll ever be able to walk past without wandering if something's lurking.'

'Mum! Didn't you hear me? Surely the man must have been done in by someone.'

'Some *thing*, the police say.'

Ice seized Chris's spine and his stomach contracted. 'Some ... *thing*?'

Julie put the fingertips of one hand to her lips and pressed, as if she expected to vomit some time soon. She swallowed hard. 'PC Chapel said there've been reports of a huge dog – more like a wolf really. He said the police had been treating it as a hoax. But now they're ... not.'

'I guess a guy with his throat ripped out is pretty strong circumstantial evidence.' Chris took a few steps towards the bushes before his mother shrieked. Just what was he *doing*? Didn't he *know* there would be blood, and ... stuff?

'Mum! The police took the body away, and the dog's well gone!' On the other hand, it was getting dark, and Chris didn't want to upset his mother any more than she already was. He'd wait until morning and then do some rooting around. He had no illusions whatsoever that any dog, or wolf for that matter, had anything to do with the man's death. The motorcyclist was obviously a ... now what did Sem call them? A "Wiergan" ... and Sem or one of his faerie friends had sorted him out. Far from being traumatised, the dead man served as a sign to Chris that he was being protected.

The wolf-shaped being in the bushes knew otherwise. This day it had tasted blood, and now it wanted more. It wanted more blood and it wanted Chris. Specifically, it wanted Chris and would allow nobody to stand between it and its goal. Had Chris ignored his mother and entered the bushes, he would even now be feeling hot and fetid breath at his throat, pungent with the stench of not-so-fresh blood.

Next morning Chris was first up. It was a misty grey morning and there was a light drizzle, but nothing so bad that he was put off from donning his Wellington boots and heading straight for the bushes. Mother had been quite correct: there was blood, albeit almost wholly soaked away into the ground. And there was – stuff. Chris speculated that the muddy, red-brown pea-sized globules of indeterminate matter, each with its retinue of voracious blueflies, could easily be gobbets of flesh. But there was also something else: it was just on the other side of the fence and embedded in the trunk of an ancient oak, its bole thick with ivy.

Chris took his find and waited for his dad in the work shed knowing he would stop off there before cranking up the Landrover and heading off for Wymes Park.

'Hey-up! What you doing here so early?' Richard De'Ath cleared a space on the work bench and set down the first of his daily quota of steaming mugs of tea.

'Nothing much. Just grubbing round.'

Richard fixed his son in an urgent gaze. 'Not round the bushes.'

'Afraid so, Dad.'

'If your mother finds out she'll –'

'Don't sweat it, Dad. She'll only find out if you tell her.'

Dad apparently got out of bed the wrong side. The grumpy side. 'Can't you just do what you're told for once in your life. Don't you think it's kind of sick that you would even consider snooping round where a bloke was killed not half-a-day ago?'

Chris shrugged. 'What do you make of this then?' Chris slapped his find down next to dad's tea. It was a knife of sorts, with the most curiously shaped blade of bright, polished steel. Dad picked it up.

'A knife with a moon-shaped blade. Where on Earth ...? Not in the bushes?'

'Yep! Dug into the trunk of the big oak just on the other side of the fence.'

'But ... the police searched the whole area. Bloody carrot crunchers! The Met would have never missed something like this. I'm not talking POLSA either! Any probbie with ten weeks in the job would have found a dirty great big blade like this.'

'To be fair, it *was* kind of hidden in the vines. I only spotted it when the sun glanced off the blade.'

Richard looked out the window. 'What sun? It's as dull as the inside of my cap.'

Chris reached out and took the blade back. 'Suppose it must have winked at me then.'

Richard did not look amused. They argued for a while about possession of the weapon and what should be done about it, but De'Ath senior lacked his usual confidence and authority. The blade was obviously not connected with the dead man's injuries, which were clearly cause by animal ripping rather than precision slicing, and so Chris kept the blade. Richard went quiet and sulky and acquiesced reluctantly. He did not like the feeling that he was concealing evidence.

Chris wondered if he'd guessed the real reason behind his dad's mood. 'Was it very horrible, Dad? Finding that guy in the bushes?'

Richard took a hit of tea. 'When you've scraped a teenager's brains off the motorway, not much else comes close, but it wasn't exactly pleasant, I'll grant that. The shock of it really. I mean, you get called to an RTA you have time to prepare. Whereas here I was wondering why the bushes look dishevelled and bingo! Here's matey with his head virtually off. I suppose it did kind of put me off my supper.'

'I'm sorry Dad.' Chris felt a little ashamed that he'd forgotten to consider Dad's feelings. 'I should have thought.'

Richard spun round. He really did look troubled. 'It's not what you think,' he said sitting at the bench and waving a hand in the direction of the spare chair. Chris took the hint and sat opposite. 'See, I can handle blood and gore. I don't revel in it and I don't like to dwell on it, but I can cope. What I can't cope with is all this stuff that's going on.'

'Dad?' Chris had never seen his father looking so vulnerable and awkward.

'The missing people and ... well for God's sake, all this Fey Knight stuff. I'd be a fool if I kept trying to kid everyone it's nonsense.'

'You ... you believe me?'

Richard nodded, diffidently. 'I believe you, and ... it frightens the hell out of me.'

The next half hour was full of awkward moments but father and son got through it. Chris told Richard about his various encounters and Richard reciprocated with his thoughts concerning the motorcycle jacket and the Fey Knight he'd seen running away in his underwear. He had feared to hope that his father might come to believe him, but now that he had he knew that he could want for no better ally.

'So what do we do now, Chris?'

'I just keep doing what I'm doing already, and see where it leads.'

Dad shook his head vigorously. 'Can't allow it, son. Too bloody dangerous by half.'

'You know you can't stop me Dad. I'm not a kid anymore.'

Dad looked at his boots, defeated but proud at the same time. 'Well, if I can't stop you, I'll just have to help, won't I? But for God's sake keep it from your Mother. She gets one niff of this and she'll be scarier than a whole legion of Fey Knights or ... what did you call the biker blokes?'

'Wiergan,' Chris said, smiling at the thought of his mother going into battle with a flock of succu-bitches and leaving them all mincemeat.

'Yeah, Wiergan.' Richard picked up his tea mug and looked into it. The dregs were cold, so he put it back down. 'Do you think the Fey Knights are evil, like the nurse-bloke said?'

Chris chewed on the inside of his cheek and hovered between options. 'I've given it a lot of thought, and no, I think Kostja's got it wrong. But we have to find his stone circle. I think it's important some how. And that's where you can help.'

Dad was all eyes and ears. The prospect of some action blew away the forlorn looks.

'Have you ever heard of Lady Rosemary Fennimore?'

'Lady Rosemary Wymes, you mean. I believe she was a Fennimore once, but she married into the family.'

'Of course,' Chris mused to himself. 'Have you ever met her?'

'Yes, and so have you.' Richard laughed at his son's bemused expression. 'Old Rosy? You know? Used to tell the school kids stories about –'

'Mad Christy and the Indians! Old Rosy and Lady Rosemary –'

'Are one and the same!'

Chris explained his theory that little old Rosy was a witch. Well, one more impossibility among many. Nothing was surprising any more. Dad said she had lived at Wymes Park until she went senile and was put in a home, where – he was almost sure – she'd died. Chris told Richard about the grimoire and how important it was that he should get his hands on it. The grimoire was the key to finding the stone circle. And the stone circle? Chris was sure it would lead him closer to the truth. Logic dictated that if the book existed at all it would be at Wymes Park.

'Do you think you could have a look for it, next time you're up at the House?'

'I could have a go, but it's most likely to be in the library, and I never have any call to go there. Why don't I just ask to see the book?'

Father and son realised at the same time: that would never work. *Hey Your Lordship. We understand your mother was a witch. Can we see her book, please?*

'There is this one idea I have,' Chris said, uncertainty garnished with hope. 'See, Lord Wymes's great, great grandfather was a bit of a war hero.'

'Oh yes. Harold Wymes was a general in the First World War wasn't he? There's a statue of him on the village green.'

'I don't mean him. I'm talking about Wilbur Wymes. In the 1860's he went to increase the family fortune in "the colonies" and ended up fighting for the Union. I could ask for an appointment with Lord Victor to ask questions about his hero-ancestor and perhaps get in a few questions.'

'And a crafty look round!'

'Yup! And a crafty look around for the grimoire. Think it could work?'

'No. Not in a million years. But unless we can come up with anything better ...'

A day later, Chris dropped Abe off at the museum to continue his seek and search mission; objective, news of the Unsullied Jewel; while Chris went on to keep his appointment with Lord Victor Wymes. Richard dropped him off at the grand entrance and he climbed the Portland stone staircase to be met at the top by the butler.

'Good morning, Mr De'Ath. Please follow me to the Blue Room.'

'Good morning. The Blue Room? Is that the library?'

The butler, a cheerful, stout, red-faced man whose look spoke of a personal key to the wine cellar led Chris along a wide corridor flanked with gold-framed photos of recent generation of the family Wymes. 'The Blue Room is so called because ... well, it's blue.' The butler chuckled. 'And it has been that way since the House was first decorated. Never so much as a touch-up since. As you see it, so too did Lord Charles Wymes see it in 1734. The library is in the adjacent wing.'

Damn! Chris thought. Why couldn't his interview have been in the library?

The butler left Chris while he went to notify His Lordship that his guest had arrived. The Blue Room was cold and tatty and ... well, in need of a good paint job. The laws of physics and entropy could not be changed, not even for lords. But as he had recently discovered, some laws of physics were open, if not to new discovery, then certainly to redefinition. Would Lord Charles know how to address a faerie, Chris wondered. Lord Charles looked down from a lofty oil painting, twice life size. He wore a blue velvet doublet trimmed in gold and buff riding breeches. His dark hair was held back with a black lace and lying on the table before him was an impressively large flintlock pistol. He stood before a massive fireplace. In fact, it was that very fireplace – over there! With the same wrought iron fittings and the same ornaments on the mantel. This room really was a time capsule.

Wait a minute! Chris peered at the three statuettes in the painting, and then crossed over to take a closer look at the real things. He could hardly believe his eyes. Carefully reaching up he took down a porcelain representation of Tarn, the Fey Knight he had actually met.

'Careful old boy!'

Chris nearly jumped out of his skin. Lord Victor Wymes had not come in through the door. Maybe he'd been there all the time. Maybe there was a secret entrance.

'Worth a King's ransom. Been in the family for over two hundred years, so I'm led to believe. The painting seems to confirm it,' Lord Victor said taking the figure from Chris and pointing to its painted representation at the same time.

Bad start! Chris began to apologise, but Lord Victor waved it aside as he replaced Tarn the porcelain figure back in its place.

'They're the Fey Knights, aren't they?'

Lord Victor looked surprised, and then he looked at the figures. 'Do you know, they could be, at that! I've never really given it any thought, but they certainly fit the description.' He put on a pair of half-rimmed spectacles and had a really close look. 'Bugger me! You're right. Bloody Fey Knights on my mantel shelf all my life and I never knew it. How did you know it was them?'

'I've met them.' He went for it, without hesitation. Somehow it just seemed right and natural. 'Well, I've met one of them at any rate.'

Taking off the glasses Lord Victor turned on Chris with a bemused look that soon transmuted into an avuncular smile. 'Have you by Jove? What other surprises have you in store for me, young man?'

Before Chris could answer the door swung open and a lady carrying a tea tray flowed into the Blue Room. There was a kind of warmth to her that immediately made the Blue Room seem less chilly, and far less blue.

Chris recognised her from a day – a day so long, long ago when he had gone fishing and his life had changed forever. 'Lady Wymes. Good morning.'

'Young De'Ath. What a pleasure it is to meet you once again. I understand you've been through the wars, one way or another.'

'Claims to have met the Fey Knights my dear. And, Helen, what on Earth are you doing with the tea things. That's D'Arcy's job.'

'I wanted to Victor,' Lady Helen Wymes said in a voice that terminated any chance of an argument. 'And I also wanted to meet Christopher again.'

'That's "Christian", but "Chris" is what I always go by.'

'I'm dreadfully sorry dear, but please do indulge me. I so hate diminutives. Mayn't I call you Christian?'

Chris was a little nonplussed. 'Not even my Mum does, but if you like. I suppose it does suit a place like this better.'

Lord and Lady Wymes exchanged little smiles, both charmed by Christian's reply. Lady Wymes asked how Christian preferred his tea and then began to pour. They all sat in comfortable chairs already arranged around a coffee table and chatted of weather and health. Once the polite formalities were covered, Lord Victor began with the business of the meeting.

'So, you're researching good old Wilbur, my wandering ordnance-minded double great grandpa. Hoorah for the Redlegs Colonel!'

'Well, actually, no.' Just lately, the truth seemed to be working. Chris took a deep breath and told his story once again. He was becoming fairly practiced by now, and found himself using phrases he had used before. He could now tell the whole story on automatic pilot, cutting out the bits he thought unnecessary for whomsoever formed his present audience. He thought the section about his encounter with the succubus could comfortably be left out this time.

Chris had become so used to relating the impossible that he failed to notice the effect it was having on his audience. Lady Wymes seemed to shrink into herself, and Lord Victor went red, then his eyes popped and on the first mention of Lady Rosemary he exploded.

'That is quite enough!' Lord Victor cried and he jumped indignantly to his feet. 'How *dare* you come into my house under false pretences? I've never heard such a raft of utter, idle, contemptible *piffle* in all my life.'

Chris felt his jaw flapping noiselessly. The stuffy, pompous outburst would once have made him giggle. As it was, Lord Victor's apoplectic seizure was frightening him to the extent that his sphincter was twitching most unpleasantly. He looked to Lady Wymes for support. None was forthcoming; she merely sat silently with eyes downcast. Chris knew how stupid his story must have sounded and wondered how he had ever been moved to tell Lord Wymes the truth.

'Get out, do you hear? Get out!' Lord Victor treated Chris to a stare of unrepressed contempt and stormed out of the Blue Room. He underscored his fury by slamming shut the big oak door. Chris felt wretched and drained. Lady Wymes rose like billowing silk and drifted from the room without another word, sucking the last remaining warmth out behind her.

As if his will had been removed, Chris continued to sit, wondering where he had gone wrong and how he could allow another person, albeit a Lord, to leave him feeling so crushed and lowly.

The door opened and D'Arcy, the butler, stepped in. 'Audience over, I fear,' D'Arcy said, pulling his face into a mask of empathy. 'Never mind, hey? He can be a grumpy old sod at times.'

Chris smiled weakly and followed D'Arcy back along the long hall. They arrived at the huge main doors when Lady Wymes called from a side room.

'Christian. If you wouldn't mind,' she said bidding Chris to enter by a delicate wave of her hand.

'But Ma'am. His Lordship said I was to –'

'That will be all, D'Arcy.'

The butler stood his ground – for about two seconds – then excused himself and disappeared back down the hall.

When lady Wymes was quite sure they were alone she began. 'That was unforgivable, young man.'

'I'm so sorry, miss, but I was telling the truth and –'

'You told the truth eventually, but you lied to obtain your appointment. You had no interest in Colonel Wymes at all, admit it!'

'But, if I'd said why I wanted to visit –'

'Lord Victor would have said no. Indeed he would, and I do understand your predicament, I really do. That's why I'm giving you this.' Lady Wymes held out a Harrods shopping bag with a book shaped object inside. He guessed at once, although he would hardly allow himself to believe it, that Lady W was giving him the grimoire.

'Take it away. Don't bring it back and never mention it to Victor ever again. And be warned young man. One or two of the enclosures will chill you to the bone. I can't explain, but there you are. Perhaps you should not look inside until the middle of a sunny day, for should you look at night, you will surely go mad.'

'Thank you. Thank you so much.'

'Not another word. Now off with you, and if you're caught with this, I shall say you stole it.'

Chris spun, and like a six year old with the bogeyman at his heels he ran down the stairs and didn't stop until the shingle drive and Wymes Park was far behind him.

D'Arcy's ruddy countenance had drained to grey and his kindly eyes had set into an icon of cold fury. Looking up and down to hall to ensure that he was unobserved, he pressed on the centre of a photograph of Lord Harold Wymes dressed in hunting clothes. There was a click, and then D'Arcy pushed to the side of the photo. The wall gave way, not half as solid as it had appeared, and the butler stepped into a secret passage. He followed the dark, narrow passage, dry and wisped here and there with cobwebs, passing other secret entrances: this one led to the library, that one descended by a short flight of stairs to a recess behind the ice room. He came to a spiral staircase.

By the time he reached the top his was sweating profusely and panting like a steam engine. His hand hovered over a brass handle while he caught his breath. Then he snicked the catch and opened the door.

'Ma'am?' he called softly, putting his head round the door, which on the inside was a full length, gilt-framed mirror. 'Lady Rosemary?'

'Is that you, Fatty?' The voice crept through the darkened room like a snake, smooth and little above a whisper. 'Come in man. Don't be shy.'

D'Arcy stepped into the gloom, casting round for a direction to aim his words. Finding none, he spoke into the darkness. 'I'm sorry to say that Edmund and his spies have let you down, Ma'am. The De'Ath boy has been here, and he's gone away with your book.'

Ten minutes later D'Arcy stumbled down the spiral stairs as quickly as his legs would safely carry him. Back out in the light of the hall, he leaned on the wall by Harold Wymes's hunting portrait and pressed a hand to his heart. It was racing, a fact that had nothing to do with his rapid descent.

He waited until he had reached his rooms before fumbling for his mobile and then quickly dialled a number. After two cycles of the dialling tone someone answered. 'Edmund ... Your spies need shooting. The De'Ath kid has just been here, and I had *no* warning. He's been antagonising his Lordships with questions about Lady Rosemary ... Yes, I'm *telling* you, and what's *worse* is that Lady Helen, the daft old cow, had the book all the time and has now has seen fit to give it to the boy ... *The* book you fool ... I agree. It's time we concentrated our efforts. The boy has to be secured, before he ruins us all. And we *have* to get that book ... What? ... No, I have no idea where it was hidden. Certainly not in the library, but that's irrelevant now. Assign your best man ... Oh, I'm sorry to hear that ...You'd better deal with the boy personally then, and get that book ... Yes, I think we had better meet. In one hour – usual place ... I'll tell her if I must – if you think it will do any good, but she's only really interested in results.'

D'Arcy broke the connection and before resuming his duties, he pondered as to how Edmund Warwick's best man could have ended up in the boy's front garden with his throat ripped out. Perhaps the boy was more dangerous than he looked.

CHAPTER FIFTEEN

The Demon and Sandrin Syndicate

Edmund Warwick found the 21st century entirely to his liking. The motorbike had many advantages over the horse and it had proved easy to master. Electric lightening was a thrill to use; he quickly came to understand the science behind the power and had no desire, not even for reasons of sentimentality, to return to the use of candles or oil lamps. His fears about the advanced intellect of modern people were entirely unfounded. Far from making him cower in shame from a lack of knowledge, he found himself to be superior to them in almost every way. They were mostly an uneducated bunch who didn't know John Donne from John Milton and so long as he steered clear of talk about technology and avoided 17th century idiom, he could get by very nicely. Food was an especial delight, so abundant and tasty. Edmund was a big fan of Big Mac. Yes, there was much to enjoy in this new world in which he found himself, but nothing quite caught his imagination so much as modern ordnance.

Edmund Warwick's weapon of choice was a Steyr M9 semi-automatic pistol with a laser sight. With his heavy boots thrown into a corner, Edmund sat cross-legged on the double bed in his room at the Axenwhit Hotel. The grey, high-impact plastic case with the yellow and orange Steyr logo rested in front of him, sinking into the duvet. With his back perfectly straight he folded his legs into a half-lotus and slowly reached down to undo the catches. Taking the pistol out with such care that his movements resembled a martial ceremony, he stroked it before fitting the laser sight and sliding home the 14-shot magazine. Holding the weapon up, he squeezed the trigger minutely and activated the needle-thin beam. He imagined the red dot projected, not onto the hotel room wall just below a painting of Bamburgh Castle, but right between Christian De'Ath's eyes. He visualised the effect of a 9mm tungsten-coated silver bullet smashing through the meddling youth's head.

'It will make a pink pottage of his brain, burst forth from the back of his skull, and serve the knave right justly,' Edmund whispered. The thought made him smile and he recalled a young whelp of Royalist parentage whom he had once put to the same fate with a half-inch ball from a gilded German wheel lock. He wondered if the Steyr would prove to be as messy, and as satisfying.

Easing off the pressure the laser winked out, but before lowering the weapon Edmund's eye fell on the chamber load indicator. It was flush with the rear of the slide indicating an empty chamber.

'Soon sort that,' Edmund said flowing easily into modern idiom as he worked the slide and put one up the spout. The mood broken, the pistol was no longer a mechanism to revere, but just a pistol. Checking the numerous safeties he stuffed it into a navy-blue webbing shoulder holster together with the spare magazine, pulled on a black leather riding jacket and got booted up. He looked forward to killing Chris, but first things first. In half an hour he was due to meet with a certain Master Knapper.

Chris stood in front of his bedroom mirror and ran a finger over the crossed rifle patch sewn high on the left sleeve of the combat jacket Abe had given him. He felt a little silly in all this soldier stuff, but he was meeting up with Kostja to seek out the stone circle, and if he was going to be grubbing around in the depths of the forest, it was the best gear for the job. He slid the tobacco tin with all its outdoor survival gizmos into a side pocket, wondering if Abe had got round to using the condoms yet. He hoped not; he didn't want to be the only seventeen-year-old virgin left in town. Chris hadn't yet realised that virtually all his friend were in the same condition as himself in that respect, and just like himself, they exaggerated or just plain lied about their exploits.

Sidling over towards the window, Chris put his weight on the carpet above the loose floorboard. It squeaked and moved quite noticeably. Under his foot; under this carpet; under that floorboard, was Lady Rosemary's grimoire with its terrifying contents – so sickening that he dare not show his dad, so chilling that Chris deciding to take the hefty knife with him on today's mission. Still, filter out the terrible photographs and the equally horrible written revelations, and if he came away with one thing, it was a pretty clear idea that the stone circle was pivotal in matters concerning the Fey Knights.

Chris and Abe had studied the book together and Abe recognised the location. Chris could not have done it without him and although he wanted to wait until he'd gathered a little more information, Abe had persuaded him of the importance of going to the circle, and the sooner the better.

Chris hovered by the day-sack, stuffed with other useful gear, thinking, *why the Hell not*, before swinging it onto his shoulders. Kostja would probably think he was an idiot turning up like someone out of the 82nd Airborne but in for a penny, in for a pound. Might as well get hung for a sheep as for a lamb ... and several other old saying he could think of.

'Blimey,' Dad said as he met Chris at the foot of the stairs. 'I thought you were going for a look round Wymes Forest, not deepest Borneo.' He threw the keys to the Landrover in a little ashtray on an occasional table by the front door where they lived when he wasn't using them.

Chris was on the verge of spinning right round, running up the stairs and changing into jeans and a sweatshirt, but held out. 'I don't want to muck up my stuff. I'm likely to get pretty muddy out there today.'

'Suppose so,' Dad said. 'Is it just you and this Kostja geezer, or is Abe helping today?'

'Nope. It's just me and fourth cousin Kostja.' Richard had told his son about the matching family trees. It turned out that Chris had a great grandmother whose maiden name was Gretchen Hochwalt and who just happened also to be the great grand aunt of Kostja Claussen. It led Chris to speculate that maybe all the victims of the Fey Knights really were related in some way. Charles Knapper had been correct.

'Abe's doing some more research in the museum today. Mike Ryan, the curator, has got pretty well into it too and he's giving Abe a lot of help.'

'Ride a motorcycle does he, this Mike Ryan?'

Chris stopped to think. 'Not that I know of. Why?'

'I just saw Abe out on his dirt bike round back of the supermarket. He was parked up next to a guy – dark buzzed hair, mid to late thirties – on a bike with an engine the size of a tractor's. I waved but Abe ... I was going to say ignored me, but I guess he just didn't know it was me. "Who's the nutcase waving at me from a clapped out old Landrover?" he was probably thinking.'

Chris smiled, guessing that the motorcyclist was Abe's friend – the one who either already had or was soon to get as close to Abe as latex would allow.

The phone next to the ashtray trilled out and Chris got the drop on Dad.

'Hi Abe! ... We were just talking about you ... Nah! Nothing like that ... Okay ... Okay ... Yeah, no problem ... Okay ... Okay ... Hope to be at the circle by lunchtime ... Noon or just before ... Sure, see you later.' Chris replaced the handset into the cradle.

'Everything's *okay* then?' Richard said.

'Fine,' Chris replied, missing the joke. 'Abe's dad – the vicar – wants me to meet up with some people this afternoon to talk about the Fey Knights.'

'What people?'

'I'll find out this afternoon. But Abe says they're all people who know something about the ... the goings on.' Chris had an idea. 'I'm going to ask Kostja to come along too.' He smiled broadly. At last, it was all coming together. Like ripples spreading from a stone thrown into a pond, the word was spreading and Chris was no longer alone. Not even the despicable horrors of Lady Rosemary's obscene book could dampen his mood.

'Anyway, Dad. Got to fly, or I'll be late.'

'Want a lift?' Richard said reaching out for his keys.

'No thanks. I'll just cut across by the lower pond. Kostja's meeting me at the lay-by with the picnic tables.' Chris headed for the door.

'Take care, boykie!'

'Don't worry about me, Dad,' Chris said patting the knife at his hip.

Dad noticed it for the first time. 'For crying out loud, Chris. If you're taking that dirty great thing out with you, keep it stuffed way down your trouser-leg – right out of sight. And if anyone asks make sure you tell them you've got a good reason for carrying it. I don't want the local plod getting a cheap detection for "points and blades" at your expense.'

'What's a good reason, Dad? Excuse me Mr Policeman, but I need it to go faerie hunting?'

Richard rolled his eyes. 'How about saying you're out on survival training? You ruddy great pillock!'

Chris hurried along to the end of his drive and turned left. The forest spread out before him, green, cool and inviting on a day too hot to be out of the shade. He hoped he could make the wood before any of his friends – or worse yet, enemies – saw him dressed up like this. As so often is the case when one hopes for anonymity, Chris hadn't gone fifty yards before he bumped right into someone he knew.

'Ohayo gozaimas, Cappy-san!' Chris said in his best back-of-the-throat Samurai voice.

Cappy Shirakawa flipped him the middle finger. 'Up yours, jerk-off!' he said, the wide cheerful smile negating the aggressiveness of his address. The Doberman he was walking looked intent on giving Chris a friendly lick.

'Hey! I only said good morning,' Chris protested, again in jest.

'You just have to rub it in don't you?' Cappy hated to be reminded that he knew hardly a word of his father's tongue. 'One day I'm gonna learn though and when I do you can "Cappy-san" me all day long.' Cappy looked Chris up and down. 'So what's with the soldier-boy duds?'

Chris felt his ears heating up and he hoped it didn't show. 'Got some stuff to do with my Dad up at the estate,' Chris lied. 'This gear's all the colours of a cow-field already, so a bit more muck won't show.'

Cappy nodded his understanding. 'Okay then. Just you keep away from those freaking Fey Knights though. They see a nice fresh soldier-boy coming along the trail they'll be like, yum yum, here's breakfast.'

Cappy didn't know that was about the worst thing he could have said, this of all mornings. 'How come you mention the Fey Knights, Cappy?'

Cappy pulled a face which said *how dumb are you?* 'Look Chris. I live in an old boat tied up next to Dolly Tregonhawke's pub. Come evenings I work behind her bar. I'm telling you bro, she's the freaking Fey Knight queen. Then of course here we are in Little Rillton, the Podunk capital of everything folksy and where Fey Knights is talked about more then the weather. "Oh how nice it is today Miss Dolly, and what do you think the Fey Knight's is at?" You can't *live* in L.R. Chrissy-san, and not mention the Fey Knights.'

Chris forced out a chuckle. 'I guess.' He reached out and patted the dog. 'Well, stuff to do, so see you round.'

Just before the young men went their separate ways, Cappy stopped and called. He should have told the Doberman he was stopping, for the dog did not and it jerked him almost off his feet.

'Cool it Tea-bag, you crazy mutt!' Cappy snapped. Tea-bag stood looking suitably contrite. 'Hey Chriisy-san. You seen Abe lately?'

'Yes, just last night. Why?'

'Do you think he's kinda off colour, or something? Just don't seem his usual self.'

Chris had noticed, but then Abe was doing long stints down at the museum and the library. Too much of that was bound to give you a glazed look. 'I think he's just tired. He's got all his usual stuff to do ... school, his supermarket job ... and then he's helping me with a ... project.'

Cappy looked quite concerned. 'Well, don't work the kid too hard. He's the kind of guy who'd give you his last cup of water even if he was dying of thirst. So ease up, okay?'

'Will do Cappy, but when did you turn into his papa-san?'

Cappy rolled his eyes and then turning to Dolly Tregonhawke's big mean guard dog, he tickled her between the ears. 'Hey, Tea-bag. How would you like a nice juicy soldier-boy steak for your dinner?' Tea-bag grinned a doggy grin and rolled over with her legs in the air.

'I'm off before the scary dog gets me. Later, Cappy.'

'Sure. Sya-freaking-nara, soldier-boy.'

'Up yours, Cappy-san!'

Chris and Cappy went in opposite directions, Cappy back towards town and Chris heading for the forest. Chris wondered if Cappy Shirakawa was like the Lucky Buddha. He didn't think he'd ever feel the need to "rub his tummy for good luck", but he always left his encounters with Cappy feeling uplifted and cheerful. Even today and that was saying something.

Chris was glad to be in the shade of the forest. He skirted the pond and cut through the lower wood made up mostly of pines. He miscalculated and the traverse took him much longer than he had anticipated. Rejoining an official path Chris quickened his pace.

The air was still along the bare earth paths and the weather had been mostly dry so the muddy patches had all dried up. At this point where the Park was open to the public, the path skirted a large open meadow which was an impressionist's dream of yellow buttercups and gently swaying grasses with smudges of pastel green and a skirmishing line of three freestanding oaks casting cool, liquid pools of blue-grey. At the far side of the meadow great oaks stood in ranks, vanguard of the ancient forest. In the thick of it, he felt sure, he would find the stone circle – very close to Abe Knapper's secret camp. The stones would wait as they had done for millennia; looking at his watch Chris hoped Kostja Claussen would wait too.

Kostja was sitting on a picnic table with his feet resting on the bench attached. A family saloon that had seen better days was the only car parked at the secluded lay-by. Kostja caught sight of Chris as he emerged from along one of the marked trails. Chris waved and Kostja smiled, please to see him.

'Did you bring Lady Thingamajig's whatsit book?'

'Lady Rosemary's grimoire. No, but I'm pretty confident I know where to find the stone circle. I figured it was too valuable to bring out here to the woods.'

'But what about the incantations? The ceremony or whatever, to close the gate.'

'Well, it looks like that involves a lot of blood and an altar stone, so we can forget about all that. Just let's see if we can find the place today and worry about the rest later.'

Kostja looked a little disappointed but shrugged it off. 'All that's in the book? Blood and altar stones? Any other surprises?'

Chris chewed his lower lip. 'You're not kidding!' Chris felt his heart-rate increase, but fought to control it with steady breaths. 'There were these two little black and white photos in there. Really old style of print and pretty well weathered so they are actually old in age as well as style. And the photos were … now I know this sounds nuts, but they were both of me.'

'You? But …'

'Yep! In one shot I'm tied to a tree. In the other … in the other my head is sitting on a tree stump.'

'Your head? *Just* your head?' Kostja's eyes widened.

'And a lot of blood pooled round. Bit of windpipe or something poking out from underneath. My own, chopped off head just sat there on a tree stump.'

Kostja sat heavily on the bench and scratched his head and if trying to take it all in. 'Well, I must say, you're taking this pretty calmly. If I'd seen a picture like that I'd –'

'Oh you can be sure I wasn't calm when I first saw the photos. But it only took me about ten seconds flat to work out it wasn't me … but at the same time it kind of was. Worse ten seconds of my life.' He thought of his encounter with the succubus. 'Well, almost the worst. See, in the picture of me tied to a tree, I'm wearing my Echo t-shirt and best trainers. Those are the clothes the succubus thing stole from me after she'd … you know. So it isn't me at all. It's her, only she looks like me, and she couldn't have met a better end. Ha fucking ha! I hope she saw it coming, like I did when she attacked me, and couldn't do anything about it.'

Kostja covered his eyes and shrank. It was as if Chris's description of the photos and his explanation had diminished him somehow. Another straw on the camels back, perhaps. How much "impossible" could a brain take?

'You say "she", but surely if the demon was a copy of you it would be "he"?'

'I don't know. If it starts off as a "she" and then turns into me, isn't it just a "she" that looks like a "he"?'

'On the other hand, if it's got all the bits and pieces that make it a he, I guess it *is* a he.'

'Whatever. I don't think it matters very much. Let's find this stone circle.'

The Sheldrake Memorial Museum was officially closed, but Mike Ryan had come in a little earlier than originally planned and opened it up especially for Abe Knapper. In a little while others would gather here: people who, like Mike, knew a little something about the Fey Knights; people who'd had a past fling with the Wiergan, or like Ernest Sheldrake – God rest his soul – had found cause to research the unique folklore of Little Rillton or indeed, had been a part of it. Secretive, though not a secret society, the group rarely met but events were unfolding, and demanded a response. Yes, the actions of the boy called Christian Wren De'Ath certainly demanded a response. They called themselves the Sandrin Syndicate, and they were gathering this afternoon.

Abe sat at a reading desk with Ernest Sheldrake's book open before him, several piles of other texts surrounding him like a protective wall and a mountain of bound newspapers. He flitted from page to page, from volume to volume, taking notes at a frantic pace like a man possessed. A line here drove him to the depths of the newspaper pile; a paragraph in this volume sparked something in his mind and he seized an earlier volume with such urgency that he lost his grip and the whole broadsheet-sized binder went crashing to the ground.

'Hey Abe! Be careful with those. They're irreplaceable!' Mike Ryan bent to retrieve the dishevelled newspapers. 'That is to say, irreplaceable without a long boring haul to Colindale, and I steer clear of London trips if at all possible.'

Abe did not apologise. Ignoring Mike he snatched the volume and slammed it down. Mike noticed his fevered looks and they frightened him. He was about to suggest that Abe took a break when the door to the reading room opened and in walked Reverend Charles Knapper. Mike Ryan was ignored for a second time in as many minutes.

'Abraham Knapper!' the vicar called in a voice trying hard to restrain anger and failing miserably. 'Where were you last night? Your mother and I have been worried to distraction.' Charles was dressed in a light brown suit and an open neck pale yellow shirt. Unusually for him, he had left his clerical collar at home.

Now it was the vicar's turn to be ignored as Abe spied a line in a newspaper that meant something to him. He let out a little gasp and scribbled a line in his notebook.

'Young man! I asked you a question. Mother went in to check on you last night and finds your bed virtually torn apart!'

Abe's head snapped up like a cobra about to spit venom. He almost barred his teeth and Charles Knapper was taken back, so un-Abe-like was the expression.

On the brink of something frightening and aggressive, Abe drew back. 'I told you, Dad. I'm helping Chris. It's *important* and I have to do this, so ... so give me some space.'

'Indeed it *is* important. Not denying it in the least. But you haven't answered my question. Where did you spend the night?'

Abe held back the impatience. 'At camp. My camp in the woods.'

'Jesus Christ in a nightcap and slippers!' Charles said spluttering and utterly exasperated. 'All this Fey Knight activity going on with people going missing and turning up *dead*, all centred on Wymes Forest, and *you* choose to spend the bloody night there? Have you lost your mind?'

Abe's head fell into his hands and he breathed deeply. He was on the watershed between exploding and bursting into tears. For a little while longer he managed the balancing act. 'I'm on the verge of finding something important,' he said, his voice quavering. 'Just ... just leave me in peace and let me get on with it.'

Charles shook his head, a thunderstorm flashing from under his thick white eyebrows. He muttered 'You haven't been the same since that De'Ath boy called at our house.'

Abe's intensity flew away like a flock of pigeons released from their loft. The tension left his features and he smiled. 'You don't know the half of it, Dad. My whole life changed direction that night.'

'Bit of a drastic statement, isn't it?'

Abe shook his head. 'Not at all. Just think about it for a moment. I discovered something *very* important about the kind of man I am.'

Charles took on an uncomfortable look. He knew what Abe was talking about, and he knew Abe knew he knew. He wasn't ready to deal with that and suspected he never would be. He'd had his suspicions since Abe was twelve years old and had never found the courage to talk about it or to support him.

Abe continued: 'Then I hear the most unbelievable story from Chris ... and I believe it. And following that, as if I hadn't had quite enough for one day, thank you very much, I hear you making a telephone call, in which you make it very clear you're something to do with all these Fey Knights goings on. And whoever you're talking to, the pair of you have got something nasty in mind for Chris because you and this other person are going to "deal" with him.'

Charles sat down at an adjacent reading desk. He looked deflated. 'It's not what you think.'

'Tell me then. Tell me what's going on.'

Charles looked for the words. They were not forthcoming.

Mike Ryan stepped in from the sidelines. 'You'll find out later Abe, when the others get here. The others, and Chris too.' Mike put a hand on Abe's shoulder. 'You did send him the message to meet here, didn't you?'

'You too Mike? You're tied up with all this stuff and you never mentioned *anything* to me. You've been helping me with the research, and all the time you know the answers.'

'Believe me Abe, I *don't* know the answers at all. I've barely got a grip of the questions.'

Abe did not appear to have heard. 'You're all in on it, and I've led him into a trap.'

'Only one way in, means only one way out,' Chris said looking round Abe's camp. 'That means we could easily be trapped.'

'Who'd want to trap us?' Kostja Claussen said. 'Anyway, if someone blocked off the path we could dive through the bushes. They're not impenetrable.'

Chris looked at the nearest clump of rhododendrons, the once glorious flowers now dead and withered to papery brown. They seemed to stir and something gleamed, like light from an amber eye. The impression was gone hardly after it had formed and lodged in the back of Chris's brain where it would fester and grow into tonight's nightmare.

'Okay Chris?'

'Huh? Oh yes, fine thanks. I just thought I saw something in the undergrowth.' A strong odour permeated the clearing. Fox perhaps, thought Chris. He had never smelt wolf before.

'Do bears shit in the woods? Yes, if this smell is an indication. How does your friend stay out here? It's enough to make you gag.'

Then, as quickly as it had arrived, the smell was gone. Once again, the air was fresh and heavy with the aromas of the forest. The warmth and heaviness of the air, the smells and the quiet all worked on Chris to make him feel powerful and potent. He thought of Gayle and the time together that they had never had. For the hundredth time, he made a silent vow to find her.

'Where's the stone circle then?'

Chris looked round. The grassy clearing was hemmed in on all sides by thick shrubs. Abe had made his shelter in the heart of one of the bushes weaving a wall with withies using living branches and boles as the framework and then lining the walls with mats of woven bracken. The packed earth floor was carpeted with more bracken, now browned with age, and there were several places to hang glow-sticks and stow gear. Abe's hearth, seat and dining table combined was a long, flat boulder just off centre of the clearing. Kostja sat on one end of the boulder and began caressing its cold surface.

Chris began to force little inroads into the bushes, looking for standing stones and soon found one. He called and Kostja crawled through the undergrowth on hands and knees until he came to Chris and the stone. He stood, reaching out to touch the stone which was about five feet high and covered in vine. Ripping away a small patch revealed the stone to be covered in a mass of concentric circles carved into the surface. Age had softened the lines and some of the circles were barely discernable.

'No wonder Danny and I never knew about the stone circle. All the stones must be overgrown and surrounded by bushes.'

Kostja stuck his tongue in his cheek and his eyes slid to the left. He appeared to be searching for a connection, seeking out some meaning to validate a theory. 'Maybe not *all*, the stones.' Suddenly he was crawling back through the bushes. 'Follow me,' he called. Chris followed.

He emerged from the bushes just in time to see Kostja trashing Abe's hearth. Oblivious or uncaring as to the dirty ash, Kostja swept an arm along the length of the boulder scattering hearth stones, ash and Abe's utensils.

'Be careful man!' Chris protested. 'Mind Abe's table.'

Kostja brushed the ash from his sleeve and turned on Chris with a raking glare. 'It's no table, kid. It's an altar stone.'

The world went out of kilter and dragged all Chris's senses towards Kostja Claussen's eyes, eyes which did not look human anymore.

'An altar stone,' Kostja repeated. 'And all it lacks is a little sacrifice.'

Reassured of their good intentions Abe sat on a padded green-leather chair in the conference room with his father, Mike Ryan and several other members of the Sandrin Syndicate. Abe felt a little silly that he had not confronted his father earlier. It would have saved a lot of needless heartache and speculation. Yes, the Reverend Charles Knapper did intend to deal with Chris De'Ath – by bringing him hear to meet with the Syndicate and facilitate an exchange of information. Some members of the Syndicate had been researching the Fey Knights phenomena for years, and Chris had stumbled across a live example almost by accident. There would be much to discuss.

It was small for a conference room, but the running of the Sheldrake Memorial Museum did not call for mass meetings. There was ample room for ten around the polished oak table, and the room was light and cool in décor. The predominant colour was green and the pastel walls boasted some nicely produced framed prints of the better known works by Monet. The minutes of the meetings were measured by a full case grandfather clock even as they were noted by the secretary, a task normally undertaken by Mike's wife, Polly.

Polly Ryan would be taking no notes today. Abe caught her eye and she smiled. She was younger than Mike and Abe felt certain that had he been wired for girls, he would have found her quite attractive. She was quite small and petite with lively, smiling eyes that appraised without judgment. Abe returned the smile, a gesture that was visceral rather that planned.

Next to Polly sat Adie Chapel. So the local police were involved too. Was his dog even in on the act? Abe wondered.

Mike poured tea from a big, brown ceramic pot into pale green teacups resting on matching saucers. He was asking people how they took their tea when the door opened and the Little Rillton Library librarian came in. She went through a hurried round of greetings and was introduced to Abe as Kate. She said she recognised him, but it had been some time since he'd been to the library. Her library name tag identified her fully as Miss K. Paterson. Another fine looking young lady. There were five seats left around the table, but Kate chose to sit next to Abe and he found himself thinking how Chris would be in his element.

The group engaged in small talk while Mike Ryan kept checking his watch and craning his head to look out of the window down into the courtyard. Abe was longing for the meeting to be called to order and the business of the day to begin, when throaty roar of someone double declutching an open topped red MG-T drifted up from below. Abe twisted round to look out of the window at his back. The driver was, to use the polite term, a "very large" woman.

Acting Detective Superintendent Dawn Bowman introduced herself and apologised for being late. She'd had something nasty to deal with in town which involved crime scene preservation and the coroner's officer.

'Poor chap's been dead for days,' Dawn said while claiming the end of the table opposite Mike Ryan and the vicar. 'But his family are away so nobody discovered him until the smell ... Well, I daresay you can draw the picture for yourself.' Dawn Bowman settled into her chair and took an iPAQ from her handbag. Removing the stylus she tapped in a code and readied the device for note taking. 'Now then, where is young Master De'Ath? I could be forgiven for thinking he's been avoiding me for weeks.'

'It's a bit early for him,' Abe said. 'I told him the meeting was for two o'clock. Sorry.'

Dawn looked a little miffed. 'Can you give him a call on his mobile? See if he can shift his arse a little? I can't spare much time with a murder to investigate.'

'I'll try, but the signal's not all that good in the Forest.'

Charles Knapper banged the table with his fist. 'Not him as well? Going into the Forest ... You're both as mad as March hares.'

'He'll be alright, Dad. He's with Kostja.'

Charles was about to remonstrate further, but he caught his words mid-launch and fixed an uncertain stair on Dawn.

Abe looked from a reddening Dad, to a Dawn almost grey. 'Who is Kostja, may I ask?' her voice was quiet and eyes wide.

'Kostja Claussen,' Abe said. 'He met Abe at the hosp –'

'Oh shit. Oh shit. Oh shit of a thousand shits,' Dawn whispered, her scatological references intended for her own ears. She stood and supported herself on outstretched arms, the centre of everybody's attention.

Swallowing hard she addressed the meeting. 'Kostja Claussen was the name of the man we're dealing with in town. Kostja Claussen is the name of murder victim.'

She fell heavily into her seat. 'And I'm willing to bet Kostja Claussens don't come very many to the pound.'

CHAPTER SIXTEEN

Key and Crowbar

The Unselost scion that was now Kostja Claussen held Chris is a tight, double-handed grip around the throat, but throttling was not his aim. He merely wanted to hold Chris close to observe the terror in his eyes and smell the fear in his sweat. He held lightly, just to maintain the optimum distance between their eyes as Chris stood rigid before him. Kostja sucked consciousness and self possession out of those terror-glazed eyes, and Chris weakened quickly past the point of no resistance. As Chris's will spilled away so the demon-Kostja drank greedily and grew stronger, and because increased strength requires more sustenance, he knew he would have to draw out Chris's fear for as long as his body could take it.

It was not long enough. Chris lost consciousness and Kostja threw his limp body onto the ash-stained altar like a discarded empty husk. His head made an audible crack on impact with the rock and his limbs fell like dropped pick-up-sticks. Kostja regarded the misarranged body with primeval hunger, lusting after blood and fear. There was another kind of lust too, for whenever this demon took human male form he felt an urgent pressure to be driven by the loins. Pressing a hand to the hardness between his legs, Kostja envisaged the perfect way to engender maximum fear while at the same time slaking his lust.

Incubus-Kostja could hardly wait for the De'Ath boy to regain consciousness. This boy was wanted by powerful forces far greater than Kostja, and unforgiving ones at that. But he was not needed *fully* intact. Kostja would complete the task he had been compelled to and would relieve the pressure to kill by expending his foul energies in another way. Afterwards he would make the blood offering at the Altar of Passage and pass into the other realm. Kostja laughed: oh the fear, the fear; the abject terror he would feast upon was almost too much to anticipate.

Kostja arranged Chris's body neatly on the altar, stretching it out straight with arms neatly folded over the chest, and legs as orderly as a soldier's standing to attention. He considered stripping the boy, but no, save that for when he was conscious; a nice terrifying prelude for the indignities and pain to come.

Without the need to hide behind Kostja's appearance the demon slowly began to slough it. Now it would revert, little by little, to its natural form. At the same time it dumped stolen memories, having no more use for them. The prey was trapped and helpless. The weapons could be discarded – except for one: it would retain its maleness until the job was done.

A long, mournful howl rose from deep within the thicket. Kostja laughed again. 'You wait you turn, Wolf-man,' he shouted. 'Enjoy the show, and then feast on my leavings.' Kostja picked up one of Chris's hands and let it fall back across his chest. 'And they will be precious few,' he whispered.

Chris opened his eyes. The light, filtered though it was through the canopy, hurt the back of his head. No, his head hurt quite sufficiently all by itself without having to blame the light. He recalled Kostja turning on him and attacking, closing the space between them in an instant, stop-gap movement that left him stunned. He remembered the paralysing touch and the hypnotic, yellow eyes. And he remembered thinking *Oh no. Not again.*

Chris tried to move and found, just as he had feared, that the smallest movement was beyond him. Like last time, he could breathe and blink and move his eyes but that was all. As if from a sharp blow, fire ripped through his brain and reminded him that his ability to feel pain was undiminished. He screwed his eyes shut in a futile effort to shut out the agony, and when he opened them again Kostja was peering down at him – except he was no longer entirely Kostja in appearance. The mouth was cruel and wider than Kostja's, revealing pointed and yellowing teeth. The eyes were no longer blue but yellow with no definition between pupil and iris. And the skin! The skin wore death's hue, blue grey suffusing through the previous skin tones, giving him a chilling, zombie look. When he spoke the voice had lost Kostja's tones and the German accent, and now sounded like wind through long grass.

'What have you done with Kostja?' Chris said, noting that he had retained one more capability since his last encounter with a demon. He could speak.

'No more than was necessary,' hissed Kostja.

'Where is he?'

'I have no reason to believe he is elsewhere than in his own bed, where I left him. Though by now, he is probably sharing the space with several thousand bluebottle grubs.'

Chris's imagination flashed a vision into his mind and the resulting pain far outweighed that produced by the crack on his head. He railed furiously and thrashed and fought – all internally; his body moved not in the least. He forced himself to relax and let the turmoil within him die.

'What about his family? What have you done to them?'

Kostja moved to within an inch of Chris's face and locked into him, eyeball to eyeball. 'I slit their throats. Or perhaps I wrenched their entrails out through their arses. Maybe I feasted on their flesh, or perhaps I did nothing at all to them. You should look to your own fate for any or all of the methods so far mentioned, and many others besides, may be your portion.'

Chris discovered there was another action open to him. He spat fully into the demon's face causing him to recoil for an instant.

A moment of fury transmuted into cruelty. With saliva dripping from his chin, Kostja said 'I have something for you, just as a prelude to the feast.' He squeezed at his crotch and Chris was instantly sickened. Kostja removed his shirt to reveal a grey-skinned torso, the ribs clearly defined and the stomach like a starved dog's. He began undoing the belt which hovered above an obscenely distended crotch.

'Can you see it coming Chris? Yes, of course you can! Just like my sister who lost her head. You can see it coming but you can't do anything about it! Ha bloody ha!' Kostja undid his belt and let the unclipped ends dangle as he leaned over Chris and ripped open his jacket. The hands, blackened and monkey-like went to his throat and ripped open his t-shirt from neck to navel. Chris prayed for the ability to move. Oh – how he would fight this foul creature, if only he could move. He would beat and thrash against it, and never give in, even if it meant death. He had experienced one of these creatures before. Never again.

Kostja hooked his disgusting, skeleton-thin fingers into the waist of Chris's combat trousers, just above the zip, when there was an explosion of noise from the undergrowth. Kostja pulled up with a start and then went to investigate.

No sooner was his back turned than something streaked down from an overhanging branch to land lightly on Chris's chest. It was Sem, and before Chris could utter a word Sem signalled silence, a finger laid in front of his lips. Sem scrambled up onto Chris's face. With his booted feet on Chris's upper lip, the underlying teeth giving him a firm platform, and taking his weight with a hand on each of Chris's cheekbones, he looked deeply into his eyes – first one and then the other.

There was a cry from the edge of the clearing and Kostja shot back. As Sem leapt up, Kostja slapped him from the air. The faerie dead-headed a clump of foxgloves and smashed into a thicket of rhododendrons sending up a cloud of withered petals and old leaves. Kostja ran to the scene to survey the damage, and Chris felt a tingling in his fingers and toes. He held up his hand and wiggled his fingers. Sem had lifted the paralysing spell, but Chris was too slow off the mark.

He sat up as Kostja looked over his shoulder. Seeing Chris move he leered, more demon-like than even a moment ago. Chris went for his survival knife and Kostja slammed into him knocking him back down onto the altar stone.

With unnatural strength, Kostja seized the boy's throat and slammed him hard, down into the rock. 'Looking for this,' he said holding Chris's knife first before his eyes and then to his neck, just below the left ear. With the razor edge famishing for blood a centimetre from Chris's carotid, and his other hand fumbling at Chris's trousers, Kostja leapt up on the stone and straddled his victim.

'No fun in a dead fish,' Kostja said. 'That interfering fae has made life interesting. Now you can writhe while I ride.'

The resolve was gone. The certainty that he would fight to the death was less than a memory. Chris knew now he would do anything, endure anything and even try to simulate enthusiasm, just for a little more precious life. Another minute, another second – it didn't matter. He wanted to live for just a little longer. His mind began to recede into a place where it could shut out the world, but just before his eyes closed he noticed a little insect with a bright red body, flitting manically over Kostja's chest. He found himself willing with all his remaining strength, that the insect would bite, and bite hard, giving him just a little time to escape. Suddenly all his hopes were on this little insect.

Chris was vaguely aware of a noise – tap-tap – like two rapid beats on a side-drum. And at the same instant the insect bit. Two sprays of bright blood burst from Kostja's chest, like tiny solar flares from a dying sun, and Kostja fell back and toppled from the stone.

Now was his chance! Chris sat up, but Kostja was on his feet once again. He had diminished: his body greyer and less human, his yellow eyes wide and fearful as he cradled his skeletal arms across two small wounds close to where his heart should be.

'Back! Back to your pit, foul and filthy spawn!'

Chris swung to the sound of the shouted curse to see a man advancing from the path with an outstretched hand holding a very modern-looking firearm. A broken, needle-thin bead of light was intermittently visible at the whim of swirling motes. It emanated from a device attached to the weapon and ended as a small dot of bright red light on Kostja's forehead.

'Be gone!' ordered the man who wore black leather motorcycle gear, and with that valedictory imperative, he put a round through the incubus's skull. Cut instantly from life he fell, like an inert object that had never ever possessed it.

Chris did not know whether to jump for the joy of life or fall on his knees before the man who had saved him. He did neither, running instead to the lifeless heap of grey flesh that had once been a demon. Retrieving his knife, which Kostja had dropped, he kicked his head and then stomped on it.

'That's it, my hearty lad!' the man called. 'Lay on with a vengeance! Vent your spleen righteously upon the devil's flesh. And then, if you please, take your place back upon the altar stone.'

When Chris turned to question the man, he saw the maw of a pistol barrel instead, and the needle-beam cutting the air to stain the pale skin that covered his breast bone.

'We have a need of you, not entirely dissimilar to the designs of our goblin friend over there. But ours can be met, be you alive or dead.'

Chris's emotions were being flick-flacked from one extreme to the other, several times a minute, and the trend appeared unlikely to change in the near future. Beyond the man with the gun he saw a very large woman step into the clearing.

'Don't listen to him Chris!' she shouted. The man spun and levelled his weapon at her.

'And who, pray tell, are you other than a hogshead of tallow?'

'You cheeky ... I'm Detective Superintendent Bowman, local police. Now ... drop your weapon.' Dawn held up her warrant card.

'I recognise no tipstaff, so I rather fancy I shall drop *you*, if my bullets can force their way through your elephant hide.' He aimed and fired, and Dawn's warrant card was ripped from her hand. She dived headlong into the undergrowth, an amazingly nimble manoeuvre so large a woman.

At the sound of the shot, Chris dived behind the altar stone. Then, as the man aimed into the bushes wherein Dawn had just buried herself, thunder split the air and thick white smoke filled half the clearing. The man in motorcycle leathers wheezed in pain and clutched at his shoulder. Chris peeped over the stone just in time to see Mike Ryan emerge from the bushes with a revolver that had to be more than a foot long. *Hoorah for the Redlegs colonel!*

Edmund Warwick, one time general for Parliament and present Wiergan, swayed on his feet, the red beam from his laser sights solid looking as it cut through the billowing gunpowder cloud, an interface for two weapons separated by 150 years. His eyes screwed up with pain, he failed to notice Dawn extracting herself from the tangle of shrubs.

The laser beam swayed through the cloud and every now and then, Edmund squeezed off an un-aimed shot. A bullet cracked past Chris's ear. Another took an inch square chunk of white stone out of the altar. Dawn hurried over to Mike. 'Here! Give me that!' she said taking the antique pistol. Pulling back the hammer she held it in a double-handed grip, aimed and then launched a lead ball on another peal of thunder. The round smashed the Steyr pistol out of Edmund's hand then deflected to glance off his temple and he fell, cursing. 'Felled by the butcher's daughter!' he cried.

'He's asking for *such* a smack.'

'You've shot him, Dawn. Doesn't that count? Mike replied taking back the pistol. 'Good shot by the way.'

'Bollocks was it! I was aiming for his chest.' She smiled, and then the two of them ran over to where Chris as still hiding.

'You alright, love?' she said helping Chris up.

'Erm ... yes ... I think.' Chris stood and tried to pull the two ends of his ruined t-shirt over his exposed chest when the sound of an approaching motorcycle filled the air.

Dawn checked the wounded Wiergan who was now unconscious.

'Oh bugger!' Mike said. 'Sounds like more of them.'

Events were still running far too quickly for Chris's assailed and befuddled mind. He felt safe with this police lady and Mike Ryan so close, but how long would that last?

Mike turned to Dawn as he held the Remington pistol up to the aim, pointing it towards the gap in the undergrowth. 'Do I shoot them? I mean ... is that allowed?'

'If that's what you have to do to save us, you shoot, and shoot straight. We'll worry about the consequences later.'

The engine noise raised to a level a notch below deafening and Mike took aim up along the path ... then pointed the pistol to the sky as Abe Knapper rode in on his dirt bike. He slewed to a halt, the back tyre throwing up clods of earth and describing a half-circle through the grass.

There was no time for explanations, only life-saving instructions. 'Get on, Chris!' Abe yelled, slapping the pillion seat with his gloved hand. 'They're right behind me!'

Other motorcycle engines could be heard over Abe's idling one.

'Take these,' Mike shouted slapping two items into Chris's hands. One was the pistol, the other – Chris had no idea.

'And this,' Dawn said hauling his pack from the ground and chucking it at him. He slipped the straps over his arm, did up his jacket and stuffed the other items down his front at the same time as he was rushing towards Abe and his bike.

No sooner had Chris's bottom touched the pillion seat than the bike leapt forward with such speed that he nearly fell off backwards. Abe blipped the brakes to facilitate a quick recovery, and then they were off. As Abe turned onto the main path two monster bikes roared up from the right, and the chase was on.

Abe had the advantage, except for where the bridleway was straight. He pulled away round the bends, and the two Wiergan gained on him on every straight and narrow. They twisted and turned sending up dust and clots of dry mud. Abe was one with his machine and could make it leap exposed tree roots and slew round tight bends. Chris for the most part held Abe tight round the waist and kept his eyes shut. It was the only way he could lay into such acute turns; at one stage he felt his knee scraping the ground.

The speed of the ride terrified Chris and he wondered if they shouldn't just pull up and run through the undergrowth where the Wiergan couldn't follow, until they reached another straight run and Chris forced himself to look over his shoulder. What he saw made him wish for even more speed.

There was a commotion of exploding vegetation as the trailing biker bit dust. Chris thought the rider had just lost it until he saw something leap on the remaining Wiergan. The "something" was very wolf-like, but not entirely wolf. Whatever its true nature, it tore the Wiergan's arm off in one awful rending of its massive jaw. Man bike and wolf-thing rolled over and over along the dirt sending up a brown cloud from which only the wolf emerged, and it was faster than any bike. Chris screamed and pulled himself tighter into Abe's back. Something hard poked him in the ribs, and gave him a little hope.

Reaching into his combat jacket, he pulled out the Remington. He pulled back the hammer until it wouldn't go any further and then, with one arm maintaining a sturdy grip round Abe, he half turned on the pillion, aimed as best he could and fired. The wolf, a mere bike's-length behind, snapped at the lead ball which seared past harmlessly. It bounded forward and Chris fancied he could feel and smell its breath. Its eyes were the same yellow eyes of the succubus and the demon-Kostja. Chris cocked the weapon again and fired point-blanc. This time the ball struck the top of the wolf-thing's head. Its nose was slammed into the ground and it rolled head over heels until the bike rounded a bend and the beast was out of sight.

After a few more moments of furious riding Abe pulled up and ordered Chris off. Abe killed the engine, leapt off himself and dropped the bike at the side of the road. Beckoning Chris to join him he began fighting his way through the undergrowth.

'Where?' Chris managed.

'The old tower,' Abe replied, and then a lop-sided smile spread across his face. 'I've found the Unsullied Jewel.'

The boys were soon through the border of undergrowth and into the ancient wood. Chris was relieved to feel cool after the red-hot excitement of the last hour or so. The forest airs salved him and light breezed caressed him back to strength.

The deeper they moved into the forest, the darker it grew. The cool became brooding, and the trees seemed to have eyes. He wondered if any of Sem's friends had decided to become trees or indeed, if any of demon-Kostja's fellow demons could take on tree-form. Chris hoped Sem was alright and that he had recovered from the demon's attack.

After half an hour Abe and Chris sat on the fallen merlon at the foot of the tower.

'I didn't know you knew how to find the old tower.'

Abe smiled. 'I had to get my own back, once you and Danny had ferreted out my camp.'

'I suppose.' Chris wondered at Abe's ability to smile after all they had gone through. 'So, show me the Unsullied Jewel then. Where did you find it?'

'Aha! That would be telling, wouldn't it?'

'Well, let's just see it then.'

Abe winked and then put his hand inside his red, white and blue nylon motorcycle jacket – just as the wolf-beast crashed in through the trees. It fixed the boys with its yellow eyes and its lips curled up in a lupine smile.

'Keep behind me, Abe,' Chris said drawing the pistol.

The wolf spoke, the sounds of near-human words coming from the mouth of a beast almost as devastating as physical blows. 'I can't say your leaden bullets don't hurt me, for they do. But they cause me no lasting harm, and so, you only delay the inevitable and make me inclined to prolong your suffering.'

Chris fired anyway. The huge man-animal stumbled but soon regained its footing. It shook, dog-like, and the ball, now severely misshapen, flew from its thick tan-grey main. It slowly rose onto all four paws and closed the gap.

Abe picked up a long length of fallen branch and flew at it with an intelligible war-cry. The wolf swiped him sideways with a massive paw-strike that left the boy unconscious.

'Now come,' the wolf said. 'Back to the Altar of Passage, for there your destiny awaits you.'

Chris wanted to check his reality meter, but why bother? Even if he had one, he knew it would be off the scale. Meanwhile, Abe was lying on the ground unconscious and the wolf eyed him hungrily. Chris had to put lunch out of the wolf's mind and the only way he could think of doing that was to rile the beast to such a degree that it would forget all about Abe.

'Listen. You're just a stupid dog, so don't be talking like Shakespeare. Just … just piss off!' Suddenly, bravado didn't seem like such a good idea.

A deep staccato sound came from the wolf as its shoulders quaked. It was laughing. Rising again it bounced deftly to where Abe Knapper lay. It licked and snuffled Abe's neck.

'Leave him alone!' Chris ordered, raising his pistol once again. It seemed his plan had the opposite effect, or perhaps the wolf was clever enough to see through it.

'Come with me and this one lives. Make my job difficult, and you may watch while I devour the flesh from his bones.' To underline the threat he took the collar of Abe's jacket in his fangs and ripped. Abe's body moved limply from the assault.

'Hey! Fleabag!' The voice came from above. 'Why don't you just do like the man said, and piss off?' Sem hovered below the crown of a hawthorn tree.

Chris noticed two other tiny flying beings. One he'd seen before, all that time ago on the day Marc and Shaun were taken. He was youthful of face and slim of body, and dressed in a Tarzan-like loincloth. His wings were like those of a dragonfly and he appeared to have armed himself with a large rose thorn. The third one sported white feathered wings and a complicated hair style with shaved sides and a long topknot folded over giving him the appearance of a silver-haired Japanese warrior.

'Who of the Host dares to address me so?' the wolf said, standing tall but with an air uncertainty even Chris noticed.

'My name is Semangeloph,' Sem said. 'And I am sure you've heard of me – and my sons.'

The wolf hunkered down towards the ground, its hackles raised and its tail between its legs. With no more interest in Chris or Abe, it appeared to have been seized by abject fear. It tried to run, but if such a creature had a quota of luck, today its luck was all out. The three tiny fliers flew straight through it, like bolts of lightning. As each one entered the beast's body there was an implosion; the wolf shrank in upon itself and light burst from its eyes and ears. Last in and last out, the little loin-cloth covered fellow burst from the wolf's side and the creature shrivelled and died. As Chris watched, it became a pool of oily black, which slowly soaked into the ground making it hiss and bubble as if assailed by strong acids.

The three faeries alighted on the fallen merlon and appeared to be brushing themselves down when a hand fell lightly on Chris's shoulder. Chris turned and looked into the eyes of Tarn. Tarn smiled, and the rest of the world ceased to exist.

Senoi hated the stench of werewolf. He broke off his ablutions only to watch Semangeloph and Tarniel lead the boy along the Hidden Path, and once they had melted from this world, he pulled at his wings to rid them of the loathsome residue.

His brother Sansenoi descended close by, his dove-wings white and unsullied. 'Will you watch over the fallen warrior while I join our brothers and keep him safe?'

Senoi looked over at the unconscious boy. 'Yes, that I will, though I smell no other enemies near by. I smell nothing of the Unselost Mass except that which clogs my pores!'

Sansenoi chuckled, then slipped through the ether and joined the Hidden Path.

Senoi pulled up a handful of damp moss and scrubbed his arms with it. Better to smell of forest than of werewolf. Running a finger between each toe, he was a free as he could be of Unselost residue until he could get home and bathe. Throwing his head back he laughed heartily, for no apparent reason and then springing into the air, his wings became a blur and he flew across the old tower clearing to land lightly on Abe Knapper's back. He walked up and balanced on Abe's right shoulder blade.

He looked down at the boy, a huge grin on his face. 'Sleep well, bearer of the Jewel. None shall harm you here, while I stand guard.'

Had he been awake, Abe would have felt no fear and he would have known that Senoi, armed with an impenetrable shield of joy and barely contained, benign mischief, made him safe from any scion of the Mass.

Back in another clearing all was silent. Two bodies marked it as a place of recent conflict. The earth had started to claim demon-Kostja's body as insects crawled over it and darkening blood soaked into the ground.

The other body spoke. 'One short sleep past,' quoted Edmund Warwick, his breath short and ragged. 'We wake eternally, and Death shall be no more. Death, thou shalt die!'

'Oh do shut up, Edmund. There is absolutely *no* need to be quite so dramatic.' She stooped and picked up the piece of altar stone that one of Edmund's wayward bullets had dislodged. It was pure white and crystalline, unlike the rest of the altar and she wondered if it might be special in some way.

Edmund opened his eyes weakly and looked up at the green-clad woman. 'Lady ... Rosemary. I have ... failed you. And I go to my grave ... unfulfilled in my duty.'

Rosemary hated robes, so cumbersome and impractical. She preferred the strength of waxed cotton and sensible skirts, completely reflected in her present choice of heavy duty green jacket and green plaid skirt. But she did have a sense of humour, and at the collar she had pinned a little silver brooch fashioned to resemble a besom.

'You have nothing but a scratch, silly man. And I'm not at all sure you've failed in the least.' She walked over to the demon's body and plunged her hand into the cranial cavity through the exit wound. She withdrew it and rubbed the matter between finger and thumb. 'How unpleasant,' she said. 'Like sago pudding.'

She went back to Edmund and kicked him. 'Now, up on your feet, my man, and come with me.'

He rose, groggily, and joined his mistress by the altar stone. 'Should I set a petard to lift this infernal gate to the heavens?'

With one hand Lady Rosemary took her lieutenant by the elbow and then placed her gory hand directly onto the stone.

'Certainly not! Why use a crowbar when we have the key?'

Edmund didn't understand. His looks said as much.

'Blood's the key,' Rosemary said. 'The boy's would have done nicely, but I can't see why this won't work.'

With those words, and a few others uttered under her breath, she and Edmund Warwick slipped through onto the Hidden Paths. They had no map, but they had an eternity to find their way.

CHAPTER SEVENTEEN

Flaming Nora at Flint House

It was difficult to do anything with one hand and Cappy wasn't there to help. Abe Knapper grinned at the thought of how his life had changed with such rapidity. He twirled the chocolate biscuit in the fingers of his good, right hand, while looking forward to the day the plaster could come off his left arm. He placed the bar in the protruding wiggling fingers of his left hand but there was no strength in them, and try as he might, he could not get the wrapper off. By comparison, making and pouring tea single-handed was a doddle. Determined not to ask Mum for help – she fussed and faffed around in a most annoying way – he ripped it off with his teeth.

Abe sat at his desk and disobeyed one of his own rules: he placed the mug of tea on his desk top where it could easily tip and ruin his computer keyboard. Rules didn't seem to matter very much anymore. Only two weeks ago the rules of the universe disintegrated, so why worry about spilt tea and damaged keyboards? Leaning closer to the monitor he checked the clock in the bottom right-hand corner. Just after two o'clock, so there was almost half an hour before the meeting was due to begin, and he would be expected to tell the gathering everything he knew about the Fey Knights.

Abe recalled all the extraordinary events of two weeks ago, in reverse order. First, waking to excruciating pain – a broken arm, inflicted by a blow from a ... well let's think about that in a minute; a little winged faerie-lad less than half the size of an Action Man asking him if he was alright; the attack of the ... okay, can't put it off any longer ... the *talking* wolf; the mad flight through the woods on his motorbike with Chris squeezing him so tight – he smiled at that thought; the gunfight in the camp-clearing between Mike Ryan and the police lady verses a Wiergan-biker and a half-human ... thing. Abe wondered if Chris remembered the same things, and if so, just where was he remembering them? Chris was gone, like all the others. The Fey Knights had him, and nobody knew their purpose for sure, but Abe believed it was for the good. He had to, for otherwise he had delivered Chris up to heaven-knows-what.

The faerie or rather angel, as Abe preferred to believe, hadn't given him much of clue. 'Chris is with my brothers,' was all he'd said with a miniature Mona Lisa smile. 'They will do all they can to keep him safe.' Then the cavalry arrived in the shape of Superintendent Dawn Bowman and Mike Ryan. When he looked again, the tiny angel was gone. Abe hadn't decided whether to mention the little being at all this afternoon – it was a little embarrassing. Somehow wolves that had the power of speech and demi-demons were easier to discuss than ... faeries. Abe and Chris shared similar feelings in that respect.

They all arrived in time for the meeting which was held in the sitting room. The study was too small to accommodate the Sandrin Syndicate in comfort, so they circulated and chatted and drank tea among the cut crystal and the leather suite and the professionally framed prints and photos. Prints came and prints went, but two had always shared a little nook by the cocktail cabinet. There was a young man in a railway porter's uniform and another lad looking very proud in a First World War uniform standing at ease with a rifle, the fixed bayonet of which reached the brim of his service cap. The photo frames bore little brass nameplates telling the world that the railway porter was "Napper" and the soldier "Spike". Abe had never quiet worked out how these two lads fit into the family story. Whenever broached, the subject was changed. Suffice to say the soldier must have had some connection to the family, for "Spike" was the nickname Charles Knapper often used when addressing his son.

Fed up with people enquiring after his health and making sympathetic noises concerning his broken arm, Abe was pleased when his father called the meeting to order. He certainly wished Cappy was here with him now instead of away in the woods being crazy as only Cappy knew how. The meeting broke two hours later for more tea and a leg-stretch, and then reconvened until late in the evening. Abe told everything. Absolutely everything and didn't falter when he came to the bit about the faerie. There was much discussion, a lot of which concerned the mysterious events of five years ago to which only Abe, it seemed, was ignorant. And then Acting Detective Superintendent Dawn Bowman summed up and did this by way of an address to Abe.

'You see, Abe. The Wiergan were key players until five years ago. Just like some of us were. They were on one side, us on the other in the continuance of a conflict that had been going on for centuries. And then something happened. Call it a war, a conflict come to ahead. Call it anything you like, the bottom line was the Wiergan lost their power and as for us, there was no more need for us because the Wiergan were out of it.

'The trouble is, they didn't stay out of it. They *had* been servants of a master who fell, and when he fell their purpose was at an end. But now it seems they've found a new purpose, and that purpose is not to serve, but to lead, drawing the remnants of their master's power to themselves.

'So, that's the Wiergan. But then on top of it all we get these other oddities – the Fey Knights and the … other things.'

'Wolves and demons!' Abe said.

'Precisely. Now, it all makes pretty good sense, what the character called Sem told Chris De'Ath about the … what was it? Host and Mass?'

'The Selost Host and the Unselost Mass,' Charles Knapper said.

'That's the buggers! With the Mass-lot drawing their power from the corpse of the old master –'

'I never said that!' Charles said. 'And I don't believe Chris did either.'

'I'm extrapolating. Where was I? Oh yes … with that lot getting power from the Mass, I think the Wiergan are looking for a way to get in on the act, and grab some power for themselves.'

People nodded sagely and sipped tea.

'To what end?' Charles said. 'From what I gather the Unselost Mass and its scions – the wolves and demons – are driven by hunger. But what drives the Wiergan, who are after all, nothing but men?'

'The same,' Dawn said. 'They hunger for power.'

The doorbell rang and Abe rose to answer it, but Charles fixed his eye then shook his head. 'Daisy will get it,' the elderly Reverend Knapper said. 'Sit down.'

'It's not quite like Sem told Chris then?' Abe said. 'Whereas you – us? – are kind of on the Fey Knights' side, the Wiergan aren't trying to help the Mass, they want to exploit it.'

'As far as we can tell,' Dawn said. 'And until now we weren't entirely sure whose side we were on. Thanks to the work of Ernest Sheldrake and Polly Ryan,' Dawn said, nodding and smiling towards Polly, ' ... we were fairly sure the Fey Knights were benign sorts, despite the disappearances, but then all bets were off once Marc Stockdale and Shaun Ashton were taken, rapidly followed by the other events.'

The room grew quiet while the events were contemplated: Danny, Kostja, and several Wiergan dead; several young people missing. Before the thread could be picked up there was a knock at the door and Daisy's head peered round.

'Someone to see you Dad,' she said.

'Can't they wait? I'm rather tied up at the moment.'

'Sorry vicar-bro,' said the visitor who didn't wait to be invited in. 'There's someone to see you who won't wait no longer than I will.'

'Cappy!' Abe said standing in astonishment.

'Hi, Abe!' Cappy Shirakawa said, his face beaming as if Abe was the person he wanted to see most in the whole world.

Then the second visitor stepped though. Abe and the Sandrin Syndicate stared at the spectre filling the doorway, and then Dawn Bowman rose to her feet and pressed both hands to her heart.

'Flaming Nora!' she said. 'I think we'd better give our visitors a seat.'

CHAPTER EIGHTEEN

The Olrock

From the heat of flight and the jaws of a talking wolf, Chris entered a non-place of cold and sensory deprivation. Surrounded by whiteness thicker than fog and yet without the substance of fog, he saw only bright cloudy white. A hand held an inch from his face did not register against the void and Chris wondered if his body had become one with the whiteness. He was vaguely aware of walking, but there was no sensation of the ground beneath his feet. He could hear echoes within his mind, but no sound came from his surroundings. It was as if he *were* the surroundings – like he had somehow expanded to become a massive amorphous being without boundary, drifting in an empty sea. He felt naked and touched over his entire surface by a numbing cold that had nothing to do with climate or temperature and when he breathed the air passed through him making his lungs – if he still had any – redundant.

And then he was assailed from all sides, above and below as his infinite self rushed back towards the centre that was his body, like the Big Bang in reverse. Sound and colour and feeling smacked into him from every angle and with such intensity that fell to his knees. As he hit the ground he sucked in air like a newborn and he heard himself cry out.

'You're safe, Chris. We have arrived.'

The blue blur by his side coalesced into Tarn, dressed in baggy jeans and a collarless, light blue shirt that was far too big for him. Later he would explain that he'd borrowed the shirt from PC Shadrack's washing line, but for now Chris was just glad of the supporting arm that Tarn threw round his shoulders, and he stood shakily to take his new surroundings. There were leaves; green, and not purple or scarlet as he may have imagined. There were trees, firmly rooted and not skipping around free. Bird sounds came to his ears that were quite surprisingly bird-like and the pungent aroma of damp leaf mould and the herbs of the forest, though perhaps stronger than that of Wymes Park, was not altogether dissimilar.

'Off the *olrock* with you. We don't want to be the cause of a jam,' Tarn said in a policemen's tone that must have seeped out of his shirt. He wore it un-tucked and the tails came to his knees. Tarn gently manoeuvred Chris from a rectangle of polished stone set in the ground. Like sentinels a circle of standing stones stood among the surrounding trees.

'The *olrock*? A kind of ... door?' Chris said as the shock of transition became subsumed by growing curiosity.

'More of a beacon really,' Tarn said. 'The Hidden Paths are hard to navigate.'

'He can't do it at all,' came a voice from a low branch. Sem sat cross-legged preening one wing. 'They need us to find their way through the Paths.'

'It's true,' Tarn said. 'We can get onto the Hidden Paths, but there would be no point without those from the First Realm to guide us.'

'Without us, the ones you call the Fey Knights and others like them wouldn't have a chance. They'd hop onto the Paths and come out anywhere between

1066 and a week next Tuesday. Like moles blundering round in blinding sunlight and no tunnel to guide them.'

'And so, you use these *olrocks* as beacons?'

'They do the trick,' Sem said. 'Sometimes they're at the centre of a stone circle. Others are just big boulders, often close to a path ... that's "path" in the normal sense of the word.'

'And ... the old tower?'

Tarn chuckled. 'Let's just say the fallen wallstone didn't fall without a little push.'

Chris nodded then gave himself some time to let things sink in. He patted himself down and satisfied that he, and all his gear not including the Remington, had made it intact, he began to make himself more comfortable. 'Are the others – Abe, Mike Ryan and the police lady – going to be okay?'

Another voice came from on high. The faerie with the dove wings and the silver hair in the Samurai top-knot sat on a low branch, his bare legs dangling. 'My brother Senoi will keep watch over your friend,' Sansenoi said. 'And the Mass-creatures have no interest in the others.'

Naturally there were questions that wouldn't wait, foremost of which concerned Chris's missing friends and acquaintances. Tarn explained that he would soon meet them, with the exception of Gayle. She had never been taken by the Fey Knights, and as painful as it was to contemplate, it had to be that she had been a victim of certain scions of the Unselost Mass. Whether she was alive or dead, Tarn could not say. Chris hid his fear and disappointment in needlessly checking his survival equipment. Tarn also explained that Chris's role in the struggle between the Host and the Mass would be made clear, once they reached Brikadden, the mountain village of the Ieladhrim.

Taking off his combat jacket – it was too hot for such a thick garment – Chris stuffed it into his rucksack and tied a knot at the neck and another at the hem of his sliced t-shirt to hold it together at the front. Then he took up the item given to him by Mike Ryan. It was a draw-string bag containing a belt and three black leather pouches of slightly varying size and design. One was full of percussion caps shaped like tiny copper top-hats; one was filled with lead ball and the third with cartridges. It was a shame the big old Remington was nowhere to be seen. Chris guessed he must have dropped it on the other side. He came through, but the pistol had been left behind. He thought of his recent transit and how it might have been achieved.

'Has Abe still got the key? I mean ... the Unsullied Jewel?'

Tarn exchanged glances with both the faeries. 'It's still with him.'

'How will we get back home without it?'

'We are home, my brothers and I. The Jewel is merely another kind of beacon that attracts us to the right place and the right time. Now we have you, we don't need it anymore.'

Chris did not entirely understand. 'So, we're here. What now?'

Sem hopped from his perch and descended to land on Tarn's shoulder. 'Are you hungry?'

'Now that you come to mention it.'

'Good! Then we will eat, and while we eat we'll talk. This land around you may not look very different from home, but you will soon meet beings who will test your sanity.'

'Even more than you do? No offence and all that.'

'None taken! Just keep an open mind, and don't let it get all clogged up by what you think is possible or not.'

'Erm ... got to ask. Dragons?'

Tarn and Sem exchanged looks and both began to laugh, long and heartily.

'I'll take that as a no, then,' Chris said as his ears grew warm.

'No, no, no, Chris. Don't get cross. There are dragons, but not the kind you have in mind.'

'No, added Sem. And they're a lot closer than you might think.'

They were off again, sharing their private joke at Chris's expense.

Sansenoi flitted down and hovered in front of Tarn and Sem, staring them into silence. Then he zipped through the air to hover inches from Chris's face.

'Let the land and its inhabitants impress themselves upon you slowly,' Sansenoi said. 'Be alert, and ready to act, but don't rush the ways of the land.'

Chris nodded sagely. 'Thanks for that,' he said. *Don't understand a bloody word*, he thought.

Tarn led Chris over to a clearing where the sun shone through hot and bright and motes flew with tiny flies while swifts dipped down in squadrons for a meal.

'Dragons aside,' Sem said. 'A being, so very different from anything you can imagine, is flying towards us right now. And his mission has all to do with you.'

'Me? I don't think I like the sound of that.'

'Nothing at all to worry about, once you get over the initial shock of the meeting,' Tarn said. 'Now, first things first.' Tarn spread a cloth on the ground and began to produce various items of food from a pack that had been stowed in the undergrowth. 'We'll take bread and water and a bit of dried meat – and then we'll have our magic food that raises the spirit, gives energy and tastes of heaven.'

With the meal spread out Tarn sat on the ground with Sem at his shoulder like a pirate's parrot, and Chris sprawled in the grass with Sansenoi sitting on his uplifted knee. Chris was glad of the food and gobbled down his share of the bread and dried meat. It was soon gone and washed down with cool water.

Tarn reached over and drew his pack close. 'Now for the magic food,' he said reaching into a side pocket.

Chris was all anticipation wondering what kind of delicacy would be worthy of the name magic food, when a small purple and silver pack hit him in the chest.

'Fruity Bites?' Chris held the pack in one hand and looked at it as if he was missing something. 'Mum buys these from the supermarket!'

'And very delicious they are too,' Tarn said. 'Here, have another couple of packs. Stick them in you pocket for later.'

Chris stuffed the extra packs into his combat jacket. 'But ... it's just bits of dried fruit. It's not magic.'

'Is to me! It's clean and ready-packed and just enough for a snack. My knapsack's full of them.'

'Stop rabbitiing on about magic and chuck me a raison,' Sem said.

Chris ripped open the pack and did as he was told. Sem caught the offering and munched into it, holding it in both hands like a huge piece of melon.

'Where do you get them, Tarn?'

'The same shop your mum does, I suspect. Whenever I'm your side of the Path, I pay a visit and get the supplies in.'

'And the money? Where do you get the money?'

Tarn stopped mid-munch. 'You're supposed to have money?'

Chris didn't ask; he just hoped Tarn was joking. He settled to the serious business of eating magic food.

Before the meal was complete Senoi appeared and told the diners that the warrior was safe and collected by his friends.

'He means Abe,' Tarn said.

Senoi hadn't been there long before Sem and Sansenoi departed for a sojourn in the First Realm. Sem snapped Chris a tiny salute by way of a valediction, hovered with Sansenoi over the *olrock*, and was gone. Tarn explained that the First Realm was the natural home for all those of the Selost Host, and that they were obliged to return there at intervals for their continued wellbeing.

'It is not a place we can go, the likes of you and I,' Tarn said. 'But nor is it a place from which the Host can long absent themselves.'

'What about you, Senoi?'

Senoi's dragonfly wings caught the sunlight and refracted it into rainbow starbursts at each movement. Although he sat on top of Tarn's pack, he never lost his keen, almost birdlike alertness. 'I've been home more recently than Sansenoi my brother, and Semangeloph my father. I'm safe to tarry a little longer yet.'

'Which is as well,' Tarn said. 'For once our visitor has done with us we must go to the Paths again. Brikadden won't wait for us forever.'

Tarn explained that the indigenous people of this land, which included Tarn himself, spoke a language that Chris would need to know and that the visitor would see to it he did. Tarn warned that the visitor's appearance would shock, but no warning could ever prepare Chris for his first meeting with Drone.

Drone styled himself as First of the Free Drones, and he was to all intents and purposes a five foot high cross between a man and a grasshopper. Man only in similarity of general body design – a head, a body and two pairs of limbs – he also had wings, not entirely dissimilar to Senoi's although many times the size. He had an elongated, vaguely horse-shaped head with mouth-plates instead of lips and his exoskeleton was covered by an iridescent membrane that flashed blue-green, red-yellow and bronze depending how the sunlight reflected. Drone stood upright on two legs and had two arms and hands with bony fingers. He wore no clothing save a narrow band of cloth that hid the place where his legs joined the abdomen, which extended to the level of what in a human would be his knees.

Drone's arrival from the sky, unannounced, slap smack into the centre of the clearing did nothing for Chris's digestion. He was beginning to find, however, that his recovery time from shocks of this nature was improving dramatically.

Drone addressed himself to Tarn and Senoi but not in any manner that Chris could detect. There was no sound other than the occasional staccato-hiss resulting from the tremor of wings, but from the body language of his friends there certainly seemed to be a conversation going on.

After several moments Tarn turned towards Chris. 'Drone, First of the Free Drones, greets you well. He hopes that you may be blessed with the courage of the Slain Prophet, the compassion of the Prophet Jason and ... and several other benedictions that will go straight over your head. In short, he says pleased to meet you.'

'Erm ... tell him likewise ... and stuff.' What did you do? Shake hands, or rub your knees together until they stridulated? Chris settled for a curt nod of the head. Drone responded with an altogether more graceful movement.

The introductions over, Drone moved straight to business and communicated his intent to Tarn. Tarn interpreted.

'By your leave, Drone will fit you with the devices that will make you receptive other tongues, including *Hereek*, which is what the people of this land call their language.'

Chris wondered what the device would look like and envisaged something like oversized headphones. 'Tell him to go ahead,' and then as an aside for Tarn's ears only. 'Will it hurt?'

He hadn't expected an answer in the affirmative, and was rather sorry he'd asked. Apparently there would be a certain amount of discomfort while the device seated itself into the bones of his skull. If Chris didn't already know "discomfort" was a medical term for "bloody well hurts loads", the bit about seating itself into his skull was enough to make him change his mind. He didn't though, and Drone came towards him with a tiny black object, the size of a hearing-aid battery, on the end of a bony finger. With much will power, Chris held steady while Drone reached up and placed the tiny device gently onto the skin of his left temple. He produced a second, identical device and placed it on the right temple.

'As soon as they bed down you will start to understand the local language,' Tarn said. 'When somebody speaks to you, the meaning of their words will be manifest within your mind. Furthermore, you will then remember the words they used and will be able to speak them. It will take a while to get used to the mechanics of *Hereek* – they use a lot of clicks and glottal stops – but you'll pick it up.'

Pictures then flooded Chris's mind; they scared him, for he did not know their origin, but they also caressed the thought-paths of friendship and acceptance.

'Oh, I forgot. You will be able to understand Drone as well, and others of the Kern race.'

'He speaks in ... pictures?'

Tarn smiled and nodded.

'In that case, I think I've got incoming.' It was then that the first pain struck: it was like a mild burning sensation directly under each device.

'Don't rub! You might dislodge them. The pain will pass quickly and by morning the language buttons will part of you. They will seat themselves and the skin will heal over them.'

The pain grew worse and made Chris's eyes water. Then an image of cool water came into his mind. There were other pictures too, but Chris started to feel meaning rather than notice the picture.

Take this, Drone said. He held out a small flask of green glass. *It will ease the pain and help you to sleep.*

It didn't taste like medicine at all; it tasted of honey, with a cinnamon aftertaste, but the draft soon got to work. The pain went through burning to mild irritation to a slightly warm feeling. And at the same time Chris became very, very sleepy. Tarn and Drone laid him down on a bed of quickly gathered fronds and he drifted off feeling cosy and protected, little knowing that he would wake to a new kind of terror.

CHAPTER NINETEEN

A Kumakkashi Welcome

Far to the north high in an isolated range of mountains the Spider-Queen slept in her lair protected from everything except dreams.

'Paul!' It came out as a scream, as it always did but this time it tore out from the centre of the old woman's chest. She sat up from her couch blinking away the mid-afternoon nightmare as she splashed cold water on her face from a bronze and silver bowl. She rearranged her purple robes. Once Rosemary had eschewed robes, but now that she was less mobile, she found them comforting, and they certainly impressed the feeble-minded dolts who formed her court.

The door burst open and her lifelong retainer rushed in, worry in his eyes.

'It's nothing, man. Why must you always panic so?'

'Forgive me, my lady. The servants –'

'The servants heard me call out in my sleep. That is all! Now, if you don't mind ...'

'Of course, my lady.' Edmund Warwick, held unnaturally to no more than forty years of age by his mistress's manipulations of the dark powers, nodded and turned to go.

Lady Rosemary followed him out into the cold hall. 'And yet ... stay a while. Perhaps there is a need for us to speak.' Something niggled at the edges of her mind. Not this time the writhing of the Unselost Mass, bridled and yet untamed by her sharply honed arts, nor the lingering of that old, old recurring nightmare: there was something else. She braced herself against the granite mantle-shelf above a fire of logs, and almost staggered as she raised a hand to her temple. Edmund closed on his mistress, lest she needed support. She waved him off.

'It is ... as if a little fly treads upon the weave of my thoughts, like ... Ah! I have it!'

'My lady?' Edmund was quite encouraged at his mistress's rapid recovery.

'It's him! The boy has touched the Hidden Paths. After so long, he comes.' She was carried back to another time and another world. 'Such a shame we couldn't have ended him on that altar stone all those long years past.'

'It is surely more than a century ma'am.' For some moments Edmund was lost in contemplation of the unnatural span of his years. 'I wonder if the young whelp has changed.'

'It's more than a hundred years for us, but perhaps only an instant to him. We suspected he would come. And now he is here he must die. So very far to travel for such a final and useless end.'

Edmund nodded. 'I shall assemble a company and lead it myself.' As he waited for his lady's leave a thought occurred to him. 'Shall I bring him before you, so you may witness his death?'

'It is unnecessary. Kill him, and kill him swiftly before he can do any harm.'

'It shall be done, my lady.' Still no order to dismiss: Edmund waited patiently in this hall of granite walls and oak beamed ceilings. The trappings were comfortable without being ornate, and the room spacious enough for Lady

Rosemary to conjure such phantasms as would cower the most brutish of her retinue.

'Is he a fair lad, Edmund? I never saw his face, whereas I believe you got quite close as he lay on the stone.'

Edmund's brow reflected the effort required to sift out a face from so many memories. 'As fair as many of his generation grow with good food and fresh air and not a sniff of the pox. Nothing to mark him especially, as I can recall, but for his elevation above his boots.'

'A tall lad then? Does he have the look of the German about him?'

'I know little of Germans, though once I spied Prince Rupert from a distance, but he has the Arian look that books do tell Master Hitler was fond of promoting, or so I believe.'

'Oh good,' Rosemary said. 'I do so love to contemplate the death of Germans.' Her craggy, age-worn features took on a lop-sided grin. 'You are to ensure he dies, first and foremost. But if the chance arises, draw out his death with many indignities and long agonies.'

Edmund's grin matched her own – this was *his* kind of work – and she gave her leave for him to be about his duties. But then she was assailed by a sudden and icy uncertainty. This meddlesome boy could dash the plans of decades, so perhaps it was not the time to indulge in excesses. She called Edmund up and he halted in his tracks.

'On second thoughts ...'

'My lady?'

'Ready your men, but send Master Readtoth and his pack as vanguard, and ... send them through the Hidden Paths.'

Edmund's shoulder shook in silent mirth. 'Old Readtoth is unlikely to leave so much as a fingernail to show that the lad ever existed, much less leave any work for my men.'

Lady Rosemary frowned and absentmindedly sucked the tip of her thumb as she considered another change of plan.

'Well, see to it that his instructions are precise. He must bring me the boy alive and in tact, for it occurs to me, there is a gap in my collection. And you are fully aware of how I like to collect my specimens ... personally.'

Edmund glanced up to a stone ledge decorated with a row of skulls, some entirely bony, others with vestiges of flesh and skin; one even had a fine head of hair.

Rosemary reached up and took the whitest of skulls from the line. She held it close to her face and looked into the eye-sockets, remembering the colour of the eyes that had once occupied the space. 'My dear Mad Christy,' she said in a voice filled with real affection. 'Soon you shall have a new friend.'

'May I assume you shall prepare in the usual fashion?'

'Oh yes, Master Warwick, indeed I shall.'

'Then I shall seal the room as I leave, and instruct the servants to busy themselves elsewhere about the castle.' Edmund bowed his head, glad that he still had a head to bow.

Lady Rosemary smiled and nodded minutely – Edmund's signal to leave. He slipped out silently and closed the door behind him.

Chris ran away from the tree with the spiteful amber eyes, but the faster he tried to move his legs the slower he went. It was then that he knew for sure he was in a dream. Unfortunately this knowledge did not appear to impress the monster-tree nor decrease the fear that gnawed at Chris's chest. He pumped his legs as hard as he could, but they just grew more and more leaden. He gave up.

'Okay, come and eat me ... or whatever it is you have planned ... and let's get this over with.'

The tree overwhelmed him and threw thorny branches all round his body. They ripped his combat jacket, and then his flesh, into strips. There was no pain, for this was a dream, but he felt smothered and terrified. Branches pulled him in and squeezed crushing air from his body, and then he was flung high to hit the hard ground with a bone shattering thump.

He sucked in chilly air, now fully awake. With great relief he felt the ground beneath him – he was sitting on a smooth, rocklike surface – and saw stars above, although little else; the night was inky black and somewhere a wolf howled. Weren't they supposed to howl to the moon? No moon here, not tonight. It was so completely dark that Chris felt isolated, and wanted some sign that the others were asleep nearby. He couldn't hear them breathing, or shifting in their sleep, but then Senoi was unlikely to make much noise, and Tarn probably slept like a log. One little snore would be nice, but only the distant howl of the wolf – if they had wolves in this place. He hoped they were nothing like the one he'd encountered just before Tarn took him.

A sharp pain across the temples reminded Chris about the implants. Lifting a hand and delicately probing the right side of his head with one finger, he was surprised to feel the little button was sinking into his flesh. On the left side the skin was already closing over the device.

I smell him. Chris sat up, shocked. *I smell him*, the words came again and they washed into his mind on the wave of a wolf-like howl. His guts turned to water as he realised the Kern devices were interpreting the animal noises as words, or at least meaning, and that the wolves were talking about him. He was being ... hunted.

'Tarn!' he called in a loud whisper. 'Senoi!' There was no response. He crawled round feeling the ground but though he widened the circle, he couldn't find Tarn. He was alone. The others had left him, and now there were wolves after him. Standing he blundered round blindly with arms outstretched, hoping to find a tree he could climb. He was fairly certain wolves couldn't climb trees. But then again, until a few hours ago, he knew – he thought he knew – they couldn't talk either. There were no trees. And yet, when Tarn and Drone had laid him down to sleep he was in the thick of a forest.

Suddenly his surroundings were utterly silent. The wolves were not howling, and all the other little background noises of the night were now noticeable by their absence. The night hunkered down, and waited ... for an attack. Chris felt the hairs at the back of his neck bristle and his being shrank into himself, there being nowhere else to hide. Crouching down, he tried to make himself inconspicuous to the kind of eyes that could see in the dark. The night itself became a predator, with sharp claws and dripping fangs and then a scene from his nightmare played back and Chris saw the flesh being peeled from his bones.

He tried not to move; he hardly dared breath, and the silence magnified the noises made by his body. A heartbeat like a stampeding herd, breath like a howling wind, his every movement smashing into the night like a klaxon ... and then there was another sound from outside his own being.

Footfalls. Running feet. They were coming for him! And heavy breath and a clatter of equipment. Something slammed into him hard, knocking him to the ground and piling in on top. Chris was about to cry out when an equally frightened voice quivered through the black.

'Who's there?' the person or creature cried. The voice sounded like that of a man and Chris's hand flew to his temple, for the words were not English but the meaning was clear, and once heard Chris knew he would be able to speak those same words with perfect clarity.

And so, he did. 'Who's there?'

There was scuffling as the stranger gathered himself together and caught his breath. 'I asked first. Who are you?'

Chris tried to answer, but he hadn't the words. The phrases he'd heard were now stored in his brain and ready to use, but he couldn't know words in this strange language that he had yet to hear.

'I asked, who are you?' Chris tried again from his tiny new vocabulary.

'Alright then. I'm Yukio. I'm from … the north. And though it be dark I know you're not a wolf, so come now. Declare yourself. You *sound* like my people, but are you Kumakkashi?'

'I'm Chris, and I'm from Little Rillton.'

The stranger in the dark took time to reply. 'What manner of a name is "Little Rillton"? It's not part of the Kumakkashi territory.'

'Not Kumakkashi territory. No.'

A dry, mirthless laugh came from Yukio and a smell too. There came a waft of stale sweat and wet leather. 'Then we're both in the same kind of trouble. If the wolves don't get us, the Kumakkashi probably will.'

'Probably,' Chris said, and then 'Who are the Kumakkashi?'

'Hard bastards who'll slit out your liver as soon as look at you. But they're not so brave when they're off their mounts. My blade's tasted plenty of llama-boy blood. And you, killed a few Kumakkashi in your time, I'll bet.'

Chris was rapidly getting a feel for the new language, thanks to the implants. 'Not killed Kumakkashi. But wolf, my blade has tasted.' Well, he'd shot one, but he didn't know the word for shot, or pistol.

'You … a howler? You did for a shagging howler? Here, let's get a look at you. You must be built like a bear, or maybe you've got Wiergan skills.'

There was a spark as flint hit steel and then a small steady flame. 'Wiergan's teeth! You're no bigger than me and no older neither. How did you manage a wolf?'

The light shone both ways, and Chris saw a thin, wiry almost feral figure staring at him from the darkness. Yukio looked like a starved teenager with dark darting eyes that looked for opportunity while bleeding fear.

'I don't reckon you could take me, let alone a shagging wolf.'

For a moment Chris sensed danger, and knew instinctively this was not a time to show weakness. 'A wolf, a Kumakkashi, a Wiergan … or you! My blade tastes, slits out liver.' Chris slowly drew his knife.

Yukio's eyes went wide increasing the flow of fear. 'That is one *shagging* big knife. It's white-lightning all sooted up, isn't it?'

One way of describing Parkerised steel, Chris guessed. 'It is,' he said, sheathing the survival knife.

The bluff won the day. Yukio chuckled. 'Good job we're on the same side then, hey?'

The need for an oil-fed lamp faded with the rising sun, and Chris was bemused by his surroundings. He was not in the same place as before: no forest, no trees at all and just miles of open plane with a purple range of mountains in the far distance. He and Yukio sat on a slab of stone, scurfy with lichen and proud from the soil by about a centimetre. It was like an island in a sea of tall yellow-headed grass and Chris guessed it was an *olrock*, and that somehow and for a reason he could not fathom, Tarn and Senoi had transported him here. Maybe it was some kind of test.

During the time it took for the day to pass through dawn to early morning, Yukio had spoken non-stop giving Chris a huge store of new words. Yukio had been part of a hunting party scouring the plains for *tark* and *narkell* – game animals as far as Chris could gather – but they had been ambushed by the Kumakkashi and all but Yukio slain. He had managed to escape and had survived several days avoiding Kumakkashi patrols only to come up against a pack of wolves. He'd been fleeing them, running full pelt in total darkness when he smashed into Chris.

'I brained it that I had more chance being eaten if I didn't run, than running blind into a tree, which you don't get in the plains, or falling in a river, which you do get but a long ways apart. So instead, I slaps bang-wallop into you, the only man for shagging marches who isn't Kumakkashi! What's the chance of *that*, do you think?'

Once there was sufficient light to see where they were going, Yukio led Chris towards the undulating horizon. 'If we're lucky, we'll meet up with a friendly band of my people.' It turned out that there were even enemies among his own kind, and as they covered the miles Yukio talked about the glory-times when all the bands were a great and powerful nation to the far, far north united under a God-like and powerful ruler. He spoke with misty eyes and Chris could be forgiven that this legendary period was centuries ago. When he learned that the fall came just before Yukio's birth, fifteen years ago, Chris wondered just what could have brought the mighty so low is so short a time.

Walking side by side towards the purple mountains, Chris hadn't been watching his footing and before he had a chance to ask Yukio any questions about the fall of his people, he stood in something unpleasant and almost had a fall of his own.

Yukio looked down in response to Chris's display of disgust.

'Oh shag!' Yukio whispered before grapping Chris by the lapels and dragging him into a squat. 'Fresh *kumak* crap! Can't be more then an hour old or the sun would have dried it up. The Kumakkashi can't be far off. We'll have to lie low for a while.'

Chris became suddenly and acutely aware that Yukio's sand-yellow three-quarter length shorts and billowing, hooded shirt were much better camouflage in the long, dry grass than his combats. Maybe if he stayed very still, any passing Kumakkashi would take him for a bush.

'We need to get to the river, then we can keep low – under its banks – and head upstream to the mountains. If we can reach the river soon, we'll be at the mountains by dark.'

They dare not break the height of the tall grass and remained at a crouch all the way o the river. An hour of walking thus left Chris with aching legs and shoulders and a nasty twinge in his lower back, but stripping off his jacket and t-shirt for a wash in the gloriously cool water did much to restore him. Yukio did the same, and Chris wondered if he had ever seen a lad so thin except those on documentaries about concentration camps.

Yukio unlatched his sandals and sat on the bank to wash his feet, and Chris sat on a rock close behind. 'Yukio, have you heard of the Ieladhrim village of Brikadden? It's somewhere in the mountains.'

Yukio looked over his shoulder and chuckled. 'Have you heard my arse shoots out golden stars?' He chuckled some more. 'Of course I've heard of Brikadden. The Kumakkashi tell their sprats Brikadden stories, and the towns south of the Great Mountains do too, but you don't think the place is real for shag sake, do you?'

It seemed faerie stories were faerie stories, whichever side of the Hidden Path you happened to be. 'I've heard about it, that's all. I didn't know it came from stories.'

'Well, it does, and pretty puke-making vomitty stories at that. Typical Kumakkashi! They believe in a town which isn't there and piss themselves to see a white hare dancing under the moon.'

'You don't like our stories then, Taker!'

Yukio leapt up and Chris spun round. Up on the lip of the bank above them were seven riders on seven curious mounts the size of horses but with a look half llama half horse. The men, though, they were men through and through, and under outsized turbans of many colours their eyes were cruel and their mouths mocking.

Seeking advice from Yukio as to their next move, no answer could be more eloquent than the spreading, dark stain between his legs and the frozen look of terror on his face.

The next few moments were a jumble of action and assaults directed at the two young men. Amidst a confusion of punches, shoves and rough handling, Chris found himself being dragged up the bank by a rope fastening his wrists together, and then he was being dragged behind a malodorous *kumak* with Yukio, similarly tied, stumbling at his side.

'Where're you taking us?' Chris called as soon as the turmoil settled.

The rider in front whipped him across the shoulders with the other end of the rope that bound him. 'Quiet, Taker!'

A younger rider reined back. 'You're going to get a proper Kumakkashi welcome. The sort Takers deserve.'

'I'm no Taker,' Chris yelled. He earned a riding boot in the mouth for his troubles, and spat out dirt from the rider's heel and blood from a burst lip. He felt no inclination to ask more questions. Yukio remained silent, as if the power of speech had been robbed away. He stumbled on automaton-like, a being no longer entirely human. His eyes stared wide like a beast smelling blood while being led to the abattoir. Nothing frightened Chris more then the portents signalled by Yukio's petrified demeanour. The boy had death before him without hope of reprieve.

By the time they came to the Kumakkashi camp, Chris's wrists were raw and bleeding. The *kumak* pulled up and the rider dropped the rope. Yukio and Chris fell to the grassy earth, exhausted. The camp was obviously temporary and consisted of three large, *kumak*-skin tents and half-a-dozen smaller ones, all of circular design with conical roofs. There was a pen for young *kumakkesh* and tethering lines for the older ones. The women and children who gathered to see the captives were soon eased aside by several riders and one young man who wore the same, many-coloured flowing robes but no padded turban. Yukio and Chris were dragged to their feet. Both were slapped hard across the face. There was no sense in squaring up to the man; he carried a thin, metal shafted spear with a broad, leaf-shaped blade.

Addressing the young turban-less man, he said 'Watch now!' Chris understood the words, but also knew by the sound of them that they spoke in a different language, or at least a different dialect, to Yukio.

The man walked briskly towards Yukio and then with the speed of a snake's darting tongue jabbed at Yukio's midriff with the spear. Chris couldn't tell if the blade had struck until Yukio, shocked and confused, clasped his hands above his belly and looked down. Throwing his spear into the earth the rider grasped Yukio's head in two hands and forced him to look into his eyes. Yukio's knees buckled, but he recovered momentarily. They buckled again and this time he fell heavily to the ground. He gasped three times and then quivered. Blood frothed up from his mouth, then another spasm seized his whole, thin frame before all his muscles relaxed and he was still.

'See! Perfect kill!' the Kumakkashi said. Chris was almost past hearing, his mouth agape at what he had just witnessed. He could not take his eyes from the thing that was now only a body, when moments ago it had been a living youth with whom he had shared the road.

'You must avoid the bones, the heart, and the large blood vessel that lies in front of the backbone. Aim to strike deep into the liver. You must be able to look him in the eye while he dies, and he must know that you killed him.'

Chris was vaguely aware that a spear was handed from the man to the boy. 'Now, your turn. Strike fast and deep, but not too deep. If you kill him instantly you fail the test. See the life pour from his eyes and you are Kumakkashi and you shall have your mount.'

It was only as the boy approached with the spear that Chris took his gaze from poor Yukio. If the boy had been the man, Chris would even now be on the short dusty road to death looking into the eyes of his killer, but the boy hesitated.

Now would have been a good time for Chris to reveal his true identity, to fling an insult that would draw the Kumakkashi up short and make them think again; perhaps even to deliver a roundhouse kick with such force that the spear would be flung into an unsuspecting rider, striking him as dead as Yukio. But Chris could do none of these things. He was numb, paralysed by what he had seen and with the knowledge of what was about to happen to him. As the boy approached the only conscious thought was *Will it hurt?*

'Now lad! Fast and deep! Have done with the Taker filth!'

The boy stepped closer and his spear-arm drew back.

Chris couldn't even close his eyes, but watched unflinching as his death inched nearer.

'Hold fast!' came a guttural and booming voice from somewhere in the crowd. An old rider elbowed his way through and the boy put up his spear. 'Hold off the slaying, I say!'

The younger riders paid due deference and let him through. He addressed the man who had killed Yukio. 'Is it true, he claims to be no Taker?'

'It is true, *Rukavosh*. But Takers lie and the more so to save their stinking skins.'

The old man strode up to Chris and sniffed deep. 'And yet this one smells as sweet as meadow grass.'

The younger rider shrugged. 'I suppose even Takers bathe once a year or so. And we *did* find them by the river.'

'His clothes are strange. Have you ever seen the like?'

The younger man had not, nor had he ever seen such footwear and just what was that emblem stitched to the sleeve?

'Do you speak the civilised tongue, boy?' the *rukavosh* asked. 'Good! Then what in the seven heavens are these?'

Chris looked at the old man's hands and the spectre of imminent death fled. He was holding two packs of Fruity Bites and at once Chris's mind formulated a desperate story which he thought might just save his life.

'It is food from Brikadden, given to me by Tarniel.'

The *rukavosh* stared at him and his eyes grew wide. With anger? With fear? With admiration? With wonder? Soon, Chris would die ... or he would continue to live, and what could be a better indicator as to the old man's emotions?

CHAPTER TWENTY

Master Readtoth and His Pack

The forest held its breath in the last dark before dawn. Senoi woke from a doze under a fern, wrapped in a nest of dry leaves and protected from the occasional voracious dog-sized beetle or hunting spider by squadrons of mouse-sized ants. He had used his powers to bend the ants to his will and set them as guards while he rested; they performed perfectly. One ant paused by his foot and waved its antennae at it, no doubt detecting the stink of all those wolves.

It was at moments like this when Senoi wondered why the diminutive form was so popular among his people, and how Ieldamarah, their land in the uttermost west could be so teaming with beings of like form. Fortunately times like this were few and recollections of better days made him smile. His smile grew a little brighter with the dawn but it was born of reminiscence and not joy. Perhaps joy would return when – if – he found Tarn and Chris safe.

Last night's wolf attack had been unexpected, unheralded, explosive and sudden. There was Tarn tending to the fire. Over there was Chris, the Second Realm boy, oblivious to this world or any other except the unbounded land of dreams. The crickets sawed the air and night birds called, and then came the wolves bursting from the very black of night. Senoi had shot through the leading beast almost by reflex giving Tarn time to lay a hold on the boy and leap through onto the Hidden Paths. Senoi followed close behind, but not close enough. He felt the shadow of their passing but could lay no touch upon them, so they slipped through unguided, and now they were lost. Senoi knew they had remained in the Third Realm and felt sure they were still in the same temporality, but where they were in all of S'herra, he did not know.

He *did* know, without any doubt, that the wolves were no ordinary creatures, for they had followed him onto the Hidden Paths where no natural animal save the hawks could go. And that they worked together as a team marked them above the usual scions of the Mass. No, these were not unattached Yaemonadhrim. They were *her* creatures. The Lady had sent her bound servants for the boy, and now he was alone in a land he could not begin to understand unaided. Easy prey, to a myriad of creatures: natural, Yaemonadhrim, the Lady or her servants – or mercy forbid he should stray into the land of the Kumakkashi to become meat for their dogs.

Senoi broke the link and the tiny, invisible tendrils of thought that kept the ants on a lease dissolved, releasing the insects to their unceasing toil. He launched himself into the air a flew below the high canopy of fern fronds seeking out a place where he could rid himself, once again, of the cloying smell of the wolf he had killed. His mouse-skin loincloth was clotted with its tar-like essence and although not necessary for a being of thought-energy and personality bounded together in First Realm matter, he felt the need to bathe.

He soon came across a trail of deep *narkellesh* hoof prints each filled with fresh rainwater. He stripped off his cloth and washed it, beating it out against a pebble and then setting it to dry before jumping in to the largest and deepest impression. The water was cold and contained in a print as large to Senoi as a hot-tub would be for a being of human proportions. Open to all the same sensations and feelings as a purely physical body, Senoi's tiny frame tingled and he felt refreshed and cleansed, though in reality no essence of the Mass could touch him. He could be drained by the Mass if he were to encounter too many of its scions, even up to a point where he would cease to be. In that sense, he could be killed by the Mass or any of its derivatives. But when it came down to it, for all its lustful power, a being of the Mass was a fragile thing compared to one of the Host.

Shafts of light stabbed through the frond canopy and opened up the silver water to a dragonfly's many eyes. It landed on the edge of Senoi's hoof print tub and regarded him as prey in the split-second before he threw out an aggression suppressing tendril.

'How goes it, sister dragonfly?' Senoi said relaxing again now that the insect's instinct to rip and consume was masked. 'See how our wings throw the sun's light all about, splitting it into rainbow hues?'

The dragonfly twitched her head, which was half the size of Senoi's. Her wings were of a similar configuration to his and appeared to be made of the same substance, but Senoi's were bigger. Her body, the thickness of his thigh, alternated colour by segments and was iridescent green and red.

'Would you like to help me find my friends? No arduous task I crave, simply fly above the forest and use you special vision to seek out my friend, who is Ieladhrim of the Shade and the other who is of the Second Realm.' It amused him to ask, but the dragonfly had no real choice in the matter. Her basic impulse to hunt for food, water and a mate were modified by Senoi's thoughts and she took to the air to seek out Tarn and Chris. Senoi maintained a link with her consciousness, and as he crouched drying in a dapple of sunlight, he saw the land though her eyes whilst always alert to the many dangers of his world.

Tarn sat on a large boulder that marked the edge of the forest and the beginning of the long mountain path to Brikadden. Entirely by luck and without any application of skill he had emerged here when the Yaemonadhrim-wolves had attacked along the Hidden Paths.

Dressed in the loose-fitting, off-white clothes common to the area, he had stowed PC Shadrack's shirt and Second Realm trousers for later use. He stuffed them deep into his haversack and pulled out the cloak which he would keep close to hand, should he need it in a hurry. Woven in threads of many natural hues it provided good camouflage. The last of his magic food fell out with the cloak, and he felt a sudden need for it. Ripping the packet open with his teeth he ate the contents slowly, savouring each piece as he put his mind to the problem at hand. Should he seek out Chris and Tarn? Should he go to Brikadden and arrange search parties from there? He knew there was no such thing as fate, but he couldn't help thinking the Paths had brought him to a place where the last option looked favourite.

There was a flash of green and red, and a dragonfly landed on his knee. It roused Tarn's curiosity, for it was of the species that usually preferred the shadows of the deep forest. It was gone almost as soon as it had arrived and Tarn thought no more of it until half an hour later when he was making good headway towards Brikadden, he heard the thrum of dragonfly wings – and then the voice of his friend who was Senoi, Ieladhrim of the Light.

Senoi and Tarn greeted one another with relief and not a little joy, but there was no time to linger for long. They drew into the shade of a rowan tree that grew by the side of a mountain stream, and shielded from the direct sunlight they spoke of recent events and worked towards a plan to rescue Chris from wherever he happened to be.

'I thought it strange when the wolves sprang upon us with no warning,' Tarn said. 'Especially as you can hear the wind rush of butterflies wings.'

'I knew they were Yaemonadhrim as soon as I peneflagrated the first attacker, and –'

'Peneflagrated? ... You just made that word up,' Tarn accused.

Senoi worked his wings to a blur and then froze them rigid – his way of shrugging. 'Language is a fluid thing, and I merely adapted two existing words to make up a verb that describes our method of slaying Yaemonadhrim.'

Tarn nodded. 'I suppose it is more compressed than saying "flew through the skin of the scion and then opened a rift to the First Realm from whence effulgence flowed to burn up the dark matter of the Mass, thus dispersing its body and releasing its life force". Let us use "peneflagrate" as a root verb from this day on.'

'You're behind the times Tarn. We commonly use the term in Ieldamarah.'

'Forgive me for being out of touch with the Uttermost West. Perhaps when I first set foot upon her shores I may be given a little time to catch up.'

Senoi smiled. 'Perhaps on that day when Tarn, Ieladhrim of the Shade becomes Tarn, Ieladhrim of the Light, Ieldamarah will indulge you and give you the peace you will have earned.'

Tarn laughed. 'Here's to the day I win my wings then!' He threw a raisin into the air and caught it in his mouth. A cloud drew over the brightness of his expression and soured the sweet fruit. 'Will I make it, Senoi? Are you the "me" of my future? Will I become Sansenoi or am I the brother who perishes? And if I am not to die, which of my brothers shall? Retsutsiel? Savaliel? ... Which? You know, don't you?'

Senoi flew up and settled among the fine fabric at Tarn's shoulder. 'Of course I know. But equally, *you* must know I will never tell.'

Tarn shook off the mood. 'Stupid of me to ask. Of course, I know better. So, I will continue to live my life as if I am immortal and my days as if death awaits me at sunset. And with that thought in mind, we have no time to waste in idle chatter while Chris De'Ath is lost.'

Much rejuvenated, Lady Rosemary paced the cold floor of the vaulted chamber. She looked not a day over forty, although she had hoped for younger. There was a limit, even to her powers, so Readtoth began at a disadvantage. She was already in a bad mood.

'The boy is lost my Lady,' intoned the old werewolf. The blazing fire in the hearth threw no warmth into the room nor took chill from the cold grey stones of Lady Rosemary's reception chamber.

'Indeed he *is* lost, Master Readtoth. And *you* ... lost ... him.' Her fury was contained, but only just.

'For that, my humble apology,' Readtoth said, dipping his shaggy head. 'But what I meant was –'

'I know *exactly* what you meant. He has parted company with those who seek to protect him. He is naked in a desert with no shade, and I am the blazing sun.'

'Precisely, my Lady. He is without hope.'

Rosemary smiled in mockery of sudden understanding. 'Ah! I see, Master Readtoth. He is without hope. It is impossible for him to hide from the effulgence of my gaze ... just as it was impossible for him to escape good Master Readtoth and his furry fellows.'

'My Lady, I shall –'

'Master Readtoth, you have failed. And for that, you shall die.'

Readtoth's yellow eyes widened for a moment, then drooped with his heavy head.

'Now, be so good as to descend into the heart of the Rock and present yourself to Gaoler Edward. He will find you a suitable suite of rooms while I ponder your fate.'

Readtoth dragged himself from his mistress's presence, defeated and in death's shadow. The heavy door closed behind him and Edmund Warwick stepped from behind a velvet drape. The touch of steel on steel whispered as he returned a blade to its scabbard.

'Shall I have my men –'

'Readtoth will die of his own accord, and without any assistance from you, thank you Edmund. I have spoken, and it shall be.'

'And the boy?'

Lady Rosemary waved away his question with an impatient flick of her hand. She strode out of the chamber into her own bedroom and beckoned Edmund to follow. Leaving medieval décor behind, he stepped into early 20th century comfort. The bed had a cream quilt embroidered with pink and red roses, there were matching drapes – very Laura Ashley – and there was a mahogany dressing table decked with combs, brushes and little pink perfume bulbs. There was a photograph of a young soldier on her bedside table and an open fire, with a mantelpiece. It was only the row of skulls along the mantelpiece that marked this room as unusual to the eyes of any middle-aged woman of upper middle class England, circa 1950.

'Here my man. Just here,' Rosemary said pointing to a gap in the mantle display. 'I have moved my friends in from the cold of that ghastly room next door, but there is still a space for Master De'Ath. When I have done with him, he shall live just here.' She contemplated the space for a moment, imagining it filled with the smiling head of a youth.

'And just here,' she said stepping back and sweeping her arm towards the bare stone flags in front of the fire. 'A wolf-skin rug, I think.'

CHAPTER TWENTY ONE

In the Shadow of the Pack

The elation at being allowed to live was marred by the spectacle of Yukio's body being fed to the dogs. The horror he felt while witnessing the pathetically thin corpse being torn apart and consumed by the Alsatian-like pack may have been tempered slightly if Chris had known that all Kumakkashi dead were disposed of in that manner, including their own dear departed. But he had no such knowledge, and to him the act was elevated to the summit of barbarity. That these people should not be content with killing, but had to extent their cruelty past death numbed Chris to the heart.

The dogs attacked with such fervour that Yukio's torn and bloody arms seem to be waving from shredded sleeves, calling for help. Chris fought to prevent himself from shrinking into a dark, internal place of no return while the riders laughed and enjoyed the show. Boadak, the youth who would have been Chris's executioner, increased their mirth by calling out a merry halloo and waving back to the dead boy. It was at that point that Chris decided he hated the fellow more than he had ever hated anyone or anything before in his whole life. Hate fired him up and hate pulled him from the edge of the dark pit, but he soon learnt it was a completely mutual feeling. It did not matter to Boadak whether Chris was a Taker or not. He had been robbed of his kill and therefore his mount which meant that his status as a fully fledged rider had been delayed for he knew not how long. Boadak entertained the hope that he would be able to kill Chris at some time, none too distant. Boadak was soon to become a dangerous yet furtive enemy.

Yukio's killer, Boadak's sponsor and mentor, was another of the riders who eyed Chris with near-open contempt. His name was Terren and he would continue to council Boadak and advise him in the art of conquering enemies.

The remaining riders though, they either showed mild curiosity towards him or no interest at all and it was only the *rukavosh* who approached him with any degree of friendliness. He told Chris he was to be taken to a rider they called the Heartless Warrior, a man who had knowledge of Brikadden and of the youth named Tarniel – a journey of five days if all things went fair. He would share a lodge with the young riders; the same young riders who openly shunned him or at best, ignored him.

Unlike the riders, the Kumakkashi women, especially the younger ones, showed a great deal of friendliness. If anything, the indifference of the men was outweighed several times over by the ogling, the smiles – some shy others openly seductive – and the intense interest his presence undoubtedly engendered. It was either his imagination, or he had suddenly become an object of desire.

'You are like Boadak, long limbed and slim of form. Snake-bodied, we call it, and it is a look much favoured by the women of our clan, as you may well see,' the *rukavosh* said. 'But be well warned. If you go to any of the women in the night with night-time passions, your fate will be that of your friend, only ...'

Chris listened to the old man's cautionary words, which were given in a tone of friendly advice despite the dreadful consequence. Chris wondered at the "only" but did not have to wonder long.

'Only, you will not be dead when you are put to the dogs.'

Chris swallowed hard and glanced over towards the pack which fought over gory bones, lengths of slippery intestine and strips of blood-soaked rag, all that now remained of Yukio. 'Don't worry *Rukavosh*. I won't go anywhere near any of your women.'

'*My* women?' the old man said. 'I do not *own* them, I only seek to protect them … and you of course. I would rather not see them used by a stranger, nor see a stranger put to the dogs for ignorance of our ways.'

'No, of course. What I mean is, I won't touch any of the women. At all. In any way whatsoever. It's a promise.' He would have sealed his word in blood if it might banish the spectre of death-by-being-eaten once and for all.

Chris's assurance did not appear to please the *rukavosh*. 'Ah, but *they* may come to *you*. And if they do, you will not dishonour them by turning them away.'

The old man smiled and landed such a hearty slap between Chris's shoulders that he staggered forward a few steps. This amused the *rukavosh* and he chortled until barking orders to a gaggle of young riders that Chris should have his property restored.

All Chris's clothing and gear was returned to him, including the Fruity Bites and much to his surprise, the ammunition for the absent Remington. He was allowed to roam round camp freely – he was not tethered or bound in any way – and as evening turned towards night he shared a meal of roasted *narkell* meat and honeyed bread. It was warm and cosy around the fire in the communal tent used for meeting and eating. Lamps were lit and stories told; Chris listened but said nothing. With the spectre of Yukio's fate ever foremost in his mind, he was close paranoid about committing the slightest *faux pas*. Instead he kept quiet and tried to shrink into the background, ever hopeful that Tarn and Senoi would burst in at any minute to conduct a rescue.

When it was late and stars pierced the black night, the riders prepared a drink of which Chris received a share. It was hot, creamy and highly spiced; Chris thought of it a Horlicks with cinnamon. The riders called it *creeth* and he found it soothing and sustaining. He asked about it and an elderly woman said it was gift-goods from a town from south of the mountains and east of the great lake known as Tear-of-God.

Chris slept in one of the large tents with five other young men. Boadak was not one of them: considered too young – he was yet to earn his mount – he slept with the matron and children even though he did not appear any younger than the youngest of his present companions. As best he could judge, the five young riders ranged in age between about sixteen and twenty-two. Chris was assigned the billet almost as an afterthought, when late into the night people became sleepy and took themselves off to bed. When only the young men were still about the fire, Chris was reluctantly picked by one of the groups who apparently had the most room to spare. He felt like the kid who nobody wants on their football team and always ends up as goal keeper.

Under the light of three oil lamps suspended from the poles supporting the roof, the young riders stripped to their underwear – they all wore variations of a kind of loose cotton shirt and something akin to a tight dhoti – and washed from the same wooden pail. They spoke and joked together in hushed tones, but all this came to sudden silence as Chris tried to creep under the fleeces he'd been given, fully dressed. They treated him to similar expressions a smelly beggar might receive on entering a west end restaurant, so he undressed diffidently aware of their intense scrutiny. And then they laughed out loud, apparently finding something hilarious about either his white socks or his boxers – perhaps both. An older rider from somewhere outside shouted an admonishment, so they continued to laugh under their breath, pointing and curling up and rolling on their fleeces, amused completely beyond supporting themselves upon their legs.

Ignoring them as best he could, he washed perfunctorily in the sixth-hand water and tried again. He was half expecting to find himself propelled from between the fleeces and subjected to some kind of humiliation or other, but much to his relief, the others settled down. The tent was soon an auditorium for the varied sounds of sleeping. One of the riders snored lightly, another breathed heavily and one gave a high pitched, almost inaudible whistle as he exhaled though restricted sinuses. Chris just listened and despite the exhausting day just gone, he could not settle. Every time he drifted, Yukio's smiling face hovered before him, soon to be replaced by a gory skull. Then once again, he turned his thoughts to the unknown road that led him here. The previous night he had fallen asleep safe in the knowledge that Tarn and the faerie boy were close by. And then he woke up to another place. If only he knew: was that their plan or was this all some kind of horrible mistake?

The night dragged on, each minute an hour each hour an eternity, but eventually he slipped past the bloody face of his companion-of-a-day, and would have slept were it not for the intruder. Chris was immediately alert. The tent flap admitted a cool draft and was then secured. Chris dare not peep out from under his fleece. There was whispering, giggling, cloth sliding against skin and then – there was no doubt in Chris's mind – the soft sounds of lovemaking.

At any other time, Chris may have derived a kind of voyeuristic pleasure from it all, but despite the whispered sounds coming from his closest neighbour and the night time visitor, all he could really hear were the warning words or the *rukavosh* and the baying of ravenous dogs. In the midst of all this, he eventually found sleep. He slept deeply and without dreams.

He awoke early next morning to a hefty shove. Peeping timidly out from under his fleece he was just in time to see an older rider exiting through the tent flap which was deliberately left open to the cool morning airs. He wasn't the only one to receive such a rude awakening, and the others were stirring. His youngest tent mate, about sixteen, was first to brave the chill; he threw off his *kumak* fleece, scurried to the pail and threw a handful of water over his face. The others followed until the lad closest to Chris, a wiry chap of about eighteen with a wisp of chin whiskers and a black ponytail, threw off his covers and stood, completely unclothed. He posed like a footballer who's just scored and the others laughed and cheered – one threw a riding boot at him – and from all the banter it didn't take Chris long to work out that if you went to bed in your underwear and got up next morning without it, it was a sign to all that you'd had a visit in the night from one of the young women.

When the others had all splashed their faced and all but the favoured lad had started to dress, Chris ventured out and made a feint at the water. He made sure only the smallest amount made contact with his face, for he was certain the water would do little to clean him after so much use.

The youngest rider left and returned with several rounds of unleavened bread and Chris was given a share. They sat round a newly kindled fire in the centre of the tent and tucked in, the one rider still nude and showing no sign of dressing soon. He appeared to revel in his nakedness as if it were a trophy of last night's adventure.

Chris though he had better join them, although he hadn't been invited. He started to dress and the naked rider told him to stop. Chris started to get a very bad feeling. The rider told him his name was Jacken – which was all very well but the fear of what was to come next made any introduction redundant.

'Today we break camp,' Jacken said. Chris looked him in the eye, determined not to let his gaze fall below chin level, let alone navel. 'You will ride a spare *kumak*, and if you do so with that stupid garment, your parts will be pinched black and blue. So, take it off.'

This Jacken geezer was telling him to drop his boxers! Chris was having none of it. Far from removing them he took hold of his waist-band as if his life depended on it.

'You're a fool! I should let you ride and then you'll swell up like two bladder-balls and learn the hard way. But – well – I am soft hearted and hate to see a fellow suffer. So off with it! And Stas,' the last called out to the youngest rider. 'Dig out your spare garment. We'll clad this traveller as Kumakkashi!

'Why mine?' protested Stas. 'Give him yours. It's your idea after all.'

Jacken looked at Stas in a certain emphatic, not to say threatening way, and the protest was over. Within five minutes Chris was snug in his new Kumakkashi pants and Jacken was tucking his boxers into a pack.

'That's not fair!' called Stas. 'He gets mine and you take his! Give them to me and it's fair swaps!'

Jacken shook his head. 'Such a child, Stas. But if it makes you happy ...' He threw Chris's boxers across the tent and Stas snatched them up and squirreled them away just as an older rider – the one who'd awakened them all with such enthusiasm – stuck his head into the tent.

'Jacken!' he called in gravely voice. 'Such a child! By now we all know you got lucky last night, so hurry and get dressed. The sun is almost up and I fear I shall be blinded if it glances off your fleece-white flanks.' The older rider pulled his head out and smacked the flap shut.

Jacken's tent-fellows allowed themselves some cautious laughter and suddenly Jacken looked less comfortable. He dressed quickly.

There was more re-cladding to come. Chris was supplied with a pair of weave and leather boots, smooth-soled so if he fell from the saddle he would be less likely to get hooked up on the stirrup and dragged along. Finally Stas and Jacken fitted him with one of the brightly coloured, outsized doughnut-like turbans. He was surprised to learn that they were more of a hat than a turban, and required mere placing on the head rather than a lot of winding. Stas told Chris the turban had belonged to a boy who had died in a Taker attack. It was red and white, the white panels rich with a tapestry of tiny green leaves.

Chris was actually beginning to relax when two events reminded him how precarious his situation was. When he was being taken to where the *kumakkesh* were tethered they passed the dog enclosure. Only the contented looks of the dogs and a blood-brown stain in the grass remained to tell of Yukio's existence and as if to magnify his thoughts the old *rukavosh* sidled up to inform him that if he had lied about knowledge of Brikadden or Tarniel, the dogs would have him.

Such well fed dogs and so many the offences that kept their bellies full. Terren and Boadak witnessed his discomfort and exchanged smiles.

It took two hours to break camp. Without a rider's skills in the task Chris was put to work with the children and found himself fetching and carrying. When it was time to move out, he was introduced to a worn out and very aged *kumak* with matted yellowing fleece and an improvised harness. He soon picked up the rudiments of control and riding, and although he had never in his life been on more than a seaside donkey, he imagined the skills needed were the same as those required to ride a horse. This *kumak* stumbled and bumped often and Chris immediately saw the benefits of Kumakkashi underwear. Just out of the old camp area he caught Jacken's eye and Jacken gave a fat wink – the first real sign of acceptance from any of the riders. Once again though, he was acutely aware that the girls and young women could hardly take their eyes off him. At home he would have been on cloud nine, but in the land of the Kumakkashi every girl's smile seemed to reveal the ripping jaws of dogs and far from enjoying his newfound popularity it made him shiver and shrink.

Apart from to short meal break, the day was spent in the saddle and Chris was glad when the *rukavosh* called a halt and ordered 'off saddle up tents.' One-night stop-over it may have been, but there were no half-measures in setting up camp and as much care was taken as for a long stay. Again Chris found himself with the children performing the simplest of tasks, which was just as well for his inner thighs hurt terribly from the day's riding and it was all he could do not to hobble feebly. That night he slept soundly, all through, and his neighbours gave no sign next morning that any of them had been as lucky as Jacken the night before. On the following morning, the youngest rider was the centre of attention but he was not as brazen as Jacken had been. Once his credentials were briefly proven, he breakfasted with his fleece pulled firmly about him and refused to confirm any speculation as to which young lady had complimented him with a visit.

Chris's legs didn't hurt half so much on the third morning and he ventured to lend a hand breaking camp, and after careful observation over the last two mornings, he managed to make himself useful and be at the right place to loose a hook or secure a rope and such like. Although they said nothing, Chris thought he detected a certain amount of approbation from the riders. Jacken at least spoke to him about the weather and one of the young ladies approached him with a sunny smile, gave him a honey cake and introduced herself as Sundami. For all the innocence of the encounter, he felt the breath of dogs at his neck and he acquitted himself rather badly. A girl at home encountering such a dim witted response to a friendly gesture would surely hold her finger and thumb, just so, and mumble 'loser', but Sundami gave every appearance of finding his diffidence endearing.

For the rest of the day Sundami conspired to be near Chris, or so it seemed, and the indifference of the majority of riders warmed to mild acceptance. Jacken was the most friendly towards him and if it is true that every aspect of life has its flip-side, then this was provided for amply by Boadak and Terren who skulked together, the boy and the man never failing to display their loathing for him in one way or another, by word or by gesture. Whatever their intention, the behaviour they displayed seemed to alienate them from the other riders and at the end of the second meal stop, although his words were not clear, the *rukavosh* raised his voice in their general direction, and his tone was not friendly.

That night, the young riders, washed and ready for bed, were gathered in a circle around the fire in their tent, when Jacken invited Chris to join them. Having acquired a cotton undershirt – it was one of Jacken's spares – Chris was only distinguishable from the others by his less weather worn face, short hair and lack of straggly chin whiskers, but for all that he was beginning to feel one of the crowd. Not so much so that he had the confidence to initiate a subject of conversation – the dogs' breath hadn't cooled that much – but he was at least happy to answer their questions and keep his ears open, the better to build up a vocabulary in the riders' tongue.

'So Chris,' Jacken began. 'How came you to be unsaddled in the vast plain and chummy with a Taker?'

'Yes,' joined in the youngest rider. 'For whatever you be, it's clear you're not a Taker, and yet you suffered to breath in his stink.'

Things had been going so well. Now they mentioned Yukio and Chris felt his spirits chill. He had known Yukio for only a day, and yes he did need a bath, but he was a nice guy, and Chris had liked him. Perhaps it was not time to voice such feelings. Maybe Chris should have taken the opportunity to deride the dead boy for the sake of his own security. But he would not; the quality of standing by a friend was central to Chris's sense of self and even the spectre of the pack wouldn't smack down the defence he felt rising. 'He was just a boy. He was nothing more than a frightened boy, and you killed him.'

The young riders exchanged looks, not quite sure how to respond, until Jacken took up the loose and flying strand of the argument. 'I didn't kill him. But I would have done, as quickly and as surely as Terren did. He was a Taker, and Takers do no more than pollute the land. And another thing – if the spear was in the other hand, he would have killed me without a moment's hesitation and I daresay he would have tortured me first if he had the chance.'

'All Takers must die!' cried Stas the youngest rider, only to be hushed up by Jacken.

'All except one, that is,' Jacken said. 'Never forget the one honoured Taker.'

Stas blushed and cast his eyes down. 'Oh yes. I shan't forget again.'

Now Chris was really confused until Jacken explained. 'Marhonaz, the Heartless Warrior – the man we are taking you to see, his woman is of the Taker race. She once served the evil Kar'akhen, their great leader – a kind of slave, she was – but she also encountered the Prophet Jason who visited that monster's den. Put with child by another slave – the evil one used to make them couple for his entertainment – she somehow survived his fall when many another did not, and escaped from the great city which was far to the north of the Arkenark Mountains. Through many adventures she came to our lands. Heavy with child and with knowledge of the Prophet Jason, she was spared, and when Marhonaz came among us from the west, he took her under his protection. By that action, and no other, it is known that he is capable of mercy. But for the most part, he is worthy of his title.'

Chris didn't want to know how Marhonaz earned his title – the Heartless Warrior. He still thought of Yukio and his horrible fate. 'How do you know Yukio wasn't a slave? You killed him without so much as asking his name.'

Jacken shook his head slowly. 'You really are a strange one, ignorant of Taker cruelty. I can almost believe you do come from Brikadden and sup with The Three.'

'I have only been in this land a short time, and the only cruelty I've seen was the killing of Yukio – and then ... and *then*, you *fed* him to the *dogs!*'

After a period of uncertain silence during which Chris wondered if he'd gone too far, at least one misunderstanding was cleared up. Jacken explained the Kumakkashi custom and method of disposing of the dead.

'So, our dogs will eat the dead,' Jacken said. 'Try keeping them off! And they will rip apart a hooded man, for that is how we deal with transgressors, but they fear to so much as bark the wrong way towards any, living rider.'

Chris listened impatiently, eager to put another question. 'Tell me what you know about The Three,' he asked, certain the Jacken referred to Tarn and his brothers.

'You claim to be acquainted with at least one of them. Why ask me?'

'I know one of them ... quite well, but I'm curious as to what you may have heard of them.' Chris hoped this explanation would satisfy.

'Very well. My knowledge is vague and I have never met them, but I believe they come from the Town of Leaves on the banks of the lake called Nenrilluen, east of the mountains that border our land. They are rumoured to be the triplet sons of the Oracle of Nenrilluen and the Prophet Jason. They travel freely through all the lands of the world, for all people wish to call them friend.'

'Even among the Takers?' Chris interrupted.

'The Takers have no land. They merely infest the lands of others – but there is a rumour that even the Takers think kindly of The Three, for their flesh is the blessing of the Prophet and the wisdom of the Oracle and everywhere they walk goodness flourishes and evil dries to dust. They are three and they are one and in them is the hope of the world.'

Chris tried to pin down the moment when fact became fiction; certainly Jacken gave the last information in a voice dripping with something akin to dogma, and Chris very much doubted Tarn or his brothers could be quite so highly revered. He thought it best not to press for more information about the holy triplets.

'What about Brikadden then? Tell me about Brikadden.'

Jacken gave Chris a curious look. 'Surely you know already. You claim to be from the place.'

'No I don't. My food comes from there,' he said whipping out a pack of Fruity Bites. 'But I've never been. Where is it and what's it like?'

'It is a town for the likes of The Three, not for common folk such as us. It is a town that ... moves about. Sometimes it is there, sometimes it isn't.'

'Have you ever seen it?'

'Of course not! It's a place ordinary folk cannot see. That's how it was described by Tarniel himself to our *high rukavosh* and it was he that passed it on to our own *rukavosh*. The Three live there when they are not abroad in the world ... or so it is said.'

Jacken changed the subject to other legends and a period of story telling began, whispered deep into the night so as not to disturb the riders and women in the tents all about. At length the lamps burnt out and the six young men buried themselves in their fleeces. Chris drifted away quickly with the niggling fear that Sundami might come to him in the night, and she wouldn't understand that he loved Gayle and he was faithful – or that if he was inclined to be unfaithful, there was no way he could make out under a fleece with all those others in the tent.

He woke early next morning, relieved and disappointed at the same time that Sundami had not called.

By mid morning of the fifth day's journey, the flat plains had erupted into a sea of gentle, rolling hills which became loftier as the day wore on. Chris was relieved when Terren and Boadak rode on ahead; he was sure he was the subject of their furtive whisperings and in no doubt at all that their spiteful looks were always directed at him. Good riddance to them!

It was three hours past the afternoon break when Chris first spotted the high white walls of a Kumakkashi town. Tassat-sarai it was called, and it was set on the top of a steep sided hill like a circlet upon the brow of a medieval prince. The steep slopes leading to the settlement were scattered with thick swathes of gorse-like bushes through which the path wound a snakelike route. Chris was no military historian but even he could see that an assault up these slopes would be most uncomfortable for the attacking side.

His *kumak* slipped and huffed through its nostrils, clearly irritable at having to make such an ascent. When it swung its flank into a clump of bushes causing cruel thorns to pierce Chris's trousers and skin, he felt sure the grumpy animal had done it deliberately so he dug his heels in without guilt. It responded by twisting its head round, squealed and launching two gobbets of snot that Chris just managed to duck. He kicked again and the *kumak* appeared to get the message; it plodded on responding sluggishly to Chris's commands, head hung in reluctant acceptance.

The young Kumakkashi were getting excited now. They jumped down from the *narkell* carts and ran towards the settlement. A watchmen standing atop the wall waved and did a little dance causing the children to laugh and copy the moves. Chris shared some of their excitement. After all, Marhonaz the so called Heartless Warrior may have knowledge that would help him find Brikadden. Find the town and it was sure to lead to a reunion with Tarn. His excitement was clouded by fear though: Marhonaz might prove himself to be heartless in the face of anything Chris had to say, and the pack of dogs was never far from his thoughts.

Chris had dwelled much upon his response to fear over the last few days. He had never failed to face it … and he never failed to freeze to absolute inaction. Luckily – and it was no more than luck – someone or something had saved him each time, but he had witnessed the fatal consequence of allowing fear to kill your mind. Yukio had frozen in exactly that way, and Yukio had died. Chris vowed that he would not allow himself to shut down in face of fear. If there were to be attacks in the future he wouldn't go down without a fight.

As the walls loomed Chris noticed a single cloud above, like a hot air balloon floating but he had no time to dwell on it. Several armed Kumakkashi warriors hurried out of the open portal and surrounded him. This time he did not freeze; he didn't have time to: they dragged him off his mount and his struggles were quelled by several hard slaps to the face. One warrior came up to him with a raised cudgel but he was pushed to the ground by Jacken.

'Hold back with your stick!' Jacken cried. 'We have the lad's parole! There's no need to rough him up!'

'There's every need. Marhonaz has ordered it. We're to pen him and if he resists, we're to knock the fight from him.' The warrior dusted himself off and retrieved the weapon he dropped. Whereas Chris's captors wore robes predominantly of red, this chap had blue trimmings and looked to be in his late twenties. He wore a thin moustache and narrow stripe of whiskers down his chin.

'If Marhonaz gave those orders, you have broken them, for your attack preceded any kind of resistance.'

The warrior strode over and wound his fist in Chris's collar. 'Allow me to establish the rules. A little roughing up now and he'll be no trouble later.'

Jacken struck his forearm and broke his grip. The warrior and his comrades squared up to Jacken, but Jacken too was supported. For a moment it looked like there might be trouble between the two bands of Kumakkashi. A hush fell; the children, melted away behind the lines of *kumakkesh* and even the dogs hunkered down in subdued expectation.

Chris, true to his vow, had found it within himself not to give in to whatever others might have in store for him. All this time he had been quiet but entirely centred. He had watched developments and now, mustering as much confidence as he could, he made his play.

'There is no need to rough me up,' Chris said to the warrior. 'Lead me to where I must go, and I will follow.'

The warrior sneered and Jacken looked crestfallen.

'But touch me again, and I'll break your arm.' Chris bored a gaze like two nails, straight into the eyes of the warrior.

The warrior held his countenance … until Jacken began to laugh and then his eyes fell to the ground, briefly but with the flicker of defeat clear for all to see. 'Follow me,' he mumbled, and pushed through the ranks of his fellows.

Chris winked at Jacken who was still chortling, then followed the defeated warrior. Chris thrust his hands deep into his pockets, lest anyone notice them trembling.

Surrounded – at what they considered a safe distance – by warriors, Chris didn't get much opportunity to take in many details, but it was clear that the settlement was little more than a walled enclosure for the Kumakkashi to set up their tents. There appeared to be only one permanent structure, and that was a sturdy three storey building in the same whitewashed stone as the walls. Chris mentally labelled it as 'the keep' although it was not crenellated nor did it possess loopholes, a portcullis or any of the other fittings he associated with castles back home. It was more of a square tower with a pitched roof, tiled in red stone.

The enclosing wall was similarly un-crenellated, and stood about 5 metres in height. The inner face had various wooden lean-tos and animal crèches abutting, and there was a general air of industry and business among the people.

If the keep was without all the usual features of a late Norman or medieval keep, it certainly had a dungeon, and once he was shown in, the warrior vented all his humiliation and anger by slamming the prison door with excessive force.

Once his eyes grew accustomed to the low levels of light – there was one small opening high above his reach which let in daylight, and a brace of flickering oil lamps – Chris took in his surroundings.

'At least there're no skeletons manacled to the walls,' he whispered to himself. 'And the place doesn't smell of crap.' He walked slowly round the cell with its iron studded, black oak door. He ran a hand over the smooth wood of the small table and appreciated the fact that the single chair had a thick cushioned seat. It was decorated with brass studs which hinted that Kumakkashi furniture was made by the same craftsmen as their saddles. There was a stone ledge with a thickly padded soft leather mattress, and a couple of off-white blankets and along the wall opposite the door was a chest-height shelf lined with books. He took one down and sniffed the binding. It was leather. Opening the book he found the sturdy pages were covered in a curios form of writing that reminded him of Japanese kanji. The Kern devices, now fully embedded into his skull, had never yet failed to provide a clear understanding of the languages he had heard, but they did nothing to help him interpret the written word. There was an opening in one corner that opened into a tiny space where there was a stone toilet set into the wall. It appeared that any wastes were carried away by no more than gravity, and Chris made a mental note to stay clear of the keep walls if ever he was allowed outside.

Chris threw his pack onto the bed and made himself comfortable in the chair. Surprised they had put him in here with all his gear and without so much as a pat-down, he guessed the Kumakkashi weren't experienced gaolers. He had all his stuff, including the cartridges. Maybe they would come in useful if he had to devise some method of escape. Helping himself to some water from a pottery pitcher he finished off the open pack of dried fruit and tried to keep his mind from inventing various horrible scenarios for the immediate future. After an hour of so, he began to doze, until …

He sucked in sharply as he caught a movement at the corner of his eye, and he would have frozen had he not applied his newfound resolve. Spinning round ready to fight he drew back as he saw the frightened creature in the far corner. It was a large, white hare and it sat on its haunches regarding him with yellow eyes. Yellow eyes. The hare was quite beautiful, but the yellow eyes unnerved him, for he had looked into similar eyes before.

CHAPTER TWENTY-TWO

The Cold Stone Cell

Chris held down the revulsion that tried to surface as he recalled the attacks of the succubus Lillian and incubus Kostja. He fought the terror that came with a vision of the unnatural wolf that had threatened to devour the unconscious Abe Knapper. But this beast in front of him, it was just a cute little bunny. If only its eyes were blue, or green or even red, for then it would be like the albino rabbit he'd once had as a pet.

'You're … you're not going to turn into anything nasty, are you?' he said in the tone of voice he'd often used when Arnie was a pup. 'If you're looking for food, all I've got are a couple of packs of dried fruit.' He tried to remember what kind of food rabbits, and supposedly hares, took in the wild and decided that dried fruit was not on the menu. The hare sat still, not even twitching her nose or black-tipped ears. Chris decided to go for it anyway and taking out a pack of Fruity Bites he ripped open the top with his teeth. He poured some of the mix into the palm of his hand, ate a few raisons and held out a large chunk of dried fruit towards the hare.

'Here you go Bugsy. Here's a nice bit of pineapple.' He inched towards her with his arm outstretched, crouching close to the floor to make himself less intimidating. The hare didn't budge, but not wishing to push his chances Chris stopped advancing and rolled the pineapple piece along the stone floor. It fell a foot short of the hare, which resumed all fours and sniffed the offering.

'Go on, try it. Genuine guaranteed magic food from Little Rillton in the Shire of the Shrop.'

A loud bang from the direction of the door diverted Chris's attention. He stood up straight and pocketing the remaining fruit he waited to see what would happen next. Glancing quickly down he noticed the hare was gone, and so was the little piece of pineapple. A rather nervous looking blue trimmed young warrior pushed open the heavy door and stepped to one side to allow the majestic entry of a woman dressed in white silk riding trousers and matching blouse and jacket. Her riding boots were also white and appeared to be made from soft leather and a white cloak of heavy material – wool cloth or similar weave – was held at the left shoulder by a silver broach shaped like a crescent moon. All this white lent a healthy hue to an otherwise pale skin and emphasised the darkness of her black hair which she wore long and over her right shoulder. When she spoke, the Kern device planted the words into Chris's head but did nothing to take away her Taker accent. Chris guessed at once that she was the woman spared by the Heartless Warrior.

'You have made a great impression with the riders who found you. They are quite distraught that the warriors of Tassat-sarai have received you with such ill mannered boorishness.'

Chris shrugged. 'No harm done.'

The elegant woman smiled and Chris was affected by her beauty. It was a beauty that could lay dormant, hidden within, but fired up and released at the will of the possessor. 'I am glad to hear it,' she said holding something up to her nose and apparently sniffing it. 'They tell me you had a friend whom they killed, perhaps a little recklessly.'

'He died, I think, because he was a Taker. No more than that.'

The beauty died and now sadness flowed from the woman affecting Chris every bit as much as the beauty had. 'Takers are not suffered to live in the land of the Kumakkashi.'

'He was just a boy.'

'He would have died if he were just a baby, for babies grow into men and Taker men a cruel beyond measure.'

Chris frowned deeply. 'Are they men, or are they some other kind of creature?'

'They are men – just. But they are also something else. They are the remnants of a once mighty evil.'

'So Yukio died because of something that is in the past,' Chris said. He tried to fathom her age: from the flecks of grey in her hair forty at the very most, probably a lot younger.

She smiled sadly. 'We try to hoist up the fallen honour of the world before we have introduced ourselves. I know they call you Chris. I am called Moon.'

Chris nodded an acknowledgment.

'I also know that you are not of the Taker race, nor are you of any race from this side of the Tear-of-God.' She glided round Chris in a sweeping circle observing him all the while as if trying to draw an opinion from his appearance. 'I once met another from under the water, and that other brought great changes to our world.' Moon walked closer and eyed him up and down. 'What will you bring us?'

Chris frowned then dragged something from his pocket. 'Fruity Bites?' he ventured. Receiving only a bemused look in return, he put them away again.

'A cold stone cell is not the place for you. My man would flay every last inhabitant of Tassat-sarai if he returned to find you incarcerated so. Let us find somewhere more suitable.'

Moon gestured towards the door and Chris was about to move when she stopped him. 'Before I entered the cell I spied upon you through the peep hole. You were crouching down, and appeared to be talking.'

'Oh,' Chris said smiling. 'There was a hare,' he said pointing to the corner.

The guard balked and colour drained from him like his throat had been slit. 'A ... a *white* hair?' he asked.

'Well, yes.'

The guard's eyes bulged. He looked into the corner where Chris had pointed then lost all decorum and ran away.

Chris cast a bemused look towards Moon and motioned for an answer.

'The Kumakkashi have some very strange beliefs,' Moon said, and offered no more of an explanation than that. Once again she waved him towards the door. As he past close by she sniffed in his scent, a combination of roll-on modified sweat and old *kumak*, and her eyes flashed yellow. Then she looked down towards her closed fist. Opening it, she examined the little piece of dried fruit before popping it into her mouth. She had never tasted pineapple before. Not in this world, at any rate.

It was bright and warm outside despite a powerful, steady wind. His erstwhile travel companions and captors were having trouble with one of their tents so he asked Moon if he could help them and she consented, saying she would send for him when the camp was secure. Within moments he was pitching in with Jacken and Stas who were both pleased to see him.

'Thanks, Jacken,' Chris called against the wind while securing a guideline.

"What for?'

'For taking my side against those fellows who wanted to hurt me. And I *think* you had something to do with my recent release.'

Jacken laughed. 'These Tassat-sarai riders lost their sense of humour when they took to living under stone and cast away their tents. Sometimes they have to be reminded that they're still Kumakkashi and they don't rule the rest of us.'

'And my release?'

Jacken laughed again. 'Shout a little, cut a few guidelines. Let the dog in with the *kumakkesh;* it's easy to get people's attention. Moon's as good as *high rukavosh* until Marhonaz returns, so once she came out and heard what we had to say ... You know the rest.'

Jacken winked at Chris. Chris winked back, and then they pressed on with their work until all the tents were secure. Then it was time to eat and Chris was invited to share a meal with the young riders. By tradition the young women were also invited. Chris learned it was customary to share the first meal at a new camp with the girls and he soon found himself the centre of attention. Jacken, Stas and the other lads were keen to hear about his short experience in the stone cell and Sundami and the other young women wanted to know all about Moon: what she had looked like, close up; what she had said and all the minute details of her dazzlingly white costume. But conversation was ended and silence ruled at the first mention of the white hare. Sundami who had shuffled close to Chris, so close that he felt the warmth of her body, moved away and took on a concerned, frightened look.

Jacken was the first to speak. 'A guard came out of the tower like a fox with his tail on fire. He was yelling something about the white hair, but we thought Moon had put her curse on him for mistreating you.'

'Yes,' added Sundami, her voice little above a whisper. 'Who could have guessed you would be visited by the White Hare?'

Chris looked from face to face. None could hold countenance except young Stas whose eyes filled with tears. 'You don't know about her, do you Chris?'

'The White Hare? Not a single thing and I am beginning to wonder whether I want to.'

Stas carried on regardless. 'She dances under the moonlight, to steal away your life.'

'What? A *hare*? A cute, furry, little *hare*?' Chris suddenly had a vision of the ridiculous, recalling a scene from the film *Monty Python and the Holy Grail*. 'All I need is the holy hand grenade of Antioch then', he whispered to himself.

'When she dances, she takes the form of a woman,' Stas continued. 'But if you see her in the form of a hare, it is a sign that she will come for you, next full moon.'

'Which is tomorrow,' Sundami added sadly.

'It's all *kumak* crap!' Jacken roared. 'Nobody's going to steal your life. It's all a legend.'

It was clear from the others, few agreed with Jacken.

'It just means a little bad luck, that's all. You'll probably get nipped by a *kumak*, or fall and break your leg. Nothing serious.' Jacken looked round for support, finding none. 'Have any of you *ever* heard of a *single* person being taken by the White Hare?' he demanded.

Again, it was Stas who broke the silence. 'I never heard of anyone seeing the White Hare before.'

Chris took up his mug of *creeth* and held it to his chest. He took a draught of the soothing, hot drink and put on a brave face. He figured all he would have to do would be to get through to the day after full moon without too much bad luck, and then they would all forget about the silly white hare and all the superstition that went with it.

'Oh well,' Chris said. 'Full moon isn't until tomorrow. Why let it spoil today?' Chris had apparently said just the right thing, for the gloom immediately dispersed and the young men and women were all smiles and cheerful banter.

'And so should we all be,' Jacken said close to Chris's ear. 'When night approaches, savour the last of the sunlight. Whoa! What ...'

Sundami pushed Jacken aside and closed with that same ear. Her hot breath made him tingle, and her whispered words only added to the effect. 'Tonight, you must leave your tent flap untied, for I will visit you once the camp sleeps.'

Sundami's words were like a bugle call to arms and Chris felt himself responding immediately. He shifted his knee to hide the evidence, but Sundami recognised the manoeuvre and smiled. Jacken notice too and winked.

Sundami leaned in and whispered once again. 'You must keep your dragon tame until the time is right, then I will come to release him.'

It was all very well, and if Sundami had ventured a feel right now, she would have discovered Chris's dragon to be fully rampant – but later, in a tent full of other people ... He wondered how she would react to a terrified and shrivelled little dragon.

Chris swallowed hard, and then their was a flurry of activity as a rider came in with several rounds of unleavened bread and threw them about to be caught and eagerly devoured. There was no more talk of white hares or impatient dragons.

Just before dusk, a Tassat-sarai rider came for Chris and showed him to his quarters. Sundami went with him, eager to discover where she would be heading for, late in the night. Chris had been assigned a small but well appointed individual tent, and he felt his excitement rise as he realised the main barrier to his night time adventure had been removed: he would not have to worry about others in the tent.

Having stowed his gear he returned to the young men's tent for the rest of the evening. Sundami accompanied him and held his hand. It reminded him of those early days with Gayle.

Later when Chris was under his fleece stripped to his Kumakkashi underwear, he lay awake, aroused and expectant. He kept seeing pictures of Gayle in his mind, which he found uncomfortable. But she wouldn't begrudge him an opportunity like this, would she? Of course she would! But, he didn't even know if she was still alive. And then that little voice in his head started up. If he made love to Sundami that would be as good as saying Gayle was dead. If there was any hope of her still being alive, Chris knew he had to turn Sundami down. That damned, bloody damned horrible voice! Why couldn't it mind its own business? He had waited nearly eighteen years for this night. Nobody, but nobody would expect him to be quiet so saintly.

Round and round the voices went, tilting at each other within Chris's skull. Right up until he recalled the words of the old *rukavosh*.

Ah, but they may come to you. And if they do, you will not dishonour them by turning them away. That clinched it! He was going to do it with Sundami. He was going to go all the way, as often as Sundami wanted, as hard and as passionate. If not, they'd feed him to the dogs. With the decision made and backed up by the perfect excuse, he stripped off and then fell asleep almost immediately. As sleep came he was smiling.

He dreamt, but not of sex. He dreamt of rescue. There was a huge hot air balloon floating over Tassat-sarai and hanging from the basket dressed in the uniform of a Union artillery colonel was Tarn. He was directing the attack and Senoi, dressed in tiny modern combats (that would be too small for an Action Man), and several other similarly clad faeries, complete with tiny M15 carbines, abseiled down on several dangling spider threads. Why they didn't simply use their wings was a question that did not arise to Chris as the spectator of this dream sequence.

On striking earth, the faeries were assailed by a hoard of white hares and Kumakkashi riders, but beat them back with the help of Tarn who fired hard pellets of dried fruit from a weapon resembling a Gatling gun. Things began to look desperate when the gun jammed, and Tarn began to rip at the fabric of the balloon to secure sufficient rag to clean the mechanism. He ripped and ripped ... and Chris woke up.

The ripping sound softened to the noise of someone undoing the tent flap. Sundami! Chris sat up. This was it. It was really going to happen. He flung back the fleece and rose on his knees to greet her as he saw her shadow cross over from the entrance. She moved quickly and he opened his arms to enfold her. She was close now and he shuffled forward on his knees, just as a powerful blow caught him under the solar plexus and knocked all the wind out of him.

There was more than one of them. He was held and pummelled, and scratched hard down the left cheek. Then when they had him subdued, his right arm was held out and something smacked down hard across his knuckles. Pain, like fire, shot up his arm and he would have cried out but for the fleece wrapped round his head.

A voice rasped, 'Lay still or I'll tear out your throat.' Chris laid still. He heard a scream far off and then distant commotion. And then, with a final blow, his attackers left.

Chris lay back on a fleece and pulled another over the top. He breathed heavily trying to regain his wind. Pressing his damaged knuckles he winced at the pain. But there was no more time than that for recovery. He heard running feet and shouting, and then his tent was torn open. There were torches and Tassat-sarai riders and hard grasping hands and more angry blows. He was dragged and bundled and dragged some more until at last he was cast down onto a cold stone floor. For a second time he found himself in the dungeon, but this time he was naked and injured and had none of his gear.

For a long time he laid still, frightened to move. But as his mind began to clear he remembered this was no longer his way. He sat up and took stock of his injuries in the soft light of the old lamps. The knuckles of his right hand were skinned and swollen. His left cheek stung from several long scratches, but they were not deep. He was sore in the middle from that initial blow back in the tent, and there were a number of scuffs and bruises but nothing too serious. He took a drink of water direct from the pitcher and poured some more over his head. The scratches stung like hell, but otherwise he was glad of the refreshment. Shaking droplets from his hair he went over to the bed and taking one blanket, he wrapped it round and fastened it like a bath towel. The other blanket he threw over his shoulders and then he flopped down on the mattress and tried to take stock of his situation. He could come up with only one fact: somebody disliked him – very much. Boadak came to mind, but he was a squirt and Chris couldn't believe he had it in him to be part of the attack.

Chris tensed as the door lock rattled and rose upon the entry of two guards. The younger of the two held back, keeping a safe distance, but the older man owned the room by his presence. He was fat in the face and had a five o'clock shadow of grizzled whiskers. His turban was finely woven with gold threads.

'Your reckoning will be held tomorrow after breakfast,' he said gruffly.

'My ... reckoning?'

'The *high rukavosh* will hear about the crimes you have committed and then he will assign a punishment.'

'I haven't done anything,' Chris said. He was disappointed in himself, for the whining tone was unmistakable. He cleared his throat and started again. 'I haven't committed any crime, and for the second time I find myself in your prison.'

The old guard looked at him with contempt but said nothing.

'Will you bring me my clothes?' Chris asked trying to imbue his words with the authority of a demand.

'It is my job to inform you that your reckoning will be in the morning, nothing more. It is not my task to tell you tomorrow will be your last dawn, neither to bring you food nor take away messages and is certainly not mine to bring you clothes. You will go before the *high rukavosh* just as you are.'

'Actually,' the younger guard added diffidently. 'It's against the rules for the blankets to be removed from the cell.'

For the first time the old guard showed something similar to a smile. 'It looks like you will answer for your crimes dressed in nothing but your own skin and hair. So we will all see what the dogs will soon taste!' he looked Chris up and down, cracked a cruel grin and left, slamming the door behind him and making much of throwing the bolts.

Chris slumped back onto the bed and recalled the dream he'd had earlier. If ever he needed rescuing, the time was now. He wondered if he was forever doomed to be caught up in situations from which he needed rescuing and then his mind drifted towards another apparent constant in his life. Whenever he got close to losing his virginity, something terrifying *always* seemed to happen: from the day in the woods when Marc and Sean had been taken, to the encounter with Lillian and now his promise from Sundami.

'A guy could wind up with a complex,' Chris said to himself. 'If he gets to live long enough.'

He swung his feet up onto the bed and lay back. He closed his eyes and deliberately conjured up images of sex; himself with Gayle, with Sundami, with all the girls of the college netball team – simultaneously: anyone and any situation, as long as it kept his mind from the tearing jaws of the dogs.

Despite the underlying fear, sleep did come for him and he was successful in summoning dreams of a sexual nature. He was just beginning a session of French kissing with Gayle when the intensity of her lips upon his woke him – and there, licking his chin, was the white hare. He sat up with an involuntary cry which scared the hare off to the other side of the cell.

'Have you come to steal my life away?' Chris heard himself say.

The hare sat on her haunches and cleaned first one long ear and then the other. And then she hopped warily to the middle of the room and sat on what Chris at first thought was a silken cushion. She scrabbled at the material a couple of times then ran into the guarderobe. Chris ran to the little room, but she was not there. He looked all round the stone privy but there was not a sign of her, nor was there any hole or crack through which she might have made good her escape. He wondered if she could have hopped down the crude plumbing, and concluded that must have been the case. Either that or he'd still been dreaming.

Wandering to the centre of the cell he bent to examine the cushion and much to his delight, he found the fabric to be a full set of clothes, including – under all the silk – a pair of soft leather riding boots.

Chris discarded his blankets and washed as best he could. He dressed himself in the Kumakkashi underwear, pulled on the socks and placed the trousers, shirt, jacket and boots on the table where they could remain, un-crumpled until the morning. Crawling under the blankets he quickly dropped off for what was left of the night.

Chris slept soundly, but not for very long. He woke with the various noises of dawn, splashed water on his face and got dressed. The Kumakkashi clothes were a perfect fit – the trousers were massively baggy but they were meant to be – and he could tell they were of the highest quality. With no knowledge of how they came to be in his cell, he developed the silly notion that the hare had somehow brought them.

Light began to seep in through the high window together with sounds, such as the running feet of a young child trying to outrun a matron's scolding voice; the guttural rumblings of hungry *kumakkesh* eager for feed – and the occasional barking of a dog, no doubt equally famished and hungry for flesh.

Chris was strangely calm. He had no idea what the morning would bring, but if it brought rough handling he would deal as good as he got. Being a brown belt in jujitsu *had* to count for something. He had a fleeting vision of PC Chapel dressed in his *gi* and calling out Hajime! It made him smile and so it was that he felt ready for anything when the cell door was thrown open with commotion design to instil fear. Today it didn't work; Chris was all out of fear.

Fat face from the previous day and his now very bleary eyed younger companion burst in, and immediately the smug features of the older guard dropped.

'Who brought him those clothes,' he barked to the young man.

'Nobody! I've been at his door all night! Nobody came past me … I swear!'

His oath did not prevent the older man from slapping him hard across the face. He turned his attention to Chris. 'Take them off! You must be brought to your reckoning in the same condition that you were found.'

'Yeah, right,' Chris said in English, then reverting to the local tongue, 'I'm not taking anything off.'

'Then I'll do it for you. Eless, go tear his garb from him.'

'Who, me?' said the young guard. 'I can't –'

'Do it! Now!'

Eless shrugged and then pulled a face toward Chris that said *sorry but I have to do this* before advancing upon him. Young maybe, but he was well muscled and although reluctant to carry out his orders he clearly believed himself capable of the task – right up until the point where he found himself crumpled and upside down in the angle between the flagstones and the stone wall. Chris had executed a perfect throw with such speed and precision that the old guard had missed it when he blinked.

It was insane, but for the first time in many weeks, Chris felt absolutely in control. Neither the spectre of dogs nor the entire Tassat-sarai army held any fear for him. He was living right on the very edge but he felt like the ultimate trapeze artist; if his martial skills were insufficient, he'd talk his way out and that belief was instantly put to the test. The old guard yelled at the top of his voice – yes, there was a good measure of fear mixed in with that command – and after a short few moments half a dozen Tassat-sarai warriors piled into the cell, and all carried bladed weapons. Chris laughed. These guys looked like they were about to kill him. He laughed again and longed for them to understand the phrased that strained for release. *Am I bovvered?*

'I will tell you one time only Taker,' blustered the old guard. 'Take off those princely clothes, which have no place on your putrid carcase, or my men will rip them from you together with a good measure of your skin.'

Chris looked at the warriors, every one, and made sure he locked eye to eye with each one in turn. Just as the guard was about to speak again, he held up a hand to silence him.

'First, I am *not* a Taker. Second, which of you will dare to take these clothes away from me?'

Two warriors exchanged glances and leering smiles before beginning their advance upon Chris.

'These fine and princely clothes were given to me by the White Hare.' His timing was perfect. The two warriors blanched and quickly fell back. 'She came to me in the night, through these stone walls. So I have her favour and you will earn her anger if you lay but a single finger upon me.'

Eless stood up rubbed where his head had smacked the wall and did his best to tidy up. 'It's true,' he said. 'Those clothes weren't in there when I locked him up and him all naked. *Nobody* came by me, not even a mouse. I slept across the threshold with the keys in my shirt – and then this morning ...'

Couldn't be better, thought Chris. He stepped out towards the door and the warriors parted for him. He breezed straight out without the slightest impediment – only to turn and pop back in again.

'I won't be touched, but someone should lead me for I don't know where I am to go.'

Eless volunteered and Chris followed him out of the dungeon and up two flights of stairs. They came to a large room with a polished board floor and many scattered fleece rugs. There were several tables and wooden chairs upholstered in red and gold weave. Eless took Chris on a tour pointing out the various significant items.

'That chair is where the *high rukavosh* will sit when he comes in. A warrior will stand either side of him. You will sit over there.' Eless pointed to a small chair at a table set with a pitcher of water and a plate of dried meats, fruit and bread. 'That's you last meal,' he said with a light tone of voice that did not match the meaning of his words. Chris felt the first tiny dent in his confidence.

Two warriors will stand either side of you, and see that hood on the chair behind? That will be pulled over your head once the *rukavosh* orders your death. You'll be gagged so we shouldn't have to suffer your words and once the hood is pulled over your head you will have looked your last time upon the world, for it will be pulled off only by the teeth of the pack.'

The tiny dent became a somewhat larger rift. 'I don't even know what it is I'm supposed to have done, and anyway, I might be proven innocent.'

Eless laughed. 'Not a chance of that!'

Chris swallowed hard. 'How do you know?'

'Well, you did it and you can't deny it. I've seen the proof and anyway, the White Hare only visits those about to die. It's a shame though. I would like to have learned your fighting skills. I still can't work out what you did to me.'

'What did I do? I mean ... what am I accused of doing?'

After a long silence, the old guard made his presence felt. 'You went to one of our women in the night, and you forced yourself upon her,' he said in a voice of chilled venom.

Chris went slack-jawed and was too shocked to answer. All he could think of was the irony of being a virgin and being put to death for rape. The reins were slipping again. Time to take a firm grip! Chris forced himself back onto the high ground and thought once again about Yukio. Yukio gave up. Yukio died. He raked his rekindled gaze across the old guard's face and then looked into his depths. The guard quailed visibly.

'You will *not* place that hood over my head. The dogs shall *not* have me.'

Shortly after making a good inroad to the food before him, his reckoning began. *High Rukavosh* Marhonaz entered and the room hushed. He was not a tall man, perhaps in his mid-thirties, and was dressed in the standard garb of the Tassat-sarai, his flowing clothing and Ali Baba trousers all heavily trimmed in blue. He wore his doughnut-turban high at the front and low at the back so it formed a kind of halo about his face, which was round without being fat, and dominated by sad eyes. He had an olive complexion and, unusually for the Kumakkashi, no facial hair apart from his thin eyebrows.

Marhonaz approached Chris and waved the guards to a distance outside earshot. 'You are Chris? And from the land of prophets,' he said, his voice soft, perhaps weary.

'Yes, I'm Chris De'Ath. But I'm not from the land of prophets.'

The sad eyes smiled, just a little. 'My second phrase was a statement, not a question. I rode into battle with the help of Prophet Jason. Like him, you are from under the Tear-of-God.'

Chris began to speak but Marhonaz cut him off.

'A crime was committed, but not by you. Sadly I must act as I will, but when all this is over, we shall speak.' With that he took up his own place and the guards resumed theirs.

They had certainly worked a number on him. Sundami was brought into the reckoning. One eye was closed and puffy with a purple swelling. She told of her ordeal in which she was attacked in the dark of her own tent and beaten before her attacker forced himself upon her. She had managed to hit him once, but he had been too strong for her and in the end she suffered the assault until riders, hearing the commotion, came and he ran away like the coward he was.

Chris had deep scratched on his face. Chris had bruised knuckles. Chris's strange and singular underwear – his boxers – had been found at the scene.

Chris had been taken so shortly after the act he was still undressed and he had cried to his captor for forgiveness – so swore Terren and so swore Boadak.

Chris's story of attack by unknown warriors was derided as the frightened ramblings of a man who sees his own death approaching. He was so obviously a liar. It was the old guard who gagged him roughly and tied his hands behind his back, and the old guard who pulled the hood over his head.

'Your eyes will see no more unless the dogs rip off the hood while you yet live. But in my experience they go for softer meat first, and they eat you alive, strip by bloody strip.' The guard moved his mouth so close to Chris's ear that he felt his hot breath through the cloth of the hood. 'And in cases such as yours, we expose the offending flesh before turning you over to the pack. I am sure we will hear your screams, gagged or no.'

These words roiled round Chris's head as once again he felt cold stone beneath him. This time though, his room was the condemned cell. Chris cried, but not for long. Blindfolded and with hands tied all movement was difficult but he managed to sit, and then to stand and to feel his way to the bed. He sat on the edge of the mattress and willed Tarn to rescue him. But no! He must rescue himself. Surely he had not come to this other world to be a victim, a pathetic creature who needed to be rescued time and time again. He could not believe that a bloody and painful death was hours away. That just *could not* be! And then he found himself wondering if that was exactly how those young soldiers felt in the First World War, who had been condemned to be shot at dawn. As the minutes ticked by, did they not all believe in some last minute reprieve? Was this not all some colossal, sick joke?

But the soldiers had been shot, and maybe – the thought threatened to send him into deep freeze – maybe the dogs would tear him apart. Would he go quietly – or would he scream and rail against the world?

And then came the familiar rattle of the keys in the lock and the throwing of bolts. Chris stood. His time had come.

CHAPTER TWENTY-THREE

Execution

The dogs were restless. It was customary to starve them all day before an execution, but they were troubled by more than hunger. The people of Tassat-sarai were restless too, for outside the walls and securely barred doors, a wolf pack roamed.

Terren patrolled the wall-tops with several other riders. All kept their hands close to their weapons and their attention fixed on the wolves with the almost glowing yellow eyes. There were a dozen of them and they lurked among the gorse bushes and formed a loose circle surrounding Tassat-sarai.

Terren threw a stone at the closest wolf. It caught the stone in its mouth the spat it out as its haunches shook.

'Did you see that Jacken? The stinking beast is laughing at me.'

Jacken ran a finger along the blade of his spear and gestured for Stas to stand away from the edge. 'It appears so. These are like no wolves I've seen before.'

'No. If I'm not mistaken they're a northern breed, known for their cunning. Neither plains nor forest wolves will attack men unless crazed, but it's said this kind from the northern mountains favour man flesh above all other.'

Stas was frightened but hid it well. 'I thought those wolves were just from stories.'

'Maybe,' Terren replied. 'But where prophets walk, legends live. A little boy who was early from bed said he saw a man with the wolves when they first emerged from the morning mist. We laughed at him and told him he was dreaming, but ...'

'You think the man was ... is ... a prophet?' Jacken asked.

'If there was such a man, he was the legendary wolf-master, not the prophet.'

'Chris!' Stas said. 'You think *he's* a prophet, don't you?'

'Don't speak his name!' Terren barked. 'He is condemned. He is nothing but dog fodder and must no longer be spoken of as a man.'

'Or as a prophet?' Jacken said. 'Are you telling me that Chris ... sorry, the dog fodder ... is a prophet?'

Terren shrugged. 'I think it's likely.'

'Then should we have condemned him? Won't there be ... consequences ... if we throw him to the dogs?'

Terren turned on Jacken, angry. 'Prophet or *high rukavosh*, nobody is above what they deserve. A ravisher has offered himself up to the pack by his evil deed.'

The old, fat faced guard had been listening to the exchange, and now he spoke. 'Perhaps the dogs should go hungry for the wicked boy's flesh.'

'What?' Terren said, his words coming out on a spray of spittle.

'No. Let us not give him to the dogs. Let the wolves have him. It would be good sport to watch, and maybe with full bellies the wolves will leave us in peace.'

Terren thought about it, a wide smile slowly splitting his face. 'Sundami is of our clan, so the final word will be with our *rukavosh*. But I like the idea, and I shall commend it to him.'

The old guard smiled and slapped Terren across the shoulders. 'In that case Terren, speak to your *rukavosh* now. We can throw the ravisher down to the wolves as soon as we have his word. Otherwise we must wait until sunset, when the dogs are famished, and each moment longer the filthy little Taker lives is an affront to every rider who calls himself Kumakkashi.'

Jacken and Stas exchanged glances. It was true that Chris deserved his fate, for what he had done could never be excused, but he had been their friend and it gave them no pleasure to contemplate his fate.

Terren, never one to miss the slightest nuance, spotted their silent exchange. On the verge of deriding them, he changed his mind. 'Hey you! Stas. Go see if you can find Boadak. I haven't seen him since breakfast.'

With one last look at to the nearest wolf, Stas scooted down the stone steps and ran a meandering route to see if he could find Boadak. Terren followed down the steps at a more measured pace and headed for the tents of his own clan to seek out the *rukavosh*. Passing through the buzzing throng, he soon came to the *rukavosh's* tent and was surprised to find a tearful Sundami emerging. He took her in his arms and hugged her.

'There, there. You bear no guilt for what happened last night. Do not cry so.'

Sundami cried all the more, her head on Terren's shoulder, until with one long sniff, she pulled herself up to full height.

'Tonight, or sooner if the *rukavosh* allows, the world will be rid of your attacker. You can watch while he screams his last as the dogs ... or the wolves devour him.'

'I do not wish it!' Sundami said. 'I am not upset because of last night! Do you think I am soft like a *kumak* fleece?'

Terren realised she had been shedding tears of anger and frustration.

'I have told the *rukavosh* Chris must be spared, but he forbids a reprieve. I was so angry I ... I struck him.'

'You ... you hit the *rukavosh*? Why? It makes no sense at all.'

'Because Chris was not the one who attacked me.'

'That's ridiculous!' Terren answered a little too quickly, eager to smother the truth.

'No, it is not! I *was* attacked. But I did not see my attacker, and although I was yet to know Chris's body, I knew his heart. Such an act was ... is ... not within him.'

Terren took her shoulders and shook. 'Are you forgetting, Sundami,' he said with an edge to his voice. 'It was me, me and Boadak, who found him and chased him. We caught him before he'd had time to dress and he was marked in keeping with the facts. His face was injured where you struck him and his knuckles skinned from punching you. Do you ignore what is so clear to see?' He looked at Sundami askance. 'Do you call me a liar?'

Sundami bit back her words. She wanted to say she believed Chris's version of the story. 'I desired Chris,' she said. 'I had told him, that night I would visit his tent. Tell me why then, he would choose to force upon me that which was about to be bestowed with all good favour? It is *that* which is ridiculous! It is *that* which makes no sense at all.'

Terren ground his teeth together. 'Then the boy makes no sense and it is he that is ridiculous. He is a fool as well as a ravisher, and I shall laugh to see his limbs torn from him.' He turned his back on Sundami and entered the tent of the *rukavosh*.

To the disappointment of the fat-faced guard, Terren's *rukavosh* did not like the idea of throwing Chris to the wolves. He had been sentenced to die by the dogs, and so that is what must happen. And even if it were not for the word of the reckoning, suppose the wolves were Chris's creatures, the old man reasoned: they might help him escape justice. No, he would die at sunset, when the pack was famished. It was just as well, for by late morning the wolves had vanished, as mysteriously as they had appeared.

Terren helped to prepare the enclosure where the execution would take place. The area was roped off and a podium was set up for the *rukavosh* and dignitaries from any other clan who might wish to witness the spectacle, and sand was spread liberally for nothing was worse than the dogs trailing bloody footprints or dragging slippery intestines between the tents. Whip-boys were stationed round the perimeter to discourage any of the pack from straying from the circle with scraps of flesh, or to push the condemned man back should he stumble, in blind panic, near to the edge.

As evening meals were ended and utensils tidied away, a crowd began to gather. There was an atmosphere of respectful anticipation as the people gathered, as was their duty, to see justice done. Terren was not surprised to notice that Sundami had chosen to stay away, but at least Jacken and Stas were in attendance. He knew they would both rather be somewhere else but had made it very clear that their absence would earn them dishonour. Where was Boadak though? He hadn't seen him for hours.

Lamps were lit and fires stoked as the sunlight softened and shadows grew long, and then the buzz of the crowd fell to hush as the condemned man was brought from the tower, a strong Tassat-sarai man at each arm and the old guard parting the crowd. It was quite within the rules to mistreat and abuse a condemned prisoner, who was, after all, no longer a man, and blood stained the hood in front of his face where several riders had felt it there right to punch him as he passed. Spittle coated the hood and shoulders and the air was filled with derisive laughter and cruel invective. Still dressed in the fine silk clothes, for no man had risked incurring the anger of the White Hare, nor had anyone dared to rip open the crotch area to "expose the offending flesh", the boy trembled as he was dragged into the prepared enclosure. As the guards propelled him into the centre the crowd fell silent – then roared as the pack was released. The boy stood, head bent in fear and knees little able to take his weight.

It was poor sport, and those in the crowd whose blood-lust has been peaked were disappointed. As the first dog struck the boy fell to his knees, then keeled over onto one side as two other seized his arms. Then the lead dog seized the boy's neck ripped out the carotid, almost as if he wanted to give him a swift end. There was blood aplenty, and ripping silk and the shredding of skin and flesh, but never once did he cry out nor even move once he had fallen to the sandy ground. Without the terror and the struggle for life and the screaming, the crowd might as well have watched the butcher at work. Why, one old lady was heard to day, she'd seen better sport with a corpse and an already well-fed pack.

Four dogs fought over a mess of innards that one had ripped and dragged from the abdominal cavity – the one highlight of the event – and Terren found himself cheering when someone grabbed his arm.

'Boadak! Where have you been all day?

'Sorry Terren. I was hiding.'

'Hiding?'

'I kept thinking what we'd done. I wanted to think of a way to stop *this* happening.'

'Keep you voice down, fool. Do you want us both taken for speaking false at a reckoning? I hope you know what they'd do to us.'

Terren didn't have time to enlighten his young friend, because the crowd let out a sudden, unified cry of shock and horror. With Boadak close behind, Terren elbowed his way to the enclosure rope to see what was going on.

'What is it?' Terren demanded to nobody in particular. He cast his eyes quickly over the scene of blood soaked rags and body parts, but noticed nothing unusual until a dog, it maw red with blood, trotted up with something dangling from its jaws.

'That! I see what it is!' cried a man from the crowd. 'See what the dog has torn from the body?'

And all of a sudden Terren could see, only too well, and a sickening feeling gripped his stomach. The dog was holding the pendant of the *high rukavosh*. It could mean only one thing: if the *high rukavosh* gave his pendant to a condemned man, it was a sign that he took serious issue with the accusers. It meant that he had given sentence reluctantly and only because the law of the Kumakkashi had tied his hands. Chris, the Taker scum was dead, but Terren and Boadak were as good as banished, and banishment onto the plains the Kumakkashi Plains was itself a kind of death sentence.

Terren wished he could turn time and make it run backwards, at least back as far as this morning's dawn. Then, instead of punching the hooded Chris, he could have searched him and found the pendant before it was all too late.

CHAPTER TWENTY-FOUR

The Dance of the White Hare

Was this not all some colossal, sick joke? Chris thought as he sat, hooded and bound. He sensed dawn's first light creep into his cell.

Maybe the dogs will tear me apart. Would he go quietly – or would he scream and rail against the world?

And then came the familiar rattle of the keys in the lock and the throwing of bolts. Chris stood. His time had come.

As the footsteps drew close, Chris anticipated his immediate future. Rough hands would seize him at each elbow. They would drag him out of the cell and he would find it difficult to keep his balance but *fuck them*, keep his balance he would. He wasn't going to have them think he was scared, because in all honesty he wasn't. The crowds would part and he would hear their mockery. They would probably throw rotten vegetable at him, almost definitely rough him up a little – maybe a lot. Then there was that thing about exposing the offending flesh. That would really give them something to laugh about. So much pain, so much humiliation, but none of it seemed to matter. Chris felt as if a heavy, wet blanket woven of resignation and acceptance had been drawn over him, suppressing the horror that bubbled somewhere, deep inside him – suppressing everything: killing fear, stamping down the will to act, extinguishing the tiny spark of hope. At the same time his thoughts ran at maximum speed, but they ran through treacle. And from somewhere deep inside came the one emotion that buoyed him up, and that was defiance. Futile though he knew it to be, he would be defiant until death – or until agony imposed its immutable imperative.

By the time his captor stopped in front of him he had contemplated all that his loss to the world would mean: whatever his role in this war against the Mass, it would have to go unfilled. What *had* happened to Tarn and the faeries? There! He could say it now. Faeries: he'd never been comfortable with the word until now, always feeling somehow tainted by the fact that he had seen them. To see a faerie, much less speak the word, dented the macho part of his ego. If red-blooded guys were going to have to choose to see something from legends, faeries were not exactly at the top of the list. But now, with death a short walk away, none of that ego stuff mattered any more. Nothing really mattered very much.

When the footfalls ceased and Chris heard his visitor's voice, the cloying blanket was ripped away and his senses were no longer dampened.

'Sit down, Chris,' Moon said. 'We must talk.'

Chris heard her soft voice – it fanned a residual spark of hope within him – but in his mind he saw the White Hare. 'Can you untie me, and help me get this hood off?'

'That is not why I'm here.'

'Not ... not here to rescue me?'

'The law has been spoken and I must not interfere. But ...'

'But?' Chris was ready to hold on to any piece of flotsam that passed by.

'I have brought you my man's pendant. Here ... bend your head forward. Let me slip it over ... There!'

Chris took a deep breath sucking the material of the hood towards his mouth. 'Thank you,' he said without enthusiasm. 'Won't it get a bit bloody?' Maybe that was the point, he thought. Maybe after today the *high rukavosh* would wear his pendant decorated with dried blood.

'I hope it will not become sullied with your blood. It is my hope that none of your blood will be spilled.'

Here we go again, thought Chris. Hope, no hope, and hope again. He couldn't be bothered to ask.

'When a condemned man is presented for execution wearing the pendant of the *high rukavosh*, it is a sign that he was displeased with the outcome of the reckoning. He is not above the words spoken in judgment and nor can he order a reprieve, but he can make his displeasure known, and if the people so wish, they may reprieve.

'So, all they have to do is see this and I'll be alright?'

'Perhaps, but even if they don't reprieve you, it is said that the pendant will save your spirit and guide it to the Realm of Light. Your body may be torn and consumed, but you will walk with the First Ones.'

And finally, no hope. If they didn't reprieve him, he'd be ripped apart – end of: no heaven, no land of light, no nothing. What the dogs left behind would be worm food. Chris felt the blanket enfolding him once again. They all thought he was a ravisher. There would be no reprieve for him.

'There are wolves outside the *sarai* walls,' Moon said. She laid her hand on Chris's knee. 'They are there because of you.'

Chris nodded, the rough cloth of the hood rubbing his nose. 'I dare say they are. I've met a couple already.'

'They are led by a man who calls himself Wierchan.'

'I think the word is "Wiergan" and yes, I've met one of them too.'

'Words change over the centuries, but style himself as he may, he is no wierchan, although his lady is.'

'His lady?'

'She came from your world, long years ago, and used her arts to ensnare the Mass.'

'The Unselost Mass?'

'My, my! You *are* well informed. I assumed you would be ignorant until you ...' Moon cut herself off as if she had said more than she intended. 'Anyway, I came to warn you. If you are reprieved, you will caste outside the walls, so unless you are careful it will be but a short stay of execution for you will fall to the wolves.'

'What do I do? Wave this pendant at them?'

Moon did not notice the sarcasm in his voice. 'No, but should you see a white hare, you must turn your back upon her and walk the other way. She will dance the wolves to their deaths, but if you gaze upon her, you will have to follow them and share their fate.'

Chris shook his head. If his hands were free he would have placed his head in his hands. He whispered under his breath: *I'm a celebrity. Get me out of here.*

Moon's hearing was acute. 'You have no wierchan skills to rely upon such chants. Just remember, if you survive the dogs, you may best the wolves by leaving them to the White Hare. But, do ... *not* ... look upon her.'

'You're a wierchan, aren't you? That White Hare and you – you're the same. You are her and she is you.' *And I am the walrus, coo, coo, ca-choo.*

'Many wierchan have animals with which they are familiar,' Moon answered without directly addressing the question.

If nothing else, at least the conversation was keeping Chris's mind off the dogs. 'Wait a minute! Are you a *witch*? Is a wierchan the same thing as a witch?' Chris suddenly had a face in his mind; it was the young woman who ran the garden centre back home. Why her face should come to him in the midst of all this was a mystery to him.

'I don't know that word, "witch", but as I said, words change over the long years.'

'Yes, but are you a witch, or a wierchan or whatever?'

Moon's reply was a long time coming, and blinded by the hood Chris began to wonder if she had slipped away.

'I have been called wierchan, but that is not strictly the correct term. Perhaps I am "whatever" for I am no wierchan, at least, not in the same way as the Lady. She is of your world, and I –'

'You're from the Mass!' Chris said, remembering the yellow eyes of the hare that had visited his cell, the same eyes he had seen many times before: the succubus, Kostja, the wolf – they had all had those eyes.

'And yet, you must believe me when I say, I mean you no harm.'

Words were cheap. Bound, hooded and completely helpless Chris brought his knees together waited for the attack. Maybe he wouldn't die a virgin after all, and if Moon was going to make a move on him, he'd do his best to enjoy himself. He'd close his eyes and think of Gayle. In spite of all he faced, he actually began to feel aroused.

'I must go,' Moon said.

'W ... what!' Hope, no hope; up and down like a bloody yo-yo. He heard the soft caress of silk on silk as Moon walked away.

'Have faith in the pendant, and remember, do not look upon the White Hare.'

'Whatever,' Chris managed under his breath in English. There was an exchange between Moon and the guard, then the door slammed and the keys were turned. Once again, Chris was left with his thoughts. Swinging his legs up onto the bed he laid back and tried to let his mind settle. In that he was successful, for in five minutes he was asleep.

He woke with a start and sat up. Someone was in his room, although the heavy door had not been opened. The White Hare?

'Who's there?'

'It is me, Marhonaz, and a friend.'

'How did you –'

'There is no time for questions. It is late and soon they will come for you.'

Chris felt himself hustled to his feet; there was fumbling at his throat and someone worked on the knot which bound his hands. Although the light was dim Chris's eyes smarted when the hood was pulled. He blinked and looked down at Marhonaz while his friend struggled with the knot at his back.

'You must undress quickly and put on your own things,' Marhonaz said indicated, with a nod of his head, a bundle of mainly green clothing and his boots on the table. His arms suddenly free, Chris turned to thank the stranger and found himself looking at a very short young man who was wearing no shirt. He was naked to several inches below the navel – further down Chris did not care to look. He was perhaps in his late teens for his beard grew no stronger than Chris's own. His eyes were hazel, bright and intelligent and he moved his head at different angles to get a better look at Chris; there was something almost birdlike in the way his head moved, but most curious of all were the horns which curled out from thick, chestnut hair. Or perhaps the pointed ears were more striking yet.

'May I introduce you to my friend? His name is Agronal and he is of the race called s'tyradhrim.'

Agronal inclined his head while keeping his eyes locked into Chris's. Chris nodded back and Agronal stepped closer to the dim lamp light. The horns and ears paled into insignificance as Chris noticed the young man's legs. What he had taken as a pair of shaggy trousers was in fact long hair and the knees bent the wrong way. As if that wasn't enough, the legs terminated in hooves rather than feet.

'You're a ...' Chris didn't know the right word in the *Hereek*, so he said it in English. 'You're a centaur.'

Agronal and Marhonaz exchanged smiles. 'There's no such thing,' Agronal said. 'People from your world call me a satyr, which is close enough to the true name of my kind.'

Well, well, well, thought Chris. *A satyr. How very interesting.* He was no longer surprised by the diversity of sentient life forms in this world, although he rather hoped he wouldn't bump into a Telly-tubby some time soon.

'Forgive me,' Marhonaz said. 'But there really is no time. Change quickly!'

Chris needed no more encouragement. If rescue meant changing, then he'd change in record time. Apart from the huge relief at the diminishing possibility of being eaten, it felt really good to back in his clothes. As for the princely Kumakkashi garments, Marhonaz discarded his own clothing and put them on.

'Now, give me back my pendant and then you must go.'

Marhonaz placed the pendant over his neck and picked up the hood.

'Are you going to pretend to be me?' Chris asked as the penny dropped.

'The pendant will save me.'

Chris wasn't convinced. 'What if it doesn't?'

Marhonaz smiled. 'Events will unfold as they will, and schemes and plans will succeed or fail. But however the future sets, I will have kept a promise I made many years ago to another like you.'

Chris nodded. 'The Prophet Jason.'

Marhonaz smiled and nodded.

Heavy footfalls echoed in the hall outside. 'They come!' Marhonaz said, and then nodded towards Agronal. As Agronal approached Marhonaz pulled the hood over his head.

'Now we must take to the Hidden Paths,' Agronal said. He put his arms round Chris's waist, squeezed hard and then Chris expanded to fill the Universe. One again he was experiencing the Hidden Paths. This time there was a short interlude of fear and pain along with the timelessness and absence of sensation during which there were shouts and blinding lights and finally a sweetly sung song. When the world coalesced around him, Chris was standing in a scrubby wood, Agronal at his side and a strange creature huddled by the twisted roots of a tree. It was dusk and it was hard to discern the outline of the creature, but it emitted a low, steady moan and it appeared to be in pain.

Night fell at Tassat-sarai. Terren and Boadak shared the cell that had started the day as Chris's. The situation had not been good for either of them once the pendant had been ripped from the dog-torn corpse. How much worse it was when the hood came away and instead of the Taker's features, the light had fallen on those of the *high rukavosh*. As soon as the pack was hungry, Terren and Boadak were to be their next meal. The council of their reckoning had spoken. For the contrived murder of their leader, they were to die by the same means. Terren appealed to his own *rukavosh*. The old man simply turned his back.

The pack howled, hungry once more, and Terren cried and beat at the cell doors. How could they be the victims of so great a miscarriage of justice? Could nobody see this was a work of evil magic?

Boadak sat quietly for the most part, and it was he who heard the cries of excitement from the riders outside. Later they were to learn from the fat faced guard, that the White Hare had been seen, dancing in the moonlight, and that wolves followed her into the darkness. Early next day, riders came in from an outlying camp, their mounts loaded high with the bloody pelts of wolves, the whole pack found crushed by a herd of *narkellesh*.

Strange goings on, and the dancing of the White Hare was central to the last conversation shared between Terren and Boadak. In the end they were spared the pack, for someone – perhaps Jacken, or so Terren surmised – threw a thin blade in through the cell window. They made their peace with the world then Terren ran the blade between Boadak's ribs and into his heart before slicing though his own throat. When he found them the fat-faced guard was consumed with anger. Once again he had been cheated of his sport.

CHAPTER TWENTY-FIVE

Out of Time

The wood was unwholesome; it stank of corruption and the bleached, skeletal branches of the trees gathered fetid mists about them. Chris pushed all this to the back of his mind and edged forward towards the unhappy creature, for as his eyes adapted to the gloom he could tell that it was human. Agronal had drawn a moon-shaped blade identical to the one Chris had found thrust into the tree near his front garden back home. He scouted round trying to get his bearings.

From far off came a sound like soft-edged rasping wind. Chris correctly guessed he was hearing the noise made by the footfalls of many hundreds of people, but now he had come to the side of the piteous man huddled in the tree roots, sound claimed little attention.

'He's got a gash across his forehead,' Chris said to Agronal who was visible as a pale shadow in the mist. He was crouching, an ear cocked towards the sound of the marching men as it died away to nothing, and he appeared not to hear Chris at all.

'It looks infected. I think he's dying.' From the stench that arose from him he could already have been a week dead. 'Agronal! Help me!' Chris reached out to move a clotted shank of hair from the man's eyes but withdrew at the last instant. There could be disease.

Agronal moved silently and seemed to appear at Chris's side instantly. 'Stand clear,' he said, testing his moon-blade. 'He is of the Taker race. I shall put an end to him.'

'You bloody well wont!' Chris said in English, putting himself between the unconscious man and the satyr. Reverting to *Hereek* he continued. 'We'll help him. Got any water?'

'None to waste.'

Chris looked at the man and saw Yukio. 'Look Agronal, I appreciate what you've done for me, but I really think we should help this man. I don't know what Takers have done to your people, but it doesn't mean *we* can treat *them* like insects.'

'Come here a moment,' Agronal said walking off into the mist. Chris reluctantly followed, not only because he didn't like to leave the Taker, but because Agronal seemed to be leading him closer to the source of the sickening odour.

'This is the work of Takers,' Agronal said pointing to a mound that seemed to writhe by some trick of the mist. Chris walked closer to find that it wasn't the mist that animated the mound, but a veneer of rat-like rodents, mice and insects of numerous kinds. He caught his breath when he saw a human arm, glistening wet and green, standing out above the living carpet of vermin. And then through a gap he saw a smiling row of teeth which was all that identified a decomposing ball of slime as a human head.

'There are probably close to a hundred dead in this heap, some a week or two from life, others like this one slain within a few hours.'

Chris followed Agronal's gaze to the corpse of a very old man in clothes of silk with his belly slit open. The eyes stared, lifeless but not free of accusation.

'Takers deal only in death, and in this period more so than ever before. Look there – through the trees. Keep staring until the wind shifts the mist.'

Chris scuttled up over fallen trees and balanced on a stump to increase his vantage point. At first he could only make out a dark shape, like a distant mountain, but then a gust of wind lifted the veil for just an instant.

'It's a city,' Chris said. 'Or at least a large town.'

'And in the temporality to which I belong, that city is an ivy-clad ruin.'

'It doesn't look like a ruin to me. I only saw it for a second but everything looked solid and well built.'

'That is because when the Yaemonadhrim attacked, they pushed us off the Hidden Paths, in course, distance ... and time. We have come back some fifteen years, to a period when the Takers were still powerful and their abominable king yet lived.'

While Chris thought about the young satyr's words he made his way back to the Taker and Agronal followed.

'The demons attacked? You mean the wolves?'

'They have the appearance of wolves but they are of the Mass, and they can run along the Hidden Paths. They attacked but – with help from an unexpected quarter – I managed an escape for us both.'

'Who helped us?' Chris said, believing he knew the answer.

'The Paths are not like the worlds of leaf and blade, and neither vision nor hearing is the same, but I fancied I heard singing and saw –'

'A white hare?'

Agronal darted an enquiring look towards Chris, then nodded.

'Let's get back onto the Paths then. She ... the White Hare may help us some more.'

Agronal shook his head. 'The Hidden Paths are being watched by something more powerful than wolves or white hares. I felt something dark and evil, as if the Mass itself had developed eyes. We cannot risk further use of the Hidden Paths except to get us back to our own time. That I think we *must* attempt. After that we go on foot. Come! Make ready.'

'Help me with this man,' Chris said.

'We cannot take him with us. Surely now, after I have shown you their handiwork –'

'I don't think he did any killing. If anything, he's another victim.'

'Takers kill their own. He is one of them. Takers do not pass into adulthood without a string of murders to their name.'

'And yet ... do they usually dress in gold silk?' Chris pulled a shred of fabric out for Agronal to see.

'Not usually, but garb is nothing but wrapping. The man inside is a Taker and he must be left. To bring him with us would be likened to let a bear into your family retreat.'

Chris stood and took the skin that hung from a leather strap across Agronal's shoulder. 'Water?'

Agronal nodded and sensing determination in the young human, handed it over.

Chris took a handkerchief from the thigh pocket of his combat trousers and a black plastic 35mm film pot fell out with it. He popped the lid to check inside.

Good! Tarn's tooth was still safe wrapped in a tissue. Putting the pot back in his pocket, he uncorked the water-skin, wet the hanky and wiped away the dried blood from the Taker's face. The injured man showed some response and opened his eyes. Death was chased from his features by the delicate smile of relief and he tried to speak, but the effort was too great. Words were beyond him and sleep took him once more.

Minutes later, when argument and counter-argument was exhausted, Agronal leaned into the void to step once again onto the Hidden Paths with a human tightly held in each arm. Chris would not go without the Taker and to leave Chris was unthinkable.

Emerging from the Hidden Paths, Agronal was drained by the transit but satisfied that they had come back to their own time. The intervening years had been a healing tonic for the wood which was now fresh and lush, and looking from the wood's edge the city of the Takers was indeed a ruin. Could nature reclaim so much in just fifteen years? Buildings were hardly discernable: time had rounded all sharp edges and added a blanket of vegetation, so what had once been a city now resembled tumble-rocked mountains.

Agronal explained that his kind maintained retreats in all parts of the world and throughout temporal levels, and that he could sense one nearby. Soon Chris found himself safe within a s'tyradhrim shelter which they came to through the gnarled and twisted roots of a great tree. Chris noticed no walls or other recognisable structures, and fancied himself to be in a cave hollowed out under the wood, but for comfort this little retreat was the equal of any log cabin or stone built dwelling. The chairs and table appeared to grow from the living wood, and there were beds and stores of food. There was also a hollow in the floor with sides of polished, auburn wood filled with water that Agronal heated up by what Chris could only think of as magic.

Together they peeled off the stinking rags of the Taker, bathed him, dressed him in the hooded cloak that Agronal kept for cold weather and put him to bed. Semi-conscious throughout the process, he fell into a deep sleep the moment he was laid out.

Then Agronal prepared a meal comprising a stew of meat and vegetables and a large hunk of bread. Agronal was reluctant to take his eyes from the sleeping Taker. While Agronal watched the Taker, Chris took in all the strange and inhuman details of the satyr. Facially he could almost have been a human of perhaps twenty, but of very small stature. Chris estimated him to be no more than five feet tall. His cranial hair was human-like, bushy and if Agronal wore any clothes it could be called collar-length. His intelligent, vital eyes were set in a narrow face and the slightly curved horns emanated from just above the hair line and were about eight centimetres long. His torso was weathered and well muscled without being heavy. Then came the legs with their thick covering of shaggy, red-brown hair, quite sufficient for the sake of modesty, and reaching down to what Chris thought of as his fetlocks. The hooves were cloven, and Chris wondered why so devil-like a creature should actually be part of the Host rather than the Mass. He wore a dagger round his neck and several items of equipment were kept in a leather haversack slung over one shoulder. The moon-blade was sheathed in a moon-shaped scabbard usually hidden from view under the haversack.

'Can you do that thing again, Agronal? With the water? I don't smell much better than the Taker did, so I reckon I'm overdue for a bath.'

'The water flows through the tub, so now it is fresh and clear of the Taker's scum, but it has run cold. Get ready and I will heat some for you.' He took a slender dowel of turned wood from a brushed leather pouch.

'I suppose that's a magic wand?' Chris said, feeling very silly for saying so.

'It is a *cambralik*, and it is used for channelling the light.'

'Channelling the light? You mean, casting spells.'

Agronal smiled. 'You speak like Jason did. He was ignorant of our ways and spoke of "magic" and "casting spells".'

'You met Jason? I've heard his name quite a lot.'

'I met him when I was just a little faun. I danced for him! But it was from Caedmon, my older brother that I have since learned of his questions about our ways. I was too young to take much notice of anything that was not fun, and talking of our ways was ... boring.'

Chris began to undress. The clothes couldn't go long without a wash, but they'd wait a little longer than him. Pulling a towel from his pack he wrapped it round and went over to the tub, suddenly very conscious of his feet. He wondered if Agronal was as fascinated by his feet as he was by Agronal's hooves.

Agronal pointed the *cambralik* at the water and a gentle glow emanated from it, and kept flowing until the water began to steam. 'There! That should be sufficient for a comfortable bath.'

Chris stepped in and sunk into the hot water. The warmth seeped into his bones and he relaxed, feeling better than he had so far since before the pursuit though Wymes Park. Was it really only a week since his encounter with the incubus Kostja?

'So Agronal. Can anyone learn to ... what did you call it ... channel the light?'

Agronal sat on the floor by the rim of the tub. 'All the s'tyradhrim can draw both the light and the dark. Some humans can, but very few, and I do not understand how this can be. But you can't.'

'Why not?'

'We can sense the ability within people, and in you I do not sense it.'

While he soaked Chris continued to ask questions until he had quite an understanding about the drawing the powers, which he still thought of as casting spells. After all, that was the term Tarn had used when they first met in the hospital. Chris was surprised to learn that each spell was a kind of individual being, drawn either from the Host – the light powers, or the Mass – the dark powers. It would be drawn from its own realm, perform a specific task and then dissipate or return to its realm.

Chris was puzzled that a being of the Host could draw powers of the Mass and asked Agronal about it.

'I am not of the Host. I am a being of blood and bone, the same as you. There were the First Born, from whom the beings of the Host spring, and then us. S'tyradhrim came to the world before it was torn into three, and then came the Last Born – people of your kind.'

'Where do the Takers fit in?'

'They're Last Born, like you.'

'And their evil king?'

'Ah. He was First Born, but perverted by the Mass.'

Every answer led Chris to another batch of questions, and the water was cool by the time he had a basic grip on how his universe worked. The First Born, the s'tyradhrim and the Last Born had all shared the world, until it was torn into three. The First Born were to inhabit the First Realm which they called Ieldamarah, which was the source of the powers of light. Humans lived for the most part in the Second or Middle Realm, and the s'tyradhrimmen were to have the Third Realm. The spaces between became known as the Hidden Paths and it was never intended that they should ever be walked by the Last Born. But the rending of the worlds was not a precise thing, and people of all kinds were stranded in the wrong worlds. Furthermore ways and portals were left to the Paths, and therefore there was limited access between the worlds.

Chris reluctantly dragged himself from the water which Agronal had boosted back to comfortable warmth, and wrapped himself in the towel. As tired as he was, there was one more question. 'You said the First Realm was the source of the light and where the Host come from. What about the Mass?'

'The origin of the Mass is a mystery, but it is seated in the far reaches of the Hidden Paths, and there it feeds and grows fat on the substances of the three worlds.'

Chris towelled down. 'And I've been brought here to go sort out the Mass.'

'If you have been brought here to fight the Mass, it will only be to help. You will not be expected to best it all alone.'

'Oh good. Because I *was* beginning to wonder.' Chris gave a wry smile, and Agronal was not blind to the humour. Chris slipped on boxers and t-shirt and sorted out some spare clothing for the Taker.

'First though, we must travel to the western coasts and then across the sea to my land. There are many Takers to the south of these woods, and we cannot use the Hidden Paths.'

'Do you live at Brikadden?'

'No. That is usually to the south, not far from the land of the Kumakkashi, but we were hurled far to the north in our encounter with the wolves, and now we dare not tread that way until I have taken council with the Govern of my people.'

'How long will that take?'

'It is a long journey by foot. A month, perhaps, if you have good stamina.'

A month would be far too long. Chris thought of Gayle, stuck in some demon prison waiting for him to come for her. He didn't know if that was his purpose, but he did know his answers were at Brikadden.

'Well, you can go west Agronal. And I wish you a good journey. But I'm going south, and I hope you will tell me the way to Brikadden, even if you won't take me.'

After failing to impress upon Chris the impossibility of a fifteen day march through arid plain, open to the sky and thick with marauding Takers, Agronal sat in silence for some time as he contemplated another route.

'I see you have the language stones fused to your temples,' Agronal said pointing to the side of Chris's head.

'Do they still show?' Chris said raising a finger to his left temple and pressing lightly.

'They show in your mastery of several tongues. Even Jason only spoke basic *Hereek* and the tongue of my people with an appalling accent, and that after much study. Yet you speak with Takers, Kumakkashi and ... when I have slipped in the occasional phrase from the language of the s'tyradhrim you have never once stumbled in your understanding.'

Chris nodded, his thoughts back home in French class. What a shame he hadn't had a pair of these devices fitted before he got an unclassified in his French GCSE.

'My point is that you must have met the Kern.'

'Those giant grasshopper-people? I've only met the one called Drone. He's the one who stuck the devices on me.'

'If you have only to meet one of the Kern, Drone would be a good choice. He is eminent among his kind and well known to the other races too. Once the Kern served the same master as the Takers and Drone was one of those who first broke away from his control.'

Chris grinned. 'Good old Drone. I get to meet the best people, present company not excepted.'

Agronal was unsure of the syntax and was not sure if he was being complimented or insulted. He decided to respond to the smile, if not the words and grinned back.

'Anyway, I mention the Kern because there is one way we may travel south and avoid the Takers.'

Agronal explained that the Kern were magnificent engineers and over hundreds of years they had constructed underground tunnels which served as roadways for pods that moved about without the need to draw the powers and with no animals to haul them. The way the system was described made Chris think of the London Underground railway network on a much grander scale.

'The pods are propelled to great speeds by the interaction of power fields natural to the earth, and there is ... or was ... a terminus on the edge of the Taker's city.'

'You're talking years ago Agronal. The system will have been turned off or broken down by now, won't it?'

'The Kern still use it in places, and it was maintained by automatons ... little boxes that wondered through the tunnels seeing to repairs. Yes, the Kern tunnels my no longer work, but we should try them. The other options are far too dangerous.'

'Let's get some sleep then, and in the morning go looking for tunnels.' He sat on the bed which was soft and springy. He noticed an aura of warmth emanated from the bed, so there was no need for blankets. Perhaps the aura was a soporific too, for he was overwhelmed with fatigue and slept at once.

Agronal approached the Taker and with a minute movement of the hands he summoned a form of power that would keep the young man sleeping until he withdrew it. With safeguards now set against nocturnal treachery, Agronal too made use of a bed. All slept soundly until morning.

CHAPTER TWENTY-SIX

A Path of Bones

Edmund Warwick had half an eye on the distant resting place of his quarry: Chris De'Ath, the goat-boy and a mysterious third person. The remainder of his attention was taken up by the dying wolf. It lay up against a soft grassy mound that was pierced here and there by sun bleached human bones. Long years had passed since the place was used to discard the dead of the City, but Edmund Warwick knew well enough where he was, for across a grassy plain the bones of that City were visible, though as completely entombed in greenery as this old ossuary.

Edmund lifted the wolf's head and put a flask to its lips, letting a little water flow forth and tease the black lips and trickle between the yellow fangs. The beast was past swallowing, and it would be dead within the hour. Edmund cursed under his breath. He had no love for the wolf men, and precious little respect: sometimes fear, perhaps, but never respect. This wolf though, he would have it live, for without it Edmund could not navigate the Hidden Paths nor even enter upon them. When this one died, which would be very soon, Edmund would be stranded in the Forest of the Dead, far away from his mistress.

There were compensations. Stranded he may be, but before the wolf succumbed to its crushing injuries, it had followed the goat-boy and Chris De'Ath along the Hidden Paths, so it was thanks to the wolf that he was close to the same place and temporality as his quarry. And as this was Taker land, it would be an easy matter for him to gather to himself a rag-tag company to pursue and capture them. He had no choice; take them he must for without Chris he could not return to the Lady, unless he was keen to have his head stand in line with her other friends of the mantle shelf. He had served her faithfully for many years, but so had old Readtoth, and he had no doubt that for one mistake, Lady Rosemary now wore his pelt on chilly evenings.

The wolf-man began to wheeze, and then bubble deep in the throat. The sound of dysfunctional respiration increased, rose to a crescendo and then stopped abruptly, only to end in one final and lengthy exhalation. With that last breath, the beast's life left its body. One final corpse to the pile, soon worms would take it beneath the grass to be with the other bony folk.

And now the quarry was on the move. Edmund gathered his gear together and slung a pack over his shoulder. Ready to set off in pursuit of Chris and the satyr – they were heading north, how strange, and now there were three of them – he paused to bring a booted heel crashing down into the dead wolf's gaping jaw. He yanked out a loosened fang and checked the stump. Satisfied, he pocketed the gory trophy and set off, keeping his prey at the edge of sight, while ensuring that they would not see him, should they care to cast a backward glance. He could only trust to fate that they would refrain from entering the Hidden Paths, for if they did he was lost and could do no more than follow his erstwhile companion into the land of the dead.

Agronal found the old City Hive quite easily. Though abandoned when the Kern left and the city fell, it was the most distinctive of structures and it had survived fairly much intact. It was a tower-like structure shaped like a fat cigar and they were fortunate in that there were several openings at ground level. The ground floor had become the abode of wild animals which were aggressive only in their odour. The floor was rank with nesting materials, droppings and the bones of smaller prey.

The Taker, now dressed in old tracksuit pants, a t-shirt covered over with Agronal's cloak and wearing Chris's trainers, sniffed the air and pulled a face. Chris thought this pretty rich, as the aroma was not half as offensive as the Taker had been when they'd found him. Now he was cleaned up, he appeared to be in his early twenties. He was shorter than Chris, whose spare clothes swamped him, and was sparely built and malnourished. His eyes were dull in a narrow face, and he was cowed and jumpy, ever expectant of attack from either Chris or Agronal, but nevertheless he followed them eagerly and Chris began to think of him as a little whipped pup frightened of its master yet more frightened of being left alone.

The lower levels had remained free of animal intruders simply because the unlocked doors had been kept closed. The three companions wound down and down activating short-end-of-the-spectrum lighting as they came within range of unseen sensors. Long abandoned perhaps, but the building had maintained its basic functions. Its corridors were soft-walled tubes or tunnels; like the eerie red lighting, no doubt perfect for the Kern, but strange and uncomfortable to navigate for human and s'tyradhrim alike.

With so much evidence of neglect to be found on the upper floors, it came as a great shock to find the lowest level, not only spotlessly clean, but occupied. As Chris and Agronal passed through a door to the base level, they came face to face with a dozen Kern. One had a double-set of wings, the others were wingless.

With his devices, Chris was able to communicate with them quite easily, more to their surprise than his. They were a maintenance party involved in the re-commissioning of City Hive. When Chris spoke of Brikadden they had heard of it, and told them they should travel by pod to the Hive of the Alchemists, also abandoned after the war, but still with a functional terminus. They were helped on their way and soon found themselves in possession of a tiny control device and huddled in a pod of very organic structure and hurtling towards the Hive of Alchemists.

The journey was long and completely without on-board entertainment. Being designed for the insect-like bodies of Kern it was also dreadfully uncomfortable. It was impossible to relax, much less to sleep, so Chris and Agronal swapped stories of their journeys to Tassat-sarai, of the war and of the oft-mentioned Prophet Jason from under the Tear-of-God. The Taker appeared to listen although gave no hint of understanding, and he made no attempt to speak. Chris began to wonder if he was dim-witted or mentally numbed by his experiences. He certainly did not look at all dangerous. A pity the same could not be said for the Taker-band Edmund Warwick had quickly gathered about him. As Chris's pod drew close to its destination, Edmund and his retinue boarded another having slain every last Kern in the City Hive.

Chris's party came to their intermediate destination after an hour of travel and alighted into the base level of the Hive of Alchemists which was in the midst of towering mountains in a range to the north of the Kumakkashi Plains. Choked with cobwebs and dust it had withstood invasion by any animals apart from invertebrates, but the hive was just as miserable, and they were happy to find a way out onto a high mountain path, open to bright sunshine.

'This path winds for a march of five days, and it has been out of use since the war, so it may be hard to follow, but eventually it comes to a great monument of the Slain Prophet, and there we shall join the path to Brikadden.'

'My boots are up to it, and it looks like your ... feet?'

'Hooves!'

'It looks like your hooves are tough enough, but I don't think those old trainers are much good for mountains.' The Taker did not appear to realise he was the subject of conversation. 'They're not even a good fit for him.'

'No they are not. I have met many humans and your feet are quite the biggest I have ever seen. I have also noticed, from when you bathed last night, there appears to be a correlation between the size of a human male's feet and his –'

'Yes! Yes, but what are we going to do about the Taker? We can't trail him along for five days with blistering and bloody feet. It would be cruel.'

'I could still kill him,' Agronal said fingering the hilt of his moon-blade. 'This *dookalik* has the keenest of blades and I would dispatch him quickly and without pain.'

'It's not going to happen. I'll carry him on my back before I let you kill him.'

'That is a very silly idea, Chris. It would be akin to a llama allowing a bear to ride upon it. Sooner or later, the bear will become hungry, and food is more important than a ride.'

Chris pulled a wry face. 'You seriously think he's going to try and eat me?'

'It is not unknown for Takers to indulge in cannibalism.'

The Taker did better than Chris expected. By the time they came to a region of small caves where they camp they had covered twenty-five kilometres. The oversized trainers did not appear to cause the Taker any discomfort. The trail had been narrow, often with a sheer fall to one side or the other as they followed the contours around lofty peaks, but the paths were smooth and surprisingly free from loose rock and the detritus of weather erosion. Once or twice they had to scramble over the results of a minor rock slide, but for the most part the going was good.

When the sun first showed signs of dipping below the mountain tops Agronal summoned a bird of prey. Seemingly from nowhere, Agronal assured Chris it did not involve any drawing of the light or of the dark.

'She is my hawk, and she responds to my call. Most every grown sa'tyr and many ma'tyr have hawks, and as you will see they are invaluable on long journeys.'

'Ma'tyr?'

'The females of my kind. Many of them think it frivolous to keep a hawk especially those who have a voice in Govern, but they would go hungry without one on treks such as ours.'

The hawk proved her worth and provided for the cooking fire. She caught a large hare-like animal which had ears shorter than a true hare. Agronal called it a *tark* and once roasted it tasted delicious. The Taker would not eat until Chris and Agronal had finished, and then he took his share of tark meat into the dark, away from the small fire, to consume it.

'I may have to draw the light to enfold us in a little warmth,' Agronal said, drawing the *cambralik* from its pouch. 'It will be cold tonight. See how the moon shines forth.'

'Moon!' came an urgent response from the Taker. Chris jumped and Agronal hunkered down as if preparing to spring. Both were surprised because neither had heard the Taker make any sound before.

'Is she here?' the Taker continued in the Taker dialect which Chris recognised from his day with Yukio. 'Have you seen her?'

'Who do you mean?'

'Moon. The goat-footed boy said her name.'

'You know Moon, the ... the White Hare?'

The Taker burst into tears and could not be consoled for several minutes. He curled at Chris's feet and held onto them, his tears dampening the bottoms of his trouser-legs. While Chris bent forward and tried to comfort the young man, his thoughts raced; the separate threads of two distinct parts of his journey came together and wove round each other to form a fast bond.

'She brought us to you,' Chris said. 'Moon brought us to where you lay dying. She brought us to you so we could help you.'

The Taker's tears subsided and then they spoke, he and Chris, and the horrors he had endured spewed from him like poison. She was Moon, and he was Sun – both had been to-hand servants of the evil ruler of the Takers. Moon served him at night and Sun had to bow to his every whim during the day. At dawn, dusk and at other times when ordered, both Moon and Sun had to be ready to do his bidding. Sun did not know where Moon came from, but Sun had been ripped from the midst of the war and at first he had thought himself dead.

They had served for what seemed like many years, though it may have been months or even weeks, and although the king never suspected, there was something special about Moon. She was not just a beautiful young woman dragged from the flesh-pots of the City. She came from elsewhere and she watched. She bided her time. She had a mission, although Sun did not know what it was. He did know she was very kind to him, and that without her he would never have lasted.

And then, one day, Sun dropped a platter of food and the king flew into a rage and struck him unconscious. He woke to rough handling and beatings from the king's soldiers and one in particular, who was called Angus. Beaten unconscious again his eyes next opened to find himself in the Forest of the Dead laying upon the fetid corruption of many corpses. Using the last of his strength he dragged himself clear and wound himself into the roots of an old tree, there to die alone. He dreamt that Moon had come to him in the shape of a white hare, and at last he woke but not to Moon's care. He woke to see Chris above him and to feel his face washed with fresh water.

Chris and Agronal helped Sun into the cave where they all settled down and made themselves as comfortable as they could. Agronal worked his skills to bring them a little extra warmth and Chris could tell he was glad he hadn't slain the Taker, who was really no Taker at all.

Edmund Warwick led his band along the mountain path deep into the night. He estimated the De'Ath boy had a head start of less than two hours and he intended to close the gap despite the danger of negotiating such a high and narrow place with only the light of the moon to guide them. The moonlight inverted shapes, so that small rocks appeared as holes in the ground and holes appeared as rocks. There was much stumbling, and one of the Taker-band complained. It was his last act in life; Edmund stepped over the body which oozed blood from a single thrust wound to the heart and struck out along the path, the others following with renewed respect. The last in line tipped his erstwhile companion over the edge with a sharp kick – after taking his boots, weapon and other trinkets that might prove their worth next time he had any bartering to do.

Edmund was sickened by the Takers and thought them but a step or two above lowly and savage beasts. They had certainly regressed from the days when he had commanded a Taker army. Their enemies called them "Spider-people" and they were feared throughout S'herra. Now they were still feared, but only as one feared the bear or the mountain lion. Needs must though, and they were fit enough for tonight's purpose. They had only to track down De'Ath and they would be amply rewarded – reward being their sole motivation – and then released to their own affairs. Should they fail, Edmund would call upon others, and these Takers would die. Edmund did not like to contemplate the 'others' while he walked a high path with a precipitous decline to one side. His power over them was limited, and they frightened him. He would summon them only as a last resort for he was uncertain he could bend them entirely to his will as his Lady could. The scions of the Mass were reluctant servants to Wiergan and Wierchan-kind and would as soon attack the conjurer as the intended target.

As Edmund's thoughts were on Yaemonadhrim he fingered the little piece of altar stone which hung on a silver chain round his neck and recalled that day in Wymes Forest when he'd had Christian De'Ath in the sights of his pistol. He projected his imagination into the darkness before him and saw Chris's head explode and his lifeless body drop to the ground. If only ... if only ... He knew how much trouble the so called Prophet Jason had once caused, and now the De'Ath boy was almost as annoying: to think that he could have ended it with one tiny movement of the trigger finger. If only he had done it. If only his Lady did not want him alive.

'Lord-Wiergan,' whispered the Taker scout who broke through the darkness ahead. 'We have them!'

'You have them? Caught and bound?'

'As good as! They're sleeping in a cave a short way up the path. I've left two of my men guarding the entrance, so there's no escape.'

Edmund grinned and relief was mixed with the glow of success. He'd have the De'Ath boy for his Lady and without the need to summon the twisted hoards of the Mass.

'Lead on, scout! And savour thought of your reward.'

The path jinked left and entered a hanging gully with steep, high walls both sides. They passed several caves with mouths like gaping maws, the darkness within deepened because the moonlight could not penetrate. Within five minutes Edmund came to the scout's men who guarded the lair of his quarry.

'Listen,' whispered the scout. 'You can hear one of them snoring.'

Sure enough when Edmund cocked an ear and cupped it with one hand, he noticed a soft snore and smiled to think of Chris De'Ath, deep in slumber with no thought as to the agonies he was about to suffer.

'Take the boy I have described. The other human, kill him, or if he be one of yours, keep him just as you wish. And kill the goat-flanked fiend for I'll not suffer the likes of him to breathe clean air.'

The scout signalled two men to stay by the entrance and all the others to follow him. They drew a variety of weapons, mostly short blades but one or two had metal-headed clubs.

'Lord-Wiergan. As part of our reward may we not have a little sport first? Draw out the killing of those we must kill and have some fun with the boy you want alive. We can deliver him unbroken but ... softened up and shall we say.'

Edmund smiled at the visions that filled his head. 'I don't see why not. Make De'Ath watch the death pains of the others, then hurt him and humiliate him as much as it pleases you. But deliver him to me whole and breathing, otherwise you will answer to the Lady.'

The leer suddenly dropped from his face. 'Perhaps we'd best leave the boy then. We wouldn't want to upset her in any way.'

'Don't deny yourselves the reward you've earned. Have your sport, but be careful not to go too far. Now – to it!'

The scout lit a torch and led half-a-dozen Takers into the cave. Edmund stood outside with the two who had been set as guards and waited to hear the screams. He wondered if the goat-boy would scream like a human or bleat like a sheep. The thought made him chuckle and then as the first screams came he laughed out loud. It was a death-scream, high, full of terrified surprise and then cut off short, dying with the victim who had produced it. The Takers had decided to deal swift death after all. A second scream came and was followed quickly by a third ... and then ... a fourth?

Edmund drew his blade. Something was wrong. The screams were coming from the Takers. And then the earth reverberated to the sound of a furious and explosive roar.

Bear! Edmund ran from the mouth of the cave as a gaggle of terrified Takers burst forth, a massive dark shape on their heels. A bear from his own world would be bad enough, but these Third Realm beasts were of a more primitive breed, with huge, wide heads, long forelimbs and short back ones, so that they resembled hyenas, six foot high at the shoulders. Edmund ran for his life, headlong in the dark hoping that he wouldn't leap out over a precipice, while screams and savage growls and the sound of limb being torn from limb split the night behind him.

The bear was not content with Taker flesh and Edmund Warwick heard the lumbering pursuit and the rasping breath. He ran on blind but the bear was gaining on him until he felt warm breath at his neck. Turning he threw his sword at the dark mass that reared up and saw a flash of white claws in the moonlight as the blade was swiped aside.

Edmund Warwick, once general for Parliament and once *Ordin-Marshal* for the great Kar'akhen, faced his death. Of all the glorious ends he had contemplated, to be killed ignominiously by a wild beast was not one of them. But there was no escape ... unless –.

In one flowing movement Edmund drew his moon-blade, sliced a gash in his thumb and with the bloody hand seized the altar stone pendant. The fear of imminent death lending him absolute concentration, he let his mind pass through the stone into the between realm of the Hidden Paths and called out and order to the scions of the Mass. And in an instant the call was answered. Edmund was thrown to the ground by a tremendous gale which tore through him and round him before sensing the direction he intended and hitting the bear with the force of a speeding truck.

The moon was blotted out by a dark cloud-like shape and then the bear let out a high pitched yelp, a sound totally at odds with its size and ferocity. The yelp stretched into a high pitched, terrified bellow, but only for a little while. Silence came quickly and there was an interval before screams from further down the path rose quickly before dying just as suddenly. Then there was silence and absolute stillness. The demon had done its work. It had heeded Edmund's bidding, saved his life and gone back to that between-space where it lived.

All this happened in the dark and Edmund Warwick saw very little until morning. When daylight came it was to illuminate a scene of utter carnage. The bear was a clotted mass of bloody flesh and fur, its head no more than a skull and bones visible in several places through the gore. Unfortunately his Taker band had fared no better. They were all dead and there was little to tell which had died by the bear or which by the demon. If Takers bothered at all with the niceties of family, it would be true to say that not a one of this pack could be recognised by his mother. Some of them could hardly be recognised as human.

Far from cowing Edmund, the morning's revelations made him feel powerful and potent. If he could summon demons and do this to bears and Takers he had nothing to fear from De'Ath or the legend associated with his coming. The power he felt inside came out as a wide grin, and he no longer felt quite so loyal to his Lady. Still, he intended to track down De'Ath and deliver him, or perhaps just his head, to Lady Rosemary. And then ... well, time would tell. If he felt like it he would serve her still. If not, he would follow his own path.

CHAPTER TWENTY-SEVEN

Bones of Brikadden

Agronal was awake a moment before the screaming started. Once those cries of death split the air, he did not need to wake the others. Chris jumped to his feet banging his head on the cave's low ceiling and Sun sat up with his usual frightened, bemused look. Agronal had conjured a tiny sphere of orange light which hovered in the air and illuminated the interior sufficiently for them to gather their things. Agronal voiced his suspicions that an attack, meant for them, had disturbed a bear, but there could be no tarrying to see if he was right. He smelt Wiergan, and that was enough for him to grab the others the moment they were ready and leap. They came out onto the mountain path and Agronal held them tighter and leapt again, aiming for a high peak against the moonlight. They landed in a sprawling heap of entwined arms and legs and it took them a few seconds to extract themselves.

Chris zipped up his jacket against the chill night air and adjusted his pack. 'I thought you said it was too dangerous to use the Hidden Paths.'

'We didn't use them, as such,' Agronal replied. 'We simply slip-shifted and we barely scraped the Paths at all. Slip-shifting is a lesser art and requires no skills of navigation. You simply look and leap, and then you are at the place where you looked.'

Chris grimaced at a pain shooting up to his hip. 'Clever! Especially seeing through the cave wall for the first leap.'

'Ah! That you could call a leap in the dark. I knew where the path was – roughly – so I looked with my inner eye.'

'You'll have to teach me that one day.' Chris rubbed his knee where it had struck the rocky ground.

'That might be possible if you have any First Born blood in your veins. Nevertheless, I shouldn't like to use the method too often while the Hidden Paths are being watched.'

'I suppose it got us out of a scrape. You think it was Wiergan after us?'

'At least one of that breed, and several Takers.'

'Let's hope the bear gets them all.'

'The bear will give them something to occupy themselves while we make a better escape. Meanwhile, there will be no rest for us until we reach Brikadden. We cannot rely upon the bear taking all our enemies. If they can follow us through the Hidden Paths and along the tunnels of the Kern, they must be powerful indeed.'

At first light Agronal guided the others through three more slip-shifts to successive peaks, and then they walked down to the path having saved themselves two days travelling. Agronal had exhausted himself. Slipping through the ether was apparently not free of effort but neither Chris nor Sun felt any the worse for their trip.

Noon found them in the shadow of an immense statue. It had stood the weather of centuries and all the features were wind-blasted, but it looked like the Slain Prophet had been a very young man. Both stone feet were firmly rooted in the living rock of the mountain – one bare and one booted and each big enough to provide a comfortable seat for travellers of natural size. Chris sat on the bare foot and something reminded him of the merlon back in Wymes Forest, in the shadow of the old tower. The monster foot was covered with a similar array of mosses and lichen.

'We will rest a while. We shall eat, and then we take that path, which leads up to Brikadden.'

The path looked steep and Chris was disheartened. He had hoped their way would be along the lower path that wound gently down towards a green valley. He tried not to show it. 'How far?'

'A walk of three hours – maybe four. We shall arrive well before dark.'

Chris wondered if Tarn would be there, and Sem and Senoi. He hardly dared to hope that he might find the missing people waiting for him: Marc and Shaun. Gayle! Not wishing to jinx the possibility, he kept his thoughts to himself.

'Cold,' mumbled Sun wrapping his arms about himself and looking up towards the sky. Clouds were drawing in and what was left of the morning's blue sky was being squeezed out of existence.

Agronal sniffed the air. 'We must press on. There will be rain soon, and driving winds.'

The winds came first, when the statue of the Slain Prophet was an hour behind them. They were by now on a decaying stone path which ran up the centre of a wide, rising valley. Here the grass was dry and yellow as if long in drought and perhaps the grass rejoiced when the rain came but the others did not. It attacked them, sheet after sheet of heavy rain driven hard on the wind. There was no shelter to be had and the only option was to press on into the face of the weather which seemed to oppose them with malevolent deliberation.

Agronal could have made good use of his hooded cape, but he made no move to retrieve it from Sun who wrapped himself against the deluge. Chris was soon wet to the skin and Agronal's shaggy quarters lost all shagginess and took on the look of a seal's pelt, slick and oily-wet.

Leaning into the onslaught Chris bent his head and forced himself to continue, wondering if he was experiencing nature or something else – something deliberately set against him. After an hour the wind dropped and the rain lost its sting but none of its volume. They plodded on thought deep puddles and spongy moss until the path came to a ruined village. The stones that had once formed its walls were strewn all about so that no grass could be seen. In some places the walls had survived to hip height, and there were gaps where doors and windows had once been. One wall rose even higher so that a grey stone lintel was still in place.

A few brave ferns struggled to establish themselves here and there, green in the grey, and patches of lichen covered old stone. Chris stooped to pick up a stone that was not as grey as the rest and he rubbed at the wet veneer to reveal a dark red tile. He found himself exploring the place, peering over a wall, squeezing through a narrow doorway and padding around a grassy interior that had once had a floor. The village had originally been built up the steep sides of a hill and so there were ruins at many different levels. He found a deep well and crossed many little rivulets, whether they were permanent or resulted from the torrential rainfall he couldn't tell.

A bleak and drear place for a village, but how Chris wished it was not a ruin and that they might find shelter here, and food and friendly company. Looking round he noticed Agronal had made himself comfortable sitting on an old window sill, flanked by the walls which had once formed the casement. Sun stood nearby rocking to and fro like a mind-numbed animal kept in all too small a cage. He also noticed it had stopped raining, and the sun was trying to come out.

'I'm just going to look round. Is that alright?'

Agronal waved and nodded. 'We are safe here. Be careful not to fall into any deep holes. There were mines here once.'

Like Chris, the walls dripped. There was a chill about the place. Not just the damp fug resulting from the bad weather, but the echoes of aeons old laughter, reverberations of work long ceased: old sounds echoing below the level of hearing and sights at the corner of vision. Ghosts and memories enveloped the stones with as much reality as the rain. Suddenly Chris didn't want to be alone.

He hurried to rejoin the other two and reached them, slightly out of breath. 'Spooky place,' he said looking over his shoulder. 'I don't suppose you can conjure something up to make out clothes dry?'

Agronal looked down at his hairy legs.

'Well, our clothes,' Chris said indicating himself and Sun. 'And your ... fur? ... hair?'

'I could, but I prefer not to draw the powers unless absolutely necessary. We shall dry off soon enough,' Agronal said waving a hand up towards the sun, which was now winning the battle and scattering the clouds.

Chris nodded half-heartedly, resigned to staying damp for a little while longer. 'How much further until Brikadden?'

'No further at all,' Agronal said. 'We are here. This place is Brikadden.'

Chris couldn't hide his disappointment. 'But ...' His vision of warmth and roasting fires, hot food and comfortable beds, not to mention the re-unions he had hoped for, was cruelly shattered.

'This pile of ... this utter pile of *crap* is Brikadden? *This* is where the Fey Knights live? For *God's* sake!'

Agronal was surprised at Chris's anger. He jumped up from the windowsill, his face full of concern and an explanation on his lips when he spied something behind Chris and smiled widely.

Chris spun in time to see a tiny bottom being wagged in his direction at just above eye level. The little flying figure spun and blew a raspberry at Chris, tongue stuck out and a thumb in each ear. Chris swiped at the faerie never intending to make connect.

'Temper, temper!' Senoi called dodging the playful feint. 'Brikadden won't come to you if you call it rude names.'

'Senoi!' Chris yelled, happy again and all traces of his angry flare-up gone. 'It's good to see you, even if you are pulling faces.'

Senoi re-adjusted his mouse-skin loincloth and smiled broadly as he landed on Chris's outstretched forearm. Chris gazed at him intensely noticing for the first time that the faerie wore a tiny silver torc on his left upper arm and what appeared to be an animal's tooth on a sinew about his neck. On his right wrist was a little piece of black twine, loose at the ends as if someone had tried to tie the little being down and failed.

Chris introduced Senoi to Agronal – they had already met – and Sun and then they spent some time bringing each other up to date with their individual stories, covering everything that had happened since they were parted on the first night of their arrival into the Third Realm. After that Senoi explained the mysteries of Brikadden, or at least some of them. In short, it phased in and out of existence, but always centred upon the old ruins that were drying out in the sunshine. If you came upon the ruins and waited long enough, Brikadden would come to you.

It was warm now and Chris stripped off his damp jacket and spread it over a low wall to dry out while Senoi flitted off along the bed of a brook that emerged from a tiny cave at the end of a gully with a grassy hill rising above it. He flew into the cave and after a moment emerged again.

'Still too soon. Brikadden hasn't come,' he said making a comfortable seat out of Chris's drying jacket.

Chris asked about Tarn and the others and was delighted to learn that as soon as Brikadden returned he would meet a few old friends and several new ones. As for Gayle, there was news of her but it wasn't entirely good. She was alive at least, but still not with Tarn. She had been seen at Atolak, the fortified house of the Wierchan who styled herself Lady Rosemary.

'Old Rosy?' Chris said hopefully. 'It shouldn't be too hard to rescue her from Rosy. She must be in her eighties by now.'

'I hear talk that with the passing of years she grows younger,' Senoi said laying back in a fold of camouflage material and spreading his wings to catch the sun. 'She draws and manipulates the dark, and she has found a way to use it which sloughs the ravages of time. Semangeloph visited her uninvited, just three days ago, and he tells me she looks no older than forty.'

Sun sidled over, his brow deeply furrowed as if fishing deep into his store of thoughts. He was beginning to smell again, and Chris wondered if he would need permanent care and looking after. Dismissing the thought for now he turned again to Senoi.

'It'll be good to see Sem again. It's funny though, as he looks like one of you, but talks like most of the guys I used to hang out with.'

'There are many paths to the First Realm, and not all pass through the times of long ago.'

'I know. He told me that once he'd been like me. So ... maybe one day I'll shrink down and grow me a set of wings.'

'And hunt mice for clothing?' Senoi laughed. 'But unless you have a full measure of First Born blood inside you, your path will not take you to the First Realm. You will follow all your kind to dusty death and eternal rest.'

Chris pouted. 'I'd rather be a faerie than worm food.'

'Yet we must all be what we are, and never waste a second worrying about what we cannot.' Senoi sat up and emitted a tiny burp. Bringing a hand to his stomach he said 'Do you still have a supply of magic food?'

'Sorry. I ate it all.' Come to mention it, Chris was feeling rather hungry too.

Agronal called over from the gully close to the mouth of the cave. He thought Brikadden was back. Chris looked all round; still nothing but strewn rubble, crumbling walls and fallen roof-stones.

'Follow me!' Senoi said though a grin. 'And bring your bemused friend.' Senoi flew towards Agronal and they both entered the cave, so low that Agronal, as short as he was, had to duck almost double.

'Come on Sun,' Chris said taking the young man's arm. 'We have to squeeze into that little hole.' He chuckled. 'Maybe I can find a little bottle that has a label saying "Drink Me".'

Grabbing his jacket and pack, Chris led Sun down into the gully and splashed along the brook.

'That's it Sun. Duck low and mind your head.'

Sun was swallowed up by the dark and Chris bent low to follow. Shuffling along a few feet, the cave opened into a high vaulted cave with a sandy floor and pale, luminescent light emanating from slime which covered the wall in places. No sooner had his eyes adjusted to the new levels of light, than Senoi darted rapidly towards the entrance but as Chris followed his flight, he was surprised to see him fade into nothingness before he completed his exit.

'Where'd he go?'

'Calm yourself, Chris,' said Agronal. 'He merely leads where we shall shortly follow. Now, to me! Let me hold you both, just as if we were going to leap onto the Hidden Path.'

'And are we?' Chris asked as Agronal slipped an arm round his waist.

'Not quite. Please close your eyes, or at least stand very still.'

Chris kept his eyes open, but wished he hadn't. The cave walls appeared to regress to a place slightly out of focus and then fade back in again.

'We are here,' Agronal said releasing his hold. Sun stumbled and held both hands to his temples.

'But ... nothing's changed. We're still in a damp old cave and –'

Agronal smiled and held a finger to his lips, before crossing to the cave and ducking out. Sun followed and then Chris. He still had to bend double and shuffle along the brook. He still had to clamber out of the little gully. And the buildings were all still there, but they were no longer ruined. They were as bright and whole and pristine as the day they were built, with whitewashed walls, heavy wooden doors and casements painted green and roofed over in red tile.

'Brikadden!' Agronal said waving an arm that encompassed the whole village.

'And most welcome you are!' came a voice that Chris recognised. Tarn stood a little way up a grassy hill with his identical triplet brothers Ret and Sav ... and the air was full of faeries. Chris made a start towards Tarn but the multitude of faeries made him stop and stare. There were so many varieties. There were boys and girls with either butterfly wings, bird wings or dragonfly wings like Senoi's; there were older looking faeries the diversity of their clothing – or lack of it – too great to take in. There were green faeries dressed in mosses whose tiny heads were acorn-capped, there were ones as black as slate wearing clothes of matted, miniature oak-leaves and there were whimsical faeries who had not chosen to keep an entirely human form of body. Some of these had disproportionate features, or stick-thin bodies – a myriad of forms which boggled the imagination – and Chris was mesmerised. But even these many beautiful and fantastic creatures failed to hold his attention when he heard an excited voice bellow his name.

'Chris! Chris De'Ath!' Chris swung round to see Marc running towards him, and Shaun a little further back. Chris had never been so happy to see anyone before in his entire life. He grinned widely and grinned even more at the inappropriate thought which rose unbidden. He would never speak it for fear of causing hurt, but there was no malice attached so he allowed the pun to increase his joy. *All kinds of faerie fully accounted for.*

As Marc bowled into Chris and hugged him tightly another emotion took hold, and Chris was suddenly holding sobs at bay. Hot tears threatened as the emotions of many, many months were released. Marc and Shaun were alive! But Danny was dead, and Chris knew it would fall to him to break the news. Screwing his eyes tight against the insistent pricking and swallowing hard, Chris stepped back forcing himself from Marc's bear hug.

'Danny ...'

All the joy of reunion fell from Marc's face. 'I know Chris. I know.' He too fought back emotion. 'Let's not talk about it right now, okay?' Marc grabbed Chris again and held him tight for a few moments more until emotion was checked and held under control.

'So, Tarn tells us you have quiet a journey,' Shaun said while shaking Chris's hand.

'Yes,' added Marc. 'Shaun and I have had things pretty easy in comparison.'

At a subtle signal from Tarn, Shaun led the small group towards one of the cottages. 'We hear you've encountered a succubus, an incubus and a virtual pack of were-wolves! For us it was just three nice young chaps and a trio of flying pixies.'

Chris wasn't sure if he imagined Senoi bristling at the misnomer, or if he really had. 'Yeah! Pretty scary at times, but nothing so bad as nearly being torn apart by dogs.'

Tarn pulled up short. 'The Kumakkashi captured you?'

Chris nodded.

'And here you are, all in one piece? That's quite some achievement, and something that should give our enemies something to ponder.'

'I did have quite a bit of help.' He started to talk about Moon and the White Hare but Tarn suggested stories could wait. Taking Agronal with him, he excused himself and asked Shaun to see the other new arrivals the rest of the way to their quarters.

'I see your clothes are sopping, and you're shivering, so I suggest we do as Tarn said and exchange news this evening. Right now we should think about getting you a hot bath, clean dry clothes and something to eat. Which order do you prefer?'

Chris didn't need to think about it. 'How about something to eat, something to eat and then something to eat?'

Marc laughed. 'Same old Chris.'

Shaun smiled. 'Can't blame you putting off the clothes option,' he said waving a hand down his own attire of knee-length breeches and a sleeveless leather jerkin over a thick, cream coloured cotton shirt with baggy arms and no collar. 'Not exactly best bib and tucker, is it?'

Senoi hovered by Chris's ear for a moment, his wings making the air hum, and landed on his shoulder.

'Your faerie's a lively little beggar,' Shaun said. 'No offence ... er ... what's your name?'

Senoi introduced himself with a wide grin, apparently quite happy with Shaun's description of him.

'Senoi's a nice guy,' affirmed Chris. 'But I wouldn't say he was mine.'

'Well, he's *is* yours – or you're his,' Shaun said. 'Certainly one of the two at any rate. Ours has long white hair and wears boots, breeches and a gossamer-thin white shirt.'

'Sounds like Sem,' Chris said. 'I've met him.'

Shaun nodded and then continued. 'The German chap's faerie thinks he's a Samurai. Sansenoi he calls himself.'

'I've met him as well.' Chris ducked under the low lintel of the doorway to the little cottage to which Shaun had brought him.

'And have you met all three Fey Boys yet?' Marc said stepping in after him.

'Meet one you've met 'em all,' Shaun said showing Chris, Sun and Agronal to a set of seats by an open fire.

'Apart from their hair styles,' Marc added.

Chris sat on the oak chair closest to the flames. 'You mean Fey Knights?'

'Well, yes,' Shaun said. 'But it turns out "knight" comes from the Old English "cnicht" which means "boy", so it looks like successive generations have elevated the trio higher than their original station. Now, going back to my original question ...'

'Have I met all three? Well, I've seen them all from a distance, but I've only really met Tarn properly.'

'He'll be *your* Fey Boy then. Marc and I have got Ret and the German boy has Sav.'

'Just a minute,' Chris said. 'German boy? *My* faerie? *My* Fey Boy? What's all this about?'

Shaun made a start but Marc cut him off. 'Like Tarn said, it'll keep until tonight. We'll leave you lot to get comfortable. There's a tub through there,' he said pointing to a door to the right of the fire. 'And oodles of hot water – just turn the spigot – and three bedrooms. Rummage round in the wardrobes and you'll find something to wear.'

'If you're lucky,' Shaun said. 'But don't hold your breathe while you look for the drawer full of Diesel pullovers and CK knickers.'

Marc chuckled. 'There nothing you might call fashionable, but it doesn't seem to matter. We all look like tramps round here, so just go for comfort, and in the morning your own stuff will be dry.'

'Lucky you've got your own things Chris. We arrived with ... not a lot.'

'We'll leave you to it then,' Marc said. 'We'll call round for you in a couple of hours. So you can get used to your new home.'

'New home?'

'For as long as you stay at Brikadden, this cottage is "Chaz Chris". Our place is across the way, up on the next level.' Marc pointed out the window.

'And Marc forgot to say,' Shaun added. 'The whole village is absolutely safe from all those demon-types who gave you such a hard time. So you can sleep easy.'

Marc had the last word before closing the heavy wooden door behind him. 'There's a very tea-like drink you can sort yourself. All the makings are in the kitchen, and there plenty of bread and cheese. That should keep you sorted until dinner at our place. In thee hours, okay?'

Chris forgot Senoi was on his shoulder. He jumped when Senoi spoke and that made Senoi chuckle. 'What are you going to do with Sun?'

'What am *I* going to do with him? Is it really down to me to do anything?' Chris whispered, sneaking a glance at Sun who was standing, apparently in a catatonic state facing one corner of the room.

'He needs a healing sleep,' Senoi said.

'What he needs is care in the community!'

Senoi frowned. 'He needs sleep! I can induce that, but you'll have to get him out of his dirty clothes, wash him and change him, for those simple tasks seem beyond him.'

The task was easier than it sounded, for Sun only need to be guided in the right direction and encouraged. Step by step, the job was done although it took almost an hour to bathe him and find him some suitable clothes. Chris made him some tea and they shared part of a freshly baked loaf, and then the traumatised young man was helped to bed. Moments later, Senoi had induced a deep sleep.

'Whether he shall be much cured when he wakes is doubtful, but he shan't be any worse.'

'Do you think he'll ever be back to normal?'

'His mind is much scarred, but I have seen similar cases recover fully. Time and patience – and we shall see. Now! I'll leave you while *you* bathe, for of the two of you, your pong was by far the strongest. And after, I suggest you have a nap too. Then we shall meet at Marc and Shaun's cottage on the hill.'

Senoi asked for Chris to open a window, and then he flew out; for the first time since his incarceration by the Kumakkashi, Chris was alone. He stripped off and drew some piping hot water, and after taking a long bath which forced the ice from his bones, he sorted out fresh clothes, some from his pack and some from the heavy polished oak wardrobe. There was well over an hour before dinner and while dressing, he decided to wash his and Sun's smelly clothes, and then explore the village.

It was bright and warm in Brikadden and the sky directly above was blue. But there were no visible horizons for they were hidden in dazzling mists. To look far into the distance was like driving in fog with headlights set on full-beam. There did not appear to be a source of light and yet Chris found it hard to look without screwing up his eyes. It made him cross with himself – and not for the first time since his arrival in the Third Realm – that he had neglected to pack a pair of sunglasses.

There were faeries about, although not so many as when he first arrived at the village. Every now and again one or a pair would zip past, noisily if they sported dragonfly wings, almost silently if their choice was for butterfly wings, and they all acknowledged him. He came across a nest, for want of a better word, of the green variety who were busy feasting on berries in a little hollow at ground level, and near the edge of the village a lone male asleep in the fronds of a stand of bracken. It was while he was peering at the exhausted little being who appeared to be recovering from a busy night of revelling, that a voice called out.

'Hey Christy! Is that you,' a man called out, the words English but dampened down with a German accent.

Chris peered curiously at the young couple who approached from the mist. The man was beaming a warm smile and quickening his pace.

'I knew there was more to Mad Christy than a brain fuddled dumb-head!'

'I'm sorry ... I –'

'It's me! Karl! Karl Hochwalt!'

Chris maintained his uncertain look.

'From up at Donnington Camp. I'm one of the prisoners! How can you not know me after all the potato sacks we've filled together?'

Chris's jaw dropped and his eyes grew wide. One hand shot up, almost involuntarily, to cover his mouth. Kostja's great-uncle, his war time relative who should be something approaching eighty was standing in front of him looking closer to twenty.

'Aha! At last you recognise me, no?'

'Not quite,' Chris said. 'But I know who you are.'

Karl introduced Chris to Beverly and when they had found some warm rock to sit on, Chris began his story. He told them he was not Mad Christy and then what he knew of Karl and the old stories surrounding his disappearance and everything he knew and suspected about Rosemary and the efforts of Karl's brother – Kostja's grandfather – to get to the truth.

'It's so horrible to think that such a seemingly sweet little girl could spread such a wicked lie,' Beverly said.

'Well, it looks like it was the beginning of a long career.'

'To think what she has become,' Beverly mused.

Karl was sitting, quietly and very subdued.

Chris empathised. 'You okay, Karl?'

'Oh yes, very fine, but trying hard to line things up inside my head. You see, for Beverly and me ... well, it is only a week since we were together in Wymes Forest and the soldiers were coming for me. And for you ... those days are so many years before you were born.'

'And yet,' Beverly said. 'By now we should be getting used to all this time-twisting business. See, Marc and Shaun, those two nice young men who are from your time, they've been here longer than us but they were taken a whole lifetime after we were.'

'Now you're here though, the Fey Knights will tell us everything. You are the last and now there is one group for each of the boys.'

They all agreed it would be good to know exactly why they had been brought to Brikadden and what part they had to play in subduing the Unselost Mass.

'I have to be getting back to the village. Just ten minutes to dinner.'

'Then we shall see you later,' said Karl.

They had started off on their separate ways when Beverly turned. 'You know, I've never seen two people so alike as you and Mad Christy. Do you want to know what I think?' She did not wait for an answer. 'You may not be Mad Christy at the moment, but I think one day you will be. What with all this time-twisting going on I shouldn't wonder if we all fetched up with the Romans, or perhaps go the other way and come to a time when big rocket ships go to the moon.' Beverly laughed at her own silly imagination.

'As if!' Chris said through a wry smile.

CHAPTER TWENTY-EIGHT

Demon Dressed as Girl

Edmund Warwick had changed his mind. He couldn't be bothered to go chasing after Chris De'Ath. Now that the boy was safely tucked away in Brikadden there wasn't much point anyway. Edmund knew he could never get in to the mysterious Host-protected village and he certainly wasn't going to wait amongst all these tumbled ruins with some small hope that Chris might return. He kicked at the rubble then faced north, towards Atolak and presumably, his Lady – only he didn't think of her as "his" Lady anymore. She was the woman who had held him in thrall for several lifetimes, or so it felt. It was strange how devotion could sour so quickly and congeal into a kind of contempt.

The noise of the second piece of debris Edmund kicked put a tark to flight, and in an instant he had seized the stone about his neck – he no longer had to wet it with blood – and summoned forth his demon. It split from the air like a cloud of dense black smoke, and faded back to nothing only when the tark was nothing but scattered bones. The whole process took no more than ten seconds, and Edmund thrilled at his newfound power. His particular demon was in actual fact a vast swarm of tiny demons, each black, bat-winged, razor-fanged and the size of a small pipistrelle. They reminded him of flying *lutai* – those tiny creatures natural to the plains of S'herra which could strip the flesh from a man's bones in a matter of minutes – but they were far more efficient at their task, and unlike the *lutai*, could be controlled.

Edmund suspected the many hundreds of tiny demons that made up the swarm represented only one being and that the demons were incapable of operating as individuals, like a huge shoal of fish directed by one mind. There was much concerning the Yaemonadhrim that he did not understand. He knew they were of the Mass, yet independent of it; he knew they had a will of their own and resented being manipulated by those who could draw the darkness and he had an uncomfortable feeling that they would as soon tear him apart as any target assigned by him. But most of all he felt the confidence to draw and direct. As long as he held to this, the demons would not dare to oppose him.

His Ladyship's house, called Atolak, lay far to the north in an isolated range of mountains halfway between the Arkenark Mountains and the once great city of Kar'akhen. Without his band of Takers he would not risk invading the Kern subterranean highways a second time, so he would have to embark on a journey part foot and part intra-ethereal. Being Wiergan he had the power to slip-shift, although he had never much cared for it. Rather a horse any day, or even one of the beasts of S'herra that served the same purpose. But needs must, and if the devil was not driving, at least Edmund was driving devils.

Two days later Edmund's final shift brought him to the sunny sward of mown grass that fronted Atolak and bordered the final mile of the long, wide path that wound up from the plain. He felt week and clammy and he had to sit for a while in the shade of a rowan tree. He had overreached himself with that last jump and the confidence to wield demons had left him. Not for long though; he rested for an hour, ate some of his way-meat and took a draft of fortified water. His strength came back like an impatient tide and he was soon ready to face Rosemary.

Atolak stood high on a rock like an Edwardian folly, an impressive three-storey house part German *schloss* part black-beamed manor, with high balconies and a trio of conical towers peering above an honour guard of pine trees. The warm, welcoming approach belied Atolak's cold heart and the colder intent of its mistress.

When Edmund Warwick stood before Lady Rosemary he found it hard to conceal his shock. She had been drawing deeply of the Mass and applying its substance to her arts; now she no longer resembled a woman of forty but rather a girl of half that age. For a moment Edmund wondered if he could be a youth again, vigorous, lusty and full of life. How would it be to have the body he'd had when his father rebuked him as a sinner and made him wear black, stole away all the joy of being young and healthy? It was no use: a young body ruled over by an old, cynical mind would be something of an abomination, just like this simpering harlot before him. He wondered if his demons would come and do his bidding, right there and then.

'The boy? Lost again?' Rosemary circled Edmund and twirled in her blue and white frock. 'No matter. He would have provided amusement for a while, but he is no real loss. Let the Host have him!' She laughed, her tone high like chiming bells. Edmund considered the possibility that she may have damaged her mind.

'I thought we had to be rid of him. There is the legend –'

'Which I no longer believe. "The boy will come through rock and hail de-dah, de-dah, de-dah and all the Lady's plans will fail. He brings with him the rarest gift, rhubarb, rhubarb, rhubarb, and he will seal the yawning rift."

'Well, let me tell you Edmund of Warwick. There are no less than *three* rifts now, all in the same temporal layer within the Hidden Paths – and even little golden-bollocks himself can't be in three places at once!'

Edmund hated it when his Lady used coarse words. And anyway, the term was pronounced "ball-locks". If she had to use unladylike language from the peasant quarter, at least she should use it correctly. He kept his thoughts to himself.

'Three rifts, you say?"

'Yes, three! And each capable of providing me with all the substance I require to fulfil my plan. Soon, so very, very soon I will bring my Paul back home.'

'And then what, my Lady? You and your brother will live happily ever after?'

Rosemary stopped twirling and playing to her apparent age. 'Do you mock me, Warwick?' Her voice echoed through the hall.

Edmund paused, perhaps a moment too long, before replying. 'Indeed I do not, my Lady. I merely ponder the aftermath of your success.'

Rosemary circled Edmund again, this time menacingly: in spite of her apparent youth she conjured a fear inducing aura about her. 'And yet, there is something different about you since we last met.' She smiled and clapped her hands, once. 'Something I rather like! You are no longer quite so toady.' She continued to circle. 'Could it be you have come into power? After so long in my shadow, have you used that pendant I gave you long ago to draw upon the dark and control the scions?'

Edmund stood tall and could not help the corner of his mouth turning up into a slightly leering smile. 'Perhaps my Lady. Just a little.'

'As little as this!' Rosemary screamed as she threw her arms out before her towards the empty hall. There came the crackling noise of raw power splitting the air and all the wind rushed from Edmund's lungs. Substance leached from all around – from the walls, the floor, the high vaulted ceiling – and all came together in a huge living form that filled the space inside the hall.

Huge and black, with orange coals for eyes and wings that spanned the hall, the dragon opened its mouth, a maw wider than the main gate, and let forth a roar the reverberated to the foundations of the earth. If the monster drew substance from its surroundings, it took spirit from Edmund: once again he was the beaten little boy, berated by his puritan father for misquoting the scriptures and failing at his lessons. He trembled at the knee and his face dissolved, beyond any bidding of the will. Had his bladder been full it would surely have emptied, so complete was Edmund's loss of control. And through it all Rosemary laughed, a keening, mocking sound heard as if through a gale.

And in an instant the monster was gone and once the wall stones had ceased to tremble, all was silent. Edmund swallowed hard and fought to regain composure.

'There, there, my man. For you still are *my* man, Edmund. But never forget to whom you owe your loyalty.'

Edmund dipped his head in acknowledgement and cast a wary eye about the now empty hall. 'That was no conjured vision, was it?'

Rosemary smiled, still young but with an ancient look behind her eyes. 'The scions take such forms as they will. But as for Black Angus, let us just say I have cast him to a shape that suits me.'

She could really do this thing? She had the skill to manipulate the Mass to such an extent? Her powers had truly waxed. 'Black Angus?'

'My dragon has at the core of it the spirit of a Wiergan who fell during the War. He formally took the form of one of the living dead, with a body torn and bloody. But I have remoulded him and … the name amuses me.'

Was it all for the sake of amusement? Edmund hadn't the courage to voice his thoughts, but that such power should be squandered in amusement. Whereas a little while ago he had no respect for Rosemary, now he hated her every bit as much as he had once hated his father.

'Would you have me prepare a party to accompany us to one of the rifts?'

'Oh no, my dear Edmund. Wiergadhrim of our abilities need no retainers. But we must wait until I have plied my mind to the Paths and determined which of the three rifts best serves my needs. Three days – maybe four – and then you must stand ready to come with me at a moment's notice.'

Edmund inclined his head. 'You may rely upon me, my Lady.'

Little Rosemary – Edmund felt sure she appeared younger now than at the beginning of his audience – bobbed a curtsey and skipped off up the wooden staircase. As he watched her go Edmund's left hand rose to grip the stone pendant, and the fingers of his right hand twitched with the effort to withhold a cloud of demons.

After a sustaining and hearty meal Marc Stockdale and Shaun Ashton led Chris up through the village and past its perimeter towards what looked like an old war memorial. Sun stayed behind with Agronal who undertook to ply some of his healing arts in the hope of helping the young man emerge from the sea of pain that seemed to drown him.

Marc and Shaun knew their way about and showed a lot of confidence for a couple who had only arrived at Brikadden a month ago. From their perspective they had been taken from the old tower in Wymes Forest just four weeks ago and when they had discussed their journey over dinner, they had been surprised how much time had passed for Chris. Marc knew about his brother's death. The Fey Boy Ret had broken the news. Marc and Chris spoke of brother and best friend, but they did not dwell on his death. Instead they remembered happier times, and when they came to change the subject, both young men were smiling, though each had moist eyes.

They came to the memorial-like monument. There was a three metre tall white marble pillar which rose to a point like Cleopatra's Needle on the Thames Embankment. It stood at the top of a plinth made up of a set of twelve steps, surrounding the needle and serving as bleacher-like seating. Tarn wasn't there, but as far as Chris could see all the others were. Tarn's triplet brothers, Ret and Sav, sat on the top step with their backs to the needle. Karl and Beverly sat near the bottom holding hands and half twisting to look up expectantly at the Fey Knights, and Marc and Shaun took places a step further up.

And then the faeries came. Senoi sat on Chris's knee, Sansenoi the little Samurai took up a similar position on Beverly's and Semangeloph perched himself upon Shaun's shoulder. There were other faeries too and soon the steps were teaming with many different kinds and the air seemed to thrill to many others who were yet to land. It was then that Chris realised Senoi and his two faerie companions were among the heavyweights of faerie kind, for whereas Senoi, Sansenoi and Semangeloph stood some fifteen centimetres tall – when they chose to stand at all – the vast majority of the rest were far smaller, some hardly bigger than Chris's little finger.

The air-sounds grew almost palpable and Chris flinched as something huge came in a little above his head. Two Kern passed over him and made a light touchdown at the top of the stairs close to Ret and Sav who both stood to greet them. Chris checked the two human couples. Although Karl looked a little nervous, nobody appeared too surprised by the appearance of the Kern so Chris supposed they had all encountered their kind before.

Turning from his conversation with the Kern, Ret held up his hand. Semangeloph flew to join him and at the same time Sansenoi joined Sav. The audience fell silent, and Ret began. First of all, he welcomed everyone to Brikadden Beacon. Then he introduced himself very formally as Retsutsiel, Ieladhrim of the Shade and firstborn son of the Warrior Prophet and the Oracle of Nenrilluen. Sav followed suit as Savaliel, Ieladhrim of the Shade and second son of the same. Sav went on to inform the audience that Tarniel, the youngest child of the Prophet and the Oracle, though only by a matter of minutes, would join them soon. He introduced the two Kern who had names that would hardly cling to the mind and had no chance on the lips, and then he declared the meeting open and underway.

Much of the information Retsutsiel opened with was already know to Chris: he had picked it up here and there through his early meeting with beings of the Selost Host. Ret spoke of the Unselost Mass feeding on the barriers between the Realms and insinuating itself ever more intractably throughout the Hidden Paths. It had broken though in places resulting in cataclysmic events in parts of each Realm and it had even extended part of itself into the First Realm from which it sucked substance and drew strength.

Another result of the Mass's feeding frenzy was the empowerment of vast hoards of its scions who were intruding into parts of the Realms and wreaking havoc with the inhabitants. Chris began to imagine the source of many tales from folklore: they were directly as the result of scion incursions.

'Now, we have recently discovered there is another element to these temporality-arcing troubles. The Lady of Atolak, neither Mass nor scion but known to us Wiergadhrim, seeks to source the Mass for her own purposes. This we know from Semangeloph's recent reconnoitre into her house.

'It also appears very likely that she has enthralled certain scions by use of her powers to manipulate the very essence of the Mass. We cannot determine her purpose and she has not been factored in our plans to seal the rifts. Without knowing what she wants we still cannot calculate the effects she may have, so we must carry on with our plan and hope for the best, while ever being on the look-out for surprise intervention.'

Savaliel took up the mantle of speaker. He stepped forward and brushed aside a strand of hair that had come loose from his long ponytail. 'I should add that there is a body of evidence, as yet untried, that suggests that it may be the Lady is responsible for the rifts in the first place. It appears the Mass has been led to certain points along the Hidden Paths. For many years the hand that leads has been hidden, but increasingly, the signs point to Lady Rosemary of Atolak.'

Little old Rosy of Little Rillton, Chris thought. He tried to remember what she looked like from the time she'd come to his junior school class to talk about local history.

'The strange little girl whose lies nearly cost my life,' Karl whispered to Beverly. 'See what she has become.'

Retsutsiel asked if there were any questions so far, and Chris wanted to know when they would be told the role they were each to play in sealing the rifts.

'Well,' Ret answered. 'We will be divided into teams. I will go with Marc and Shaun. Semangeloph will accompany us.'

'Told you so,' Marc said leaning close to Chris and winking.

'My brother Savaliel and Sansenoi, Ieladhrim of the Light, will form a team with Karl and Beverly and –'

'I'll go with Sun, Tarn and Senoi,' Chris said, interrupting.

'Er ... no!' Retsutsiel said. 'You may have noticed that each team comprises an Ieladhrim of the Shade, one of the Light and a pair of lovers.'

'Excuse me!' Beverly yelled, blushing profusely. 'Give a girl a little privacy, won't you?' And then she looked over towards Marc and Shaun who, she noticed for the first time, were sitting very close. As realisation dawned she blushed a little more and held a hand to her mouth. 'Ooo-er!' she said under her breath. Karl smiled at her and winked.

'I ... er ... well now that you come to mention it,' Chris mumbled.

From his vantage point near the top of the steps Retsutsiel looked over the heads of the audience and grinned. 'Right on time!' he said. From the direction of the village came a small group of three people. It was hard to tell from the distance, but it looked like a girl and two boys – and yes, one of the young men was Tarn.

Ret continued. 'The third team will be made up of Tarn, Jamie McDowell, Lillian and Senoi. You Chris, have a special role to play.'

Chris's guts knotted around ice. He didn't take in the part about his special role. All he could think about was that *she* was here. Lillian the demon-bitch had somehow bluffed her way into Brikadden. Jumping to his feet he ran down the steps and flew towards the group bourn upon wings of fury.

Of course, she saw it coming a mile away – anyone would – and when Chris took a swing for her hoping to knock a demon from the illusion of a girl, Lillian blocked the blow neatly, brought her foot up sharp into his groin and put a straight jab into the centre of his face for good measure. Chris crumpled and fell to the grass, but as the pain burned through his lower belly he managed to scream: 'She's a succubus!'

Senoi streaked through the air like a burning arrow and struck her in the chest, but he did not shoot through her or end her miserable life. Here merely – bounced off.

'Ouch! You little bastard!' Lillian yelled before stomping on Senoi and grinding him into the soil.

She lifted her foot to stamp again, but Tarn took her by the shoulders and held her tight.

'Let me at him! The little git's just bruised my boob!'

'It's a misunderstanding,' Tarn said. 'I'll explain it all soon.'

'No,' Chris wheezed from a foetal position the ground. 'She's a succubus. She's the one who got me.'

'A suck-you *what*?' Lillian cried, still ready for a fight.

Senoi extricated himself from the soil, one wing bent, the two on the left apparently broken and looking completely battered. He pulled some dry grass from his hair, and he was laughing.

'What's so funny?' Chris managed while trying to sit up. 'She's just knackered me, and you ... you look like a piece of origami.'

'I'll recover. And so will you,' Senoi said, one wing already pumped back into shape. 'But she's no succubus, for she withstood peneflagration, and no scion of the Mass could do that. She's as human as you are. Your previous attacker must be a succubus who took on her looks.'

'Hold on a minute!' Lillian said with hands on hips. 'I can cope with faeries, and lanky tossers like him,' she pointed to Chris. 'But if you keep talking bollocks and I'm out of here!'

The young man she had arrived with and who had been quiet up until now stooped to help Chris up. 'It's all too weird,' he said. 'I'm sure we'll sort all this out before long.'

'You must be Jamie,' Chris said, squeezing his eyes shut to get rid of the tears of pain. 'I'm your cousin Chris. Nice to meet you.'

The boys shook hands, but briefly because Chris needed both his hands to support himself, bent forward, on his knees.

'How d'you do Chris? ... No! Don't answer that one. Count it as rhetorical.'

Chris chuckled. It hurt to chuckle.

'But, I don't have a cousin called Chris.'

'Ah but you do. See, I was born half-a-dozen years after you went missing from Wymes Forest.'

Jamie frowned. 'But ... that was only yesterday!'

'Well, to *you* it was only yesterday. To *me* it was more than my whole life ago.'

Jamie nodded slowly and frowned. 'I guess the weirdness doesn't stop right away.'

'Hey Chris,' Lillian said stepping closer. She had been watching and listening carefully. 'How about we start again? I'll forget you tried to clobber me and your little pervert pixie friend bashed me in the boob. And you can forget I toe-punted your goolies. Deal?'

'I'll try, but it will be a lot easier for me to forget as soon as I can stand up properly.'

Lillian caught his eye and drew her tongue over her lips. 'Have to find someone who can do you a massage down there.'

For the first time Chris discovered that sudden and painful impact to those most delicate parts of his body was no impediment to arousal.

'And then,' Lillian added losing her seductive tone and becoming angry again. 'You can tell me where I can find the bitch that's going round impersonating me. I'll rip her apart!'

Chris had no doubt that Lillian was fully capable of being as good as her word.

Tarn and Jamie helped Chris back to Brikadden Beacon. Chris noticed that Jamie looked younger than him; tall and slim and light haired but no more than sixteen. He wore tight Levi jeans and brown walking brogues with a dark blue turtle neck pullover over a blue and white check shirt. Lillian had to be in her twenties and was as beautiful to Chris as that succubus who had used her likeness to seduce him. It all seemed so impossibly far off, but in reality it was no more than about three months. He wondered if her body looked the same, beneath her jungle-green combat trousers and black and silver Black Sabbath sweat shirt. Her hair was shorter now, and it looked darker – almost black. He wondered if her lips were as soft, and warm and wet and as ... He had to give himself a mental slap to concentrate on the proceedings in hand.

Tarn completed the new round of introductions and Ret went over the teams again for the sake of the newcomers. 'You Chris,' he continued. 'You have a role which is no less important than the others. There is one team per rift, but you have a part to play in connection with each rift.'

'What, on my own?' Chris didn't like what he was hearing. 'What do I have to do?'

'We're not sure, but we do know without you the quest is doomed to fail. You have to provide a focus in the First Realm for the other teams. They must all align towards this point before the light is drawn and directed, otherwise their efforts will be for nothing.'

'*I'm* going to the First Realm? I thought that was impossible for humans.'

'It usually is, but with the help of the Kern engineers, we have found a way. You see, Brikadden is a kind of vessel, and the Kern are confident that within the week, they will have perfected the means to navigate to the First Realm.'

'And then I'll be taken there, so I can hang about near the rifts waiting for inspiration to do something.' Chris had completely forgotten the pain radiating from his loins. 'What if I can't work out what to do? I mean, I can hardly get my head round "Hidden Paths" and "rifts" and all this other stuff about the Realms and the Mass. How is it suddenly all going to make sense? Will it be like, "zap!" and I suddenly know what to do?' There was mounting panic in Chris's voice.

Tarn ran up the stairs three at a time and entered into communication with the Kern and then he turned and called for Chris to join them. Chris climbed the stairs, a twinge or two of pain reasserting itself between his legs and in his lower abdomen. He wondered if Lillian had done him any permanent damage, but there was no time to dwell on it.

'We talk of the Realms as three planes or levels,' Tarn began. 'First Realm is Ieldamarah and home to the First Born. Second Realm is your world Chris, and here we are in S'herra which is Third Realm. Between the Realms lie the Hidden Paths. It is a way of putting reality into a form of words which may be grasped and understood, but it is actually far from true reality. That is far more complicated and there are no words for it, but Zearik-Klah has agreed to show you another form of the reality, which may help you to understand.'

The shorter of the two Kern approached and Chris felt a tiny vibration in the Kern device embedded into his left temple. There was a little pain, and then as he screwed his eyes tight shut his head was filled with a vision and in an instant he saw.

The Realms were like three different colours of clay squashed into one sphere, crushed and manipulated and twisted in and out and around each other in many convolutions with the Hidden Paths as a mycelium shot throughout, nowhere left untouched by its influence but looking nothing like a path. To complicate the picture further the ball was divided into many temporal segments with the colours of each Realm twisted back and forth across segments and the mycelium spread everywhere at every level. The sphere and all its implications filled Chris's mind and he saw and understood, and as if the revelation was not enough already, a wider knowledge came to him: this twisting and turning of the Realms did not only affect his little world, but the entire Universe. In theory, at least, the Hidden Paths could take a person to all the worlds in time and space – if only one could live as long as the journey would take.

When Chris opened his eyes he noticed that Tarn was smiling, and Ret and Sav too. They were all smiling in response to his own wide and sublime grin. For just a moment, Chris had understood the Universe and everything in it.

'I get it,' he whispered. He started to laugh. I *get* it. Everything!' And then, he was not so sure. For a little while the veils had been lifted, but now they were falling back into place, gossamer-like but becoming opaque with every successive layer. 'At least, I think I do.'

'Did that help?' Tarn asked.

Chris nodded. 'Could we visit other worlds – not just other Realms, but other worlds – inside this vessel you call Brikadden?'

'Of course,' Tarn said very matter of fact. 'You don't think the Kern come from any of our Realms, do you?'

Chris looked the two five-foot grasshoppers up and down. 'Suppose not. Space ships ...?'

'Think of them as Hidden Path ships!' Tarn answered.

'Brikadden ...?

'A flying saucer ... of sorts.'

Chris started to jump up and down with excitement and laugh like a boy half his age.'

Near the bottom of the steps, Lillian watched. 'I thought I'd just kicked him in the nuts, but it looks like it's affected his brain,' she whispered to Jamie. She shrugged. 'Oh well, proves the old theory about where a boy keeps his brain.'

'As if you needed any more proof,' Jamie mumbled, blushing.

CHAPTER TWENTY-NINE

Atolak!

'Why don't we call her the *Shitake Maru*?' Chris said. 'It's Japanese for "mushroom ship" – well almost.

Jamie smiled. 'Cool!'

The cousins were in what Chris thought of as Brikadden's bridge. It was certainly a control room, or centre of operations. Accessed via the same cave through which they had come into Brikadden, the control room was situated at the end of a long, low tunnel leading from the back. No bigger than Chris's bedroom back home, the walls were chocolate brown and organic – rubbery to the touch – and like everything else about the area, perfectly suited to the Kern controllers. There were six of them and they attended to various control panels that sported columns of different coloured lights rather than buttons and levers. Once the young men had heard that Brikadden was a vessel of sorts, they had both been keen to see how it was controlled and Tarn had arranged it for them.

Jamie reached a hand into the holographic display that served as a viewing panel or monitor, and tried to touch the hovering mushroom shape that represented the ship.

'Chris! Ask him how big it is?' Jamie hadn't been fitted with the Kern communication devices, so he could not ask for himself.

'Bloody massive! It has to be to fit a whole village in it.' Chris asked anyway and was shocked when the answer came in pictures – a comparative illustration with the mushroom shape juxtaposed with a human male.

'Blimey!' Chris said. 'It's not much bigger than a Tranny van! Hang on a mo. The Kern's putting some words into my head ...'

Jamie looked from Chris to the little Kern and back again.

'He says the ship is subject to ... dimensional inversion ... whatever the hell that is.'

Jamie laughed. 'It's like the Doctor's TARDIS! It's bigger on the inside than on the outside. That is *so* gear!'

Chris could believe anything now, although he was surprised at how accepting all the others were. Maybe he was just naturally sceptical. 'The Kern says the ship travels mostly through the Hidden Paths, but if it ever manifests in one of the Realms, it looks like a little bright light ... I think he's just explained about eighty percent of all the UFO sightings that have ever happened.'

'I can't believe I'm part of all this Chris. It's really is *the* most!'

Chris nodded. 'I wonder if I should ask him about the Loch Ness monster while I have the chance.'

The Kern overheard and slid another burst of pictures into Chris's mind.

'Mystery solved! Old Nessie is a being of the Host who decided not to be a faerie. And here I am thinking she was a left-over dinosaur. How stupid of me.'

Jamie laughed. 'Maybe there was a real Catweazle too. He used to go through time – like we have.'

'Catweazle? Who's Catweazle?'

'It was a TV program. Used to be on when I was really young – about this old wizard who ends up coming to our time. Well, my time, I suppose.'

Chris turned his attention back to the hologram: it now showed the ship hovering above a rocky desert, but Chris was thinking that the earliest TV show he could remember would have come out years after Jamie disappeared. Steer clear of TV and music though and they had lots of common ground. They both knew Wymes Park well – that had hardly changed in a century so half-a-generation was no problem – and Dolly Tregonhawke didn't seem to have changed much from the boys' relative perspectives. Jamie even remembered Chris's dad when he used to zip round town on his motorbike on his visits up from the smoke.

Chris lapped up stories about Little Rillton and its people in the 1980s, but he was very reluctant to reciprocate. He knew from his conversations with Tarn and some of the others that it wasn't a good idea to talk to people about futures they were yet to live. There was nothing they could do to change the future, but knowing certain fact could easily lead them to living there lives differently, or becoming despondent and resigned that events would happen with or without their help. The world turned easier for people when they put their shoulders to it. No; giving up wouldn't alter a thing in the world but could easily rob a person of the zest that made life interesting.

Chris thanked the Kern for their time and he and Jamie squeezed through the tunnels back to the part of Brikadden that was the village. Jamie went off to find Lillian and Chris scouted round looking for Tarn. After the meeting at Brikadden Beacon, they'd had a long conversation together, and Tarn had made certain promises that Chris meant to see he kept.

In short, Chris was willing to help in anyway he could, although the prospect frightened him and he rather resented the feeling that he, and the other people from his world, had been press-ganged into service. In return they would assist him in his quest to find and hopefully rescue Gayle. Sem had recently infiltrated the spell-woven walls of Atolak and had seen her, so at least there was a location.

Tarn helped Chris gather some equipment. It was just the two of them in Chris's cottage now because Sun had been taken to another house where his needs could better be served and healing arts applied. Chris was relieved that he no longer had the burden of looking after Sun.

'The east gate of Atolak has been walled up,' Tarn said as he went through Chris's things, sorting out what should be left and what taken. 'That's because prophesy tells of Atolak's impregnability, except via the east gate.'

'Not more prophecies,' Chris grumbled. 'Who makes them up, anyway?'

'Some are just that: made up. Others are the result of people who have already lived through the times of which prophecy speaks. They find themselves in an earlier temporality and then find it impossible to keep their mouths shut about how certain events will unfold. The difficulty is telling the two kinds of legend apart.'

'How *do* you tell them apart?'

'It's difficult because both kinds become distorted over the years. So you don't put much reliance upon anything that calls itself prophesy – but nor do you entirely ignore it.'

'Seems to me if it's the kind of prophecy someone's already lived through, it hardly matters what you do, it'll end up happening.'

'True, but it is the manner of its happening that becomes important, and those are the very details that are lost over the centuries. So we still make plans and we must still be careful. And bear in mind that false prophecies may be sewn to bring about events that have never been foreseen.'

Chris frowned and chewed the inside of his cheek as he ruminated. 'We'd all be a lot better off without prophecies altogether.'

Tarn did not disagree.

'How about this for an idea? We go to Atolak and you do that slip-shift thing and we shoot straight through the walls and wind up inside.'

'I won't be going with you. I'm required elsewhere, and anyway, Atolak's walls are proof against slip-shifting. Senoi will go with you and Agronal has also volunteered. You should meet with them and plan your next steps.'

The following day when the sun was still climbing towards noon, Agronal, Chris and Senoi emerged from the Hidden Paths and already their plan was awry. It was true that Atolak's walls were proof against slip-shifting, but the same arts that made them impenetrable also made the Paths in that area dark and immune from remote monitoring. In theory, at least, a small party with the right skills could slip through the Hidden Paths and emerge close to the house. On that morning, theory did not convert to reality in the expected manner.

'Where's the house?' Chris said. 'Where's Atolak?'

Chris and Agronal crouched into long grass in a narrow sward with mountains rising sheer to one side and the land falling to a large lake held in a high mountain valley at the other. Senoi hovered low.

'Something went wrong,' Agronal said. He sniffed the air and scrutinised the surroundings. 'We have emerged on the wrong side of the mountain. I was pulled off route by a brightness I have only seen once before.'

'Did she do it? Has Lady Rosemary shunted us into a backwater?'

'No, it wasn't her. It was as if … When I was a faun my people used to raise a great light in the between-Realm spaces to blind Kar'akhen's eyes against our presence. We called it the Kraken's Lamp and since that last lighting I have never seen the like – until today. There was a kind of beacon-like effulgence, and it called to me and I could not resist.'

Chris looked all round, shrinking deeper into the grass as the hairs at the back of his neck bristled. Agronal seemed to shrink too, but Senoi was flitting about furiously, dipping into the long grass and rising again, quartering an area of land closer to the lake like a hawking dragonfly. His actions were hypnotic to watch, and Chris became totally absorbed until there came one last dip, a rocket-leap into the air and a shrill call of triumph. Senoi was calling the others to him, as excited as Chris had ever seen him.

'It's here! It's here!' Senoi kept repeating until Chris reached him. At first, Chris couldn't see anything, but then he bent close to the ground and rooted through the grass.

'What are you digging at, Chris?' Agronal said moving his head from side to side to see past Chris's rapid movements and the roiling grasses.

'I … don't … know. Seems to be a … long piece of –'

'Have a care! That object you're wrestling with is the source of the light. A solid object in a Realm which resonates into the Hidden Paths is usually a –'

'Got it!' Chris said pulling the object free of the tangled grass roots.

' … a thing of the First Realm.'

'It's a sword,' Chris said wiping the soil away from its gleaming blade. 'It must have been there years, but there's no rust, and even the wooden bits are okay. Just needs wiping.'

'It's not just *any* sword,' Senoi piped, zipping in for a closer look. 'It's *the* sword. It first belonged to an Ieladhrim of the Shade, and then to the Warrior Prophet.'

'Jason?'

'The very same!'

Agronal leant forward and gently but insistently took the blade which had the form of a gladius of the late Roman Republic. He held it to his ear and cocked his head, and for an instant he seemed to fade from this world as if light had refused to fall upon him.

'It is indeed a First Realm blade. Though it be in the earth a thousand years, it would show no sign of age.'

'Maybe not,' Senoi said grinning. 'But it's only been down there for fifteen years. It was on the shore of this lake that the Warrior Prophet fought his nemesis and having fought – for good or ill, win or lose – it would appear he had no more use for his weapon.'

'This blade is the mightiest relic of the world, ranking above even the Bow of Ar'zhuna.'

'No Agronal. It's just a sword, and Chris found it, so give it him back.'

'Of course,' Agronal said handing the blade over with something approaching reverence.

'And what am I supposed to do with it?'

'Hang on to it, and we might find out.'

'But ... I can't sword-fight.'

'Nor could the Prophet Jason, but I believe he may have found it useful. Stick it in your belt, and forget about it for now. It's time we thought about crossing this mountain.'

They began for the high peaks and though there was no true path they at least found a way through clinging to a fault line which provided footholds almost as good as a narrow path. As they climbed and came to the ridge that divided two high valleys, Agronal kept dipping his consciousness into the Paths to note the effect of Jason's sword. As late afternoon came and they began to descend into the Vale of Atolak, Agronal smiled for he has fathomed at least one of the sword's secrets.

Lady Rosemary stood on the highest of her balconies which faced north towards the ridge that divided her valley from the Vale of the Lonely Lake. The air was crisp and cold, and the sun bright casting shadows over her right shoulder. She had a feeling of foreboding which she could not shake, and had sent for Edmund Warwick. She was moved to irritability that he did not come as quickly as usual, so that when he did arrive she dispensed with the formality of greetings.

'Now that you have truly joined the ranks of the wise, do you *feel* something this day? Something ... palpable. Something in the air?'

Apart from being ill at ease with his lady's ever more youthful appearance, Edmund could detect nothing amiss, neither within the ethers nor about the physical land that surrounded him. He was glad at least, that she had chosen to wear her robes, for they lent an air of authority that her girlish looks no longer did.

'I feel nothing amiss, Lady.'

She turned her eyes on him, and they were not the eyes of a little girl. Neither were they the eyes of a woman, but with her plummeting age came the eyes of demons. Edmund's lady was becoming an abomination, and he was sickened.

'Do you yet have the ability to look upon the Hidden Paths?'

'It is coming, but I am not yet proficient in that skill.'

'No, I thought not,' Rosemary said wearily. 'It is just that the Vale of the Lonely Lake has been hidden to my gaze this last fifteen years – and now, today – I see it all quiet plainly. And yet ...'

'My Lady?'

'And yet, there are places once clear that are now cloudy, or fully encompassed with an impenetrable darkness. And –'

Lady Rosemary shuddered, and Edmund moved in to help, caught unawares by an old loose thread of devotion.

'No Edmund! Thank you, but I need no support. It is just that I have the strangest feeling that something approaches, like a ship wreathed in fog. I see the fog, but the ship is nothing but a vague sense of ...'

Lady Rosemary turned from the balcony, took two paces towards the door and stopped again. Turning, her smile sent ice to Edmund's spine.

'It's him! He's coming.'

Edmund Warwick peered towards the far mountain range. He saw neither fog nor ship.

'We must prepare the little surprise we arranged in case of such eventuality.'

'The girl?'

'Yes, Edmund. The girl.'

With the ridge behind them, Chris, Agronal and Senoi began their descent into the Vale of Atolak. The valley, nestled between the arms of the mountain which stretched out either side, looked green and peaceful with several small copses of coniferous trees crowning little hills. A river meandered between the hills and the smell of wood smoke and pine scented the clean air. The house called Atolak though far below and at the other end of the valley, stood proud and inviting on a granite prominence which jutted from the left arm of the mountain.

'That's Atolak?' Chris asked. He could hardly believe the nexus for so much evil could look so at one with nature, and appear so warm and comforting.

'A spider doesn't spin an ugly web,' Agronal said.

''No,' Senoi added from his perch on Chris's shoulder. 'But when the Lady passes the need to maintain physical form and cease to desire comforts of the body, this land will wither and the house shall fall in to disrepair. At that time, the Vale of Atolak will begin to look like it really should.'

'Another prophecy?'

'Not really. It's happened before. When Kar'akhen became essence rather than form, his seat of power assumed the look of long neglect and the stench of decay.'

'Maybe we can stop it happening,' Chris said, one hand drifting to the sword.

Senoi stepped off Chris's shoulder and let the air carry him to Agronal. Resettling on Agronal's shoulder he spoke. 'We are not here to make war on the Lady of Atolak. She is in much too powerful a position. We have to sneak in, find

Gayle Merrill if we can, and then make good our escape. My advice is, put sword-play out of your mind and trust to stealth.'

Agronal chuckled, drawing the attention of the other two. Chris asked a question with a frown.

'And yet the sword is key,' Agronal said. 'The Lady has the power to see through the Hidden Paths, but she cannot look towards the sword. The blade is woven with First Realm spells that cast her eyes away, and the eyes of all who draw upon the darkness.'

Chris though about it for a moment. 'So instead of seeing us coming down the path, she sees a big blob of nothing. She can see everywhere else, but not here.' Chris rounded on Agronal. 'Won't that be a bit like being invisible but waving a big fluorescent flag? The very fact that she can't see will tell her something's coming.'

'He has a point there,' Senoi said to Agronal.

'Yes, but the sword casts its masking effect far further than our immediate surrounding. The whole valley will be invisible to her powers.'

'What about her proper eyes? She can still see – as in *see* – can't she?'

'Of course, and so can her servants.' Agronal said. 'The sword doesn't solve all our problems but it gives us one more advantage.'

'In addition to which, it's so frakkin sharp it's just put a hole in my combat pants. Shame it didn't come with a scabbard.'

The party continued their descent keeping out of a direct line of sight from Atolak wherever possible. The lower slopes where the path petered out were boggy. Chris got his feet wet and it was particularly tough going for Agronal. Senoi of course, had no problem crossing the few hundred yards to the first little copse. They decided it would be quicker to slip-shift from copse to copse until they were close to the house, and then Senoi went to scout out a likely place of entry. He was back in the shadow of the pine trees within twenty minutes.

'Were you seen, Senoi?'

'No Agronal, at least not as far as I am aware.'

'What's the news then?' Chris asked. 'Can we get in?' Curiously, although he was fired up and on edge, he did not feel scared.

'There is a large gate with a closed portcullis at the base of the rock upon which Atolak stands, but it is well guarded. I could get in but you two ...

'The main door of the house, opening onto lawns growing atop the rock is likewise protected by guards, some scions and some human – probably Takers in the Lady's service. Likewise three other smaller doors have guards.'

'Windows?' Chris asked.

'There are none that may be reached from the ground, although there is a way up onto the main roof.'

Chris nodded. 'Don't suppose we could play Santa Claus and go down one of those chimneys? Or find a soil outlet and climb up the guarderobe shaft?' He remembered doing just that at an old ruined castle in Wales once, but that particular facility hadn't been used for its intended purpose in seven hundred years. 'On second thoughts, forget that last one.'

Agronal suggested that they wait until dark and keep a close eye on the comings and goings of the guards, and perhaps work out their routine. Chris had a better idea.

'Why don't we just slip-shift to the East Gate? You know what the prophecy says, and you can't beat a good prophecy.'

It's a start,' Senoi said, and two minutes later they stood in the shadow of the eastern wall of the house, the walled up gate before them. The stonework was made to withstand huge forces, but strangely it was no longer proofed against slip-shifting. Once Senoi had flown high to find a way in – through a gargoyle's mouth into an intramural airspace and then into the interior of the house, proper – it was a simple matter for Agronal to focus on him and pass through both ether and stone. Now just inside the walled up gate, they found themselves in a dark, disused antechamber. The only light was that which crept in through gaps in the wall left by mouldering mortar and a little from under a door opposite. The space was dense with cobwebs and the party had to be careful not to trip over badly placed piles of furniture and old trunks.

'They must use this area for storage,' Agronal whispered.

'I don't know,' Chris said. 'But compared to outside, it's far closer to what I'd been expecting the place to be like.'

The room smelt of dust, mildew and old straw. Echoes of voices came to them, and the sounds of far off footsteps. A guttural laugh bounced off the walls around them, the harshness dampened by distance and the intervention of several walls. Chris half expected to hear the screams of a tortured captive rip the air. Instead it was something heavy striking the door from the other side which made his hand fly to the hilt of the old sword.

There was a shout of admonishment, and more laughter – this time much closer. But whatever the cause of the noise, the door stayed firmly shut.

'The Lady's retainers are an uncouth rabble,' Senoi said flying back from a spying mission through a large keyhole. 'It appears to be their common room, so there's no way into the rest of the house in that direction. They would tear us to shreds. At least two of them are wolf-men.'

Agronal and Chris crouched low behind some packing cases while Senoi flew up to make himself comfortable on a wrought iron candelabrum. There they all remained for several minutes listening to the ebb and flow of Atolak's noises as their eyes grew accustomed to the dark. It was then that Senoi, from his vantage point, noticed a deeper darkness behind the shadows of packing cases, which he correctly suspected to be another doorway.

Squeezing behind the stacked cases with Agronal close behind Chris came to a narrow flight of stairs, wall one side and open to a fall on the other. Ascending ten metres and becoming more and more aware of the drop – for the steps were narrow – he was relieved when the stair turned inwards and took him into the thick wall for several rises before he was faced with another door. Feeling about in the dark he found a doorknob and turning it found the door to be unlocked. It opened onto a dimly lit, narrow corridor, carpeted and with polished wooden panels along both walls. Taking one nervous step he turned to the others.

'I think we're in boys!' he whispered.

CHAPTER THIRTY

Secrets of the East Wing

Edward Warwick concentrated hard at his new-found power to look through the Hidden Paths. 'The boy, the fae and the goat! I think they are inside, my Lady.' Edmund stood with his back to an open fire watching the little girl Rosemary had become, as she sat on the edge of her bed. Her face was relaxed – she looked no older than fourteen – and her eyes were turned inward, no doubt looking through to the Hidden Paths and thence onward to horizons further than any physical eye could see.

Rosemary's eyes fluttered and she refocused on the solid world. 'I *know* they are inside!' Rosemary jumped from her bed and giggled. 'And the girl is in the next chamber so I will soon wrench his friends away from him. Oh, it is all going so well.'

'I should like to try my newfound powers upon the abominable carcase of the goat-fiend, if your Ladyship permits.'

'Yes, yes, if you wish,' Rosemary said waving off the question with a flap of the wrist. 'And pull off the faerie's wings if you want. I really don't care so long as the boy is mine.'

Edmund couldn't see why she just didn't kill the lad straight away. Surely if the legends marked him as a potential danger, she shouldn't risk all just to have her sport with him.

'I am unclear as to my role. Won't you let me kill the boy, thereby foiling the legend?'

'Absolutely not, Edmund,' Rosemary said facing him with a look of incredulity. 'Oh he will die, and I will have his head. But first the girl will seduce him. She has the likeness of the girl we took, who was the boy's little slut-in-training, so he will be easy game for her. And when he is undressed, at the rut and at his most vulnerable – then I will bring him pain and humiliation.' Rosemary jumped up and down like an excited little girl, and then stopped again with a frown on her face.

'What became of the real girl, Edmund? Gayle, wasn't it?'

'The guards had her, and then the werewolves. Her only remains are cracked and marrow-sucked bones.'

'But she didn't die a virgin,' Rosemary said, leering.

'Indeed not. She was most experience after the guards –'

'Yes, yes,' Rosemary said, bored again and turning thoughts back to her next victim. 'We've no time for this. Instruct our friends to take the faerie and the goat.'

Edmund turned to see to the task, but hesitated. 'Remind me Lady Rosemary. What is it you have against the boy?'

She fixed Edmund Warwick with her eyes which flashed yellow for an instant. Just as Edmund believed he had been judged insolent to ask such a question, Rosemary gave an answer.

'There are three reasons. First the De'Ath boy is youthful and alive, whereas Paul, my dear brother is youthful and dead. Secondly, all my powers shall soon be bent to snatching Paul from the jaws of death, and there must be balance. Paul will live again, and the youth next door will die in his stead. And finally,' Rosemary smiled mischievously. 'I may look like a little girl, but you know me for the woman I really am. I have needs, and I will place my consciousness into the body of the demon-girl while she takes him and enjoy the pleasures as if it is I who lies beneath him.'

Edmund Warwick actually blushed. His lady had descended into the pits of Hell and was no more than a harlot. He struggled to keep his features even, and he managed a smile, but inside he seethed with loathing.

'Isn't this all a bit too easy?' Chris whispered from behind a huge potted palm. So far the party had managed to reach the top floor without so much as a whiff of a guard or the hint of a dark spell. Semangeloph had briefed Senoi on exactly where to look for the girl, and she was to be found somewhere on this floor towards the East – exactly where they happened to be.

'We draw heavily on our stock of good fortune,' Senoi said, but no sooner than his word were out then they seemed premature: a door a little way down the hall began top open. They would need more than a potted palm to hide them if anyone should come their way.

Through the fronds Chris saw a tall figure step out of the room down the hall and recognised it at once. It was that fellow who had first saved him from Kostja, and then turned a gun on him. In desperation Chris look back the way they had come, and quickly tried the knob of the nearest door. It was open and cracking the door just a little he found the interior to be quite dark. With no time think further on the matter, he scooted inside. Agronal and Senoi followed and the door closed – with an all too audible clunk. Chris held his breath fearing that the man – he felt sure "Edmund" was the name – must have heard and would come to investigate. After several seconds of hearing only his own thumping heart and his all too noisy breathing, it appeared to Chris that his store of luck was holding. Until …

He found himself quite alone. Neither Senoi nor Agronal would answer his urgent whispers and he was reminded of his first moments in this land: in the dark, all alone, not knowing what to do next. Fear crept up from his guts and inched ice up his spine. The world, black as it was, contracted upon him and all he could think was that if something had got his two friends, it would soon get him. He slid the gladius from his belt and held it tightly.

The place might be new to him, but emotionally he'd been here before. These were the feelings that overcame him, that laughed at his resolve and made him a shivering wreck meekly waiting for whatever happened to be incoming. Time and again since his whole world turned crazy, he found himself feeling like this: useless and unmanned. This time though he nipped it in the bud. Clenching his teeth tightly together, he stood up to full height and took a deep breath. He had no idea what shared the darkness with him or when the attack would come, so he stopped caring and came up with his own, personal litany against fear. Not quiet as eloquent as that of Dune's *Bene Gesserit*; perhaps not as stirring as Henry V's "Once more into the breach …" but for Chris at least, just as effective.

'Fear's bollocks!' he whispered, and then stepped forward into the darkness.

With his sword firmly gripped in his right hand he stepped along, his left hand held out to feel the way. He soon came to another door and found the knob. Slowly, slowly turning the catch gave and the door sprang forward minutely. A vertical ribbon of light marked the edge of the door and the sweet smell of oranges reached his nostril, but as sweet as may be, the sound he heard next had no comparison. A voice called, falteringly and uncertain, but it was the voice of Gayle Merrill. All danger forgotten Chris burst through and dropped the sword onto the heavily rugged floor. All dignity withered, in the next instant he was holding Gayle tightly to his chest holding back the sobs as he buried his face in her hair. Over his shoulder, Gayle smiled, and her eyes flashed yellow. Reaching up she ran her fingers through his hair ...

And then Chris felt the thrill of her touch as she gently caressed his ears, and then his neck. Instantly and fully aroused, he made no move to resist and Gayle led him to a large, heavy quilted bed across from the door.

It wasn't until an hour later, exhausted, drained and tingling with the afterglow of full, fervent and adventurous lovemaking that Chris spared a thought for Agronal and Senoi. He lay on top of the bed and Gayle snuggled close to his side. It had happened at last, and it was everything he hoped it would be, but it was also quite absurd. He had made love in the midst of danger, painful discovery by the Lady's servants – or at the least embarrassing discovery by his friends – a real possibility, and yet he had not once worried about any of it until now. *Surely the need for sex doesn't outrank the imperative to survive, even for randy little bastards like me.* Too late to worry about it, Chris thought.

'Gayle, are you awake?' Chris whispered letting his eyes fall upon the round firm breasts he had so recently been between, and the still-hard nipples he had gently nipped and sucked. He had to look away again quickly and swing his legs off the bed to ward off a renewed call to arms. It didn't work and the dragon was on the rise once again.

Swinging his legs back onto the bed and turning towards Gayle, she was indeed awake and she seemed pleased that the dragon was so obviously untamed.

'You still have some energy left?' Gayle said through gentle laughter.

'I haven't, but he has,' Chris replied flicking his eyes downwards.

'Well,' Gayle said rising to her knees and straddling Chris who now lay on his back. 'So far you've done all the hard work. This time you lay back and relax.'

Once again thoughts of anyone bursting in on them was the furthest thing from Chris's mind. As Gayle's cool fingers wrapped around him he gasped and closed his eyes, fully intent on giving himself up to just one more session of pure pleasure. But there was something ...just something about the way Gayle made love; the way she used her hands: he had a flashback to his encounter with the succubus.

'What's the matter, Chris?' Gayle disengaged and looked concerned.

The moment of fear passed. 'Oh – it's nothing. It's just that ... I'll tell you later. Don't stop.'

Gayle smiled, and then took up where she had left off, and a thousand demons could not make Chris worry for the next little while.

He woke up much later. Gayle was up and dressed and had put a cover over him.

'Hello sleepy head,' she said through strands of long hair. Despite the fact that they had so recently explored each other's bodies so thoroughly, Chris felt shy as he slipped from under the covers, and he kept his back to her as he got dressed.

'Has there been any sign of my friends? One's a little guy ... with wings and the other has kind of ... well, goat's legs and horns.'

Gayle shook her head and poured two mugs of *creeth* into earthenware mugs. 'Honey?'

'Yes please, one spoonful. I – er – guess you've seen strange things, like faeries and goat-boys since you've been here.'

'Not faeries. But a satyr was captured by the patrol last week. The guards had great sport with him, and then finished him off when they were bored. Lady Rosemary kept the head. She collects heads.'

'Oh God! That's horrible,' Chris said, pulling on his socks. 'Nobody's hurt you since you were taken, have they?'

Gayle didn't answer, but crossed the carpet towards the bed, her feet bare, and handed Chris his beverage.

'The thing is, one moment we were all three of us together, next it was just me.' Chris pointed to the door leading to the dark hall. He finished lacing up his boots and took a draught of the sweet, soothing drink.

'It's one of the Lady's tricks. She can drag people onto the Hidden Paths. If she hasn't killed them, which is most probable, then she'll have dumped them in some dark wood at the edge of the world.'

Gayle was so matter of fact about it all, that it made Chris very uneasy. Maybe it was her way of screening out the horrors. Gayle screened them out, and Chris chose to ignore them: he would not believe his friends had been harmed and imagined them escaping the Lady's trap. Even now they would be regrouping and making plans for his rescue – although he wasn't sure he wanted rescuing ... just yet.

Chris flopped onto the bed and sat on the edge drinking his creeth. He slapped the space beside him. 'Come on Gayle. Plonk yourself down here and we'll talk about all the stuff that's happened since you were taken. How they got you to Wymes Forest, what happened when you arrived here. All that kind of thing.'

Gayle smiled and winked. 'Trying to get me back onto the bed so soon.'

'Not for that!' Chris chuckled. 'Even the dragon is too tired to come out and play any more. Come on Gayle. You're safe from me and Mr Dragon.'

'But are you safe from me?' She sat next to Chris and he kissed her cheek.

'So, how long have you been here? I suppose you know time is all to pot in this place.'

'There's nothing I can tell you, Chris.'

Chris felt cold again.

'Remember just know, you asked if anybody had hurt me. Well, they have, in the worst possible way.'

'Oh Gayle. I'm so, so sorry. And you just let me ...'

'No, nothing like that. Much worse. Now, I will tell you my story, but you must be prepared for the worst.'

It was right then that Chris felt that familiar stirring of ice in his guts. Little, insignificant pieces of the puzzle fell together and made an all too horrifying picture. There was no need to ask; he knew, but he asked anyway.

'You're not Gayle, are you?' In that moment of absolute certainty, Chris sank inside for he also knew the real Gayle had surely perished, and he did not want to know how.

Gayle – not-Gayle – shook her head. She stood and crossed the room then turned, cradling her hot drink in a very Gayle-like way. From the highest peaks which follow pleasure, Chris was cast into the depths, but his little litany helped him keep his head. *Fear's bollocks!*

Chris couldn't stop himself from recalling that other sexual encounter with a demon and that the assault upon him had been with a specific intention. The demon wanted to assume his physical form and using the residue of their intercourse as a template, had done just that.

'Well, in the last hour or so I've made love to you four times. You must have enough of my – genetic material – to do me in right now and turn yourself into a near perfect copy.'

'I'm not that kind of a Yaemonadhrim. The Lady used her powers to shape me like the Gayle you knew. I was to be a lure for you, should you ever come to this Realm. So I am not the kind who can take on looks just by absorbing the essence.'

'Just another kind then, that gets off on shagging a human boy cross-eyed and ... and then what? Are you going to kill me? Cripple me? Flay me and use my skin for a handbag. Or maybe just –'

'None of those things. I am as much a prisoner as you, and now that I have disobeyed the Lady ... Well, let's just say she is not renowned for her understanding nature.'

'She'll kill you?'

'Probably. You see, she compelled me to seduce you, and then I was to show you my demonic side while you were at your most vulnerable. Actually, I was supposed to emasculate you with my teeth ...'

Chris flinched visibly and felt a cold asexual stirring in his pants.

'... and then she would enter the room to your screams drawing pleasure from you pain and terror before taking you for her own purposes.'

'Her own purposes being ...?'

'A little matter concerning the collecting of heads ...'

Chris swallowed hard. 'So, why didn't you?'

For the first time Gayle's face took on a look the real Gayle had never shown; she looked hard and cruel. 'I object to coercion, and I do not enjoy being a prisoner. If the Lady wants me to act in a certain way, I shall surely act contrary-wise.' Gayle's face softened once more and she licked her lips. 'And ...'

'And?'

Her smile became mischievous and her eyes sparkled. 'You were very, *very* good.'

Chris hid his surprise well and for once he didn't blush. 'I've had plenty of practice – if you include my right hand, my left hand and several hundred megabytes of porny video.'

Gayle did not understand the last reference. She had never visited the modern world of Chris's Realm. 'I found you most considerate and keen to please. You exhibited a sound knowledge of my womanly parts and knew exactly how to maximise my pleasure. Many men, especially young ones, care only for their own feelings during passion.'

'Like I said, you can learn a lot from a movie.' He wasn't sure he wanted to think about how Gayle had picked up her skills. He couldn't imagine there existed a woman with more knowledge of how work a guy so perfectly.

'Are you telling me, that was your first time?'

Chris covered a self manufactured cough. 'Let's talk about more important stuff, shall we? Like, how can we get out of here?'

Chris and Gayle both jumped as the door to the dark hall opened and a young girl walked in. She was dressed in an old fashioned frock and she carried a human skull under one arm.

'There is no escape for either of you,' she said with girlish glee. And then she looked at Chris – and screamed. She screamed with such gut wrenching terror that Gayle was rooted to the spot. Then she dropped the skull which fell to the uncarpeted part of the floor close to the door, and striking hard it shattered. With the scream echoing up and down the halls, the girl raised a shaky finger and pointed full into Chris's face.

'Mad Christy,' Rosemary blurted, her trembling voice laced with fear and her face a mask of uncertainty adding years to the fourteen-year-old girl she had chosen to be.

Chris seized the moment, for he knew it was possibly all the time he had left. Grabbing Gayle's arm he dragged her straight towards the door hardly interrupting the flow of movement as he bent to snatch up the sword. He brandished it in passing and Rosemary screamed again and leapt aside covering her face with both hands.

He burst through the door but had hardly reached the other end of the dark corridor when a voice, full of hatred and vitriol but with no more trace of fear slapped into him from behind like a physical force.

'You're not Christy!' Rosemary screamed, and Chris felt the crackling of a power that seemed electrical at the exposed skin of his neck.

Through the next door and into the will-lit hall he turned to the left trying the retrace the route he and his friends had taken, but he had only gone two steps before he remembered that without the skill to slip-shift, the best he could do would be to reach the antechamber at the walled up East Gate, where he would be trapped. So executing a rapid about turn he ran back past the potted palm still dragging Gayle behind him.

The door he'd see Edmund come though opened again up the hall and Chris soon found his way barred by a trio of surly-looking men dressed in dark colours and fumbling at their belts for bladed weapons. But through their insolent looks Chris saw the uncertainty in their eyes and instead of turning once again he ran towards them, faster and with the sword held aggressively to the fore. Barring his teeth he bellowed a cry of attack through the fiercest face he could muster. A blood curdling shrill scream of aggression rose from his back as Gayle added her voice. The guards fled back into the room and slammed the door behind them giving Chris and Gayle an unrestricted route to run past.

They encountered no more guards and with several changes of direction down seemingly labyrinthine halls without number, they came to one last long room with a pair of large French windows at the far end opening onto a balcony. With no more plan than to get to the open air, Chris made a dash for it with Gayle, no longer being dragged, keeping close behind.

When a handful of metres from the windows, Edmund Warwick stepped across their path, and with one hand clasping something at his neck and the other raised, he let forth a huge, swirling dark cloud which immediately raced towards Chris.

As the cloud was about to engulf him Chris raised his First Realm blade, and the air was split with a staccato screech of such high frequency that it hovered on the threshold of audibility.

'They won't come near your Ieladhrim blade,' Gayle said. 'And I am of their kind so they won't harm me. Charge on!'

Chris plunged into the cloud that burst before him, fearing to touch one who carried such a weapon, and Gayle followed.

Confused by the failure of his demon-cloud to tear the couple to ribbons Edmund jumped out of their way and they ran straight though the French windows as if they were paper. But such was their momentum that they also ran through the wooden balustrade and together with splintered wood and glass smithereens they plunged off the balcony with a fall of three storeys and the height of Atolak Rock beneath them.

At the instant that gravity took hold Gayle threw her arms round Chris and slip-shifted them to the ground.

'I didn't know you could do that,' Chris said, breathlessly.

Gayle looked high above to the tiny figure that stood on the balcony peering down. 'No time! She's not done with us yet. Run for the trees!'

'Slip-shift us.'

'Not while she's watching. She'll rip us apart with her powers. We must run and hide if we can.'

Lady Rosemary stood a little back from the smashed balustrade and peered down to the grassy valley fifty metres below, and at the two figures that scurried like little mice. They were running towards the woods, but they would never make it. She would call upon her powers, crush the demon-girl and catch the boy alive. She had so enjoyed casting her mind into the girl's body while he did those things to her, that now she wanted his flesh – his real flesh – to produce those feeling once, well at least once, again. Of course, she would grow bored with him after a time, and then she would have to think of a way to send him back to the temporality of the Second World War. There, by means she was unaware, he would come to be known as "Mad Christy" and there her little-girl self of so long ago, would use cheese-wire to sever her first head and start her collection. But that boredom seemed a long way off and her need for physical pleasure blinded he to everything except her mission to bring Paul back from the dead – and even that could wait a little longer.

The dragon. Ha, ha! Rosemary thought with such delight. She would call forth Black Angus and cast him into their path so they would have to turn back. She would let him eat the girl, although she was not certain he would have a stomach for other demons, but the boy would be herded to where her servants could take him. The usual rules would apply: batter the boy a little, bruise him if you must but don't break him. He had to be taken in full working order.

She looked down and squirmed with joy each time a frightened face peered up. She watched their futile flight and wondered what solace they had thought to find in the wood. Trees could not protect them, and though the Ieladhrim sword stopped her looking through the Hidden Paths, no forest shadow would hide Chris from the gaze of her eyes. She considered letting them reach the copse and settle deep into the leaf-mould for a few minutes to enjoy their illusion of safety, but she was too impatient.

Lady Rosemary raised her arms slowly and opened herself to the flow of the darkness. Black Angus heard the summons.

'We're nearly there. Just a few more ...' Chris was cut off by that feeling of power once again. He'd felt it when Rosemary had begun her pursuit along the dark corridor, and here it was again only this time, far more intense. It was almost painful. The air condensed into thick cloud and blotted out the sun and a grasping wind howled delivering more and more substance to the heart of the rapidly forming dragon.

'We are lost,' Gayle said giving up the flight. She turned to face the little silhouette that was Lady Rosemary. 'She calls forth a great and powerful demon. I will try to intercede ...'

Matter appeared to leach from the grass and the earth beneath and the trees nearby to amass into a fearful shape between them and the woods, but before the shape had become solid, there was a mighty flash like a ball of lightning. The incandescent light hovered for a moment between Lady Rosemary's forming demon and the couple. Then, at the same moment, the light and the demon were gone.

'That light, it was a thing of the First Realm,' Gayle said.

'I know,' Chris said caught between terror and hysteria. 'It was the *Shitake Maru*.

'This way!' called a voice from above, and Senoi darted rapidly towards the wood buffeted on the wind. 'Hurry, for she is calling forth the dragon once again.' He lost height as a huge brown leaf wrapped itself round his bird-sized body and he only just freed himself of it before hitting the ground. Chris and Gayle ran after them as a far away scream of Rosemary's rage and the roar of her re-formed dragon reached their ears.

They felt safer as soon as they were among the trees, and they followed Senoi to a small brook running into a cave. 'Through here!' Senoi said.

Chris knew exactly where it would lead and went to plunge through until Gayle caught him by the arm. 'I cannot follow you there. I think you know why.'

Chris imagined he did. 'But ...'

'Thank you Christian De'Ath. I could never have escaped the Lady's grip without you. One day I will repay you.' She stood on tiptoe and kissed him lightly on the lips.

'Hurry up!' Senoi shouted. 'You must come inside. There is no time to waste.' A tree creaked and split in two, the halves crashing through the canopy.

'I'm coming!' Chris called to Senoi, and when he looked back Gayle was no longer there, but he caught a glimpse of a white hare bounding over the fallen tree – and then it was gone. Gayle's last words echoed quietly though his mind: *One day I will repay you.*

'I think you already have, White Hare. Your future is my past,' he whispered.

'Now!' Senoi screamed, 'This instant!' and Chris threw himself into the tiny cave. Seconds later the wood was ablaze with dragon-fire as the monster strode through, immune to its own flame. Black Angus pressed his snout to the cave mouth and exhaled huge volumes of searing white-hot gasses, but it was too late. The cave was just a cave again, and Brikadden had slipped away to another place.

CHAPTER THIRTY-ONE

Time Out

'You have the aroma of a performing seal,' Senoi said as he flitted along with Chris towards the cottages of Brikadden.

'Nice to see you as well,' Chris replied. 'And just in the nick of time too. What happened to you back at Atolak? One moment you and Agronal were there ...'

Senoi explained: just as Gayle had suspected, Lady Rosemary had dragged them onto the Hidden Paths and would have killed them if not for Agronal's powers to draw the light. He fought back at the attacking demons but was not strong enough to prevent Senoi and himself from being dumped far, far to the west in the ruined and long abandoned city of Lansitark. The found themselves stranded and also thrown slightly out of temporality. Their journey home to Brikadden had taken many days, but luck was with them at the end, for they came back to the roving village just as the Kern had completed their esoteric modifications of its motive forces.

'If Rosy had thrown you to a future temporality instead of a recently past one, you wouldn't have been able to get back to Brikadden and come to the rescue,' Chris said sniffing at his armpit. 'Not with her blocking the Hidden Paths.'

'The lady often acts on the moment. It's is our good fortune that she sometimes lacks foresight.'

'But not so great a lack that she doesn't make certain preparations, such as taking Gayle, on the slight off-chance that I might turn up at her front door.'

Senoi did not voice his suspicions that the Lady had long had plans for him.

An hour later and Chris relaxed into deep, hot, perfumed water thick with soap suds. He had the cottage to himself and decided to use the time to take stock of his most recent experiences and to assimilate Tarn's words of warning about the mission to come. But first he had to clear out the clutter: as the residues of adventure and sex floated away and hot water eased into his bones, Chris let his thoughts drift and take him where they would.

After the initial euphoria of being once again safe, and warm and enveloped in the healing water, Chris sank for a few moments into a place of despair where alone at last, he did not fight the tears. *A man can cry*, he excused himself, *but only when there's nobody about to see.* He allowed the hot tears to flow, crying for Gayle, whose pains he could not bare to imagine, and Danny and Yukio and for the unfairness of it all. He heaved great sobs for the knowledge that even in such a place as this Second Realm, there had to be death and misery, just like back home in the world he was born to.

Without the intellectual equipment to philosophise, time and solitude opened up the philosopher's path as he tried to rationalise the tears he could not understand. As long as a child grew up hungry when others grew fat through over indulgence; as long as a mother watched her children pick through garbage while others threw away heaps simply to make room for the newest model or the latest craze; wherever the words of prophets were seized, perverted and made into creeds of hatred: here would follow unrest and misery and violent death.

Chris stopped crying for those who could never return – not for all the manipulations of time or drawing of powers, dark or light – and let his mind drift along the road it had found: comparisons between the Realms.

By the time he concluded that, on the whole, life was simpler and dangers more obvious in this land of faeries and demons, where enemies were bolder than the terrorist's bomb and the threats less insidious than lies and greed and lust for power, the bathwater had grown quite cool.

Chris drew off more hot; he was not ready to get out and face Brikadden or its inhabitants. It was time to think selfishly. His time with Gayle – he smiled at the memory – his time with her had been real and intense. Although a demon of some kind, Gayle had let him experience what he might have had with the real Gayle. Strangely, he did not feel as if he had been duped, or cheated. His memories were good, but he recalled the experience as one of making love to the woman who called herself Moon, and who could assume the shape of a white hare. He put it to the back of his mind that for all that sensual experience he had yet to make love to a human woman.

He wondered what his friends back home would say if they ever heard of his adventures. He knew that he could tell Abe Knapper about it all, and maybe Cappy Shirakawa – but the rest? They'd laugh him all the way home from the pub.

And then at last, as the water was cooling for a second time, Chris looked towards the future, realising that everything before had been mere prevarication. The past was gone. Comparisons were pointless. The future and the reason for Chris's existence, was a sunrise away.

Before Chris had been allowed to see to his comforts, Senoi had led him to Tarn and Tarn told him, all was ready. Tomorrow the final struggle would begin – and Chris would be at the centre of it. He tried to convince himself that in another week or so, he would be wallowing in another hot tub with his battle-to-come no more than a memory, and maybe one or two scars mental and physical – if he was lucky. He dried and got dressed and began to think of food, while at the same time concerns for the next day robbed him of his appetite.

'Anyone in?' Jamie said, popping his head round the door after a single, sharp rap.

'Only us super-heroes, cousin.'

Jamie took that as leave to enter. 'Amazing co-incidence number one,' Jamie said ticking the air with his finger. 'Jason used to call himself that for a joke.'

'Maybe I get to be Jason. Maybe he's me a couple of streets up my future map.'

Jamie shook his head. 'Don't think so, somehow. Phew! You smell like a girl.'

'Better than stinking like a polecat. You wouldn't be complaining if you got a niff of me an hour ago. So, tell me what you've heard about Jason.'

'Okay but let's walk. I want to show you something dead funny. I just discovered it.'

'What? Teletubbies exist after all. Frak!'

'What's a Teletubby, and how comes you swear like a colonial pilot from *Battlestar Galactica*?'

They walked and talked. Chris told Jamie about toddler's TV of the twenty-first century and then came round to *Battlestar Gallactica*. Chris had never seen a single episode of the 1970's version, and of course Jamie was in total ignorance of Chris's favourite sci-fi series with the new characters and adult themes. They compared notes on the two shows before Jamie brought the subject round to football. They walked in a straight line, out of the village and towards the misty distance where the landscape became ill-defined.

'So how's Manchester United doing in the year two thousand and whatever?' Jamie asked. 'We've been rubbish for yonks and now we've gone and got a Scottish manager.'

'Sir Alex?'

'Sir? I didn't know he was a sir.'

'Well, he is now. Your team's been virtually top of everything for years, and Fergusson's still with them.'

Jamie was delighted his team were doing so well, and a little incredulous that Alex Fergusson was still with the team after more than twenty years.

'I'll tell you this funny Man U story,' Chris began. 'Until a couple of years back they had this really brilliant player – David Beckham. He's probably not even born in your time, but anyways, a friend of mine – Cappy Shirakawa – went on holiday to Thailand a couple of years back, and he didn't stick to the touristy bits but went way out into the wilds. He comes to this Buddhist temple and he's looking round and there's this room full of orange robes hanging up to dry – all billowing round in the breeze with the sun shining through them. He said it was like walking through orange mist.

'So he's walking through this orange mist and he comes face to face with a teenage monk. Cappy says hello, and the monk says 'You English?' which is funny in itself because Cappy looks Japanese and sounds Yank but Cappy says 'Yes' and the monk gets this big wide toothy smile all across his face and he punches the air shouting "Da-vid Beck-ham! Da-vid Beck-ham!"

'He can hardly speak English but Cappy gets out of him that he supports Man U and David Beckham is his favourite player.'

'My God. Some little monk the other side of the world supports Man U? That's terrific.'

'*And*, he knows about David Beckham. He must be the most famous guy in the world. But carrying on, Cappy asks how he can ever see the matches, and the monk looks at him as if he's crazy. 'Television!' he says and points up to a satellite dish.' Chris started chuckling but it fell flat. Jamie looked bemused.

'Satellite dish?'

In certain respects, twenty years *was* a long time. 'Ah, never mind. Hey! Where are we?' Chris found himself in thick mist with visibility of a few tens of yards.

'This is my discovery. Don't worry – just keep walking.'

They kept walking with Jamie a little ahead, and as the mist cleared Chris thought they were approaching another village. After a little further he knew it was still Brikadden, but they were heading towards the far side.

'See what's happened, don't you Chris? I've done it seven or eight times now and it's the same every time. You walk out the village, keep going straight and you find yourself coming back into Brikadden from the other side. Is that ace or what?'

Jamie seemed quite delighted by his discovery. 'How d'you think that works Chris?'

'Don't ask me anything about pixie-physics. Brannon Braga could explain it, but I can't – and before you ask,' Chris added noticed Jamie's furrowing brow. 'Braga writes sci-fi scripts. He's one of my favourites – together with Moore and Thompson and Weddle – all the *Battlestar* bunch really.'

'It's not the faerie-physics. It's the bug-people.'

'The Kern?'

'The Kern are ahead of us times ten to the power one zillion. I got to ask one of them loads of questions – through Tarn who translated for me, which was great, but I still couldn't understand a word. The only bit that stuck was that the *Shitake Maru* is an extension of First Realm matter around a bubble of Third Realm substance and it doesn't really move, it just arrives and –'

Chris held up a hand. 'Stop, before my Second Realm brain explodes all over your nineteen-eighty-six Ben Davis top and your Levis red tabs.'

Jamie pulled a face and fingered the gorilla logo at his shirt pocket.

'I haven't got a clue how the *Shitake Maru* gets about, or how a whole village fits inside something the size of a Transit van –'

'It's not really the size of a Transit, or a village. The dimensions are fluid between Realms and –'

'Like I said! I don't understand any of it, but I do know it takes me to faerie-land tomorrow and you lot to various places up and down time.'

Jamie stuck out his bottom lip. 'Maybe we should have called it the good ship *Hickory-Dickory-Dock*. Get it? Up and down time!'

Chris did not smile.

'You know, like the mouse … running … up and …Oh well. Forget it.'

'I already have. And don't sulk. It's just that I'm a bit preoccupied to laugh at … jokes.'

'You were going to say "lousy jokes" weren't you?'

'*Frakkin* lousy jokes, more like. Aren't you even a little bit worried about tomorrow?'

'No use worrying. Anyway, Tarn says you've got the most dangerous job. Oops! Sorry. Not very tactful.'

'Well, here's another lack of tact. The Fey Knights have been trying to sort out the problem of the Unselost Mass for hundreds of years. Tons of young people have been kidnapped up and down the centuries. We've all read the stories, yeah?'

'I suppose.'

'Well, how many ever come back? How many of those stories end "and they all lived happily ever after"?'

Jamie shrugged and shook his head. 'I don't know. None I suppose. But … they might all end up happily ever after in another Realm.'

'And that's okay by you? Never getting home, to the right place and the right time?'

Jamie shuffled awkwardly and rested against a nearby cottage. 'All I know is it's no use bothering to worry. I'm a bit scared, of course, but we've got a lot of people on our side, and they can do stuff that's amazing.'

Chris didn't want to point out some of the amazing things their enemies could do, and didn't like the fact that he found himself being rather negative.

Jamie continued. 'Tarn says he's brought two kings of England to this Realm and one of them stayed a while.'

'Which two kings?'

'Louis and ... one of the Edwards. Not the randy one who was Victoria's son but one of the medieval ones.'

'King Louis's from *Jungle Book*. There never was an English king called Louis.'

'Tarn says there was. He just got bad press and they decided to leave him off the king-list.'

'Kidding me?'

'Nope. It was in the days of old, when knights were bold –'

'And toilets weren't invented.'

Jamie laughed. 'Nice to see the best jokes survive into the two thousands. *God* that sounds weird. Two *thousands*!'

They completed the last hundred metres to Chris's cottage in silence, watching the people – human, fey and Kern – come and go, and at last they got onto the subject of the Warrior Prophet Jason. To Chris's disappointment, there wasn't much to tell. Jamie had heard a couple of stories about him and recalled the odd snippet or two, such as the fact that he sometimes called himself superhero, with tongue firmly in cheek, and that he came to be loved and revered by all the people of S'herra. Almost as much as the Slain Prophet.

'I've heard him mentioned once or twice,' Chris said, hoping that his future didn't lead him to acquire that particular title.'

'Yes, they've got a good share of prophets, that's for sure.'

It was getting late, and Chris had preparations to make for next day's journey. 'Thanks for the walk, Jamie. And the talk – even though I don't believe there ever was a King Louis of England.'

'Look him up when you get home on that computer thing you were telling me about.'

'The web? Yeah – I think I will. See you then. Breakfast tomorrow.'

'Ah – that reminds me. Lillian wants you to come over to ours for dinner tonight. It's the little grey and white cottage with the green tile roof.'

'Sure she doesn't just want to get me cornered, so she can kick my head in?'

'Nah! She knows that was all a misunderstanding.'

'And I won't be getting in the way, if you know what I mean?'

'Hell no! We're not a couple. Once I thought we were, but she was pretty mean to me back at Grayes Forton. First I decided I wanted nothing more to do with her. Then I thought, she still wants me and I'm desperate for my first ... you know? So, kind of, "wham bam thank you mam – now go away", except straight after the "wham bam" we got taken by the Fey Knights.'

'No time for "now go away"? Must be a pain having to share a cottage with her.'

Jamie grinned and winked. 'Has its advantages. But it's pretty obvious we don't mean much to each other, except for the sex. In fact, I rather think she likes you.'

Chris didn't take in the last comment for a moment or two. He was still internally smarting that this barely-sixteen-year-old was more experienced than him, excluding demon-women, or probably even including them if Lillian's appetite was as big as it seemed.

'Okay. Eats at yours. Seven?'

'That'll do. Bring King Louis if you happen to bump into him.'

'I'll bring Baloo and Baggy as well.'

CHAPTER THIRTY-TWO

First Pedestrian of Ieldamarah

Edmund Warwick had never been down to the dungeons before. Lady Rosemary led him down the spiral stair into the depths of Atolak Rock. The walls down here were as heavy, cold and dark as the walls of the house above were light, warm and full of lively colours. The contrast gave the illusion of two different worlds. Rosemary was wearing her robes, but now they were far too big for her and she looked like a little girl playing dress-up.

'De'Ath made a mistake coming here, because I saw into his mind. I know their plan.'

Edmund concentrated on keeping his footing; a fall could be very painful. He didn't bother asking the question that Rosemary's declaration had placed in the air. He knew it would come to rest all by itself.

'They mean to form many teams and seal all the three rifts all at once.'

'Can they do that?'

'Yes, but they will need an anchor. Or a bright beacon shining from the First Realm, otherwise they will not be able to direct their powers.'

Edmund stumbled, his foot sliding off the thin edge of a stair. Rosemary giggled before Edmund steadied himself.

'The Fey Knights have learnt lessons from the past. They have never split forces before.'

'That's why they have never succeeded. They are slow to learn – how many centuries has it been? But this time it shall be the last. I am powerful enough to end them all, and for good. And so, I shall, but we must form three teams of our own.' Rosemary stopped and turned, looking up into Edmunds face.

'I shall lead one, and you shall lead one.'

'Honoured, my Lady. And the third?'

'Ah, that is why we visit the dungeons,' she said, turning once more and skipping down into the gloomy depths.

The stair came to an end and they squeezed along narrow, winding corridors until they came to a cave-like room. An elderly human guard, swathed in a voluminous grey cloak sat hunched at an oak table with a single candle. He barely managed to turn his head for the great weight of his rust-pitted sallet and the greater weight of his boredom. He acknowledged his mistress with no more than a grunt never bothering to stand or offer the usual compliments. Edmund would have kicked the insolent dog to his feet, but Lady Rosemary didn't appear to care.

'The middle door,' Rosemary said to the guard.

He tossed her a bunch of keys on an iron ring and said, 'The one with the silver shank.'

Edmund felt his face engorging with blood and fury, but still Lady Rosemary was calm. There must have been an understanding between her and the old man.

Rosemary presented the silver-shanked key to the middle lock and turned. Throwing back the heavy door with a tiny movement that belied the strength involved, she stood back in deference to the stench. It was ammonia, and rotting blood and dung. Edmund threw his head back as if he'd been struck, and the old guard chuckled. Edmund made a mental note to deal severely with the old fool once Lady Rosemary had quitted the dungeons.

'My Lady,' came a voice of rolling gravel from the depths of the open cell. Edmund recognised the voice, and he turned to see an old friend emerge from the darkness.

'Do you wish to redeem yourself, Master Readtoth,' Rosemary said.

Readtoth bowed, but even bent double he was taller than Rosemary. 'I trust you have not encountered ill-fortune my lady, for I only recognise you by you scent. You have lost stature.'

'Care not for my lack of inches. I have never been better, despite yesterday's fright. I thought one of my boys had returned to claim his skull.' She shivered as she recalled the terror that had robbed her of power – just for a moment. 'But sometimes I forget how the Paths mock time's barriers. Now Readtoth, are you ready to serve me?'

'Command me.'

'Good!' Rosemary said as she clapped her hands. 'I command you, and I *have* a command for you. You shall command a team and you shall taste the blood of enemies.'

Readtoth's lips drew back in a yellow-fanged leer, and he bowed once again.

'Readtoth, Edmund: come to the Great Hall at dusk, and I shall give you your orders.' She threw the key in the direction of the old man. They hit the side of the table and dropped to the floor noisily. Rosemary was already running up the stairs.

'After you, Warwick,' Readtoth said, offering Edmund first place behind the Lady.

'Thank you, but I have a little business to complete.'

The wolf-man bowed his head, ever so slightly, and then bounded up the stone flight none the worse for his long confinement.

Alone but for the guard, Edmund Warwick circled the old man while deciding upon a suitable punishment. Lady Rosemary may well have been so preoccupied with the scent of her longed for objective that she failed to notice rank insubordination, but Edmund was not. This old fossil deserved the ultimate punishment for his rudeness. No sense tarrying, or drawing it out though.

Edmund slipped a roundelle silently from its sheath and approached the hunched fellow in six rapid strides. He drew back his arm and thrust towards the kidney – and found his wrist gripped as if by an iron shackle, the dagger dashed from his hand and the old man's fire-lit eyes boring down into him from a head-height above.

Without warning the old man butted Edmund to the ground, iron helm onto unprotected head. The pain split through his brain, but he was an old war-horse and he sprang to his feet quickly. He went for his sword but the old guard was faster, and the tip of a cross-quillioned hand-and-a-half broadsword nuzzled Edmund's Adam's apple before he could unsheathe his own.

'I am sworn to service, but without the obligation to give fealty or respect. Should I let a captive free, then I shall submit to chastisement, but not before!'

Edmund unhanded his sword-hilt and backed off a pace. The old man put up his own blade and Edmund caught a glimpse of a surcoat that lay beneath the cloak. It bore the device of three leopards rampant-guardant that might show gold in daylight, against a field of brown that may have been scarlet when touched by the sun. Edmund had not felt frightened since he first drew the demon-cloud, but this old man frightened him.

'If your service satisfies the good Lady, I am quite sure it satisfies me,' Edmund said hiding his humiliation in polite words. 'If the day comes when it should cease to satisfy, then neither bastard-swords nor royal devices will save you from my wrath.'

The guard smiled, and he did not look quite so ancient as before. 'Then fellow, prepare yourself for such a day, for you will have no time thereafter to put your affairs to rights.' He inclined his head in minute acknowledgement before resuming his place at the table. Once again he was a huddled old man.

Edmund Warwick hoped the day would come soon. He had an almost pathological aversion to English kings. Past the first flight, he ran up the stairs two at a time.

Chris made haste towards Brikadden Beacon. He was late for the briefing. He'd been up until the early hours after dinner at Jamie and Lillian's and forgot to set the alarm in his watch when he got back to his own cottage. He'd dressed quickly, thrust the old sword into his belt and made a dignified dash up the grassy hill behind Brikadden.

Something was odd, and he soon realised it was an absence of faeries. He had grown used to seeing them all over Brikadden but there were none about and Chris wondered why. The others were gathered in three indistinct groups near the bottom steps of the Beacon.

'Wotcha, Tosser,' Lillian said. He didn't mind the south London greeting, but he did wish Lillian had chosen a different nickname for him. 'You're late. Can't take the night-life?' She winked and did that thing where she licked her lips. Jamie blushed a little and looked down, shuffling his feet. Chris greeted them uncertainly while wondering if he should gravitate to one or other of the loose groups.

He didn't have to wonder for long, because Agronal ushered him towards a small gathering of Kern and two other sa'tyrs. As they approached, the Kern melted away to attend to other duties leaving Chris and the three s'tyradhrim.

'This is my brother, Caedmon,' Agronal said, introducing Chris to a tall, slender sa'tyr who had the height of an average human, and therefore towered above the other two of his kind. 'He is my brother. And here, is Tadouwig.'

Caedmon nodded diffidently and in complete contrast, Tadouwig bowed low and looked at Chris from under thick brows with eyes that sparkled with sexual energy making Chris feel quite uncomfortable.

'Unlike Caedmon I am not of this young faun's family,' Tadouwig said rising. 'Not even of his nation. I am of the Gybs of the Westernmost Govern.'

Chris acknowledged each with a nod of the head, wondering for a moment if Tadouwig was a scion of the Mass.

'Another of our kind was supposed to come, but he has not arrived so I am to take his place in the group led by Tarniel.'

Agronal looked quite excited, an exuberance that betrayed his youth. 'It's fortunate that I was called to bring you to Brikadden, for no group would be complete without a sa'tyr.'

The sa'tyrs gravitated towards their groups each of which was joined by a faerie.

'I thought you'd all gone,' Chris said when Senoi left Tarn's group to join his for a while.

'Only the three of us remain, and soon we must leave too. We shall pass into the First Realm by a usual Path. The Kern are not keen for us to cross the barriers in the *Shitake Maru*. Ah! You smile. The village will ever remain "Brikadden", but the encapsulation of the village as a moving entity is now known by the name you gave, even among the Kern.'

'Fame at last,' Chris said, preening, and not entirely in jest. 'So, where do we go from here?'

Senoi hovered slowly towards the little cave that was the exit to other worlds and times, depending on where the *Shitake Maru* came to rest. Chris followed.

'The groups will be formed, and told what they might expect. And then they will be taken to different temporalities within your world, the Second Realm. They will go to times that are close to the origins of the couple involved.'

'That means, Jamie and Lillian will wind up in the nineteen-eighties, Karl and Beverly in the Second World War, and Marc and Shaun in my time.'

'Correct.'

'And me?'

'In all those times, and none of them. You will go to the First Realm and all will be explained to you there.'

'I was rather hoping all would be explained to me now.'

They came to the little brook that led into the gully and the cave entrance. Senoi flew to an ancient rowan, bright with red berries, and clung to the bark.

'It is better for you to be told stage by stage. Things are very different in the First Realm, and no human has ever set foot there in human form. Until the Kern adapted the *Shitake Maru*, such a thing was impossible. But as you will be the first, we cannot be sure how you will perceive it all.'

'Will anybody be going with me?' Chris asked, pretty sure he knew what the answer would be.

'No.'

Bingo!

'We will be there soon, and all you have to do is leave here by the usual route.' Senoi pointed to the cave. 'Once you have left the cave, you will be in the First Realm although I cannot say how it will appear to you. When you are there, I would advise you to be still for a moment. Take your time to adapt, and wait for someone to come for you.'

'Someone?'

'Probably me, but maybe another. Nothing is at all certain. This is a very historic event, a human in human physicality touching the First Realm.'

'I'll probably make it explode, like antimatter or something.'

'I don't think so,' Senoi chuckled. 'I *do* think might like to take your clothes off when you arrive though,' Senoi said.

'I think I might not!'

'It's just that nobody suffers the encumbrance of clothing in the First Realm, and you wouldn't want to stand out.'

'You right about not wanting to stand out. That's why I'm keeping my stuff on,' Chris said emphatically. Then, with a little more uncertainty he added 'Unless it's against the rules.'

Senoi pushed off from the tree trunk and hovered, his wings whirring noisily. 'It isn't a matter of rules. When I cross to my Realm I shall leave my rude garb on this side. There are no clothes in the First Realm, or the makings for them. And ... there is another reason.'

'Let me guess. Everyone in faerie-land has heard what a hot bod I've got, and you all want to get an eyeful?' Chris was trying a little too hard to appear cool about it all.

Senoi laughed his wings going through a rapid fluctuation of speeds. 'You have almost strayed upon the correct answer, in that it does indeed have something to do with your "hot bod".' He landed and sat on a little rock, wet with moss, at the side of the brook. 'The nature of our struggle with the Mass will lead to changes in your body. The best I can describe it is that you will become incandescent, and any clothing you may have on will simply incinerate. Better you grow accustomed to nudity slowly than to have it forced upon you, mid-battle.'

Chris was suddenly very jealous of Agronal's shaggy legs and flanks and wished he had his own natural pair of trousers. The prospect of fighting the Mass naked was appalling to him. 'Will my hair burn off too?'

'Nothing of your own self will suffer from the flame. Rather, you will become the flame and thereafter be restored without the singeing of as much as an eyelash. The conflagration will mark your success and if it happens, all will be well. If not –'

'I'll be stood round naked.'

'I'm afraid you won't be standing around at all. If we fail, it will be because your body has failed.'

'I'll be stood round dead then.'

'In event of the worst possible case, yes.'

Chris sat next to Senoi and braced his feet against a water-lapped rock in the middle of the brook. He felt anger rising, and not for the first time he was annoyed at the cavalier way these Fey Knights and faeries treated the taken youth of Wymes Park.

'To you lot, I'm not really a person at all, am I? I'm just a weapon of some kind. Nobody *ever* asked me if I wanted to do this. It's always "you will" and never "will you?" – even though I might die. I might *die*, and nobody's ever given me a choice. You lot are as bad as the frakkin Mass.'

Senoi's face reflected Chris's anger in miniature. 'Keep your clothes on then!' he snapped.

'It's not about my clothes, you little shit, and you know it. It's about choices and being able to make my own decisions.' Chris took a swipe at Senoi who leapt out the way. Chris's hand passed harmlessly through the space that Senoi had occupied, and Senoi leapt up and backed into Chris at head level giving him a face full of rapidly scything wings. It was like being slapped with a food mixer on top speed.

Chris's anger peaked and he leapt to his feet, assumed a boxer's stance and faced Senoi who flitted just out of his reach. Almost at once Chris felt ridiculous and dropped his hands to his side. He was standing in the brook and icy water topped his boots and soaked his feet, making him feel even sillier.

'That was for trying to hit me!' Senoi said, landing again.

Chris rubbed his stinging face, his anger all used up but still feeling a good measure of resentment. Surely life, in whichever Realm, was more than just doing what people told you to do, or following other people's expectations. He sat on the rock again.

'Is that what happened to all the others before me? Their bodies failed and they ... they died or whatever?'

'As I said before, no human has ever set foot in the First Realm. And, I hope you will be pleased to hear, we have never failed before.'

Senoi went on to explain that there were many points in locations and temporalities back through the centuries, each with a team who would attack the Mass from their points in time and space.

'And all, yes all, will be focussing upon you as you carry the fight to the Mass from within the First Realm. No matter how bravely they fight, no matter how successfully, if you fail, so shall they all.'

Chris took a deep breath and let it out slowly. 'No pressure then?' he said softly, to his knees. *It would still have been nice to ask*, he thought, wondering if he would have the courage to say yes. He looked up to discover that they had been joined by a pair of Kern who shook their wings in greeting and squirted a sequence of pictures into Chris's head.

'We're here,' he said making sense of the pictures. 'And we're ready.'

Senoi wished him good luck and disappeared into the mist that surrounded Brikadden. A warm feeling infused Chris's body and he interpreted it as the Kern's way of wishing him luck. Throwing a casual wave toward the others up by the Beacon, and not stopping to see if they had noticed, he splashed along the brook and ducked into the mouth of the cave.

He stood up straight, stretching tall in the cave and casting an eye back, he wondered if Brikadden was still there. Resisting the urge to go back and have a look, he continued towards the other exit and with a final glance towards the control room door, he bent double and shuffled though.

The cave mouth at the end of the tunnel was overhung with wet mosses and he received a baptism of sorts when he emerged into the First Realm. The tingling feeling, born, Chris believed, of anticipation and excitement was real enough and intensified as he clambered out of the soft-edged gully. In fact all his senses intensified, and he recalled the time in the lane outside his house back home, when everything had felt more alive and no detail too small to notice.

Pushing strands of wet hair back over his head, he sucked in the fragrant air and took a moment to look all round. The vivid greens of this dense forest were visible, and the many scents quite noticeable; the moist air carried sounds to his ears and he could taste sweet water where it trickled down from his hair. But seeing with his eyes was not enough: he needed to feel the Realm around him, he craved to merge into it so that he and the Realm were one, and with all these clothes on, his skin was blinded. He felt stifled and boxed in, and before he recalled Senoi's suggestion about taking off his clothes, he found himself doing just that. Only when he kicked off his boxers and stood naked did he feel as if he was able to breathe properly. His skin seemed to suck in the light and rejoice at the touch of the air. He gulped in a deep lungful of air, and the land claimed him for its own.

Every leaf, every branch, the grass beneath his feet: it all carried its load of silvery dew and no surface was dry, so gathering his boots and clothes he took them back into the cave, which was now only a cave, blind-ended and completely disconnected from the tunnel that led to Brikadden. He wasn't particularly surprised. He found a dry place to stow his things and slipping his belt from the belt-loops of his combats, he arranged it across his chest as a baldric and attached the sword to it. As he stepped back outside, he felt like some kind of a Viking berserker, clothed only with his weapons, but strangely he felt not a jot of self consciousness.

He stood in the high, wet grass that grew between ivy-clad trees and fallen trunks slick with moss and toadstools and he waited. He saw no obvious path to follow, and detected no sign of civilisation or habitation. He might just as well be the sole human dropped into the depths of a primeval forest.

It was no good. Even the home-made baldric was an encumbrance and his skin rebelled, no part of it willing to be separated from the land to the least degree. Slipping the belt off over his head, he wrapped it round the scabbard and held sword and belt in one hand. His skin rewarded him by tingling all over with pleasure that was more intense than sexual. The feeling went so much deeper than arousal, and without any physical manifestation, he felt that the very essence of the land was making love to him.

Chris took a few steps, felt the wet earth rise up to receive his feet, lapping at them like something alive, something animal. This intensity of sensation made him think of sex because in his world nothing was as raw, nothing as sensual. But here it had nothing to do with sex. It was all connected with belonging and being. He was of one essence with the Realm. He felt what it felt and as he merged with it, he added his own experiences and the Realm was greater, increased by his being. Making love was the palest of shadows to this magnificence of this oneness, this Nirvana. How could the faeries ever bare to part from their world, even for an instant? How could he in a time yet to come?

But then something went wrong. As he walked deeper into the lushness of feeling, he began to feel discomfort deep inside his chest. Discomfort became pain and then agony until Chris was forced to drop to one knee. Pressing a hand to his chest his head dropped and he focussed on the tiny mosses and the shapes of the sundews that grew among them. He tried to order his breathing in an effort to control the pain, but still it increased.

A bare foot pressed moisture out of the plant life in Chris's line of sight, and a second joined it to make up the pair. He looked up slender, lightly haired legs, past the mark of a male, up a flat belly with a hint of a six pack and then to a well-formed, not overly muscled chest finally arriving at a handsome face that seemed strangely familiar. Chris stood and the young man before him was a little taller than him, with a double pair of transparent wings that had a span at least the equal to his height. It was not until he spoke that Chris recognised the well formed youth.

'We had no idea your body would open up so readily to the Realm or that it would match stature with our own.'

'Senoi!' Chris managed through the pain. He even smiled a little. 'Have I shrunk or did you grow?'

'I don't know, but I do know I must lift the pain from you,' Senoi said reaching out with both hands and taking Chris's head between lightly pressed fingers.

'What's happening to me?'

'Like the rest of us, you feel everything the Realm feels. The pain at the heart of your body, it is the Mass attacking the Realm. Now, hold still.'

'I will if I can. It just hurts so much.'

Senoi pressed and almost at once the pain diminished, but so did Chris's connection to the Realm. At last there was neither trace of pain nor the oneness with the Realm and Chris felt isolated, desolate and alone.

'I can't feel the Realm anymore.'

'A body of flesh and blood cannot endure either for long. We're surprised that you almost became one with us. It is not within our experience, and we cannot explain it.'

Chris began to feel something akin to the shock of grief, cut off so suddenly from something so beautiful.

'Give it back!' he demanded. 'It's like my guts have been ripped out of me. I feel hollow, and empty.'

Senoi was concerned for Chris. 'You cannot have the connection without the pain, and I fear you will not bear the pain well. I do not know the effect prolonged connection will have on your body.'

'I'll accept the pain, now I know what it is. I know I shan't succeed in my struggle with the Mass if I can't feel the Realm. Don't ask me how I know – I just do.'

The smooth black bark of a tree close by shimmered, then turned and parted from the tree and in a series of fluid movements became a woman, skin as black and as solid looking as polished coal. Her wings had the appearance of slate-grey strips of bark intertwined with black feathers. Like Senoi she was slender and to Chris's mind, perfectly formed. Her round face was framed in back, soft hair that looked like teased wool. She came to Chris's side; she was slightly shorter than him.

She brushed his arm with hers and her skin was soft and warm. Without the connection to the Realm Chris felt the early tingle of arousal, his body craving the lesser form of connection, poor substitute though it may be.

'Give him back the connection, Senoi, and I will lend him my strength against the pain.'

'Do you think it wise, Jazar? Shouldn't we wait and consult with Raphael?'

'Do it now, Senoi. Can't you see, he is drying out, like a fish inches from the river. It is cruel to cut him off once he has been the Realm.'

Senoi nodded, and then quickly took Chris's hand. Slowly the connection re-established itself. Chris was refreshed and lesser needs extinguished once again. When the pain came he felt Jazar become him, although her physical manifestation remained a little apart, and the sharp agony became a dull ache.

'Thank you. I can cope with that. It's not too bad, especially now I can feel again.'

'Take him straight to Raphael,' Senoi said and then turning to Chris. 'I must go join Tarniel, Jamie, Lillian and Agronal. We will meet again soon. Meanwhile, allow Jazar to lead you to Raphael. It is he who co-ordinates the struggle against the Unselost Mass.' Senoi smiled and Chris was infused by Senoi's warmth as he leapt high and took to the wing.

Flight looked so much more impressive at this scale, and Chris no longer thought of Senoi as a faerie. Instead, he saw an angel. Smiling, he thought of Abe Knapper who was right all along.

'Come Chris,' Jazar said. 'We must walk quickly, for though you are one with us and with the Realm, she did not give you wings.'

'And even if she had done, I think I'd still prefer to walk.' There was something very sensual, in the old fashioned, Second Realm sense of the word, walking barefoot in wet moss. With his body of flesh and blood and his connection with the Realm and all who dwelt within it, Chris wondered if he had the best of both worlds. When Jazar poured herself into Chris and he allowed his being to mingle with hers, he knew he was right. They walked together maintaining their relative distance and keeping within their own physical forms, while at the same time merging beyond any joining of bodies and filled with pleasure greater than any stimulation of sexual parts. No human had experienced such intensity, but for all the newness and feeling of utter completeness, Chris De'Ath kept both feet on the ground.

It was a question of perception, or perhaps it was reality, but as Chris walked through the forest it seemed as if the forest crowded in to meet him. Trees appeared to move in close as he passed, or turn their great canopies to face him. It was a thing more of feeling than sight, and with Jazar at his side he was not frightened. Occasionally a tree trunk would slough away to become another being and Chris would find himself being greeted by an olive green boy, whip-thin, with dry mossy hair and hawk's wings, a girl white as marble with dappled butterfly wings of red and black or a gnarled sprite who had chosen a more whimsical appearance with twig-like fingers and skin like wind-polished wood. The meetings swiftly grew beyond count and the forms and colours he encountered were diversity incarnate, but for all the variety, each individual was clearly either male or female and except for the whimsical forms, nearly all were young in appearance.

Some part of his mind wondered about this until Jazar implanted an answer: male and female were complimentary and adversary, different poles that completed the magnetic field, the universal constants that were the heart of existence. He understood Jazar's explanation, but in his state of oneness he understood everything. All newcomers touched him with their essence, absorbed his and increased his sense of belonging and with each new meeting Chris's being expanded.

Chris and Jazar walked for hours and met many thousands of faeries, or perhaps they had journeys mere moments: time had no meaning in the Realm, but be it moments or hours, miles or a hair's breadth, they came to an opening where the trees held back from a rock pool at the foot of a waterfall, where a wide sward opened to bright sunlight. Chris found himself alone at the centre of the glade as Jazar melted into the shadows of the trees, and in all the many shadows Chris discerned a multitude of the fair folk who had greeted him and followed him to this place.

Walking to the edge of the rock pool, Chris looked up at the cascading column of water. The weight of the thunderous waters on his ears and the cool spray on his skin compelled him to sit and hypnotised him into staring deeper. With spongy moss for a cushion he dangled his legs over the rim of the pool and looked deep into the white foam of the waterfall until the column split into two. Just as tree-bark had assumed the bodily form of the many faeries he had recently met, so the smaller column condensed into human form and parted from the waters. With the upper body of a man and legs of cohesive water the being walked across the surface of the rock pool. His legs and feet formed proper only when he touched the rock below Chris.

Unlike the majority of Realm-dwellers he had met so far, who were youthful or even childlike in appearance, the waterfall man had chosen the look of a man in his prime. He appeared to be in his mid-thirties with long, black hair flowing wet and reaching down past his well muscled shoulders.

'Raphael?' Chris felt himself to be in the presence of unimaginable power, as if this man were the Realm itself.

Raphael inclined his head in the affirmative. 'I am Raphael. I am the Realm. And I am you.'

For the first time since setting foot inside the Realm, Chris groped for understanding.

'You have travelled many roads, suffered many pains and indignities. But here you are, and here all things begin. And here they all end.'

'I don't really understand what that means. What do I have to do? Can't you just tell me, without any riddles?'

Before Raphael answered he saw what Chris was carrying and was taken aback for a moment. He smiled as if to a long, long lost friend and held out his hand.

'May I?'

Chris handed over the old sword and Raphael let his fingertips trail close to the blade without actually touching. The blade shone with such intense light that Chris had to screw his eyes tight. The light only faded when Raphael re-sheathed it.

'Where did you get the scabbard from?' Chris asked. 'I could have done with that a while ago.'

'It came to me some time ago.'

Chris couldn't imagine what time was in this place, but he did conjure up an image of the scabbard making its own way to the Realm on spindly little legs. He pushed the image to one side.

'Do I have to use that sword on the Mass?'

Raphael shook his head. 'Relics and old talismans have no part in the battle you are about to fight. I feel this blade has now served it purpose – many times over – and it has come back home. For that, I thank you.' Raphael bowed his head gravely, without loosing the mirth in his eyes.

Chris shrugged. 'That's okay. My pleasure. And now ...?'

'Come, human lad. Take my hand and come with me through these wild waters, and leave behind what you can't understand. Soon the battle will begin.'

Chris braced himself against Raphael's strong grip as the weight of the water tried to force him down into the rock pool. The icy waters purged him of fears and preconceptions, so that when he came into the dark cavern behind the curtain of water he was calm and expectant, his mind empty and open to whatever might follow.

'Where are we?' Chris asked looking round the black emptiness that was relieved only by several horizontal and crossing shafts of light which served to illuminate nothing at all, but merely passed across the vast cavern.

'We are nowhere. This location is an allegory which has no true existence.'

'Well, that certainly helps. Do we exist?'

'Yes, we exist. This place has been formed so that your senses may adhere to points of reference which are non-existent. Let me take you to the dais.'

'What, that one over there, which isn't there at all?'

Another shaft of light slowly formed, this time vertical and throwing a small pool of light onto a raised, rocky platform two metres above the stone floor.

'Do I climb on top?'

'There is no need to climb.' Raphael let go of Chris's hand.

Chris's perspective changed and he found himself standing high on the dais. He sat knees up and arms wrapped round.

'Good,' came Raphael's disembodied voice from somewhere in the impenetrable dark.

Chris looked round warily at the only points upon which he could fix his gaze: the roving, horizontal beams of light.

'Each beam of light represents one of the teams that are in place throughout the history of your Realm,' Raphael said from somewhere and all-where.

Just then, one of the beams touched Chris, wavered and then held steady, throwing a little circle of light on his chest, about the size of a tennis ball.

''See! One of the teams have fixed upon you. Now, all you have to do is hold your position until all the many beams are focussed and ...'

'And?'

'And concentrate on fighting the Mass.'

'Which is ... where, exactly?'

Silence stretched for the minutes it took for two more beams to lock onto him.

'Where is the Mass, Raphael?'

'I think you know,' Raphael said.

And with Raphael's answer came a pain in Chris's chest so great he cried out. At the same instant three more beams found him, and the pain diminished slightly.

Chris gulped his words through waves of deep pain. 'The ... the Mass ... is inside me?'

'It is inside us all, and in the Realm. But here all is one, so overcome the Mass within you, and you will overthrow it in all places and within all beings.'

'What if I can't beat it?'

'In that the Mass feeds on the Realm it feeds upon us all. If you fail all will be consumed. You have to open yourself to the light, and endure the pain. If you can do these things, we will prevail.'

Chris tried to centre himself into a kind of meditative state, aware that with each new beam that found him and bathed him in its light, the pain grew less. He began to relax into the meditation when the cavern echoed to an unearthly scream and the noise of explosions so immense Chris's body and the rock he sat on and the foundations of the Realm itself shook. Chris was nearly shaken off the dais and he felt, rather than heard Raphael's words.

'Something is wrong. Something ... or someone, is tapping into the Mass.'

CHAPTER THIRTY-THREE

Many Threads Make the Tapestry

'Ticky-snack pie! Ticky-snack pie! Let's all have another Ticky-snack pie!' Corporal Wally Gable kept up his tuneless little song, like a kind of mantra as he huddled deep into the landing craft hoping that the shells would keep screaming overhead. Better that than land splat in the middle of the platoon.

'Ticky-snack pie! Ticky-snack pie! Let's all have another Ticky-snack pie!'

'Do us a favour and shut up, Corp!' called another soldier. 'I'm close to chucking as it is without having to think about fucking pies.'

There was a little rumble of assent from some of the others – someone even laughed – and then the landing craft came down hard, flat bottom against choppy water, sending a noise like thunder through the little iron craft.

Private Paul Fennimore didn't mind listening to the Corporal's ditty; it kept his mind off other horrors. Could it have been only two days ago when Paul and all his friends were keen to set off and get the job done? An explosion split the air above. Two or three lads screamed as shrapnel hit and Paul hunkered down to the bilge-plates. One of the boys kept screaming, and Paul wanted him to be quiet. He screwed his eyes shut and felt his chin and bottom lip begin to quiver uncontrollably and the boy kept screaming. Better he die than make all that din. Better he fade away quietly than call down the wrath of cordite onto everyone else.

'Ticky-snack ...' Wally began, loud and tremulous, but the mantra faded. Only Paul, who was so close to the Corporal heard the rest of the whispered refrain. A rapid succession of loud metallic impacts indicated that a German machine-gunner had found their range. They were raked again, the thick metal plates of the craft protecting them, but everything adding to the impression that the tiny craft was the very centre of the battle.

Somebody puked and the smell of blood and vomit and something else – had someone messed himself – assailed Paul as the helmsman called out that there wasn't long to go now. He started to yell something else, but he was cut off as a heavy machine gun round took the back of his head off. The platoon was flecked with bone and brains and the landing craft slewed to the right.

Paul started to cry silently and he shook uncontrollably. Someone put an arm round his shoulders and squeezed.

Wally Gable roared out an obscenity then rolled the sailor's body away and took the helm singing Ticky-snack pie at the top of his lungs. Others joined in and Paul clenched his teeth hard and forced himself to get a grip. He thought of Mum and Dad and little Rosemary and he decided that somehow they could all see him, as if they had a ringside seat way up in the clouds, and he was going to make them proud.

Then the air began to thrum as a low noise quickly grew to a crescendo. Wally broke off from Ticky-snack pie and just had time to say 'Oh bugger!' before the world went black.

Rosemary's scream touched all the Realms. 'I've lost him!' She shouted. 'I had him for an instant, and now I've lost him!' She looked round at the others, recognising Lillian but barely aware of the others or the injured sa'tyr at her feet. Her eyes burned with hatred. Spittle flecked her lips and quickly froze in the icy weather.

'I had him at my finger tips, and someone snatched him away.'

'Who are you?' Jamie McDowell asked inching in front of Lillian.

'The enemy,' Senoi said. He flew at her, but she was more than a match for a single faerie, although she looked no more than a little girl. He bounced off and fell into the light dusting of snow in the shadow of Orford Castle. It was four o'clock, but at the end of December, and it was very dark.

'You,' Rosemary sneered as she pulled Agronal up by his left horn.

'Leave him alone!' Jamie shouted pulling out of Lillian's restraining grasp.

'Don't be a nutter, Jamie! She'll flatten you!'

But it was too late. Rosemary raised her summoning hand, pointed it in the direction of Jamie and called forth Black Angus.

At the highest point of Brough Law, the ancient hill fort, Tadouwig directed the lights towards the beacon that was Christian De'Ath. Retsutsiel, Tarn's brother, drew the light through Marc and Shaun setting it with the resonance that only a very few could provide. With the light drawn by the Ieladhrim, given pitch and resonance by the humans and directed towards Chris by the sa'tyr, there was every chance that the rift could be healed.

It was late evening after a hot summer's day and those few visitors who tarried were descending to the valley floor. Any one spying the group from afar would discern only a party of four standing close, with Semangeloph too small for any to see, as he sat on a rock that was once a lintel beam. Half his job was done, getting the party to the right place and the right time. It only remained for him to get them home again.

'It is done,' Tadouwig said just as the ether parted and Edmund Warwick leapt from the Path and ran towards the group.

Retsutsiel rushed to intercept the Wiergan but he was enveloped in a dark cloud and at once began to scream. The cloud whirled round him like a tornado throwing a spray of blood, pieces of clothing and flesh in all directions. Marc and Tadouwig were flecked with gore as they ran towards the rending wind and still the screams came. Semangeloph darted time and time again through the cloud trying to disperse it.

Sean Ashton, looking for another option, picked up a fist sized rock and threw it hard towards Edmund Warwick. It hit the side of his head and broke his skull. Edmund fell unconscious, but the dark cloud gave up none of its fury.

Suddenly the cloud swerved, dropping the bloody remains of Retsutsiel, stripped of all skin and much flesh – in many places down to the bone – to engulf Tadouwig. Again came the screams. Marc and Shaun both threw rocks at the cloud. They passed through doing nothing to diminish the attack on the sa'tyr, but then from the core of the cloud, there was an explosion of white light. When their eyes recovered from the glare, the cloud was no more.

The two young men rushed to the injured and very bloody sa'tyr. He looked at them. He smiled with satisfaction that his drawing of the light had finished off the cloud once and for all, and then he died.

Edmund Warwick made a noise, a deep moan, as he came round. Marc and Shaun looked at each other, and then looked at the ancient stonework. As if of one mind, they crossed to the bronze aged wall stones, picked up the biggest one they could manage as a pair, walked it steadily to the injured man and held it above his head.

Edmund opened his eyes in time to see the rock falling towards him. By the time the heavy boulder thudded into the ground, Edmund Warwick was no longer there. Marc and Shaun were alone with the torn bodies of their friends. Warwick was gone and Semangeloph was nowhere to be seen.

'It seems longer than a week since we were last here, doesn't it love?' Beverly rested her head on Karl's shoulder. Wymes Forest enjoyed a warm spring day.

'Certainly, much has happened. But now we've done what we came to do, I hope we can get back to Brikadden soon.'

Sansenoi sat on Caedmon's shoulder and Tarn's brother Savaliel led the way.

'As far as I can tell, we have healed the rift,' Savaliel said. 'But we won't know for sure until we get back.'

Sansenoi leapt into the air and hovered. 'Someone's coming. Hide!'

Beverly jumped onto a tree stump. 'It's soldiers! Just Home Guard I think. You lot make scarce. I'll brazen it out!'

Karl and Savaliel hid amongst the thick bracken and Caedmon slip-shifted into the depths of the wood. Sansenoi flew into an overhanging branch and hid among the green leaves.

'Hello love!' the leading soldier said. He didn't look a day over fifteen. 'You're lucky day running into us. All Hell's let loose down by Bowen's Farm.'

'Ooh, whatever can you mean?' Beverly said.

'It's only a bunch of wolves – except you've to keep it secret. Don't want people to think Jerry is landing wild animals on us.'

'The idea *was*,' chipped in a very elderly corporal; 'that *you* was to keep it secret. Pardon him Miss. He just an idiot!' A big pack of dogs, just as like.'

The boy pretended to be contrite, but when the old corporal looked down the path, he winked at Beverly and mouthed *Wolves!*

'Well, dogs or wolves, thank you ever so. I'll chip off straight home.

'See you do that Miss,' the corporal said.

'What big eyes you've got,' the lad said, earning himself a clipped ear from the corporal.

As soon as the soldiers had passed out of sight, the little group reformed and made a dash for the old tower. When they got there, someone was waiting for them, sitting on the fallen merlon and holding a wriggling bundle in his arms.

'Tarn! Where ever did you get that baby?' Beverly said.

'Long story, but shortening it: a young girl gave birth to him and left him in the woods for the Fey Knights to take. An old, old tradition for girls in trouble. So I have come to oblige.'

'Who was the father?' Karl asked.

'Well, the girl thinks it was Chris – or rather Mad Christy. She also thinks she killed him – having cut his head off.'

'He looks well on it, I don't mind saying,' Beverly said sarcastically. 'I wonder if anyone's told Chris not to nod his head.'

'Let's just say the father looked like him ... a lot like him.'

'Wolves! Abandoned babies! Whatever next?'

Tarn and Sansenoi exchanged secret glances and half-smiles.

'Anyway, I think we should get back so everything can be sorted out,' Beverly said.

'Good idea,' Tarn said. 'But do like the girl wanted, will you, and take this baby to Brikadden. There is a little more for me to do before I move on.'

Beverly took the little boy into her arms. He looked no older than four of five weeks and Beverly's heart melted. 'Oh, the perfect little dear!' she said.

Tarn walked away and turned, just in time to see thick oily tendrils shooting out of the merlon to wrap round Beverly, Karl and the baby. Sansenoi and Tarn's brother were nowhere to be seen.

Rosemary pointed her summoning hand at Jamie and called forth the dragon, but Agronal used the last of his strength to draw the light and fashion it so that the dragon, pulled from the ether, was redirected to the rift and swallowed up by the Mass.

The Unselost Mass reacted by expanding explosively and sending out tendrils from all rifts, drawing people in, thrashing them about and spewing them out again, not concern for either locality or temporality. Not even Rosemary herself escaped from the random, whiplash tentacles of the Mass. Each rift grew in upon itself until each was sealed, each healed and the tendrils cut off forever, but not before displacing people to places of no return.

CHAPTER THIRTY-FOUR

Lights Over Rendlesham Forest

Chris bent all his will into staying put on the stone dais as a maelstrom raged about him. In the blackness of the cavern only he shone bright. He appeared to be a human shaped beacon rather than a man of flesh and blood, and all the beams were like radiating spokes, stretching into the darkness, his body as the hub. He was completely unaware of Raphael crouching next to him and holding his shoulders, on guard to protect him against the incursion of the Lady, for now Raphael knew that she was the cause of the storm.

Chris felt no supporting hands gripping his shoulders. He became oblivious to the tearing winds that howled round him and echoed throughout the cavern, knowing only the white-hot pain in the centre of his chest, and the feeling that his insides were being plucked at and sucked out.

Other faeries appeared in the cavern – scores of them. Some came out of the air, smoke-like before assuming solid form, while others poured from the sides of the cavern like molten rock into invisible moulds. All rushed to help Raphael in his struggle to support Chris.

Chris kept his eyes tight shut. His features were screwed up with concentration and pain that would start to subside, and then rip into him with renewed cruelty and razor-edged intent, while the beams from many places and many times poured their accumulated light into him, only to be sucked out by the greedy needs of the Unselost Mass and tapped into by the Lady.

Being careful to leave holes for the beams to pass through, the faeries formed a living cocoon round Chris and shielded him from much of the Mass's fury, but although it was not truly a thinking being, the Mass was possessed of instinct and the desire to be free. Suddenly it withdrew into the centre: the centre of the Realm, the centre of Chris, the centre of all the gather faeries and all those who were not gathered. And then it released itself explosively, shattering the cocoon and sending the faeries flying in all directions as if from a mighty explosion within.

Thick black tendrils shot out from the spherical mass that hovered above the dais where Chris had been. They filled the cavern and shot along the beams of light, thrashing their extremities into other places and other times until the sphere and the tendrils faded away. The raging winds ceased at once and Raphael stood, moving both hands to his chest. Hardly able to believe it he began to smile. All the other faeries were the same.

'No pain,' Raphael whispered. 'Christian De'Ath has prevailed. The rifts are sealed.'

Jazar joined him, forming from a mist. 'But at what cost?' she said, pointing to the dais.

Raphael looked, but there was no sign of Chris.

The pain stopped and Chris took a deep breath – but the air was icy. From the Realm, where he had been unaware of temperature, either hot or cold, Chris was plunged into freezing air that shocked his naked body.

Opening his eyes he found himself laying on frost covered grass in the dark. Jumping to his feet he instinctively wrapped his arms round his body, knowing that he had little time to find clothing or warm shelter. In the ambient light he noticed a high tower and wondered for a moment if he had somehow come back to Atolak. The tower was a different shape though, but maybe he could get inside out of the biting cold.

He ran to the walls but the only entrance he could see was high up. Skirting round he was suddenly blinded by bright light.

'What the ...?'

Chris hoped he recognised the voice.

'Come here Tosser! You need to get something on before you freeze.'

'I've got spare stuff in my rucksack,' Jamie said. 'But hurry, in case she comes back.'

'Looks like you had an interesting time in faerie-land. Didn't they like your clothes?'

'Something ... like that,' Chris said, beginning the shiver. 'Hurry up with the stuff.'

Chris found himself being bundled into a variety of spare clothes, Lillian's and Jamie's, and had never been so glad of clothing before and never so unconcerned as to how he looked. While they helped him dress, they told him about the little girl with the terrible powers who had come from nowhere while they worked to seal the rift. She had attacked them, hurting Agronal and then she had drawn on powers they could not understand.

'She kept on about reaching out for someone,' Jamie said as he stuffed the ends of a woolly scarf down the front of Chris's newly acquired shirt.

'And then she was cackling like a mad witch and black stuff, more like liquid than smoke, was swirling all round her, Lillian said pulling a bobble hat over his head.

'It all ended when she got dead cross with me and reached out her hand all abracadabra-like,' Jamie said.

'I thought she was going to turn him into a toad – well, hoped really.'

'Shut up, you! Anyway, she got grabbed by these tentacles that just came from nowhere –'

'And dragged back into nowhere! Just vanished. Poof! Just like that.'

'Come on and lets find a pub or something. You need to thaw out and these clothes aren't great.'

Chris let himself be led down the grassy hill away from the castle tower and told Lillian and Jamie that he had a feeling his mission had been accomplished. He went on to speak briefly about his other experiences in the First Realm.

'Where's Agronal and Senoi?'

Jamie and Lillian exchanged worried glances. 'Well,' began Jamie. 'I'm sorry to be the one to have to tell you, but I think Agronal might be ... you know ... dead.'

Jamie trailed off and Lillian finished the story. The strange little girl had conjured something immense and frightening, but as it was forming, Agronal somehow caused it to implode and slapped it back from where it had come. That was when the tentacles burst from the air, and when Agronal died.

'At least I think he died. His eyes just didn't look alive anymore. Senoi took him to the ... where did he say Jamie?'

'The Hidden Paths. Senoi said he'd try and get help too, but we haven't seen him since, and that was a few hours ago. When you popped out of nowhere, we though you were either help, or the girl back again.'

'Until I flashed my torch at you, and you flashed your danglies at me!' Lillian laughed. 'Then I knew you were no girl. Any chance of seeing you like that again in the not too distant?'

Chris didn't answer.

They found their way to a road sign telling them that Butley and Sudbourne were in one direction and Capel St. Andrew and Boyton in the other. Orford was just down the road though, so they ignored the sign and headed for the closest signs of civilisation. They soon came to a pub – the Jolly Sailor – and Jamie and Lillian were all set to dive in until Chris pulled them up.

'What're we waiting for Chris?' Lillian said. 'I can smell chips!'

'We'll eat and get warmed up,' Jamie said enthusiastically. 'And then we can sort out what to do next.'

'Has anybody worked out *when* we are?' Chris asked looking at all the very new looking old crocks parked nearby.

Jamie followed his gaze. 'Well, that brown one's an Austin Allegro. There's an old 1800 – the white one with a busted wing mirror. Wow! An SD1 – I like them. Some sort of American pick-up and … These are all cars I recognise. It all looks pretty much like my time.'

Just as it should be, Chris thought. He didn't like the idea of going in and having to converse with people from another temporality, but he was still very cold despite the donations. 'Okay. Let's go for it. But watch what you say.'

The interior was warm and comfortable, and all done up with Christmas decorations. And much to Chris's relief it wasn't particularly busy. There was a group of young men in one corner with short hair cuts, American accents and casuals that suggested to Chris that they were off-duty soldiers and there was another group playing darts.

Lillian ordered a round of soft drinks and scampi-in-a-basket three times. Chris was thinking that his mish-mash of borrowed clothing didn't look too stupid in the light, and all seemed to be going well until Lillian paid the barman with a twenty pound note.

'What's this then, sweetheart? Flaming Monopoly money?' He held out the note. Lillian, for once, was at a loss for words. Chris wasn't much better. But just as the situation looked unsalvageable and the scene started to attract attention, Jamie saved the day.

'Sorry about that,' he said sorting out the correct money from his wallet. 'My sister's just got back from Hong Kong.' He rolled his eyes conspiratorially, as if to say 'Girls!' The barman smiled and took the 1980's currency.

They found a seat near the fire and sat self-consciously, waiting for their food and listening to the Americans converse: they were trying to keep their voices low, as if trying to keep something secret, but at the same time failing because of their excitement about the subject matter.

In moments Chris, Lillian and Jamie had heard enough to guess that Senoi's efforts to get help had produced results. Very visible ones.

'They're trying to say it's something to do with the lighthouse, but that's *bullshit*, man!' a young, dark skinned man said. 'Lighthouses are made to shine out to sea, not inland. They have freaking great screens on the landward side to stop them shining inland and blinding all the folks.'

'Couldn't it bounce off a cloud or something,' an older man said.

'You saw it yourself, same as me. You really think that glowing mushroom was something bounced off a cloud? Nah! That was solid!'

Jamie kicked Chris under the table and hissed '*Shitake Maru!*'

'Shh! Keep listening,' Chris whispered back.

The soldiers carried on chatting. 'There's another lame-ass theory doing the rounds here abouts. Some of the locals think it has something to do with us up at the Air Base.'

'The others chuckled. 'Yeah right! If we could put something like that up in the air the Ruskies would have something to worry about!'

The last comment had been delivered at particularly high volume, causing the soldiers to look round self consciously and lower their voices. They became aware of Chris and the others and reduced to a series of whispers.

'I can't hear them anymore,' Jamie whispered. 'Shall we try and get closer?'

'No. I think we've heard enough to know what they're talking about. We'll just have to come out in the open and ask a few questions.'

'Let me try the barman,' Lillian said. 'He looks the kind who might respond to some friendly female company.' She winked.

'Go do your thing,' Jamie said.

The boys sipped their drinks slowly, watching Lillian work her magic and the barman fall under her spell. She returned to the table with a big grin, just as the scampi arrived.

They ate hungrily, making short work of the chips. Lillian spoke between mouthfuls, and sometimes with mouthfuls – her story was too urgent to hold back, and her hunger equally unwilling to take its turn.

The previous night there had been a mass sighting of a UFO. Villagers had seen it, a policeman saw it and half the staff at RAF Bentwaters had too by many accounts. There were even rumours that something had showed up on the radar. The strange, bright object, the description of which exactly matched that of the *Shitake Maru*, had hovered through Rendlesham Forest – a little to the north – and frightened a military patrol half to death.

Chris looked out the window. It was dark now and Chris sank deep into thought for a moment. The barman turned up the ambient music and *There's No One Quite Like Grandma* began to play. The soldiers made disapproving noises.

'We got get to this Rendle-whatsit Forest,' Chris said, suddenly animated. Rising, he made a rush for the door and Lillian and Jamie grabbed their things and followed him. The barman looked over just in time to see the door swing shut behind them.

'Charming!' he said. 'And goodbye to you too.'

'What do you expect!' called one of the soldiers. 'That noise is enough to drive anyone out!' The soldiers all laughed. After considering turning the music off, the barman went the other way and turned it up in defiance. The soldiers stopped their ears and made a comically over-the-top show of aural suffering.

It was over eight kilometres to the Forest. Lillian smiled her knowing smile and told the others she'd thumb a lift for them all in no time flat. It is true that a few minutes later, they were all bundling into a rickety old Landrover, but not thanks to Lillian's skills.

The driver was an elderly lady who was once a Captain in the Woman's Royal Army Corps. 'Never pass a khaki shirt!' she told Jamie. Which regiment?' she asked indicating Jamie's combat top.

'Oh! Not the Army. I'm a corporal in the Air Cadets.'

The elderly lady chuckled. 'I'm putting you down for a party of UFO hunters. Am I right?'

She didn't wait for a reply, but assumed she was correct. 'Damn quick of the mark, I must say. I thought it would be two or three days at least. Our little incident hasn't even made the nationals yet.'

Jamie explained that he had a friend whose father worked at the local base, and the word was out for those with contacts.

The lady seemed happy with the story, and went on to explain her theory: weather balloons catching the moonlight. She dropped them off by a Forestry road that plunged deep into the dark of the wood. She told them they were mad and were quite likely to get lost and freeze to death. With that, she bid them all a good night and tore off towards the next village.

'She's probably right,' Chris said. 'I haven't got a proper coat and I can hardly see my hand in front of my face. 'We could get lost within fifty metres of the road.'

'Jamie's got a torch,' Lillian said.

'Well, yes I have. But it's best to let our eyes get used to the dark. If we use a torch we'll stay night blind and … and we'll show up like a beacon to anyone else who might be about.'

Jamie made sense, and they were surprised at how quickly their eyes adapted. They couldn't see far, but it was easy enough to pick out the road and the surrounding wood. They were also able to see several other groups at a distance who used flashlights without restriction.

'If we were sniper's we could pick them off from a mile away,' Jamie said. 'No field craft skills at all, that lot!'

Lillian sniggered and nudged Chris. 'He's very fond of his night exercises.'

Chris could almost feel Jamie blushing.

'Our Jamie never gets fed up shooting and he just loves me to rub his barrel.'

'Lillian! Shut up!' Jamie said in a strained whisper.

Lillian chuckled some more. 'Nothing like a bit of spit and polish, hey Jamie?'

'Okay Lillian, you've killed it.' Chris said. 'Good joke, but not funny any more.'

Lillian opened he mouth to fire off another round, but Chris's admonishment had left complete out of ammo. She clicked her tongue and looked huffy.

They walked slowly, ever deeper into the forest. It smelt of pine and damp and the fallen needles underfoot made the going springy. They all jumped when a large bird took to the air noisily from close by, and again when a large animal – probably a deer – dashed across the path just ahead.

They had been walking for almost three-quarters of an hour when Lillian asked if there was a plan, and what made Chris think the *Shitake Maru* would return a second night.

'Because he trusts us,' came a voice from high up, accompanied by the thrum of rapid wings.

'Senoi! Is that you?' Chris said peering up towards the sound.

'Who else? And be careful. I'm small again.'

Senoi told them there was no time for explanations, but they must follow him off the path to a natural clearing in the wood where the *Shitake Maru* would come for them.

'It can only manifest itself in this Realm for a short time. Every moment it spends here is injurious to all the realms, and I'm afraid to say that the Lady of Atolak's meddling is not at an end.'

They rushed unseeing through the dense coniferous plantation trusting entirely to Senoi's guidance. They all tripped and fell numerous times, but they were imbued with a sense of utmost urgency and nobody stopped to count the bumps and bruises.

They felt the *Shitake Maru* before they saw it. Their skin tingled and their hair felt as if it were standing on end. And then came the bright light, suddenly and blindingly. Unfortunately they were not the only party to see it, and a chorus of gasps, expletives and cries of disbelief alerted them to the presence of a patrol from the base.

The *Shitake Maru* appeared to be reacting with the surrounding air. There were sparks and flashes, like an electric train running along on a rainy night, and the brightness of the mushroom shaped vessel was inconsistent, fading in and out.

'How do we get aboard?' Chris called, raising his voice against the crackling sounds of electrical disturbance.

'Just stand still, and keep this side. There is another group of people at the opposite edge of the clearing.'

The *Shitake Maru* hissed and spat and crackled its way towards them and Senoi told them all to crouch down.

And then Chris felt the night closed in around him; the light was instantly extinguished and the darkness became solid. He peered through the gloom and realised he was in a familiar place.

'We're in the entrance-cave,' Chris said, relaxing and feeling very relieved. In the next moment he followed Senoi along the low, wet-walled tunnel and out into Brikadden.

'Not a moment too soon,' he said. 'The vessel had exceeded its safety parameters. A moment longer it would have failed and you would all be stranded, out of time.'

Chris stood tall and stretched in the misty sunshine. 'Surely you could have found us and taken us along the Hidden Paths?'

Lillian looked round, frowned and then ducked back into the cave.

'I'm afraid not,' Senoi said. 'There have been changes, and the Paths are no longer navigable without a vessel such as this. But luckily we have managed to bring everyone aboard, though you were spread across the ages.'

Chris had no time to ask about the welfare of the other teams before Lillian charged out of the cave.

'Jamie's not here! And he's not in the cave either!'

Senoi darted into the cave, and emerged moments later. He landed on the bank of the little brook and his wings drooped.

'Where is he, Senoi?' Chris asked.

Senoi's worried look was answer enough. Somehow Jamie must have missed the pick-up. There was only one place he could be and that was back at Rendlesham Forest, stranded in the wrong place and the wrong time. As to where he was now ...

'We have to go back for him!'

'It's too late. The vessel will be destroyed and we will all be thrown out of time and place. Poor Jamie will just have to make the best of things.'

'He'll be all alone,' Lillian said. 'He can't come home. He's stuck five years before his time. Even if he went back to Little Rillton he'll bump in to a baby version of himself, and his parents will flip.'

'Well, whatever he does or doesn't do, in *our* time he'd be in his forties if he managed to survive,' Chris said, and no sooner were the words past his lips when an image of Jamie as an old man flashed through his mind, and he knew at once who Jamie was in his own time. He was caught between smiling and crying, but kept the new found certainty to himself.

'You need to rest, Chris,' Senoi said. 'The others are tired enough, but you must be exhausted.'

'Now that you come to mention it ...'

'Go to your cottage. I brought your own things back from the First Realm. Put them on and sleep fully dressed. There may be no time to prepare if Brikadden fails.'

Chris took in the frantic activity all round. Kern were rushing about and the air was full of flitting faeries. One hovered close to his nose for a moment and smiled. It was Jazar, now tiny and dressed in dark dry moss.

'Why would Brikadden fail?'

'We are attacked, by forces who manipulate the Mass.'

'I thought –'

'Yes Chris. You and the teams were successful, although some suffered sad losses, and all the rifts were sealed. The Realms are safe. But Brikadden itself has become the nexus for the Lady's attention.'

'And you want me to sleep?' Chris pulled a wry smile.

'You can do nothing else. If not sleep, then try to relax. If Brikadden fails we will all be plunged into the unfamiliar, and we will need all our strength.'

CHAPTER THIRTY-FIVE

Infiltration

Their strength fails,' Rosemary said as she directed more and more of the Mass into the First Realm walls of the *Shitake Maru*.

'And then what?' Edmund Warwick said. He wished strongly that his lady had not bothered to snatch him from the Hidden Paths to be by her side again. He'd hoped to be free of her.

'And then we take punitive action. We make them all pay for interfering. I had Paul, grasped by my very fingertips, and then they closed the rift and I have lost him again, this time without hope of ever touching him again.'

Edmund allowed the darkness to channel through him and stream into the walls of the strange vessel which hovered before him in the nullness of the Hidden Paths, while at the same time feeling that he was serving a mad wizened, evil woman who had the body of a girl. He had no love for any who might be within these incandescent walls, be he saw no profit in killing them either.

'Perhaps it was not meant to be, my Lady. Paul died long ago. Many millions have died in wars throughout history. He was just one.'

Rosemary's eyes flashed power and anger. 'But he was *my* one. He was my brother and I care nothing for the millions. I care for only the one, and they have stolen him from me again.'

Lady Rosemary screamed with rage and pain as she opened herself fully to the flow of the darkness. She cried for Edmund to redouble his efforts, and he did so.

'There!' Rosemary shrieked. 'The walls break down! We have them!'

'And may the Lord have mercy upon them,' Edmund whispered.

It always felt good to be back in his own clothes. Chris flopped back onto the bed. He rubbed collar of his jacket between finger and thumb and remembered in great detail how Abe Knapper had taken it from the basket drawer in his bedroom wardrobe and held it up for size. Drawing his feet up he stretched out along the bed, imagining what his mother would say if she caught him laying on his bed with his boots on back home. Running a hand down to his combat trousers he felt through the material of his pocket to check that the film pot containing Tarn's tooth was still there. It was, and there was something very reassuring about that. The tooth was solid. The tooth was real. If he ever lost it, perhaps everything that had happened to him would seem like a dream. If he ever got back home – real home – he thought he would take it to a jeweller and have it mounted on a chain.

Although very tired, Chris could not doze. He grabbed a pillow and hugged it close to the front of his body, and instead of trying to sleep he concentrated on remembering the details of his adventures since that fateful day in Wymes Forest. When he came to recall Gayle and Danny, he didn't think about the loss, or of their deaths. Instead he recalled happy times together and he was warmed by the thought that somewhere along the Hidden Paths they were still happy, and he was with them.

Chris had achieved a state of complete relaxation when the earthquake came. He tried to stand but the stone floor oscillated with such force that he fell to his knees. He heard screams and falling masonry and a cacophony of destruction, and then silence, and utter stillness.

He flung open the door and immediately saw the cause. A huge black cloud swirled manically down by the trail to the cave entrance, and it seemed to be sucking faeries from the air and enveloping those on the ground. The cloud appeared sentient, and then it detected his presence. For a moment, time stood still, and then Chris found himself at the centre of a maelstrom. Daylight was blotted out and he felt like hundreds of tiny needles were being driven into his skin and eyes. He flailed at the malevolent air with both arms to no avail as he felt his feet leave the ground.

Daylight returned as he was dumped onto the ground, landing painfully on his back. He sat up, winded, and took in his new surroundings. There were others round him: Lillian, Beverly and Karl; a few metres away, Mark and Shaun struggled to their feet, and Tarn was there too with several Kern and numerous faeries, grounded and dishevelled with broken wings.

'You again,' Rosemary said. She was suspended in the air as if by invisible ropes with her feet a metre from the earth and dark, liquid black power swirling about her. To her right was her servant, whom Chris had previously heard being addressed as Edmund. He stood with arms outstretched and eyes half-shut, his lips moving with unheard words and it was he who appeared to be drawing forth the darkness.

Some unseen force drew Chris roughly to his feet, and the eyes of the abominable little girl drilled into him.

'See, I'm not scared of you any more,' she said, her words forming in Chris's heard with dull, echoing pressure. 'I know that somehow you and I will meet again – my past, your future – and I will cut off your head. Whatever you do, you can't escape what has already come to pass. Soon I will enjoy your body for a little while, and then I will take your head to keep forever.'

The same unseen force that had held him up now slapped Chris back into the ground.

'And you ...!' Rosemary screamed as she spied Karl and Beverley. 'You escaped me in my past, but I shan't let you escape again.' While she spoke Rosemary was manipulating the power of the Mass and directing it towards her unknown purpose.

'German boy, your pain will be long and intense. I will keep you alive so that the torment will last years. I will never tire of hearing your screams.'

'You leave him alone you evil witch!' Beverly called, and then wished she had kept silent when Rosemary turned her chilling gaze upon her.

'Oh how sweet. The German and the traitor produced a child together. Now watch as your child dies!'

Rosemary lifted her arms but Tarn leapt between her and Beverley, who turned her back and bent over holding the baby close.

'The baby is yours Rosemary. Remember? You abandoned it in the woods for the Fey Knights. Well, we claimed the babe, just as you wished.

'My child?' Rosemary said dropping her arms. 'Mine and Mad Christy's?' Her uncertainty lasted only a moment, before she raised one hand and blasted

Tarn with invisible force. He struck a cottage wall and slid to a crumpled heap. Several faeries flew towards her, but with another wave of her hand they became tiny fireballs which burnt out quickly and scattered as fiery ash.

Edmund faltered for a moment and looked at Rosemary with undisguised contempt, but he resumed his task before she noticed.

Tarn dragged himself to his feet and Rosemary again raised her arm towards him. This time it was Chris who intervened.

'Leave him alone! Leave us all alone. We haven't done anything to you,' Chris said, realising that he sounded like a schoolboy complaining that everything was so unfair.

Rosemary's little girl face twisted into a mask of demented fury as she raised both arms. Chris realised he was in for some pain. Possibly this was the end, but for once he did not freeze in the face of death.

'You can't hurt me, Rosemary. Not until you cut my head off, and we both know that isn't now.'

Rosemary hesitated.

'If you even try to hurt me now, something will stop you. Like you said, you can't change what has already come to pass. If you try, you may even die.'

'We'll just have to see, won't we?' she spat, and then a distant voice felled her as surely as a bolt of lightning.

'Rosy! Rosy, is that you?'

Chris looked round to see Sun walking uncertainly down the path towards them.

Rosemary looked. Her hand flew to her mouth and her eyes filled up with water. A strange call, half disbelief and half lament passed though her lips and she sank to the ground, no longer directing the power that continued to flow from the Mass.

'Rosy. Why are you being so mean to everyone? These people have helped me.'

'Paul?' Rosemary said, the name long drawn out and her voice quivering. 'Paul, is it really ...'

'Yes Rosy. It's me, Paul. It's all come back. I'm *Paul*, not Sun.' He ran towards his little sister trying not to think of all the impossibilities they lay between their last meeting and this.

Chris tried to make the connections too. How had Paul been dragged from wartime Normandy to the Third Realm city far to the north? He supposed that the Hidden Paths would never give up all their mysteries. Looking over towards Rosemary, she was a little girl again, and not just in appearance.

Rosemary ran towards her brother with a smile as wide and as joyful and as beautiful as any Chris had ever seen. And then, he heard the last words he was ever to hear in Brikadden.

An instant before Paul and Rosemary ran into each others arms, Tarn called out. 'Rosemary has released her hold on the power. Nobody's directing! It will ...'

And then the daylight winked out once again, and there was no sound, nor smell, nor feeling until the pain of sudden impact.

CHAPTER THIRTY-SIX

The Molly Blackbridge

Chris kept his eyes tight shut. Sliding a hand across the back of his head he felt the slick, warm flow of blood. He had come down with such a crack. He moved slowly, trying to assess the damage. Apart from his head – and that felt like no more than a cut scalp – he thought he had probably had a lucky escape, and surely, that was the sun he could feel on his face. He pressed his hand hard on the cut and kept it there to stem the flow.

He sat up, opened his eyes and immediately recognised where he was. He was back in Brikadden. Not the Brikadden of nice cosy cottages, warm beds and tasty, hot food, but the old, ruined, fallen down Brikadden he had first come to with Agronal and Senoi.

Getting to his feet slowly, and stretching out the pains like a little old man, Chris scanned the surroundings for any of his friends. Seeing nobody, he called out. Not even an echo for a reply, Chris reasoned he was, once again, all alone.

Last time he'd been here he hadn't yet seen the living, vital magical Brikadden, so this time he was able to appreciate the ruins for what they were. Where had once been an unfathomable heap of rock, he now knew that over there, the meeting hall had been, and way over to the left – yes – those stones were all that was left of his own little cottage.

The little brook was choked up with debris and weed but still managed to flow somehow. He traced it back to the small gully and the little cave and ducked inside, not at all surprised to find that it was only a cave, dank and lined with slime mould and moss. Outside in the warm sunshine once more, he cast a glance up towards Brikadden Beacon. There was no sign of it, and running up the rock strewn slope he came to the place he thought it might once have been. There was nothing but an area of scrubby grass enclosed by a falling down square of fencing.

Somehow, the valley looked different. The ruins were pretty much as he remembered, but the distant mountain ridges and the shape of the valley – they did not look quite how he remembered.

Well, there was nothing to be done here, he thought. It would serve no purpose to hang around with the vague hope that Brikadden might suddenly quicken all around him. Chris decided to walk back down the valley and find his old friends, the Kumakkashi. Or perhaps he would just keep heading south and meet some of those southern people he had heard about. Of course, his real hope was that Agronal or Senoi or Tarn would find him first and whisk him back home. He did not like to dwell on the news that the Hidden Paths were no longer navigable and hoped the *Shitake Maru* was out there somewhere, looking for him.

It was pleasant to be walking down the valley with the sound of a cascading river on his left and the path before him. He warded his thoughts away from anything negative and tried to concentrate on the time and the place. He was warm; apart from a few bruises and his aching head, he was comfortable and he felt sure he would soon be with his friends again.

He came to a wooden fence, grey with age, which ran across the path. He didn't remember it on the way up, and when he saw the stile he knew with certainty that everything was not as it had been. He wondered if the others had all landed in ruined Brikadden, separated only by time, but all thoughts flew home to roost when he crossed the stile and saw a metal notice screwed to the wood.

It was an announcement to travellers to be careful of the dangers of exploring a disused mine. It said there were falls and advised people to keep to the safe side of any fence. And all this it said under an announcement that it was all National Trust property.

At first Chris couldn't take it in. Was he home? Was he at least back in his own Realm? He had to be! This was National Trust property, and the sign was in strong black-painted letters on a white painted cast iron sign. He ran his fingers along the top edge of the sign, feeling its hard, reassuring coolness. He pressed the raised letters and he even bent in close to sniff the wood. All this to keep down his mounting excitement; he failed miserably – or rather – joyously, and he ran down the stony path until he had to pause for breath and proceeded again at a brisk trot.

With a wide grin he strained to see another human being or a sign of habitation and all the while he was working out how to get home. He had some money so he could hitchhike if he was too far for it to meet the fares. He would certainly phone home and tell Mum he was okay and to get ready with his favourite Sunday roast. He started to chuckle before a nasty thought crossed his mind. Okay, so he was back in his own Realm, but what year was it? It might be wartime Britain, and then, he might have to spend some time being known as Mad Christy. He knew he wasn't going to loose his head to that annoying little Rosemary – that was his succubus look-a-like – but he suddenly felt that some of his future lay in the past. Maybe *this* was the past and those ruins and this path were set in the nineteen forties.

He walked on, a little more subdued, a little more concerned. He came to a house, half whitewashed and half natural stone, another National Trust property, and then he came to a well tarred road. It was only when a car – of sorts – passed him that he realised he had been looking the wrong way along time's long path. He had never seen the like of the silent little vehicle. Not in life, not in books and not even in imagination. It there was one fact Chris was certain about, it was that he had come back to his own Realm, but in a future far in advance of his own.

His money was useless, except one chap offered him a sub as he collected 'old stuff'. Chris didn't know what a sub was, and his mobile phone was beyond accepting one. His journey from Cumbria to Shropshire was achieved mostly on foot, for every contact he had with people was fraught with misunderstanding and embarrassment. He tried calling home, but none of the numbers he tried would work. He found himself in a world he could hardly understand. People were people, vehicles were strange and less numerous than he was used to, and money was a nightmare.

Even Little Rillton was different. There was a new one-way system. The shops were different. The *Moiled Bull* was under new management and the canal was busier. But worst of all, Mum and Dad were no longer at his old house, and Abe had moved away from Flint House. The old vicar had died, he was told, and Abe moved away, visiting regularly and accompanied by his friend until Margaret too passed away.

This was the kind of torture that Jamie McDowell must have known: so close to home and familiarity, but so impossibly far away.

At the end of a very traumatic day, Chris came to the *Moiled Bull*. No Dolly Tregonhawke. No familiar friends, except ... wasn't that Gary behind the bar, all grown up and with a grey goatee beard.

'Jesus Christ!' Gary said when he looked at Chris. 'You're the dead spit of a kid who used to live round here ... what? ... twenty years back almost!'

Twenty years? Twenty bloody years! 'Chris De'Ath?' Chris asked.

'Well ... yeah. Chris De'Ath. You know him.'

'Kind of,' Chris said playing for time and a good story. 'He's my Uncle.'

'What can I get you? First drink's on the house.'

'Thanks Gary. But my phone won't sub, and all I've got is some old money.'

'Money? For crying out loud, who uses money these days? Let's have a look.'

Gary sorted through the notes stating that it had been years since he'd seen a ten pound note.

'Look kid, I don't know what's going on. But for one of these,' he said pulling out a twenty; 'I'll let you have dinner and a couple of pints. I'll not ask any questions. Lived in this village long enough to know some things are, you know ...'

'Yes, thanks. I really appreciate it.'

'Not another word. In fact, that's part of the deal. Not another word about where you're from or who you are. Don't want to annoy the –'

'Don't say it!

'...Fey Knights.' Gary laughed. 'Just an old saying.'

Chris nodded. 'Sure.'

Chris finished dinner and enjoyed dessert. He sat back, too sad to be shocked or stunned. Numbed was more the word. Gary was the first person he'd met who had once known and just look at him. He was an old man. Chris wondered what had become of his mum and dad and all his friends. Were all the others from Brikadden similarly dislocated?

He had no idea what to do or where to go next. Perhaps he could walk into the police station and tell Adie Chappell – or whoever was the village policeman these days, if they had one, he had lost his memory and didn't know who he was. He knew he couldn't survive for long in this strange but familiar new world of the future.

Despondently he took his empty glass to the bar, and then noticed a colourful landscape view of a canal narrow boat with a happy looking oriental boy at the helm.

'Cappy!'

'Bugger!' Gary said. 'This is getting scary-weird. He used to call himself Cappy years ago – about when the picture was taken. But that was, well, way before you were born.'

Chris winged it again and said that his Uncle had a copy of the same photo and that he had always called the Japanese boy Cappy.

'Yes, well ... maybe he has and maybe he hasn't.'

'Do you know where he is these days?'

'Living on the water. You want to visit him?'

Chris confirmed that he did, although he had no way of telling how Cappy would react to him after all the years which must have passed by.

'Give me a minute,' Gary said tapping on a hand-held. 'If he signed up to Waterways, it'll tell us where he's berthed. Ah! Yes, got him.'

Gary gave Chris a printout with the name of a marina on it and a date and time when Cappy's boat was due in.

'I've got something else for you kid.'

Gary handed him a mobile phone, telling him it was fully subbed with just enough to get him to the marina, and a couple of meals on the way. Maybe even bed and breakfast.'

'Does it work as a phone too?'

Gary looked at Chris as if he was being deliberately obtuse.

Not wishing to push his luck, Chris thanked him profusely, wished him goodnight and set off for a journey across the country.

'Uncle indeed!' Gary whispered to himself as he watched Chris leave. 'You're Chris De'Ath, somehow, and I don't even want to think about it.'

Abe Knapper was tired and very glad to be close to home. He brought his little black VW Foxbat to a smooth halt beside the security kiosk, took up his mobile and beamed his membership code towards the reader.

'Thank you,' the computer said in a bright and friendly tone, and then 'Verify your identity please.'

Abe reached out and thumbed the live-scan plate, which appeared to satisfy the computer. It told him who he was – just in case he'd forgotten – and that the *Molly Blackbridge* was at Mooring Point Six on Pontoon C, and activated the barrier to give him access. Then like an afterthought, the machine wished him a good day.

It was a very large marina but Abe spotted the *Molly Blackbridge* almost immediately. Twenty metres of semi-traditional narrow boat with the rising sun, brilliant red on blinding white, painted on the superstructure had a way of standing out among the lesser minnows that wore more conservative, less colourful lines. Abe's heart leapt, as it always did, to see that Shinji's had, once again, navigated their floating home to a safe harbour. It was so good to know that wherever his short contracts took him, home would soon catch up. This time there was a slight tinge of disappointment though, because the steel hatch and window shutters were closed, which meant Shinji wasn't at home.

Parking the car in the lot opposite the relevant pontoon, he switched off, grabbed his briefcase and hooked the car up to a charger. He aimed his mobile at the machine and beamed his credit code which sprung the contacts and the juice started flowing. The reliable little Foxbat would be ready for another long journey tomorrow, but because home was that much nearer to the project than it had been this morning, his journey time would be cut by half.

It had been a long hard day at the project, but the build was going well: on target and no major mishaps. Abe walked along the main pontoon, glad of the fresh air and the huge expanse of water. He took in the names of the other boats, looking for one he might recognise. Here was the *Harold Washington*, moored snugly close to the *Kevin Barry*, and over there was the *Foundry's Darling* – he was sure he'd seen that one before, and then past *Mons Meg*, a nice stumpy ten metre job with a disproportionately tall stack. Then at the point where Pontoon C spurred off from the main, there were a couple of river cruisers, whose names he didn't bother to check, and so at last to the *Molly Blackbridge*.

Hopping onto the rear deck, Abe used his mobile to key an access code and beamed the modern lock; the magnetic bolt snicked open. Then he used a chunky multi-lever key on a padlock and chain that a tank couldn't shift. Fifteen minutes later he had shed his work clothes and slipped into shorts and a t-shirt, and he had opened up all the shuttered ports. A note from Shinji let him know that he was out getting supplies – which meant food, but everything had a nautical tilt to it these days. Abe smiled and wondered what was on the menu for tonight.

Walking barefooted through the galley section on polished floorboards, the chill felt good on such a sweltering day. Abe ducked through into the saloon, flopped into one of a pair of tan leather "captain's" chairs and relaxed into the luxuriant upholstery. Bringing his feet up, he hugged his knees and experienced one of those rare moment when he felt very pleased with life. Outside, the *Molly Blackbridge* was striking enough with the big red sun and its long reaching rays, but it was only a home-made paint job, more enthusiasm than skill. Even if it wasn't to the purist's tastes it did a fine job of keeping the elements from the hull and superstructure. Below decks it was a different matter, for inside, the *Molly Blackbridge* was a palace with no skimping on luxury; light wood panelling throughout, two sumptuous double-bedrooms, a well appointed galley, a study and a saloon. Except for the little square just inside from the aft-deck and the galley area it was carpeted, and the furnishings though practical were comfort itself. There was plenty of space for two to live in comfort and room for guests, and one soon got used to living in a linear fashion.

Abe reached out and picked up a framed photo of three happy, laughing men: Shinji, Shinji's Uncle Hikaru and Abe, way back ten years ago when they were spectators at the 2012 Olympics. Hikaru and Shinji's aunt had supported Japan, Abe Great Britain and Shinji Japan, Great Britain or the USA depending on who was doing best. Abe chuckled: how young he and Shinji looked, and then he remembered that Shinji was still going by his old nickname in those days.

'Good old Cappy Shirakawa!' Abe whispered, and as if answering his cue, Cappy – now Shinji – came aboard with the shopping. Abe's eyes flicked quickly from the photo to the man – still cute and slim and sexy, but now with a little fleck of grey in his black hair. After sixteen years together, Abe still felt the magic and he was fairly certain that Shinji did too. And then he noticed how excited Shinji looked, a second before realising why.

Shinji dropped the shopping bags on the deck in the galley section. 'Any sign of him yet?'

'Nothing, but it has to be today. It's the right place and the right time.'

'Any time now then! I have to take a shower. You get dinner started. Spag bog! Remember?' Shinji smile cut a ravine through his face. 'And do enough for three.'

Chris De'Ath was tired and very hopeful that he was close to people he knew, but at the same time apprehensive and nervous. He was just past his eighteenth birthday, and Cappy, who was only a year or two older than him would now be – what? – thirty two or thirty three. Oh, the time-twisting vagaries of the Hidden Paths. Would he recognise Cappy? Would Cappy recognise him? Would he feel like a silly little boy? He didn't know. What he did know was that he felt dirty and was certain he smelled. He felt faintly ridiculous in his combat gear. Luckily security computers didn't have a sense of smell. He keyed in his name as instructed, and the computer welcomed him as a guest of Shinji Shirakawa. Who? And then he recalled what Gary had said about Cappy changing his name. He shrugged internally: after the last few months he had learnt to deal with thwarted expectation.

The computer gave him directions to the *Molly Blackbridge* and opened a pedestrian gate. He walked by a restaurant and a pub with a suitably boaty name, and there was a chandlery and a couple of admin buildings. The utility buildings were all neatly screened off from the marina by a row of mature willows. The marina was vast and well set out, a huge expanse of water surrounded by trees with an outlet into the river. There were river cruisers, some looked seaworthy; there were floating homes, each made up of what was in effect a caravan on a pontoon, and of course, there were narrow boats. One of the latter stood out from the crowd. Apart from the fact that it was white and brilliant red, there was a man jumping up and down on the roof – or top deck Chris supposed it might be called – waving frantically. Chris waved back, whereupon the distant figure leapt onto the pontoon and raced towards him.

Chris would never have recognised Cappy in a hundred years. The dyed blond hair was a thing of the past. His collar-length hair was black now, with a few flecks of grey, and the piercings were all gone. His voice was the same though and being called "Chrissy-kun" in mid-bear hug made the penny drop.

'Eww – Chrissy-kun. Sorry to be so personal, but you stink like our holding tank on pump-out day.'

It suddenly felt very, very good to be with someone he knew, from his own world, albeit thrown into a new age differential. Essentially though, Cappy was the same person and the years fell away. He was all enthusiasm and excitement, like a pup at dinner time.

'It's ... it's so good to see you Cappy.'

'Dropped the "Cappy" a zillion years ago. I go by Shinji these days. Hey, let's get aboard. There's a guy be very happy to see you again.'

'Who?'

'Who else?'

Shinji took Chris's hand and led him along the pontoon. 'Then when we've done the meet-and-greet and got you outside of a mug of tea, maybe you could try out our shower.'

The words weren't getting though. Shinji might just as well have been speaking Mongolian, if there was such a language, for Chris was still trying to work out what Cappy and Abe were doing here together.

'You ... and Abe?'

Shinji chuckled. 'Yeah – who'd a guessed it? People used to say that all the time, like one of us had to be ever so freaking sensitive ... or maybe go in for musicals.'

Chris was at home. It felt good to know that if the whole world changed, Cappy – Shinji – for one would stay just the same.

That first half-hour was a buzz of excited greeting and question; all very bemusing for Chris, but the tea was most welcome. After he'd showered he padded along to his assigned cabin with a towel wrapped round, to find that Abe had laid him out a set of fresh clothing. The colours and the designs were unfamiliar, but it still amounted to briefs, board shorts and a t-shirt. He quickly slipped into them and joined his hosts who were waiting in the saloon.

'Thanks guys,' Chris said, smoothing down the shorts. 'I like the 2022 fashions. I noticed people don't do ties anymore. All the time I've been here, I haven't seen a single tie.'

'You get the occasional old gink, Shinji said, 'But for all intents and purposes the tie is a dead duck.'

'And not before time,' Abe added. 'Take a pew.'

Before he took the seat offered he crossed over to the wall panelling and peered at a matt finish ten-by-eight of Shinji and Abe in front of a high altitude Japanese temple. The backdrop was panoramic and clouds hugged the treetops in cotton-wool patches. In the photo the boys were both wearing formal, matching kimonos. They looked relaxed and happy.

'Our ... well I suppose you could call it our honeymoon.' Abe said. 'A couple of years before that photo was taken we'd invited Shinji's uncle and aunt over for the Olympics. Hikaru was heavily into gymnastics.'

'That's watching, not participating,' Shinji added. 'He's got a Buddha-belly.'

'So anyway, two years later they invited us over to Ashikaga for a holiday – as a kind of thank you. That picture was taken way up at the Gyodosan Joinji temple.'

'Uncle Hikaru had arranged this whole wedding thing.'

'And see those two little discs on my kimono? Well Hikaru-san gave me those – there's another one on the back – in a very formal ceremony he'd made up himself. They're family crests, and it was his way of welcoming me to the family.'

Shinji chuckled. 'It has to be official for it to count for Uncle Hikaru. He's one hell of a traditionalist, but if tradition don't cover it, he *will* find a way.'

It was then that Chris spoke a phrase of Japanese to Shinji, who replied with fluent ease.

'Shinji! You got you act together and learnt Japanese! Well done.'

'Well,' Shinji looked a little sheepish. 'Didn't exactly learn it in the traditional way. See –'

'Not a good idea, Shinji,' Abe said with a hint of warning.

Shinji thought about it, but only for a moment. 'No, guess you're right.'

Chris picked up on the undertones, but let it slip. If Abe thought a subject was not a good idea, he was probably right.

The three men were quiet while they ate dinner and kept the conversation light. How had the journey from Little Rillton been? Chat about Abe's job and Shinji's day-to-day life running and maintaining the *Molly Blackbridge* – that kind of a thing. But when dinner was over and the dishes stashed, they all sat in the lounge with a beer, expectant of what was to come next, until Shinji addressed the issues that were at the forefront of everyone's mind.

'Right, we haven't got a whole lot of time, so here's the deal. We'll gas for an hour. Me and Abe want to hear all about your travels. And then Abe is going to drive you back to Little Rillton.'

'But ... I only just came from there. It's not home anymore.'

'Chrissy-kun, don't you think I don't know that? Tell him Abe.'

'Well Chris, as much as I hate to do it, I've got to take you back to Wymes Forest. Your adventures aren't over yet.'

'He's right Chris! You have to go back to wartime Little Rillton and do a bunch of stuff. Like – put a curse on the *Molly Blackbridge* that'll stop her being scrapped. And ...'

'And other things. We don't know them all, but we do know you have to live for a few years as a chap called Mad Christy. The guy old Rosy used to talk about at school. Remember?'

Chris nodded, but without any enthusiasm. He was as close to home as he thought he would ever get, and he had no wish to go and live like a tramp in a time long ago. He was so tired of it all. Damn! He'd done what the Fey Knights wanted him too. Why couldn't he just go home?

'Cheer up, Chris,' Shinji said. 'We're not allowed to tell you much, not that we know too much ourselves. But we do know it will all work out okay in the end. Go back and have fun, in the certain knowledge that it all ends up fine.'

Chris couldn't help responding to Shinji's wide grin and laughing eyes.

'Really, really *fine* Chrissy-kun. One hundred percent gold plated fine with diamonds on.'

'If you say so Cappy. So here goes. Once upon a time ...'

'Who's that big boy with Uncle Abe, Daddy?' the ten-year-old asked whilst leaning out of the passenger window waving. Abe waved back. The teenager with him looked bemused.

'Oh,' replied 35-year-old Chris. 'It's just someone I used to ... know.' He swallowed hard and his eyes pricked. He watched as Abe and 18-year-old Chris climbed into the VW and within moments they were gone.

'Come on Daddy. Let's go find Uncle Shinji.'

The man and the little boy were welcomed aboard the *Molly Blackbridge* with hugs and little Danny gave his Uncle Shinji a kiss. The two grown-ups settled in the saloon and the boy played with his Playmobil Cossacks on the floor.

'Daddy subbed me a new PlayCenter game, Uncle Shinji. Guess what it is.'

Shinji frowned and put on an act of trying hard to guess. 'That's a hard question Danny-chan. Is it ... *Final Fantasy Twenty*?'

'Nope! Have another guess.'

'Erm – how about ... *Romanitas Three*?'

'Nope. Wrong again!' Danny couldn't hold onto his excitement for another minute. 'It's *Fae*! Daddy's *Fae*! They've made Daddy's book into a PlayCenter game!'

Shinji turned to Chris and smiled widely, nodding in appreciative, congratulatory manner. C'tasa man! That's – well – cooler than a snowman's –'

'Thanks, Shinji,' Chris said. 'It's all pretty exciting.'

'I'll say. First the book gets into the Electramazon top 100, then the movie and now a PlayCenter game! Hey – lend me a million bucka-euros. The old *Molly* could do with a dry dock for the winter.' He laughed.

'They do action figures too, and Daddy collects them!' Danny said, much to his father's embarrassment.

'I so *don't* collect them. MacFarlane just sends me complimentary samples.'

'And he has them all standing about on his bookshelves!'

'Well, you have to put them somewhere,' Chris said, wishing Danny would shut up.

Shinji was enjoying this. 'With "you" in pride of place, no doubt.'

'Actually the Kumakkashi Chief has pole position, right under the clock. A particularly fine piece, and just like the guy who played him in the movie.'

'Oh yeah!' Shinji said. 'They were lucky to get old Ingleby to do the part. He kind of made the movie for me.'

'I met the guy. Really nice chap. Anyway, he saw the script and liked it. He was already a fan of the book, so he knocked back a big Hollywood lead to do a supporting role part in *Fae*.'

'And walked right into the movie hall of fame. I'll bet taking the part didn't do his career any harm at all.'

'Can I go up on deck please Daddy?'

'Not unless you put a life-jacket on.'

Shinji put Danny in a jacket and set the computer onto guardian mode. It was designed to sound a warning if the jacket got wet or the wearer's vital signs deviated from normal. Danny was soon having fun topside pretending to be a pirate.

'So, what was it like to see your own self just now, aged a couple of months older than an embryo?'

Chris breathed deep. 'Hard. Knowing what he – me – has yet to go through. But at least I know it all works out in the end.'

'Why so melancholy? You know it isn't over yet.'

Chris couldn't help but cheer up. 'You know, Abe is one hell of a lucky guy.'

Shinji chuckled. 'Him and me both. Sometimes I think our love makes the world turn round.'

'Maybe it does,'

'But you know, you're part of our story too. What he feels for you, that's the key man. That's the key!'

Abe Knapper stood alone by the fallen merlon under the old tower. Eighteen-year-old Chris was gone again, taken one last time by the Fey Knights, so he could fulfil his role as Mad Christy. Abe felt a little sad and a little empty. Even though he knew it had to be. He also felt a tiny twinge of pride, knowing that without him the Fey would never have come: not this time; not the first, twenty-odd years ago. In all the vast convoluted wilderness of time and space that made up the Hidden Paths, the Fey could only navigate towards the key, and the key was rare indeed. It could only be held for one person and Abe Knapper was glad that he was one of the few who held it, and more than happy that he held it for Christian De'Ath.

CHAPTER THIRTY-SEVEN

Merry Met in Moonlight

Mad Christy sat on a tree stump on the edge of Bowen's Farm and watched the Beaufighters fly home. The sun rose on another day, a day that would be just like the last and identical to the next. Chris was heartily sick of playing the fool. He'd been Little Rillton's village idiot for the best part of five years now and the war was almost over. When oh when would his trial end? He dragged himself through each day, with the echo of Cappy's words growing ever more distant. It will all work out fine in the end. He couldn't help but doubt it, and then he was assailed with the familiar feeling that was becoming a most frequent visitor: it was all a bloody dream; none of it was real.

Plunging his hand into the deep pocket of his moleskin trousers he fumbled among the string and dirty handkerchiefs and old beech nuts until his fingers found what they were looking for: a very anachronistic plastic film pot for a kind of film that hadn't been invented yet, containing an incisor tooth.

He took the tooth from the kitchen tissue paper, now yellowed with age and disintegrating, and examined it. As usual Chris found himself talking to it as if it were a transmitter or a live person.

'Come on Tarn. I've had enough. Come and take me away from all this.' Looking deep into the open end of the tooth where the nerve had once been, he noticed something that had previously escaped his attention. Inside the tooth was a little brown blob of hardened blood, and then the tooth spoke to him.

It wasn't real. It was in his head. Chris was used to things speaking inside his head these days. He was Mad Christy by careful act and well rehearsed design. Give it much longer, and he'd be mad for real. But be that as it may, the voice whispered inside his head and it said *Take me to Abe's camp.*

In Abe's camp had been Abe's table, and Abe's table was an ancient altar stone. He remembered the time he had first met the Wiergan. Something about needing blood to cross over: none of it was clear, but enough to give Mad Christy a feeling. Maybe, just maybe: if he found that old stone, and did something with Tarn's blood he might be able to get onto the Hidden Path, and then home.

Of course, Abe Knapper was yet to be born, and Chris had no idea what state his future camp was going to be in. He found it with surprising ease; the space that would one day be claimed by a lonely boy called Abe was already a clearing within a circle of trees and the altar stone was at the centre of the clearing and completely devoid of moss or weeds.

Now that he was here Chris hadn't a clue what to do. After circuiting the stone half a dozen times, he sat on it. He wondered if there should be any ceremony, but discounted the idea. The Fey Knights had never gone in for genuflexions or strange chanting. They just crossed over. But this was different. This was not an *olrock*, it was an altar, favoured by those of the dark powers. They would probably do things differently. Their ceremonies would almost certainly require blood.

Chris took out his penknife and nicked his thumb. He let a tiny drop of blood touch the stone. Nothing happened. Then he let a drop of blood fall onto the dried blood in the tooth. He rubbed the sticky blood into the old clot and then smeared the resulting mess on the stone.

It was just like the first time he had ever entered the Paths. He was completely deprived of all senses and seemed to expand to fill the universe. Somewhere deep inside the vastness that was his being, he felt a pang of excitement and fear. And then, all too late, he remembered the two necessities of travelling the Paths. First, one had to cross onto the Paths. Second, one had to have the power to navigate, otherwise one would be lost throughout many forevers.

Just as space had no meaning for Chris, so too did time cease to exist and he drifted forever and for no time at all, until he thought he saw warmth amidst the vast whiteness of no feeling at all. Yes, over there, it was warm, and slowly Chris struggled to attain the warmth.

Cappy's floating iron hovel reverberated to Abe's annoyance.

'I can't believe you've done that,' Abe said to Cappy as he checked the drawing on his plastered arm. He held it up to the light coming in through the port hole. 'You're nineteen years old! When are you going to grow up?'

'It's me and you holding hands is all. Two little manga boys in love.'

'With a *heart* between us, for God's sake? And roses? What if Dad sees it?'

'Aren't you out to him yet?'

Cappy could tell by Abe's look that the answer was no.

'Well, let him see the drawing and break him in easy,' Cappy chuckled.

'I'll spend my whole time in the meeting being self conscious in case anyone sees it.'

'If you're that worried, take my pen and draw long hair and titties on one of them.'

Both the youngsters laughed. 'I'm not going to tell lies, Cappy. It's just that I don't feel like making statements right now either. And don't you think two weeks it's a little early for hearts and roses?'

Cappy pouted and looked hurt, but only for a moment. The cloud passed quickly and out came the smile. 'You don't know how long I've waited Abe. It's not too soon for me.'

'Maybe I'm frightened to rush things, in case it all disappears.'

'It's cool man, because I'm going nowhere – except as far as Wymes Forest. Hey, are you sure you can't slope off and come with me and the other guys? It's going to be one hell of a hoot!'

'If I could wriggle out of the meeting I would. But I'm still not sure if I want to come along and see you get –'

'Get nekkid!' Cappy laughed out loud. 'I think I'm only nekkid under some kind of a flowing robe affair anyhow. But I can hope.'

'You actually *want* to get undressed and dance round nude?'

'It sounds fun.'

Abe smiled lop-sidedly. 'I'll say just *one* thing: Dolly Tregonhawke.'

'Yuk! But ... she's a high priestess or some such, so she won't be stripping ... I hope.'

Abe took Cappy's chin and holding him still looked into his eyes. 'I can see into your soul Cappy, so don't lie to me. There's going to be other young guys there and that's why you want to go. I'm right, aren't I?'

'Hell yeah!' Cappy frowned and thought about it. 'Well, not really, but there's these other guys, see, and if I get nekkid, so do they, and one of them is *so* hot!'

Abe swiped Cappy across the arm with his good hand. 'I thought I was all the hot you needed.'

'You might be if you'd let me find out. Anyhoo, it's nice to look. There're two guys. Eric – and he's straighter than anyone you can think of – is my garden centre boss-lady's boyfriend. And then there's Matt, her little brother. Now he's about twenty-three and when it comes to Matt my gaydar says incoming!'

'And they're all ... you know ... witches?'

'You sound surprised, after all the stuff that's been happening lately.'

Abe shrugged.

'My garden centre boss is the chief witchipoo next to Dolly. Her boyfriend and brother are just sorcerer's apprentices, like me.'

'You're all a bunch of loons, if you want my opinion.'

'I'm telling you. It's a good laugh.'

Cappy gathered his things together and sniffed his arm pits. He decided he needed a bit more protection and had a couple of squirts of Abe's deodorant.

'All set then. I'll see you after the meeting.'

'Okay Cappy, but I can't help thinking you're completely mad, doing this coven stuff when weird things have been happening. It might be dangerous.'

Cappy got serious for a moment. 'I know what you're saying, but you know – all the fun and frolics aside – I can't help thinking this might be important. I have this kind of feeling about it.'

It was unusual to see Cappy serious, but almost to Abe's relief, it didn't last.

'And don't worry Abe. Whatever else might happen, my magic wand is all yours.'

'Dream on!'

Cappy chuckled as he headed off. 'Lock the boat up before you head home. And enjoy the meeting.'

In the event it was far too chilly to dance naked, and Cappy was glad of the white cotton alb, thin as it was. Eric and Matt had advanced a stage further and it was only Cappy who was to be initiated. Everyone made a fuss of him and greeted him warmly with 'Merry meet,' or 'Hail, young Curnunnos,' and soon everyone was free of modern clothing and dressed in flowing robes.

The coveners soon had a cheerful fire going – lit by the wave of a wand, six Zip firelighters and a box of matches – and fifteen good witches of both Rilltons and Axenwhit stood in a loose circle around it chatting quietly and drawing in the warmth. While Dolly and the First Covener made the Circle and drew the pentagram with Abe's stone circle at its centre, Cappy revolved slowly on the spot so the warmth could bathe him all over. He wondered if Abe had the slightest clue that the Rillton Coven had been using his campsite for many years. Probably not, he guessed; they made their fire where Abe made his, and they were particularly careful to leave things exactly as they found them.

Matt sidled up to Cappy and when their eyes met Matt nodded. Cappy nodded back. 'So, you know you have to have sex with the High Priestess?' Matt said.

Cappy knew at once he was being teased. 'Yeah, I heard that. What's Dolly like, seeing as how you've already been there?'

'Cut it out, Matt,' Eric said. 'Don't spoil it for him. Hey, Cappy. Nothing bad is going to happen. Go with the flow, and this will be one of the coolest experiences of your life.

'Just joking you, Cappy. Open up to it and like Eric says, it'll stay with you for years.'

Dolly called the coven to the Circle and after a few moments of quiet when everyone had centred down and there was a strong feeling of expectation, she began.

'With one another, once again we meet for joy of life and to reaffirm our hearts to the gods.'

The First Covener continued, 'The Lady and the Young Fey Lords have been good to us. Meet we thank them for all we have.'

'Let us join together,' Dolly said and Cappy thought that if there were going to be any rude stuff, it would start right about now.

'Let us join together and thank the God and Goddess for favours bestowed.'

Nobody ripped Cappy's alb off. The circle within the Circle remained in tact and there was no sign of an orgy. Cappy didn't really know if he was relieved or disappointed.

'And it harm none, do what thou wilt,' Dolly said with copious folds of indigo silk flowing from her outstretched arms. These robes were certainly flattering to the fuller figure.

Everyone except Cappy joined in with the reply 'And it harm none, do what thou wilt.'

'Thus runs the Wiccan Rede,' Dolly said. 'Remember it well. Whatever you desire; whatever you would ask of the gods; whatever you would do; be assured it will harm no one, not even yourself. And remember as you give so it shall return threefold, a portion from each Fey Lord. Give of yourself – your love; your life – and you shall be thrice rewarded. But send forth harm and you shall be thrice blighted.'

Lulled by the warmth of the fire and by Dolly's gentle tone he wasn't expecting the music. People began playing medieval sounding instruments, the combined effect being both jolly and ethereal. Others sang softly or chanted and someone came up from behind and gently put a silk blindfold over Cappy's eyes.

Cappy found himself being spun gently round the circle of coveners, not so much as to make him giddy but more than sufficient to disorientate him. Gentle hands but firm, guided him round and round in time with the chants and beats of the music, until he felt cold rock beneath him and he guessed he was being seated upon the altar stone. A fleeting thought shot through him as he realised his hands were bound behind him – *when did they tie me?* – that if these guys were a bunch of murder-freaks, he'd just delivered himself up on a plate.

The chanting continued and Cappy heard the sounds of dancing feet and smelt fragrances of burning, perfumed candles. Then he was anointed with essential oils – but still, to the continued confounding of his mixed feelings, no funny business.

The coveners became silent once more, and then Dolly said something about cutting the air with her athame and calling forth the spirits to bless and accept this young heart – *oh shit they're going to sacrifice me* – but no, they meant it figuratively, he hoped.

There was more chanted and many hands touching him all over, and yes that did mean all over and just for a moment Cappy thought it was all going to happen. The touches were light though, and asexual, and any hope – fear – of action soon passed away. The coveners backed away and there was more singing, and Dolly raised her voice calling upon various gods with funny, archaic names – and then shocked silence, and cries of fear, and screams.

Cappy started to get frightened. This was just a little over the top; all the other stuff he could take but this mass act of terrified hysteria was too much, especially as he was blindfolded and tied up. He wanted to yell and tell them all to shut up and get on with it. If they had aimed to scare him, they had succeeded.

But they didn't stop screaming or crying out. Oh yes, the hubbub certainly died down, but only because they were all running away. As panicked footfalls receded further and further into the wood and the cries became less frequent and ever more distant, Cappy found himself cold and alone in the dark silence of night. He could just make out the light of the fire through his blindfold and he could hear it crackling, but that was all. The bastards had left him all alone, and this was not funny and not at all fun. All alone: or perhaps, not entirely alone; through the thin material of the blindfold he saw a shadow move between him and the bright fire, and he felt a close presence. And that sound: it couldn't be wind passing through leaves; it sounded just like breathing.

Cappy shrank into himself and he waited for the blow. Those idiot witch-freaks had called forth a demon, and he was going to be demon-dinner.

'Cappy? Is that you? What the hell are you doing here?'

'Chris?' Cappy called out into the dark, hopeful but unbelieving.

Chris whipped off Cappy's blindfold and untied him in moments, and the two young men hugged and laughed until they fell out of the Circle. The fire was a better place and they both moved closer and sat by it.

'You look a lot older Chris. Where have you been?'

'You wouldn't believe half of it. What year as it? How long have I been gone? You've hardly changed at all since I last saw you.' Chris knew it would be wrong to say *the last time I saw you, you were in your mid-thirties.*

'A couple of weeks is all. Abe's at a meeting this evening where a bunch of people are going to discuss all that's happened and what became of you and stuff.'

'How's my parents?'

'How do you think? They're devastated. We've all been and especially Abe. It's all been too weird.'

Chris stared into the fire for long minutes, waiting for his mind to catch up with his body. He was home. Home at last and close enough to the time he left to allow him to settle back into his own life. He touched his face, wondering if people would accept the extra years. He was nearly twenty-three in years lived, but it would be nice to play the eighteen-year-old again, and take up where he left off. It could work.

'Best you take me along to Abe's meeting Cappy. Perhaps I can fill in some of the gaps for them.'

'No one round here who could do it better.' Cappy found his things where he'd hung them on a bush, and quickly got changed. Within half-an-hour they were knocking on the big front door of Flint House.

Chris stayed out of sight. Abe's sister Daisy opened the door and then said that she was ever so sorry, but her father was in a meeting and he'd have to come back later.

'Sorry Daisy. No deal,' Cappy said pushing gently past her. Her eyes went bug-like and nearly popped out of her head when Chris stepped from the shadows. She led the boys along the hall and slipped into the room where the meeting was already under way.

'Someone to see you Dad,' she said.

'Can't they wait? I'm rather tied up at the moment,' Chris heard from inside. Cappy pushed past both Chris and Daisy.

'Sorry vicar-bro,' Cappy said. 'There's someone to see you who won't wait no longer than I will.'

'Cappy!' Abe said standing and caught somewhere between astonished and indignant.

'Hi, Abe!' Cappy Shirakawa said, his face beaming as if Abe was the person he wanted to see most in the whole world.

Then Chris stepped though. Abe and everyone else stared at him, and then Dawn Bowman rose to her feet and pressed both hands to her heart.

'Flaming Nora!' she said. 'I think we'd better give our visitors a seat.'

And a long last, Chris knew he had come home. His chin began to tremble but he clenched his teeth hard and kept in control. But the momentary lapse did not escape the eagle eye of the law and Chris was soon being hugged hard against Dawn's ample bosom with the others closing in all around. He quickly became the centre of a group hug where the reasons and the whys and the wherefores could all just wait. Chris was home, and nothing else really mattered.

CHAPTER THIRTY-EIGHT

Notebook Epilogues

It took a couple of weeks for everything to settle down. PC Chapel hadn't given Chris too much of a grilling concerning his mysterious disappearance or fortnight's absence, and he guessed that Detective Superintendent Dawn Bowman probably 'had a word in his shell-like', as she would have put it. Naturally, Mum and Dad were overjoyed with his return and likewise, they didn't ask too many questions. They didn't even protest over much when he told them he'd be leaving college. How would he make a living? Well, of late he'd found he had quite an aptitude for languages. He felt sure something would crop up.

It would take a lot longer than a couple of weeks for Chris to lose the feeling of joy each time he woke up in his warm bed, in his familiar bedroom, in the De'Ath household on the edge of Little Rillton in the year 2005 – even if Mum was nearly always standing outside in the hall, peering in with a loving look. But there was one thing he'd been putting off, and now he was fully into his own life once again, it wouldn't wait any longer.

Over breakfast, Chris asked Dad what he needed to know, and as soon as he'd downed a mug of tea, Chris was off.

He had no fear of Wymes Forest. Somehow he knew the Fey Knights would never come again, and that faeries were once more creatures of the imagination. They should never have been in the Realm in the first place, but were a symptom of imbalance and of trauma inflicted by evil. All the evil was gone now, and so the Fey Knights and the faeries would bide in their own places. Just one then; just one ghost to lay and Chris kept his eyes wide as he walked along the dusty pathways which took him into the formal parklands surrounding Wymes Manor.

He hopped off the tarred drive onto the grass verge as Lady Wymes trotted towards him astride Tomahawk. He hoped she wouldn't cause a scene, and he was in luck, for she merely eased to a walk and smiled at him as she passed. He was certain Lord Wymes wouldn't be so amiable, so he ducked across the lawn towards the dairy and the stables.

He found old Harry, the former tramp who Dad had taken on to work in the stables, forking straw into a row of loose-boxes. He watched for a few moments until Harry became aware of him. Straightening up from his work he pressed one hand into the small of his back and stretched with a sound of relief passing his lip.

'Like to watch a fellow working, do you, young Mr De'Ath?'

Chris grinned widely, but not without a twinge of sadness in his heart. 'Young Mr De'Ath?' he chuckled. 'Knock it off, Jamie!'

Old Harry looked momentarily shocked, but something shifted, like a night cloud sliding silently to reveal the moon, and Jamie McDowell's fresh young face peeped out from behind Harry's ancient features. He broke into a happy smile.

'How did you find out, Chris?' Even his voice seemed younger.

'It was a few years ago now, when you and me and Lillian and all the others were at Brikadden. It just kind of came to me in a flash.'

They shared memories of Brikadden for a while, and then Harry – Jamie – invited Chris to the tack room for a cup of tea and some biscuits. They sat in silence looking at each other through the rising steam of their drinks, each unsure of how to bridge the lost years with words. It was Harry who spoke first.

'You know, you're one of only two of the whole blooming lot of us who managed to get back to their proper time.'

Chris shook his head, a twinge of joy shooting through him like a celebratory firework, let off in acknowledgment of his good fortune. 'No, I didn't know that. Who was the other one?'

'I'll tell you later.'

'Okay, but how do you know for sure?'

Harry chuckled and took a sip of tea, wincing as the heat hurt a nerve in one of his teeth. 'Spent my life finding out, so I did. Up and down, up and down, back and forth between the Realms and through time, until I traced every last one of you. Well, nearly every one of you.'

Chris was shocked. He'd thought that Jamie had spent his life wandering round as a tramp since 1980 when he'd been left in Rendlesham Forest, but even as the thought passed through his head he knew it was flawed. Jamie should be short of forty now, but Harry's features spoke of many more years than that. He had to be at least sixty, maybe a lot more.

'You found a way to navigate the Hidden Paths?'

Harry shook his head. 'No, not quite. But I did find some other ways between the Realms. See, there're some places that exist in two of the Realms at the same time; old buildings, mostly ruins. Hill forts mostly, and sometimes other places.'

Chris thought of Brikadden, and how it appeared that identical ruins existed in both S'herra and his own world.

'And then there're the water-gates as I call them, always under water. They're like gateways between the Realms. Not any old water, oh no, just in certain, special places see, and I traced some of them down. By accident I found the first one, but once I got the hang of gate-hopping and such like, I got to work. Fifty years it's taken me, and believe me, I have seen *some* places, and *some* times. I even met a king of England once. But now, I'm nearly done. Here, let me show you something.'

Harry put down his tea and shuffled about in a room next door, full of old saddles and rusty bits. He came out with a biscuit tin with a battered, faded scene of men in long-aprons shoeing horses.

'My life's work,' he said sitting down again. He prised off the lid and inside was a variety of notebooks held in a bundle by a red elastic band.

'These are all my notes,' Harry said taking out the bundle. 'Little clues, or the next lead to follow; plans of how to get there and what to say when I do, see?' But this!' Harry triumphantly withdrew a hard backed notebook from the bottom of the tin.

'In here, are all the results and I want you to have it.'

Chris took the book with great care. 'They're all in here? Marc and Shaun? Karl and Beverly? Lillian?'

'Them and some others, but look. This isn't the place. Take it home with you, and read it somewhere quiet.'

They finished the tea and chatted a little about the day Richard De'Ath had found Harry in the lake with all his clothes in a plastic bag. Chris wasn't surprised to learn that Dad had met Harry immediately after his last transition from the Third Realm.

'I recognised Uncle Richard straight away,' Harry said. 'I thought I'd come home at last, and it was all a little too much. I'm afraid I blubbed like a baby.'

Harry explained that he had no control over destinations when he passed through the water-gates, and he had never managed to get close to his own time or place.

'In fact, that day your dad found me, that was the closest I've ever got, and as all my work's done, and I seem to have fallen on my feet, I reckon I'll stay.'

Later that night Chris slipped under the duvet. Setting his pillows against the wall, under the little bird-drawing that Tarn had once made, he settled back with Harry's notebook on his raised knees, took a deep breath and opened it up to the first page. He had decided to read it through from start to finish, and not flick forward and back to take in the important one-liners about each of his friends. Harry had spent his life tracing them all down, and he needed to honour his work by giving time and patience.

The first line he read on opening the notebook was 'Karl, Beverly and the Baby Boy.'

Karl told me that Brikadden ceased to exist. When he gathered himself together he was much relieved to find that wherever he was, he, Beverly and the baby boy were all together. There was no sign of anybody else or of Brikadden. They had landed with a jolt in a green field with some domestic cattle at the far end and a wood surrounding thee sides. The sun was shining, the couple and the child were free from injury and the world was a peace. Karl found a track and with mounting optimism they followed it to a village. Karl's pleasure on discovering that the village proved to be set in the German state that was the Hochwalt family's ancestral home was spoilt on learning that they had come to the place at the end of the eighteenth century.

Fortunately they were taken in by members of the Hochwalt family, no doubt Karl's own ancestors, and they settled down to live as a married couple. They called the baby Robert and raised him as their own.

At the time I came to them, Robert was a healthy twelve-year-old and so it seemed to me that he would grow up and continue the Hochwalt name.

And so Karl Hochwalt, Jamie and Kostja and even Chris himself had Rosemary's blood in their veins, and far more frighteningly, the blood of a shape-shifting demon. Chris thought about all that time he had spent researching the Fey Knights, and he recalled one possibility he had contemplated. Maybe all the youths and young couples who had been taken by the Fey Knights had been related. Perhaps there was something in their blood that made them suitable for the task of resealing the rifts. Chris felt certain of it. Maybe you had to have the right blood to pass between the Realms and onto the Hidden Paths.

Chris turned the page, then closed his eyes and wished hard for a happy ever after for Marc and Shaun.

Marc and Shaun passed back to Wymes Forest, but not at the right time. The effect of the demise of the Shitake Maru deposited them in the middle of Wymes Lake, and they nearly drowned.

Ironic, thought Chris. His lie almost became fact.

They came out of the water, cold and dripping, and were found by the vicar of St Luke's who gave them dry clothes and hot sweet tea and took them to Lord Blencathra, who was a patron and benefactor to the local populous. The year was 1856. I met them thirty years after this, when they were well established in the community and lived in a modest manner as the eccentric yet inventive bachelor brothers who were known for their philanthropic works, much in the same vane as Lord Blencathra himself. They went by the names of Mark and John Ashdale and were still remembered for bringing the idea of clean water and underground sewers to the three villages, long before Joseph Bazaljette had done the same for London. Mark hinted that he had written to Bazaljette with the whole idea, but John said that was just Mark's sense of humour.

On a subsequent passing when I came again to Little Rillton, it was in the 1920's, I visited St. Luke's and was at the same time happy and saddened to find the Ashdale brother's freshly installed memorial stone. I was sad that they had lived out their lives so far removed from their own time, but happy that each had lived a long and productive life.

Chris had seen that memorial many times, a marble scroll set high on the wall in St. Luke's. He shivered as he thought that Marc must have seen it too, when he was living as a young man in his own time, never dreaming that he was looking at his own memorial. Drawing the duvet a little higher, he turned the page.

Edmund Warwick was the only person from the Brikadden incident to pass back to his own time and close enough to the correct location.

At the end of the last sentence was an asterix drawn in pencil, and a note to read the final entry. Chris flipped the pages forward and was not surprised to see that the last entry was about himself. He turned back to where he had left off.

I did not meet him, but found his name in some town records. He had, for an unspecified reason, been confined to a lunatic asylum, and having escaped to terrorize the local populous, he was beaten down by a man with a mason's maul, and subsequently died from his injury. It was the note appended to the record that was of most interest, for it told that his lunacy was thought to be the result of a curse received from a witch he had denounced several years earlier.

Edmund Warwick had led the witch hunter to a mean hovel in the woods where lived a woman who called herself Rosemary, but he said was truly named Molly Blackbridge, a name being well known to the people as a hag who spread illness and disease. The witch hunter was disinclined to believe that so fair a lady could be the infamous Molly Blackbridge, until she took up a fearful stance and called upon Black Angus to deliver her.

Of course, no demon – Black Angus or any other – was forthcoming, but she was arrested and tried for a witch. During her trial she spoke of the Fey Knights and other 'unnatural' beings which had come to her unbidden, an innocent woman who feared the Lord, but Edward testified against her that she had tried to call forth many dark spirits. She then cursed him for a liar and a disloyal servant, thereby convicted herself in front of the judge. She was burnt for a witch and her ashes scattered on the waters of Wymes Lake by some who pitied her fate.

'Serves the evil bastards right!' Chris whispered, but even as he did, he squirmed at the thought of death by burning. He couldn't work out in his own mind if Rosemary had really deserved such a fate, evil and wicked as she was.

Returning his attention to the notebook, Chris read the next heading. The next section was about Lillian, and once again Chris closed his eyes and hoped her story ended well before he began reading.

Lillian was the only person to return to a time well past her own. She had been taken with me in 1986 and we had stayed together until I was accidentally left behind by the Kern vessel. In terms of location, she came back almost to the spot where we were taken, but almost twenty years after her own time, arriving in the autumn of 2006.

Chris's jaw dropped when he saw the date of her return: it was just over a year into the future.

'November, 2006?'

Her return was probably the least traumatic, for she was met at the very point of her return by an old friend.

Chris was frustrated to turn the page, only to find a large section of writing blocked out with scribble from a biro. This mess was followed by a note, written especially for him.

Sorry Chris. I've perhaps left more of Lillian's entry than I should, as it concerns your future, and as we all know, it doesn't do to know about your own future. Yes – you are the friend who meets her. I'll show you where, but as for the rest? Well, it's all history for me, but you'll just have to live through it and find out for yourself.

He knew he couldn't argue with that. After all, it's exactly what he'd told Abe and Cappy yesterday when they had questioned him so much about his adventures.

'Just be nice to me on July the 15th, 2022.'

'What?' Cappy had yelled.

'Your future, my past. And that's all I'm saying.'

Cappy snatched up a ballpoint pen and wrote the date down on the front of his t-shirt. 'Where?'

'You don't have to know where. Just go wherever life takes you, and you'll wind up in the right place. I *know* you will, because it's already happened for me, and you can't change what's happened.'

November 2006. Well, Chris knew he'd be there and that was all he knew. The rest? He'd have to wait and see.

THE END
or
SOMEWHERE ALONG THE CIRCLE

Printed in the United Kingdom
by Lightning Source UK Ltd.
129250UK00002B/16/P